THE
SPLINTER
IN THE
SKY

THE
SPLINTER
IN THE
SKY

KEMI ASHING-GIWA

SAGA PRESS

LONDON SYDNEY **NEW YORK** TORONTO NEW DELHI

SAGA PRESS

AN IMPRINT OF SIMON & SCHUSTER, LLC

1230 AVENUE OF THE AMERICAS, NEW YORK, NEW YORK 10020

First Saga Press trade paperback edition August 2024

SAGA PRESS and colophon are trademarks of Simon & Schuster, LLC

Simon & Schuster: Celebrating 100 Years of Publishing in 2024

For information about special discounts for bulk purchases, please contact Simon & Schuster Special Sales at 1-866-506-1949 or business@simonandschuster.com.

The Simon & Schuster Speakers Bureau can bring authors to your live event. For more information or to book an event, contact the Simon & Schuster Speakers Bureau at 1-866-248-3049 or visit our website at www.simonspeakers.com.

Interior design by *Yvonne Taylor*

Manufactured in the United States of America

1 3 5 7 9 10 8 6 4 2

Library of Congress Cataloging-in-Publication Data has been applied for.

ISBN 978-1-6680-0847-8
ISBN 978-1-6680-0848-5 (pbk)
ISBN 978-1-6680-0849-2 (ebook)

For my family

DRAMATIS PERSONAE

Koriko

Enitan Ijebu, *she/her*, a tea specialist and scribe.
Xiang Ijebu, *they/them*, Enitan's sibling and an aspiring architect.
Ajana Nebaat, *she/her*, the daughter of a powerful duchess and the colonial governor of Koriko.

Vaalbara

Menkhet Ta-Miu, *she/her*, the Imperator and God-Emperor of the Holy Vaalbaran Empire.
Deora Edwan, *she/her*, a countess and amateur cultural anthropologist.
Kulta, *he/him*, a synth of Ominirish creation and head of Menkhet's private intelligence ring.
Katun, *he/him*, a synth and one of Kulta's craft-siblings.
Yehana Ta-Ji, *he/him*, an archduke and second cousin of Menkhet's predecessor.

Ominira

The High Consul, *they/them*, the elected leader of the Ominirish Republic.

FOR A THOUSAND YEARS, ACROSS THE PLANET GONDWANA, THE OMINIRISH REPUBLIC TO THE WEST AND THE HOLY VAALBARAN EMPIRE TO THE EAST HAVE BEEN LOCKED IN A BLOOD FEUD. FOR A THOUSAND YEARS, THE FLAMES OF WAR HAVE RISEN AND FALLEN BETWEEN THE SYSTEM'S TWO MAJOR POWERS. UNTIL NOW.

PEACE, AT LONG LAST. DESPITE A STRING OF VICTORIES, THE GOD-EMPEROR OF VAALBARA HAS ISSUED A FORMAL SURRENDER AND RECALLED HIS TROOPS, MOURNING THE LOSS OF HIS BELOVED DAUGHTER IN BATTLE.

BUT NOT ALL DESIRE PEACE. IN BOTH THE REPUBLIC AND THE EMPIRE, PLOTS AND COUNTERPLOTS ARE BREWING. AT THE HEART OF THE MOST SINISTER SCHEME IS THE SMALL VAALBARAN PROVINCE OF KORIKO, A DISTANT MOON HABITAT CONQUERED YEARS AGO BY THE GOD-EMPEROR.

THE FATE OF THE WORLDS WILL SOON BE DECIDED.

PROLOGUE

The Imperial mausoleum has a new occupant.

In its center chamber, a vast room glittering with obsidian tile, is a great mortuary slab of polished marble. On that slab is a woman. From the waist up, she looks like she's sleeping. From the waist down—well, there's nothing from the waist down.

"She saved us all, my Imperator," says Obara Uloyiso, her words echoing up to the towering ceiling. Rows of medals shimmer over the breast of her jacket as she rises from a deep bow.

She watches her God reach a black-gloved hand toward the corpse of his daughter. He brushes a dark curl of hair away from her face.

"I wouldn't be here if not for her." Obara's voice is careful.

The Imperator's bitter laugh is like shattering glass. "You want something."

"It's not too late," she says, drawing in a deep breath.

"For what?" He shifts, placing his hands on the slab and lowering his forehead to its cool surface.

"For us to crush the Republic. To redeem the Empire. To avenge your daughter." Obara offers her Imperator a single sheet of paper—real paper, not a datapad or even a simple holosheet. Easily destroyed, impossible to trace.

Her God stands, and his ink-black eyes flick over the nearly illegible scrawl of her plan. He looks back at her and sighs heavily. "No. This is wrong." He sets the paper down where the princess's right leg should be.

Obara draws back, just a little. "My Imperator—"

"I am so very tired." He lifts a hand, his fingertips just barely brushing against the paper. "And this—this is so very wrong."

"The war isn't over," says Obara, her voice tightening.

The Imperator's brow creases. "Did I not just sign a peace treaty?"

"I thought . . . I thought that was only a pretense." Her mouth is suddenly very dry. "They'll kill you."

"They can't."

Obara swallows a surge of white-hot rage. "The Republic—"

"Has won. It's over, Obara."

"So you want to play peacemaker now?" She sneers. "The great conqueror is tired of conquering? You subjugated Koriko for glory. Now let me use it to save the Empire."

"What you're asking—have we not already done enough to them?"

"I know what I'm asking," Obara snaps, before remembering who she just snapped at. She lowers her head. "My apologies, my Imperator. But it—it is the price we must pay."

"It is the price *they'll* pay."

"They're not even people," Obara hisses.

The Imperator blinks at her. "I know."

Obara narrows her eyes. "Is there nothing I can do to sway you?"

This time, his smile is a tight, grim line.

"Then may I go?"

He waves a limp hand at her. "Please do."

Obara bows, straightens, and watches him turn back to his daughter, eyes closed. She strides toward the doors, hands forming fists beneath her long sleeves. She knows what she must do. The man before her is weak, and the Holy Vaalbaran Empire can no longer afford a weak Imperator.

ONE

The best part of Enitan's day begins and ends with a cup of tea. She and her older sibling, Xiang, spend all their evenings perched atop their housepod with a full pot and their favorite mugs—gifts from the headwoman at their binding ceremony. Tea and the brilliant red gold of Jilessa are two of the few beautiful things left entirely untainted post-annexation. Tea because their Vaalbaran overlords share their appreciation for the beverage. Jilessa because Imperial technology hasn't progressed far enough to destroy gas giants. Enitan supposes they could always black out the skydomes over each community, but they'd hardly benefit from doing so. The provisional governor tried it once for a week or so as a punishment, but life carried on as usual with the help of lanterns, lamps, and bioluminescent flora. And as someone born and raised planetside on Gondwana, he suffered more than any of his Korikese subjects.

As the skydome begins to dim for the night hours, Enitan hands Xiang a steaming cup. "What would you do if the world were different?"

Xiang grins. Enitan asks the same question every evening; the inquiry doubles as one of several informal greetings. Xiang's answer changes each time.

"I'd go to one of those fancy schools in the Imperial interior, study architecture," Xiang says. "Come back here and design housepods." They take a sip of tea. "Oh, that's good. What's in this?"

"My own black uhie base, of course, with a little dried berraleaf sprinkled in," Enitan replies, puffing up a little at the praise. "A mix of aromatic bark, seedpods, roots, and peppercorns for spice."

Growing and preparing this particular blend was a pain. There are two primary species of tea cultivated in the system; uhie bushes thrive in the lush heat of Koriko, while the unforgiving climate of Vaalbara and Ominira's shared planet, Gondwana, can only support theehma vines. But despite the perfect growing conditions here, crafting tea-grade uhie blends is still a grueling art form. She's been fermenting this batch of leaves for years, carrying out a painstaking maturation process to produce a rich, full-bodied aroma and flavor. Achieving the perfect concoction of spices was yet another challenge. But the contented look on Xiang's face makes it all worth it.

But then she frowns. "You can study architecture at Edoga." It's the university on the second ring, where she herself studied.

Xiang gives her a sidelong look. "The only classes they have now are on how to design those ridiculous monoliths. I don't want to learn how to make Koriko look more Vaalbaran. I want to *create*. And for my designs to honor our own art."

Enitan snorts, refilling her own cup. "How profound."

"Fine, then, what would you do?"

She draws in air, and the heavy scent of home coats the back of her throat—night-blooming blossoms and savory-scented steam hinting at what the neighbors are having for dinner. And under it all, the darkly sweet musk of decaying vegetation from the marsh below the tiered city. She looks out over the wetland before them, a tumult of green mangrove and brilliant blue water, all gilded by Jilessa's reflected light.

A sudden breeze cuts through the air, and they both shiver.

"I'd craft tea," Enitan decides. She tucks her arms one by one into her poncho, switching the cup from hand to hand as she shields herself against the wind. She has to remind herself that the artificially generated air currents are necessary to spread the pollen, spores, and seed pods keeping the ecosystem afloat. "I'd perfect a hundred blends and open a shop on the first ring—"

Xiang smirks. "You just want to be closer to Ajana."

The name brings to mind faint, melodious laughter; ringed fingers intertwining with hers; the flash of a shy smile, lit by silvery lantern-light.

Blood rushes to Enitan's face. "Shut up," she snaps, putting down her cup to lightly smack their arm. Not for the first time she's grateful for her complexion, which is dark enough to hide a blush. "Most shut-tles land on the first ring," she continues. She cannot help but smile as she leans back, looking up at the skydome. Thick glass and bioplastic panels encase the dense fluid that provides radiation shielding and in-sulation for the community. Despite all those layers, the view outside is perfectly clear. "People from every community would come to sample my wares."

"That sounds nice." Xiang takes another sip of tea and settles onto their back beside her. "I'm sure a few of my friends would want to help out."

Enitan grimaces, running a hand through her hair. It's getting far too long; tomorrow she'll have it trimmed down to its typical cap to combat the heat. "How would they possibly find the time between smoking skeyroot and selling it?"

Xiang lets out an exasperated sigh, barely audible above the hum of the last few shuttles still buzzing about before curfew. "Not this again."

She looks down at them, her brow furrowing. "Yes, this again." En-itan places her hand on Xiang's shoulder. "You know I don't like your new friends. They're reckless young fools, and reckless Korikese are rarely long-lived ones."

The warm, rosy glow of Jilessa casts Xiang in rich gold. "You don't like anyone."

"I like you sometimes," Enitan says. "So I'm going to watch out for you, whether you like it or not. You're all I have, Xiang."

"You have our entire community." They grin. "And the head-woman is sort of a mother." They say the last word in Akyesi, the common tongue designed by Imperial scholars specifically for provincials. Korikesian has no word to describe parents. "I think you're her favorite, actually. You have to put up with Imperials nearly as much as she does."

Enitan stares flatly at them.

Xiang rolls their eyes. "I can take care of myself, you know."

Enitan links her arm through theirs. "But you don't have to."

◆

All fifty-nine communities of Koriko are remade for the Festival of Ten Thousand Stars, one of the few holidays permitted to the people by the Supreme Abbot of Vaalbara. Enitan and Xiang have made a tradition of going down to the upper-middle rings of the city just after sunset. At dusk, the brightly painted star-shaped lanterns that festoon every building in Ijebu Community light up the world itself. Normally, elders would walk the streets throwing smaller lanterns into the air, but not this year, and likely not the next. Many of the elders died when Enitan was small.

The siblings have special matching garb just for the occasion: robes of shimmering green to wear over tunics and trousers of sapphire-blue and sun-yellow cloth. Enitan strides out of the sleeping area and into the housepod's living room decked out in her festival best, only to find Xiang hunched over their writing desk in their everyday clothes. Warm orange light illuminates their work, cast by a single potted alabaleaf. The genetically engineered plant serves three purposes: its frilly bioluminescent leaves serve as lamps, its curling stems bear several species of snacking fruit, and all of the housepod's data is backed up in its genetic code. It was gifted to the pair when they first moved in. But now is the time to move out, at least for a few hours.

"Hurry up and get dressed!" Enitan sidles up to their side, peering over their shoulder. "We're going to miss the best part!"

"I can't go," Xiang says miserably. They gesture half-heartedly at the slowly rotating hologram before them.

It takes Enitan a moment to recognize that the spinning transparent object is a replica of a monolith, complete with a seamless black surface of solar panels, a superstrength synthetic fiber underlayer, a skeleton of carbon nanotubes and aluminum, a number of self-contained quark fusion reactors, and a discreet array of wind turbines tucked in toward the bottom. However, unlike most of its slimmer, smoother brethren, this levitating structure is shaped like a torus. It looks much like a slyythfang swallowing its own tail.

"It's the Imperial University of Opuroth. The prompt of the main essay is to point out all the flaws in the design and list the ways we would improve them."

Enitan draws back a little, seized without warning by a heart-clenching burst of anger. A vein pulses in her neck. Is Vaalbara not satisfied with crushing her homeland beneath its iron bulk and taxing the communities nearly into collapse? Is its lust not sated with the blood of all those who spoke out against the outrage? Must it extend its devouring grasp to her little home and her sibling?

"Isn't Opuroth the institute that reverse engineered our environmental enrichment technology to leach precious metals from the asteroid belt?" she says, her voice tightening. "When you said you wanted to study architecture in the Imperial interior, I thought you meant when everything was different. Which it has not become since yesterday."

"What do you think I slogged through all that standardized testing for?"

"I thought it was just to prove a point," Enitan mutters sourly. She realizes how foolish it sounds as she says it.

"It's not like I'm going to get accepted anyway." Xiang groans. "I can't find a single mistake."

Enitan's fury softens, its edge dulling to nothing as Xiang presses their forehead into their palms. "That's probably intentional," she says. "I bet they made the application impossible on purpose."

The entrance exams to Vaalbara's greatest institutions are known for being perfectly meritocratic—as long as one is wealthy enough to afford the top Imperial tutors, the dozens of rare texts needed to study for the tests, and a seat in the assessment chambers. At that point, supposedly, scores are based on skill alone. And yet, Xiang has passed each and every exam with flying colors, only to find yet another challenge set before them: a surprise essay, assigned only to provincial applicants.

"I know you're happy I'm stumped, though you're hiding it well," Xiang grumbles, but it's clear the frustration in their tone is not directed at her. "You hate the idea of me leaving Koriko."

"I hate the idea of you going to Vaalbara," she corrects. "And coming back as someone I don't recognize. Study in Ominira, if you wish. They won the war, after all."

Xiang snorts. "Their so-called victory is a hollow one, and you know it. If the Imperator hadn't lost his daughter and decided he was sick of fighting, the Republic would be ash and rubble by now."

Enitan tries a different tactic. "Why would you want to spend four or five years in a place where everyone hates or fears or looks down on you?" She jabs an angry finger at the spinning monolith. "And most importantly, why would you want to live in that stupid ring? There's your design flaw: it's stupid."

That gets a laugh out of them. "I wouldn't be living there," they say, their smile turning wry as it slants upward at one corner. "'Primitives' like us can only apply to special ancillary schools taught in Akyesi, so we don't taint their holy tongue."

Enitan quickly tamps down the urge to point this out as yet another glaringly obvious reason her sibling should stay on Koriko. She leans against the desk, gesturing again at the hologram. "Is there anything I can do to help?"

Xiang sighs with a great heave of their shoulders. "No, not really." But then they light up a little. "You could bring me back some food from the festival? Maybe a slice of spice cake?"

Food hawkers are likely flooding the streets right about now, waving trays of delicacies so their aroma fills the air. Enitan salivates at the thought of sweet fried noodles and fruit, fragrant bean pudding freckled with black salt, and skewered berries shimmering in a crunchy shell of colored sugar. She snaps herself out of it when the implication of Xiang's request hits her.

"So you're going to stay here all night?"

"I have to. The application is due tomorrow."

Enitan pulls her own chair over and plops down into it.

"What are you doing?" Xiang's eyes dart across her face. "The festival—"

"If you're not going, then neither am I," Enitan interrupts. She crosses her arms over her chest, as stubborn as stone.

"Enitan, go. I know you wanted to see Ajana. It's fine. Really." They reach out to muss their sister's hair.

Enitan deftly ducks under their hand. "Ajana's busy. And anyway, we're done. I thought I told you."

Xiang lets out a soft, exasperated sigh. "You guys were *done* the last two times."

"Well, third time's the charm." Enitan pulls her communicator from her robe pocket. "I'm ordering food. Spice cake, you said?"

TWO

The very next evening, just before curfew, Enitan returns home after a long day at work. She's looking forward to bingeing the latest season of her favorite show with Xiang. Between all the applications they've been working on, Xiang's had barely any free time in the last few weeks. But when she opens the door, the housepod is too empty. Too quiet. She can feel her sibling's absence like a bone-deep ache, but she calls out anyway, throwing off her satchel.

"Xiang!"

No response. Their home is not a large one. There's a living room, a space for cooking and eating, a washroom, a heavily blanketed area for sleeping, and a small room where Enitan dries and packs her tea. Motion-sensitive vines flicker on as she searches the pod. It takes about five seconds to confirm Xiang isn't there. *Shit.* They're always home hours before curfew. She checks her communicator; they haven't sent her anything since this morning. She calls them four times.

Enitan presses her lips together and takes a long, deep breath. Xiang is fine. They're probably just smoking skeyroot with those good-for-nothing friends and lost track of time. They are *fine.* When they get back, she'll throttle them.

Enitan stomps over to her sleeping mat, imagining all the chores she'll heap upon Xiang as punishment for not telling her they were going out. She won't be able to sleep, but at least she can meditate.

She notes that the floor is freshly swept, though that isn't particularly strange. Neither are the rearranged vases, nor the slightly adjusted ceremonial mask on the wall. Xiang's favorite thing to do while high is tidy up. Enitan drags her mat from its corner, uncovering a reddish-brown blotch at the foot of the wall.

All of her thoughts screech to a halt.

With agonizing slowness, she lowers herself to the floor, her gaze glued to the little patch of blood. She feels as though her own has stopped flowing. It's a deep, dark spot with a tapering red smear, as if something had been dragged through it. *A body?* A cold sweat beads up over her skin without warning, a sharp prickle of fear running down her back as her mouth goes dry.

A thousand scenarios fly through her mind like a holoprojector left on loop. Her traitorous brain reminds her of the last time a young Korikese person went missing. They found him facedown in the marsh, crimson pooling in the murky water around his head, face marred beyond recognition—

Enitan shakes her head, gritting her teeth. She's overreacting, jumping to conclusions. Xiang will walk through the door any moment now. She touches the tips of her trembling fingers to the bloodstain. She's almost certainly making something out of nothing, but what if she's right? The fear swells as shards of anxiety sink into her gut. All Enitan has is Xiang, and if she loses them . . .

Though it's the beginning of the summer cycle and the walls are thickly insulated with mycelium, the housepod grows cold and empty around her. Enitan's breathing echoes in her ears. It dawns on her that if Xiang doesn't come back, her home will always feel like this. She bites her lip until she tastes copper.

With the pain comes a spark of resolve. Wherever Xiang is, whatever might have happened to them, she's going to find them. She grabs her communicator and calls Xiang's closest friends. None have seen her sibling all day.

Enitan lifts her arm to smash the communicator against the floor. Instead, as a last resort, she calls Ajana. No answer.

Fuck.

Despite what the Imperial reporters say, there's been virtually no violent Korikese-perpetrated crime in decades, even before the colonization of their land. And now with the curfew, the endless travel restrictions, and the disappearance of anyone who might have stirred up trouble in the war of annexation . . . There's only one explanation Enitan can think of for why Xiang isn't here. Why there's blood on the floor. People don't go missing on Koriko unless sentinels are involved. The boy in the marsh had had his ribs shattered by a shockstaff.

Her heart's beating too fast, and there's a horrible throbbing pressure in her skull. She sucks in a breath, snatches up her satchel from where she dropped it, and rushes outside. She darts over the short, flimsy bridges connecting the community's rings, sticking to the shadows as best she can. It's after curfew, and she still has faint bruises from the last time a new sentinel caught her breaking it. Ajana had him dishonorably discharged, but she'd rather not risk a repeat event.

The tubelifts will be shut down by now; she has to go the long way. Muscles already burning, Enitan weaves between two bright-green housepods and scurries up a rope ladder, crawling through the stacked rings of the community. The trip to the governor's mansion is not an easy one. Ajana is the daughter of an Imperial duchess, after all; she cannot muck around in the swamps like a native. She lives in a monolith, like a proper Vaalbaran. Enitan can see it now, the crystalline tip of a massive night-black pillar floating just above the trees. She remembers how disappointed the provisional governor had been with the community's reaction when the massive structure arrived. He'd thought his new Korikese subjects would throw themselves to the ground and weep in amazement at the feat of engineering, which had been brought all the way from the Imperial core.

Eventually, she reaches the highest and smallest tier of the community, which contains nothing save for the monolith floating serenely above it. A light, artificially generated breeze rustles through the spindly trees surrounding the ring, making the iridescent leaves tremble. Four sentinels stand at attention around the transportation pad, hands tight around their shockstaffs by the time she reaches them.

"Korikese, what are you doing here?" barks the nearest. Enitan grimaces inwardly. He's somehow butchering the pronunciation of Akyesi. It is a simple language, intended to be easy for even savages to learn.

"Korikese," the sentinel says again. "It is past curfew." He steps toward Enitan, immediately ready to administer the recommended three strikes to the stomach, chest, and face.

Dread rips through Enitan as she stumbles backward. But before the sentinel comes within a meter of her, another yanks him back.

"That's the tea specialist," his comrade snaps.

She can't see the first sentinel's expression, hidden as it is under his faceplate, but she's certain his eyes have gone wide. She can hear the surprise and irritation in his voice when he says, "You mean Lady Ajana's—"

"Yes," Enitan grits out, even as she feels her face grow warm. "I must speak with her."

The sentinel's grip tightens around her staff. "You were summoned?"

"Of course," she lies. Whenever Ajana asks for Enitan, she always sends a sentinel or two to formally request her presence. As if she's ever really needed to ask for anything.

The second sentinel nods, a precise jerk of her head. She has a strange, nervous energy, betrayed by her constantly shifting stance. "I'll take you to the governor. Come with me."

As Enitan passes him, the first sentinel tenses, his spine going as straight as the trees around them. "Forgive me, I did not realize—"

She cuts him off with a small shake of her head. "It's all right."

It's not. It will never be, but if she tells Ajana, he'll just get replaced with someone from Vaalbara, someone who might be even more eager to punish her than he is. And if that happens, there might not be a sentinel who recognizes her there to stop them. Swallowing her anger down like bitter medicine, Enitan joins the second sentinel at the center of the transportation pad. Enitan tries not to flinch as the sentinel lifts her shockstaff and strikes the pad with the end of it twice.

The whole thing shudders as if awoken from slumber, and the pad lifts smoothly from the ground, a levitating disk as dark as the monolith above. The rumbling murmur of intercommunity shuttles fades away. The bottom of the mansion is an enormous triangle above them, blotting out the artificial sky. With that light-drinking black above and below her, Enitan feels as if she's drowning. She will never grow accustomed to this, no matter how many times she visits Ajana. Two semicircular doors whoosh open just before their heads smack the monolith.

They're in a sleek tubelift now, rising toward the governor's private chambers at the pinnacle of the structure. When they drift to a halt, the sentinel knocks her shockstaff against the pad again, and the sides of the tube melt away to reveal yet another set of semicircular doors.

The sentinel taps her weapon gently against them. Nothing happens. She hits the doors, harder this time. Still nothing.

Ancestors. It *is* a bit late. But Enitan doesn't remember Ajana ever being an early sleeper.

The sentinel turns halfway around, passing her shockstaff to her other hand. The hand closest to Enitan. "You said Lady Ajana summoned you."

Enitan moistens her lips. "Yes."

"To arrive this evening?"

"Yes."

"And without the usual sentinel escort?"

Enitan swallows thickly. "Yes."

The sentinel shifts to face her fully. The woman's frame tightens up, ready to lash out at the slightest provocation. Or perhaps none at all. "Korikese—"

The doors chime as their screen-surface begins to shimmer. A projection of Ajana's angular face appears moments later. "What now?" the governor snaps, shoving her short, onyx-banded hair twists behind her ears.

"I've brought Enitan, my lady," announces the sentinel, her voice tight. She gestures at Enitan, who steps forward, hands clasped behind her back to hide their shaking.

Ajana's face brightens immediately. "Well, don't just stand there!" And then, grinning mischievously, she adds, "Thank you for coming on such short notice."

The doors slide open, revealing a long, tiled hallway. Enitan makes her way down the dark passage. Lanterns flicker on as she nears them, splashing golden light over the mosaic story at her feet. It depicts the annexation of Koriko, worked out in astonishing detail, from the first exploratory raids to the formal addition of the moon habitat to the Imperial holdings. Around the middle is a scene showing the execution of all the Korikese foolish enough to resist the all-consuming might of the Holy Vaalbaran Empire. As always, Enitan moves quickly through the hall.

When she reaches the doors to Ajana's sitting room, she closes her eyes for half a moment to center herself. She lifts a hand to knock when the doors fly open. Gloved fingers shoot out, grab her by the arm, and drag her inside.

The governor steps back, grinning, and offers Enitan a goblet of wine. "So what brings you here, my dear?" Ajana sinks into her plush black couch, her own drink in hand. "Perhaps—"

"Xiang's gone." Enitan sets aside her cup.

Ajana arches a brow. "They're probably just getting high on skey-root or breaking into a storehouse. Or both." Her full lips curve into a small, secretive smile. "Was this just an excuse to—"

"No." Enitan's gut roils. "They were attacked. I found *blood*."

Ajana stiffens. "What happened?"

"I think . . . I think someone took them." *Or killed them*, though she can't bring herself to say it, as if voicing her fears might make them true. "But we don't have any enemies, and everyone likes them—"

"Oh, God." Ajana lets out a strangled sound. "So it's true, they've come here—"

Dread floods over Enitan in an icy wave. "Who's *they*?"

Her gaze flicks away. "There are rumors. About what the Imperials are doing."

"*You're* an Imperial," Enitan snaps. She doesn't mean to lash out, but she can't help herself.

"Not entirely," Ajana corrects, her voice low. She gestures at herself, smiling tightly. "These wouldn't be half-breed half nobles. They may even be agents of Adehkonra himself."

The name is like a slap to Enitan's face. The Imperator.

Fear lodges itself in her throat, all but cutting off her air. "That doesn't happen in real life," she forces out. "That doesn't happen on Koriko."

"I didn't want to believe it either." Ajana curls inward, dropping her head into her hands. "But it *is* happening—"

"Why would the Imperator want Xiang?" Enitan's hands are trembling.

"I don't think he does, not specifically." Ajana's eyes are so wide

Enitan can see the whole of her irises, a deep brown circled by burning white. "It seems like he just wants *people*. Anyone will do."

It takes a moment for Enitan to absorb what Ajana's just said. When she does, her legs buckle. She lets herself crumple, dropping right into Ajana's space. *Ancestors*. There's a broken cry already rising from her lungs, tearing up through her throat like a jagged knife. But she catches the sob, grinds it to dust between her teeth. She does not have the luxury of succumbing to her emotions.

"Why?" Enitan demands, cupping the governor's face in her hands. If Ajana loses her composure, Enitan won't get anything out of her but tears. "*Why?*" she repeats, trying to keep the irritation out of her tone. Only one of them has the right to break down and it's certainly not the shuddering woman before her. "Where have they taken Xiang?"

"I don't know." Ajana's voice is a ragged whisper. "I . . . I'm sorry."

Enitan stares at her, heat welling up behind her eyes until her vision flashes vermillion. "How long has this been happening?"

The question seems to bring Ajana back. She lets out a long hiss of air and pushes Enitan's fingers away from her cheeks, then scrubs a hand down her face. "It began a month after Adehkonra surrendered. They've done an excellent job suppressing the news, but many of our people have gone missing already—far more than usual."

"I thought that was just the sentinels cracking down in the wake of the surrender." A burning sensation threads itself between her ribs, displacing some of her shock. "So you've just been lounging here, drinking imported wine for *months*," she snarls, "while your own people were being kidnapped by your God."

"Don't be cruel." Ajana glares at Enitan. "I didn't have a choice. I still don't. I was explicitly ordered not to act, let alone speak of this."

There is always a choice, Enitan thinks. If Ajana tried to protect them, she'd be sent back to the Vaalbaran interior in disgrace, but at least she would do so with her life and title intact. Instead of voicing this, Enitan takes her by the shoulders. "You have to help me get Xiang back."

Ancestors, all those times she told them off for getting high on skeyroot and galivanting around Ijebu with their ridiculous friends, just for them to be dragged from the safety of their home. The Imperials would've done this to Xiang even if her sibling had heeded her constant complaints. Even if they were the perfect Korikese subject. She should have known better. Piety and proper behavior won't save any of them. It never has.

Ajana lifts her hands and wraps her fingers around Enitan's wrists. "I don't have much influence outside of Koriko."

Enitan squeezes, almost hard enough to hurt. "You *have* to help me."

"Of course I will," Ajana says, determination dawning in her eyes just before they flutter closed. "You know you're my only friend." She drags in a breath. "When I was pulled from my birthing vat, I was mentally and physically eighteen years old."

Enitan looks up at Ajana in concern. She's never spoken of her past before.

"I was dried and dressed and immediately bundled off to Koriko. I never had a chance to forge any lasting bonds. My first seven years on this moon were spent locked away in training and study, all to fortify the knowledge uploaded into my growing brain when I was in the vat." Her mouth twists. "Even my sentinels and caretakers avoided me as much as possible. Three degrees of relation from a past Imperator means nothing when the rest of me is savage." Ajana presses Enitan's hands into her own. "Without you I would be alone in this world. Just as you cannot lose Xiang, I cannot lose you. So yes, Enitan Ijebu, I will help you or die in my attempt."

Enitan bows her head, letting out a small breath. "Thank you."

"None of this will be easy." Ajana stands. "There will be a cost, whether it's some further burden heaped upon Koriko as punishment or another's life traded for Xiang's."

The thought hadn't occurred to Enitan. But she forces herself to nod. Guilt is a luxury, and she would burn down Koriko herself if it meant Xiang was safe. "Thank you," she says again. "I know."

Ajana smiles weakly. "Let it never be said that I disappointed the woman I was going to marry."

As if Ajana's mother, an Imperial duchess, would approve such a match. "Impossible," Enitan says, though not unkindly.

"We've had fun, haven't we?" Ajana's eyes are bright with mischief for half a second before her expression tightens again.

"We have." Enitan breaks into an involuntary smile as she remembers the last summer they spent together. She remembers kissing Ajana under the trees in the monolith's courtyard, and the nights snuggled up by the fire with tea and a badly acted drama. And she will do her best to forget it all. She has a sibling to save, and in her mind Ajana is partly at fault. Any rekindling of what they had will have to wait.

"So, how do we get Xiang back?"

"No." Ajana shakes her head. "There's no *we* in this. *I* will get Xiang back. Go home."

"They're *my* sibling." Enitan shoots to her feet. "I'm going to help."

"We're not dealing with disgruntled Korikese," Ajana snaps. "We're dealing with my God-Emperor. And if not him, then someone nearly as powerful." She reaches over and touches a hand to Enitan's shaved scalp. "If they find out I'm doing this for you . . ."

Then they'll know her loyalty is compromised. The sentinels ignore their relationship because they're certain it's just a dalliance. If anyone suspected the contrary, Ajana would be replaced, and Enitan might very well be killed. She opens her mouth to protest anyway but shuts it when Ajana's eyes harden. There are times when Enitan forgets just who this woman is. This is not one of them.

"Go home," says the governor, her words painfully soft. "Or I'll make you."

They stare at each other until Enitan turns on her heel with a curse and marches to the doors. She looks back, for the briefest of moments, and Ajana's eyes fall quickly from Enitan's face to her discarded wineglass.

"I'll contact you when Xiang is on their way back," says the governor, her gaze still averted. "Discreetly."

"I can't lose you too," Enitan says, the words flying from her mouth unbidden. She chastises herself, flushing. She is not some lovestruck teenager. Not anymore. "I . . . please just be careful."

"I always am," says Ajana. The words are firm, but her face betrays a note of fear.

There are as many ways to say what she wants to as there are stars in the galaxy, but right now . . . this is not the time. Without another word, Enitan leaves her.

THREE

Enitan awakens as the skydome gradually brightens, allowing Jilessa's light to splay its crimson fingers over the horizon, digging its golden nails into the firmament. She lies on her back with her hands folded over her stomach, looking up through the overhead window she forgot to cover last night. She yawns. It will be a beautiful day. She rolls over on her sleeping mat to shake Xiang awake and finds herself grasping at thin air.

The previous day comes crashing back like a tidal wave, and she nearly cries out from the force of it. Her palm hovers just over a small red smear, the last bit of blood she couldn't scrub out of the floor. Enitan stays in this position for a long time, until her outstretched arm begins to burn with exertion. She lets out a tremulous breath, sits up, and forces herself to her feet. As determined by the habitat's preset weather program, it's harvesting season, and she has work to do later at the church. Lying around fretting isn't going to help anyone. Ajana has never broken a promise, and she swore to get Xiang back. That's enough for Enitan. It has to be.

She steps into a pair of loose-fitting trousers, shrugs on a tunic, and slips her feet into well-worn sandals. Forcing herself to get dressed is excruciating; the urge to fall back onto her sleeping mat nearly overwhelms her. Her stomach rumbles for what must be the fifth time. She hasn't eaten in . . . she doesn't remember the last time she ate, actually.

She drags her feet over to the food conserver and forces herself to have some breakfast, a soft disk of flatbread smeared with cold nut paste. She chews methodically, tasting nothing and trying not to think about how Xiang always takes far more paste than necessary. Then she snatches up her satchel and woven basket from their place by the door and heads out. She knocks her fist against the doorframe for good luck and begins the day.

Her work as a tea specialist isn't the job that pays off the Imperial taxes. It's more of a hobby than anything else, something she can call her own. Something untouched by Vaalbara.

Enitan climbs down rickety ladders and winding stairs until she reaches the main plaza. At this hour, the concourse is empty, save for a handful of enterprising merchants setting up brightly colored tents in anticipation of the morning market. She reaches the line of tubelifts at the far end of the plaza, a row of slender glass cylinders that bisect the massive metal rings of the community. She hops into the nearest and presses her hand to the cool wall. A holographic circle spreads out from under her palm.

"Destination: agricultural level," Enitan says. She has her own small tea crop; she doesn't trust just anyone to grow their leaves correctly. A recorded bell dings, and the tubelift lowers her through each of the ten successive structural rings. Most layers of the community are a kilometer across, linked by vebweaver silk and plant fiber ropes. A sturdy frame of living timber keeps the whole structure standing far above the wetlands.

The lift comes to a gentle stop. The lowest ring of the community is also its widest, stretching far beyond the others, allowing for both moisture and ample light. She makes her way past vast orchards and sprawling fields dotted with shaggy wulubison, until she finally reaches her own tiny plot. The gate swings open after it scans her fingerprints and confirms that she is not, in fact, a nefarious tea brigand.

Warm light pours in from large circular windows in the fence, splashing over her small garden: six short rows, each with five deep-green uhie bushes. Enitan drops her satchel and gets to work, carefully picking pairs of leaves with the buds intact and snapping them off at the stem. She finds her rhythm as she makes her way down the first row, tossing the leaves over her shoulder and into the basket at her back. It's monotonous, tiresome work. Not exactly relaxing, but at least it takes her mind off things. Until the silence settles in, at least.

On most days, Xiang would wake early and accompany her. They never helped with the harvest, instead curling up in a corner to read or listen to their dreadful music. Dwelling on Xiang's relative unhelpfulness does little to assuage the melancholy that hits her whenever her gaze drifts over to their spot just below the window. She's not merely frightened for Xiang; she misses her sibling deeply.

Eventually, Enitan has plucked every tea leaf mature enough to be picked, so she grabs her satchel and heads home. She stops at the market on her way back and heads over to the meal stalls. But after glancing over the offerings, she continues on. She's too anxious to eat; her hunger has been replaced by a tangled ball of nerves, twisting and turning in her gut like a lineel out of water.

She kicks open the door to her housepod, a gourd-shaped domicile identical to every other residence on her ring. Once in her tea room, she pulls the basket off her back. She spreads the fresh leaves over wide woven troughs to dry before shaking them to speed up their oxidation. Then she stretches, scrubs her face with a washcloth, and changes into her frock. It's such a dark blue it looks nearly black—but only nearly, as the Imperator alone is permitted to wear the darkest of colors. She pulls on a set of matching gloves and rushes off to the missionary church.

Enitan is about as religious as a rock, but her office is housed in the church complex, and she's technically paid by the abbot. Her real job is that of a glorified scribe. It is more than a mere anomaly that she has this position. After all, Orin, the language and script of the true Vaalbaran citizenry, was a divine gift from the First God-Emperor.

But very few people in the Empire—the *actual* Empire, not including Koriko, a nearly nominal province on a distant, tidally locked moon—are willing to debase themselves enough to learn how to read Akyesi. Thus, after the annexation, the provisional governor stationed before Ajana was forced to hire a native translator and teach them Orin.

There are two framed degrees hanging in Enitan's living room. Her primary focus at Edoga was Homeworld languages. She graduated with top honors but resigned herself to unemployment after graduation. A fitting punishment for the impracticality of her chosen studies—in the eyes of Koriko's imperial masters. The Vaalbarans are great patrons of the humanities, but only so long as the scholarship flows from respectable sources. There is no such thing as a barbarian scholar. The scribe position was both a gift and a curse from the Ancestors. Winning the job was easy enough (she was one of two people in the running), though keeping it has been anything but. Half the monks in Vaalbara vehemently protested her hiring, declaring that it would be sacrilege of the highest order to bestow the gift of their holy script upon a filthy savage.

Enitan is about halfway to the church when a gloved hand grabs her wrist and tugs her around.

She wrenches her hand free with a snarl. "What a surprise, Stijena," she says stiffly, in Orin. "I suppose your transfer to the capital was denied? Again?"

Stijena's pale eyes, the color of weak green tea, track her every movement. Probably to pick out some mortal flaw if he can, so he can run off to his superiors and complain yet again. Of all the monks, none protested her appointment as bitterly as he.

"You are truly a desecration walking, Enitan."

"Out of practice?" She smiles thinly. "That's your least clever jab by far."

She knows she ought to be more careful around Stijena. He's a monk and a Vaalbaran citizen. If he called for a sentinel to arrest or beat her, they'd probably do it, no questions asked. Especially if they didn't recognize her. But he's never seriously threatened her before, and she figures that a truly powerful man wouldn't spend his time harassing what he considers to be the dirt under his feet. Part of her wonders if he takes some sort of sick pleasure in being verbally thrashed by a savage. But really, her patience is worn too thin for her to be polite.

"But it's the truest insult I've ever bestowed upon you," he retorts, stomping after her when she turns away and resumes her trek. "Have you no respect for God? For my mission? Give up your heresy and find something within your meager abilities."

Enitan stops, turns, and looks back at Stijena. His pale, blotchy face is screwed up into an expression so sour her own lips nearly pucker. He spent months clawing at the abbot's door like a starving mossicat, trying to get her to stipulate that Enitan could only be permitted to read her own people's petitions and letters and complaints aloud. He outright demanded that a true citizen be stationed to transcribe words into Orin. But as it turned out, no *true citizen* actually understood Akyesi enough to do so.

Even the sentinels, who interact with Korikese people on a daily basis, only know enough of the language to tell when someone's saying something treasonous, or to order around the populace. And the monks certainly aren't fluent, either, Stijena included; they don't have to be. They came to Koriko to purify the land through prayer and meditation, not to converse with the barbarians.

"What mission?" she snaps. "I have yet to see you do anything besides harass me and your fellow monks."

She watches Stijena try not to sputter. "One day," he says darkly, "the governor won't be around to protect you. You'll be ousted, and then I'll make you regret every word you've ever spoken to me."

"Oh, Stijena." Enitan pats his cheek, the condescension in her tone nearly matching his. "You already tried and failed before Ajana arrived. Spectacularly."

When the abbot refused him, Stijena turned to the provisional governor for help. He successfully harried the man into formally requesting an Imperial linguist trained to read and write Akyesi. Only the heads of the powerful Linguists' Coalition could actually do so, and they very much did not want to leave the enlightened capital of Vaalbara to live in the middle of nowhere. The Coalition made an enormous fuss and criticized the Supreme Abbot's more recent ideological interpretations of the Black Codex—the original Orin manuscript, penned by the First God-Emperor herself.

"No, the Supreme Abbot failed." Stijena's voice drops to a razorblade whisper. Wise, considering the Supreme Abbot could have him flogged for insolence if word of his bad-mouthing reached their ear. "If they weren't such a coward, they would have—"

"What? Issued a command for every monk to spend the next century manually redacting scattered lines from the last seven years of handwritten scripture?" She flings a hand at the church. "Your Supreme Abbot might be a coward, but they're not a fool. Their own acolytes would smother them in their sleep."

This is why Enitan was finally allowed to serve as a scribe. Forced to choose between defiling the divine script or having to comb through millions of pages of scripture themselves—which can only be written by hand on paper—the Church officially decided that a single savage, sufficiently cleansed, could be allowed to study Orin.

Stijena sniffs haughtily once he finally manages to come up with a retort. "I'll see to it that the Church commissions a language synth."

Enitan laughs outright. "Are you certain you were born in the Imperial interior?" The Empire has always prided itself on the fact that it relies on humans alone. It's the slothful Republic that makes widespread use of artificial labor with its sinfully humanoid synths. She's genuinely surprised by the suggestion, but he really does hate her that much. "Enjoy the rest of your day, monk."

She leaves him muttering curses in the path. Ordinarily, she'd be extremely pleased with herself. Today, though, all she feels is numb. She steps up to the church—a glass prism that looms over the other buildings—and sighs deeply. She'll be here until sundown. She scans her fingerprints on the gleaming doors and slips inside before they've slid even halfway open. Brightly painted minor Vaalbaran gods crowd the entrance chamber, each presiding over a smoking dish of incense. Enitan strides over a walkway of copper and colored glass and into the central courtyard, a painfully monochrome enclosure built from imported blocks of granite and volcanic rock.

From there, she makes her way to her office, a tiny box that remains resolutely humid no matter how high she turns on the cooling unit. She plops down onto her threadbare cushion and scoots up to her low, squat desk. There's a holopicture of her tiny family in the corner. It was taken eons ago, when Xiang was still trying to decide on a hairstyle that worked for them. They're sporting a bright red bob that makes them look a bit like a too-ripe lagalpear. Enitan tries not to look at the projection for too long.

Already looking forward to the end of the day, she begins to work through the stacks of records and reports and requests delivered to her, many of which will eventually end up on Ajana's desk after her personal staff reviews them. After a few minutes, Enitan wonders for the thousandth time whether her salary is worth the toil. There are towers of datapads and heaps of holosheets. And most of it is garbage, balderdash she can't wait to laugh about with Xiang as soon as they're back. She doesn't allow herself to consider what she'll do if they never return.

She throws out half of it. There are twenty-three petitions for fewer sentinels, and Enitan knows from experience that appeals like this only encourage the Empire to send more muscle. The seventy-seven letters protesting this year's tax raise are immediately deleted along with the petitions, their holosheets set aside in a pile for reuse. Ajana has always encouraged free speech, but Enitan knows she won't be able to do a thing about the taxes. Reading the endless pleas of her people would only hurt her. Mixed in are 105 anonymous vitriolic notes aimed like arrows at the governor herself. *Traitor to your people. Half-breed parasite. Imperial puppet.* These are the kindest. Enitan wipes them all. Though she knows Ajana can take the abuse and that erasing the governor's mail is a serious offense, Enitan wants to protect her as much as she can. The thing about love, she's discovered, is that the mass of it never changes, even if the bond itself changes shape. The crinkle of Ajana's eyes when she laughs will always make Enitan catch her breath. The brush of Ajana's shoulder against hers will always make her feel safe. As safe as a Korikese woman can be these days, anyway.

And Enitan wants to shield her people. Progressive governor or not, if a sentinel were to see the things Korikese say about the colonial regime . . . there would be bloodshed, to say the least.

She translates the rest, running the simplest files through an automatic interpreter—the Empire might look down on automation, but it's reasonable enough to make concessions—and looks the finished products over to ensure the sender's original meaning isn't completely distorted. Others are too sacred to go through a machine, like the prayers the few faithful among the community want the monks to impart to their God. She converts these to Orin by hand. The remainder are reports from the headwoman, which Enitan stamps so they'll be sent directly to Ajana.

By the time the skydome begins to darken, Enitan has slogged through nearly all of the mess. The rest she'll do early tomorrow. She stands, brushes off her frock, and goes home. She still has to hand roll the leaves, spread a couple of bundles out to oxidize for a few hours, and fire some of those batches in turn. Only then will the tea be ready to be sorted, mixed with native spices or flowers, and finally packed. It will be well into the morning before she permits herself to rest.

She looks forward to it. If she works herself to the bone, she'll be too busy to drive herself insane worrying about Xiang. Ajana was right; the bitter truth is that there's less than nothing she can do. If she tries to get involved, the Imperator's agents will slit her peasant throat. Or they'll take her, too, to be part of whatever Xiang is being forced into. Or they'll fashion her into a chain, a tool to keep Ajana in line. Enitan can't bear the thought of being used against her friend and former lover. So she drags herself through the door of her housepod, manages not to collapse on the floor, and rolls her leaves into perfect little pearls. She tries not to cry, but it's a losing battle.

She's in the main room forcing down a near-boiling mug of tea—the pain helps a little, distracting her from everything else—when someone knocks at her door, so hard the wood trembles in its frame. She hisses out a string of profanity, hot air stinging the burned meat of her tongue. She drags herself over to the door and lifts herself onto her toes to peer through the peephole. There's a sentinel there. Her helmet and uniform have been traded for a simple green headband and tunic, but Enitan recognizes the oddly coiled energy of the officer from yesterday. The one who saved her hide and then nearly turned on her later. This is the discreet message Ajana promised her. Xiang is safe. They're on their way home. Perhaps she *will* marry Ajana one day. Enitan nearly weeps with relief as she flings open the door.

"Citizen," says the sentinel, and Enitan immediately stiffens. No sentinel ever calls a native a citizen. A provincial, sometimes. Simply Korikese in its singular form, often. And then there's the classic *savage*, most effective when snarled in said savage's face. When a Vaalbaran sentinel calls a Korikese person a citizen, they do so to be ironic or cruel. Frequently both. But the woman before her seems sincere, if anxious.

Enitan draws closer to the sentinel, though every cell in her body screams in protest. She's never been this close to a sentinel before; in the tubelift she practically pressed herself to the wall. Even when they're beating Korikese people, they do so at a distance with their shockstaffs, lest unclean blood touch them. "Has something—"

The sentinel reaches into the embroidered bag at her hip, pulls out a small white box, and holds it out to Enitan. Ajana's personal seal is overlaid in silver on top, surrounded by an engraved prayer to Eshuik, one of the regional Gondwanan death gods that had been absorbed into the Vaalbaran faith like the rest.

Enitan's blood freezes in her veins, a horrible, all-consuming chill prickling down her spine. "This is one of her worst jokes," she croaks, her throat going tight. "This isn't funny at all."

"I'm so sorry," says the sentinel, and there is genuine sorrow in her voice. "Lady Ajana is dead."

FOUR

The sun has set by the time Enitan gathers the will to open Ajana's funerary box. It has only three things: her favorite headscarf, a copper ring with a hexagonal prism of blue goldstone, and a poignard with a large piece of quartz at the pommel. Alone now, Enitan presses the headscarf to her face. She lets out a strangled sob. It still smells like Ajana—citrus and sunlight. Shivering despite the warm evening, she wraps the length of the bright cloth around her right arm. She slips the ring into the pocket of her tunic and hides the poignard under a loose floorboard. Even if she knew how to handle it, she doesn't have a permit to possess a weapon; if she's caught outside with the poignard, she'll be shipped off to the asteroid mines and sentenced to twenty years of hard labor. She's heard of the horrors that happen in the shadows of those starless pits. The overseers lop off laborers' limbs if the monthly quota isn't met, only to have every hand and foot regrown without anesthetic. Then they throw their victims back to work with the promise to chop more off next time.

Enitan crawls over to her sleeping mat, hugs the box to her chest, and weeps. The panic and terror that filled her when she saw that smear of blood swell every second Xiang doesn't walk through the door. She's tried to shove down any fragment of emotion that has escaped, tried to work through the anxiety and the fear, but Ajana's death destroys the paper-thin control she plastered over the cracks. She is a broken dam, salt water pouring out of her in burning torrents.

Eventually, her body decides it has squandered enough water and Enitan stops crying. She feels as hollow as the housepod, horribly and utterly empty. If she breathes too deeply, she'll shatter completely. Fatigue sinks into her bones, grinding down on her consciousness. Clutching the box even tighter, she closes her eyes and lets exhaustion take her.

◆

Enitan awakens many hours later. She's still tired, now even more so. Her hip hurts after so long on her side, but she can't bring herself to turn onto her back. There's someone knocking at the door. It's probably one of the Church's new acolytes, sent to berate her for being late to work. She doesn't care. The knocking grows louder, more insistent. Enitan squeezes her eyes shut. She doesn't want to get up. She doesn't want to think about how she's lost everyone she's ever loved in just over a day, for reasons that are far beyond her control and that she barely comprehends. She wants answers, but she doesn't even know what questions to ask or to whom to ask them. And so her only option is to stay like this, curled up under every blanket she owns with Ajana's box. She's grown to appreciate this emptiness. Nothing is so much easier to deal with than everything—than sorrow and all-consuming loss.

Light floods in as the door flies open. Enitan stays on the ground, though her eyes flick to the floorboard concealing the stashed poignard. There's no point. Not to this, not to anything. The only people who can override the security on doors are Imperial sentinels. Although, now that she thinks of it, if she attacks them, they'll kill her. And death is absolute, effortless nothing. *Hmm.* Enitan looks up.

It's the same sentinel who saved Enitan's hide and brought her the funerary box, wearing her armor this time. She stands between Enitan and the poignard, so there goes that plan. Enitan closes her eyes, the lids dragging shut like steel doors.

"I thought you said I would be spared from questioning," she croaks. Ajana's death was ruled a suicide, but when the daughter of a duchess dies, someone must be blamed, even if it was supposedly her own hand that held the blade. Enitan's exemption from interrogation surprised her. Sentinels misplace legal principles as soon as they depart their home planet, so by the time they get to Koriko, they're convinced that savages are guilty until proven innocent. Usually, when there's a serious crime, nearly everyone in the community is interrogated.

"Citizen," says the sentinel. "Did you not hear the summons? All Korikese persons must assemble at the main concourse."

Enitan rolls onto her stomach, pressing her face hard into her sleeping mat. "I didn't. I was sleeping."

"You must join the others."

Very quietly, Enitan asks, "Can . . . Can I see her?"

"No," the sentinel says after a moment's silence. "Lady Ajana is undergoing preparations for the embalming rites. As a . . . non-Imperial, the monks would see your presence as desecration."

"The only desecration I see is you and your trigger-happy friends," Enitan hisses.

"As I said, this is what the *monks* would see," the sentinel says, mercifully ignoring Enitan's seditious statement. She sounds angry, though not at the woman curled at her feet.

That makes Enitan turn over and stare up at her. "An assembly?" She grits her teeth. "So they've already replaced her, then?"

"No. They haven't, and they won't be." The sentinel drops suddenly, crouching by Enitan's side. "At least not until the investigation into Lady Ajana's death is completed."

"An investigation?" Enitan scoffs. "You mean until a suitable scapegoat is found." She knows she should stop, but she can't bring herself to care.

"Until the investigation is completed," the sentinel repeats, her voice harsher now, "a child of the local headwoman will serve as a diplomatic guest of God."

"So, a hostage." Enitan flashes her teeth. "Someone didn't do their research. The headwoman doesn't have a child, not in any way that matters." Her people don't *have* blood families, at least not like those in the rest of the Empire. On Koriko there are lifelong bond-siblings, paired by the headpeople at birth and raised by the whole community until adulthood.

The sentinel leans forward. "That is irrelevant."

Of course it is. This is all for show. The headwoman could send absolutely anyone and it wouldn't matter. This is just a formality, yet another humiliation forced upon the communities. The Imperator doesn't need a political hostage to keep a hold on Koriko. The sentinels do their job, and they do it well. Besides, the Empire already does what it wants with the habitat. And the people. Little has changed with Vaalbara's surrender to the Republic, and certainly not for the better. It seems Koriko's losses have only gotten closer to Enitan since then.

Xiang. Her eyes prickle with a fresh bout of tears.

"Why are you telling me this?" she grinds out, wiping at her eyes.

The sentinel stands and offers Enitan her hand. "On your feet, citizen."

Enitan is about to snarl something rude when her still-reeling mind snags on her last thought. *The headwoman could send absolutely anyone.* The Imperator's hostage will be afforded little freedom to poke around, but if Enitan can somehow get herself shipped to Vaalbara, she'll be living among the people surely responsible for Xiang's kidnapping and Ajana's murder. She could uncover the monsters that took them both away.

She knows it's not a plan. It's just a desperate, supremely stupid wish, but she doesn't see another choice. With Ajana gone, she has no one to rely on but herself. She must confront the leviathan that took her sibling. There's no one to do it for her. And Xiang might still be alive. Better to be executed in an attempt to save them than to waste away on her sleeping mat.

Enitan bats away the sentinel's hand and forces herself to her feet. A sudden wave of nausea nearly knocks her over, but the sentinel catches her before she falls. Enitan shakes the woman's gloved hands off her.

"Fine. You found me. I'm the headwoman's daughter."

The sentinel says nothing, only nods her head as if in quiet approval. Enitan steps around her and flings aside the floorboard, retrieves the poignard, and looks up at the sentinel, defiance in her eyes. For just a moment she feels strong, immutable, though she knows that if the sentinel strikes her, she will fall. The sentinel does nothing, and Enitan shoves the poignard into her satchel. She runs around the sentinel and rummages through the rest of the housepod. She doesn't have much, but she packs her formal tunics, a handful of engraved currency chits, and her church frock—she laughs at the idea that she might use it as a disguise but brings it anyway. After a moment's hesitation, she snatches up a few tins of tea and starts toward the door.

The sentinel stops her. "Do you have everything you want? You may not be permitted to return for years."

Or ever, if she's assassinated by Imperial agents or executed by the Imperator.

Enitan swallows hard and nods. "I have what I need," she says, straightening her posture.

She doesn't ask the sentinel why she's helping her, though the question burns on the tip of her tongue. She's not naive enough to think that this benevolence comes without some sort of cost. But for now she has countless more important things to worry about.

Together they head toward the concourse, Enitan putting as much distance between the sentinel and herself as she can. When they reach their destination on the third ring, her eyes go wide. She doesn't remember the last mandatory assembly, doesn't remember ever seeing so many of her own people amassed in one place. There must be tens of thousands of them. And everyone is whispering, murmuring, snarling at each other. A few people are crying. The sentinel takes hold of Enitan's arm and tugs her through the frozen mass, shoving people aside as she does so.

At the front of the crowd stands the headwoman. Though Enitan interacts with the leader of Ijebu regularly, given the nature of her work, the woman remains utterly inscrutable to her. The headwoman is as formidable as they come, tall and wide and statuesque. Before her stands a thin man nearly swallowed whole by the deep red uniform of the Imperial bureaucracy. Behind him is a semicircle of crimson-armored sentinels. Their shockstaffs glint in the midday sun.

The headwoman shakes her head, her long locs swaying with the movement. "For the hundredth time, I don't *have* a child," she snaps. "You don't need to take anyone. We'll comply."

"Your community might mind itself, but what of the others?" the official demands. "Can you guarantee their continued amenability without some sort of incentive? The fact that we're taking only one hostage is already a mercy I'm not certain your kind deserve."

The headwoman's dark eyes narrow into dangerous slits. Among the dozens of headpeople overseeing the fifty-nine communities of Ko-riko, she's the first among equals. It's true that the other communities will do as she tells them. "I'll do my job whether or not you—"

"Look, Korikese," snaps the official. "I have my orders, and so do you. I will remain here as long as need be." He glances back at the line of uniformed sentinels behind him, each formidably armed. "Though I must warn you that my sentinels are not as patient as I am."

"Sir." Ajana's sentinel steps forward, her gloved hand tight around Enitan's arm. "I found the headwoman's daughter."

The official blinks at her, his expression on the edge of amused. "Good work, sentinel."

"No!" The headwoman surges forward, only to be cut off by another sentinel, his fingers already twitching toward the dissection gun on his belt. Her gaze snaps to Enitan. "What are you doing—"

"It's all right . . . Mother," Enitan says, her tongue nearly tripping over the word. "I'll be fine." She reaches over and pulls the headwoman into a brief, awkward hug. When she draws back, the older woman's eyes are full of wry, bitter understanding—and gratitude.

"I'm sorry I couldn't protect you," says the headwoman, cupping Enitan's cheek in a cool, dry hand. She probably means it; perhaps she even knows about Xiang.

"Don't be." Enitan wants to be angry, but she knows that the headwoman's options were even fewer than Ajana's—she could either allow a handful of people to disappear or bring about the destruction of whole communities. "Farewell, Mother."

The headwoman drags her into another embrace, one that's almost comfortable now. The second they break apart, one of the official's sentinels grabs Enitan's shoulders.

The official regards the headwoman with cold cruelty. "You should not have lied to me." He smiles, and something in the expression sends a sick chill down Enitan's spine. He turns to the sentinel at his side. "Break her arm."

"No!" Enitan screams, surging forward. "Please—"

She doesn't see it happen. All she hears is a nauseating crunch and the headwoman's strangled cry as the sentinel restraining Enitan hauls her backward out of view. He laughs as he drags Enitan onto the bridge connecting the main level to the Imperial docking station outside.

The official's ship presses against the other side of the skydome like a huge marcroaker, rotund and ungainly. It's small, though, barely larger than any of the dozen shuttles flitting like iridescent beetles above them. Certainly, it's no match for an interplanetary mining vessel or warship, the latter of which the Empire built only three. They needed very little to conquer Koriko. Before Vaalbara, the communities had never known war.

Enitan twists, trying to get a good look at the official himself. He walks a few paces behind her, flanked by the rest of his sentinels. He stares back at her, and she sees that his hint of amusement has swollen like a boil. He doesn't look even moderately convinced by her little show, but he also doesn't look like he cares whether she's the headwoman's beloved daughter or a ne'er-do-well the whole community wanted to be rid of. His slight smile tells her the whole thing humors him, while the quickness of his step makes it clear that he wants to return to what his people consider civilization as soon as possible.

"Let that be your first lesson," he tells her, his lips pulling apart into a caustic, full-blown grin. His teeth are very, very white, contrasting sharply against the russet tones of his skin. "Lying is one of the Twenty Great Sins, and it will certainly not be tolerated in the capital." He lets out a mournful sigh. "It is a shame that your mother possesses the same evil as the rest of your kind. Leaders should be the best among their lot, even if the lot are . . ." He gestures expansively with one hand.

"There was no reason for you to hurt her," Enitan hisses. She feels sick to her stomach. "She told you the truth. Our truth."

"There is only *one* truth, and it is Vaalbara's," the official replies, as the sentinel's grip around her tightens. "Take her in."

The dock's doors slide open, revealing a narrow tunnel that cuts through the skydome's protective outer fluid layer. The sentinel maneuvers Enitan through the tunnel and then the air lock; into the cold, oily darkness of the transport; and onto a cushioned seat. Jilessa looms behind them, unobstructed by the skydome's filters. The vessel isn't so different from a local shuttle, she tells herself over and over. But it's useless. They haven't even departed the skydome yet, and this is already the farthest she's ever been from home. Her heart races so desperately she can hardly hear her own thoughts.

"Secure yourself," the sentinel orders, silhouetted by the bright
window behind her. A monster in a mask, indistinguishable from her
brethren.

Enitan swallows the tightness in her throat and forces herself to
take in a breath. She drops her satchel, then reaches behind her shoulder to buckle herself in. Her hands are only trembling a little. The official strides in, hands clasped behind his back, and lowers himself
gracefully into his own seat. The other sentinels soon follow, tramping
in lockstep. With a warning chime, the air lock doors refold themselves
and begin to slide shut. Enitan forces herself back into the seat and
watches the community disappear behind the rising steel, blurred by
the skydome's sealing surface. She tries to sear that murky emerald
wedge of home into her mind. The air lock whirs shut, followed by the
vessel's main doors. The ship detaches from the habitat with a heavy
click. And then, with a low, bone-rattling hum, the spacedrive activates.

Enitan yanks against her safety belt, wrenching herself toward the
nearest window. Koriko shrinks into a tiny blue-gray ball flecked with
brilliant green, and then into nothing at all.

FIVE

The ship is truly a marvel of engineering. Its artificial gravity, too, is extraordinary, set to match Gondwana's natural tug. It's just a little heavier than the effect produced by Koriko's generators, meant to simulate the Homeworld standard. Thankfully, though the increase is significant enough to notice, it is not so great as to impact Enitan's mobility. She knew the difference was a slight one, but hearing about the shift secondhand and feeling it for herself are two very different things.

More impressive, though, is the fact that they're cutting through space at a tenth the speed of light. Every second, they cross another thirty million meters. Despite herself, Enitan is once again breathless, though for quite different reasons than before. Her awe is only heightened by the fact that this is ancient technology, scavenged from the Homeworld leviathans that brought the first Ancestors of every society to this system. The secrets of much of their forebears' technology have been lost to time and the cycle of civilization, with the last dozen generations understanding only enough to operate what few wonders remain.

Everyone else seems bored.

They've been flying for just over three hours when the official tires of his datapad and turns to Enitan. "If your Korikese brethren do anything foolish, you'll be the first to pay the price," he says in stilted

Akyesi. He reaches over to the shuttle's food conserver and produces two small bottles of watered wine. He does not offer her one. "When we reach Gondwana, you ought to ask for a monk."

Enitan ignores him. Her cool gaze does not leave the blur of space. Though the stars to either side of the ship retain their normal color, the ones at the front have a faintly cobalt tint, and the ones behind the vessel are slightly scarlet. Human eyes aren't quite good enough to register anything but a minor difference in brightness, but she's still awed. Blueshifting and redshifting in action; the compression and stretch of light waves. For the first time in her life, Enitan is grateful Xiang blackmailed her into taking a physics course with them. She wouldn't be able to fully appreciate this otherwise—

"If you don't schedule a cremation, your corpse will be used as fodder," the official finishes.

"Thank you for your concern, sir," she says smoothly, "but my people are loyal—"

"*People?*" The official chuckles, sipping at his wine.

She knows that, legally and culturally, Vaalbarans don't recognize the humanity of Korikese. Only true Imperial citizens are people, and everyone else is less. At the heart of the Empire, the distinction is a small one. It would be impossible to determine the quality of one's blood until they opened their mouth and started speaking. But everywhere else, this difference is starker. During the annexation, it was the line between life and death, between firing the dissection gun and being at the muzzle of it. And after the Imperator's surrender to the Republic, the Empire needs another target for its aggression.

But knowing that she is not a person and having someone tell her that she isn't, especially with that sneering mouth . . . Enitan entertains the fantasy of grabbing the bottle and swinging it into his head. But then one of the sentinels shifts beside her, and her anger is usurped by fear. She knows they'd eviscerate her if she laid a hand on the official.

And even worse, she would only be confirming every idea about her people that he brought with him. She will not give him the pleasure of returning to his friends and family with tales of how the Korikese are just as barbaric as he imagined. Besides, he's really doing her a favor. She has experience dealing with sentinels and monks, not regular Imperial citizens. If this is what the rest of the Empire will be like, practice at dealing with it can't hurt.

So Enitan draws in a breath and meets the official's eyes. But although she keeps her face frozen into a careful, politely embarrassed mask, anger bubbles in her chest like molten rock. She cannot break a bottle against his skull, or even yell at him, but she *can* unsettle him. "My apologies. A slip of the tongue," she says in flawless, accentless Orin.

The sentinels stiffen. The official nearly spits out his wine. He doesn't, unfortunately, but he does struggle to swallow it. "Who taught you that?" he snaps, eyes burning.

She shrugs. "The monks, sir. I'm the barbarian scribe."

He cocks his head, his brow furrowed. She watches as remembrance dawns on his face: his mouth falls open; his eyes grow wide. Enitan's smile widens. The squabble between the Church and the Linguists' Coalition was a source of prime entertainment for the Empire's rich and powerful, second only to the war. Her story has already spread across the Empire (although few know her name and face, as the Church did everything it could to minimize publicity).

Any chagrin drains from his expression, all too quickly replaced with glistening interest. He smiles at her. "You're a fascinating little savage, aren't you?"

"You flatter me," says Enitan.

The official frowns. "It was not a compliment."

Enitan's grin is so wide now it hurts. "I know. Sir."

◆

Two hundred million kilometers from Gondwana, the official orders that they stop by an asteroid station to stretch their legs and find their dinner. The conserver has nothing but wine, and the shuttle's stores have only emergency rations that, according to the official, smell like fermented sewage and taste worse. It's not the God-Emperor who's traveling across half the system—just an unlucky functionary and a quasi-diplomatic savage hostage. Whoever assigned the man to this mission thought he could go eight hours without fresh food. They were wrong.

The ship slows to a more reasonable speed a safe distance away from Lagash Mining Outpost, a lifeless imitation of Koriko clinging to the second-largest asteroid in the belt. The overgrown, silicate-rich rock might not look like much, Enitan knows, but it contains perhaps a billion or so kilograms of metal, with a hundred thousand of those kilograms being gold, platinum, and rhodium. Vaalbara's fledgling mining project has yet to pay off its ludicrous investment, but once it starts turning a profit, that profit will be unimaginable. Assuming the Republic survives long enough to see that happen, Enitan imagines its greatest regret will be focusing all its efforts on maintaining territory on a single planet, rather than expanding into the system.

The ship touches down on a mobile landing pad, which rolls them through a massive air lock and into an environmentally controlled hangar. The doors fly open with a sharp breath of air, their constituent segments sliding down into a curved walkway. As soon as the ramp hits the floor, the official complains about Enitan's stench and tells a sentinel to go "air" her. Swallowing a sharp retort, Enitan follows her armed escort outside, where they stand in the shadow of the shuttle. The rest of the force heads toward the hangar exit in search of supper.

Enitan looks around, her stomach grumbling furiously. She doubts they'll bring her back any food, but at least she can distract herself from her hunger. The hangar is a cavernous, stark space, in essence a wide hexagonal prism cut deep into the belly of the asteroid. Seamless black steel flows over the massive walls like ink, interrupted only by long, thin blue-white light panels. It's almost entirely silent now that the ship is on standby, save for the low electric purr of the engines. Empty, too, save for a handful of other Imperial spacecraft. All in all, the space is sleek, elegant, and sterile.

The mines farther in are everything but. Forget artificial gravity; she's heard the shafts are rarely even lit. She has no idea how many of her people are already imprisoned here, toiling in the unending darkness alongside the hulking machines the Empire pretends not to use off-planet. And all of it made possible by the Korikese environmental-enrichment technology Vaalbara stole and then perverted for their own aims.

She slides down against the cold chassis of the ship until she hits the tiled ground, then wraps her arms around her knees and lowers her head into her lap.

Her minder puts his hands on his hips and leans over her. "Do you require medical attention?"

"I do not," Enitan grits out. *Psychological attention, though . . .*

The official may be a condescending asshole, but his earlier words about organizing her own cremation ring true. The Imperator must know that if Koriko wants to rebel, it will do so whether there's an axe over Enitan's head or not. But the Empire first glued itself together by taking the hostages of neighboring nations; a thousand years of historical precedent aren't about to be thrown out the window just because no one on Koriko actually recognizes their biological children. At least if the barbarians decide to declare their independence, the Imperator will have one of them at hand to murder. Enitan is almost certain she's headed to her death, though that's the least of her problems. Her primary concern is that she won't be able to save Xiang. (If she's *very* lucky, she'll be able to revenge herself on whoever ordered their abduction and Ajana's death. But in the end, that is more desire than necessity.)

Enitan pulls her head from her knees and looks up at the smooth, dark ceiling. She shivers and stands. The air around her is as cold as death itself, likely to save energy where it matters least. She doubts the mines are much warmer. Enitan is about to retreat back into the shuttle when the official sticks his head out and glowers down at her from the top of the ramp. "Why aren't you with the rest of the sentinels making yourself useful?" he snaps. "There's a hydroponics deck somewhere out there. Go put your people's gathering skills to good use."

Enitan counts to five before she opens her mouth. "We have farms, sir. As you have seen yourself, Koriko is a *city*, not some half-submerged hamlet," she says, keeping her voice as sweet as possible.

The official stares at her blankly, and Enitan sighs. It's as if her words went through a filter; he only understands what he already believes about her people. "You don't know what a proper city looks like," he says. If his eyes narrow any further, he'll be closing them. He waves a satin glove at the sentinel. "Take her to—"

He doesn't get to finish the order, because his head is gone. Blood mists the air, coating the ship, the sentinel, and Enitan in crimson. A few drops land in her open, silently screaming mouth. The official's head begins to float downward in paper-thin slivers. The rest of his body collapses over the ramp in thick slabs, sliced apart as effectively as by a surgeon's scalpel. Stomach acid bubbles up Enitan's throat—she forces it down, just barely.

Six people step out from the shadows of the surrounding vessels, all masked and wrapped in filthy scraps of multicolored cloth. Pirates. Enitan jerks backward on instinct, throwing herself into the ship's hull.

Pain sinks into her shoulder as a man steps forward. The shredded blue remains of a monk's frock wrap around his muscled form. His dissection gun, aimed directly at the sentinel, is still smoking. Enitan stares at him in horror, commanding her body to remain perfectly still as he stalks toward them.

"We want the savage," he barks in Orin, and Enitan nearly lets out a breath in relief.

If the raiders spoke in Korikesian or Akyesi and it got back to the capital, the Imperator wouldn't bother with diplomatic pretense when the news reached him. He'd simply raze Koriko to the ground and send in his own citizens to repopulate it. And then Enitan realizes what the brigand has just said. Her teeth sink into her tongue, trapping a bubble of hysterical laughter—she's being taken hostage from the people who took her hostage.

"Hands up, savage," the man snaps.

Heart hammering, Enitan rises to her feet with her hands up in surrender. She looks over at the sentinel, the acrid stink of urine filling her nostrils. Well, she's not going to get any help there; he doesn't even have his shockstaff. She turns toward the pirates. "Don't kill him," she says, her voice as even as she can keep it. "I'll come."

"How heroic," says the man. He pulls the trigger, and the gun goes off with a bang and a flash of brilliant white light.

The sentinel falls beside the official, his torso sliding apart in fleshy sheets. His final expression is one of complete and utter shock.

Enitan's heart feels like it's about to burst. She swivels around. "What—"

The man lifts his arm and fires twice more, slicing apart the external cameras on the shuttle's hull. Then he shoves his weapon into the holster at his hip and rips off his mask. His face is like a block of granite, with a prominent nose that seems as if it's been broken and reset half a dozen times. His expression, though, is surprisingly gentle.

"Who—"

The man cuts her off with a sweep of his hand. "We don't have much time. Follow me." And then he strides over to the shuttle, kicks the bodies off the ramp, and saunters in as if he owns it.

One of the other pirates, still masked, presses the cold muzzle of their gun to Enitan's back. "Move," they snarl, and Enitan does.

She creeps into the shuttle, keeping her eyes resolutely off the two corpses flanking the ramp. She hesitates before she steps all the way in; the first pirate has turned off all the lights. She throws a glance over her shoulder. There's nowhere to run; the man's companions have formed a tight circle around the shuttle.

"Sit," the pirate says, the sharp crescent of his grin flashing in the darkness.

Enitan folds herself into the seat opposite the man. She clasps her hands together, resisting the urge to wipe her sweat-slick palms on her pants. "How did you know we'd be landing here?"

"That so-called official is—*was*—a wanted criminal in Ominira. We've been tracking his movements for months, and the opportunity finally presented itself for us to eliminate him. But we've also been ordered to find you."

"You're not actually pirates, are you?"

"No." The man leans forward, arms crossed over his knees. "We're operatives from the Ominirish Republic, sent by the High Consul themself."

Ancestors. Every word out of his mouth seems more absurd than the last. "All right." She doesn't have much of a choice; she decides to play along. "And what does the Consul want with a barbarian hostage?"

"They'll tell you themself." The pirate pulls a thick silver disk from his pocket—a compact hologram projector.

He sets it carefully on the floor before pressing a side button. The device flickers to life; a silvery beam shoots out from the center and flattens into a triangle, then an upturned pyramid. The prism revolves for a few seconds before contorting into a gray, transparent head. Dark, deep-set eyes. A long nose. And that charismatic almost-smile. Enitan has seen this face a thousand times, on the mocking posters and in the propaganda-stuffed "documentaries" churned out by the Empire. The High Consul's holographic head tilts amiably to the side.

"Sir," Enitan chokes out.

"I do apologize for the strange circumstances," says one of the most powerful people in the star system. "But discretion is of the utmost importance."

Enitan's gaze flicks to the offical's blood-splattered boot, just visible from her seat. "I understand."

"Good," says the High Consul. "What did you think of the war?"

Of all the things she thought they might say, that was not one of them. "I didn't," says Enitan, after an eternity. "It never touched Koriko."

The High Consul tilts their head a fraction of a centimeter further. "And now?"

Enitan licks her lips. "The Imperator signed your treaty. The war is over."

One side of their mouth quirks upward. "You don't believe that."

Enitan looks away, swallowing thickly. "Koriko has never been a part of your conflict."

"But your overlords are, and they'll drag you into it. The former Imperator's surrender has only stoked Vaalbara's hunger," says the High Consul, a tightness around their eyes now. "The new Imperator—"

"New Imperator?" Enitan interrupts, and then remembers herself. "Forgive me—"

"Yes. Adehkonra is off galivanting in the wilderness as some sort of ascetic, according to our informants. He abdicated and proclaimed his successor this morning. The coronation will be well over by the time you reach the Imperial interior." The Consul's gaze slides away for a moment, tracking some movement to their side. "As I'm certain Lwin here has told you, there's not much time. This is true on several levels. We've just discovered that the old Imperator began abducting Ominir- ish citizens years ago. Spirits know how many poor souls he took." Their brows knit together. "And it appears that the new Imperator is set to follow in his footsteps, only in far greater numbers and from her own populace."

"Korikese aren't Imperial citizens."

The High Consul sighs, a sound heavy with sorrow and shared pain. "Well, that's not exactly salve on the burn, is it?"

"What do you want?" Enitan demands.

"I want what you likely do as well: to protect my loved ones. Though in my case, that encompasses all of my nation. Help Ominira, and Ominira will help you."

Enitan jerks back, eyes wide. "You want me to spy for the Re- public?"

"No." The noise the High Consul makes almost sounds like laugh- ter. "You'd be more of an . . . independent agent."

Enitan looks over at the not-pirate in front of her. "Don't you have your own spies?"

"Most of our contacts have been compromised, and we have nei- ther the time nor the means at present to plant a new operative." Their gaze is as placid as a lake in winter. "You're the perfect replacement. To the Imperial Court, you're nothing but an unenlightened savage with the intellect of a child. No one will suspect you of political connections, let alone espionage."

How wonderful for Ominira. "My days are already numbered," Enitan says. "Without direct Imperial supervision, I expect that my people will take whatever chance for freedom they can. It'll be a miracle if I survive the month. If *Koriko* survives the month."

Enitan's stomach tightens as the High Consul's gaze grows sharper. "So you have nothing to lose," they say.

"Oh, no," she says. "I have everything to lose. My sibling—" *Ancestors*. Enitan's heart plunges.

The High Consul's brow furrows. "Was taken?"

"My loyalty is to them first," Enitan says, her voice so taut it trembles now. "I have to find them."

"And when you find them, what do you think will happen?" The High Consul arches a thick brow. "Are you hoping Vaalbara will just let you both walk free?"

"It doesn't matter what happens to me," Enitan snaps. "I'm going to find Xiang and get them out, no matter the cost."

The High Consul draws in a deep breath. "The likelihood you'll succeed alone is next to none."

"I know. I don't care." Getting herself involved in Ominira and Vaalbara's political drama is a horrible idea. Her situation is already a thousand times more complicated than she's comfortable with.

After a long moment, the High Consul says, "If you do as I ask, when the time comes, I'll organize your and Xiang's extraction myself. The Imperial capital is a floating prison, even for its noble residents. You'll need help."

"I—"

"Enitan. You need to decide now."

So they'll have time to eliminate me if I refuse, Enitan thinks bitterly. Though she hates herself for it, she has to find out more. "Assuming I agree, what would you have me do?"

"Take this disk with you." The High Consul cants their head down toward the thin holoprojector, smaller than Enitan's palm. "It's linked to my personal communications line. The signal is undetectable and untraceable, but you'll still need to take care concealing the physical device." They look hard at Enitan. "You would share any important information that you uncover, especially that regarding Ominira."

Enitan narrows her eyes. "That's all?"

"If you don't want to be in more danger than you already are, yes." The High Consul's head nods, flickering for a moment. "That's all. Now, we're aware that you speak Orin fluently. There are several paths you can take to gain both the attention and confidence of the Empire's elite."

"I'm a master of the 'strange tribal art' of Korikese tea ceremony," Enitan volunteers, surprising herself. "I imagine I could be a popular performer at aristocratic gatherings. Before they call for my head, that is."

"Wonderful." The High Consul glances away again. "We are agreed, then?"

Enitan's lips press together. "We are."

"We'll speak again soon, I hope." And they vanish.

Someone very close cries out in surprise. A string of profanity soon follows, only to be cut off by the sound of a gun firing.

"The sentinels are coming back," says the operative—Lwin, was it? "We'd better get going."

He pulls himself to his feet with a grunt. Enitan reaches down and grabs the disk. It sits heavy and cool in her hand before she tucks it into a hidden pocket in her pants. Lwin's still there; his legs are still in her line of sight. When Enitan looks up, there's a gun in her face.

Her heart slams into her rib cage, a desperate staccato. "What—"

"Don't worry, it's on stun," Lwin says, lifting his brows. "Nice to meet you, by the way."

He pulls the trigger.

SIX

Enitan comes to with a jolt. She can't move. She panics for a moment before she realizes she's been strapped back into her seat. She looks around, noticing there are four fewer sentinels than they started with. Her cheek throbs, sending spikes of pain across her face. Lwin must have punched her after shooting her unconscious.

"What—what happened?" she gasps, her voice hoarse. She remembers the attack, but she figures a few stupid questions might lower any suspicion they have of her.

"Pirates," says the nearest sentinel, now buckled into the official's seat. He gestures to his right, where the dead are piled into one bloody, sliced-up heap. "We're lucky all they did was beat you. We would've had to go back to the swamp to grab another native."

Another sentinel barks out a harsh, bitter laugh. "You're going to have a nasty bruise, Korikese."

A third huffs and turns to Enitan, crossing her arms. "Are you unwell? There should be no lasting symptoms. You were only stunned."

Enitan stretches, rolling her neck and shoulders and working her way down to her toes. "I'm fine."

"You should still probably schedule an appointment with one of the court physicians," the sentinel continues.

"I will," Enitan lies. "How far are we from Gondwana?"

The sentinel chuckles. "Look outside."

Enitan turns as much as she can, wincing from her bruises as she cranes her neck to peer outside. "Oh, Ancestors."

They're not in space anymore. Instead of a rapid wash of stars, her vision is dominated by the Imperial capital. The first thing that slips through the cracks of her flabbergasted mind is its ridiculous size. The Splinter is fifty times as wide as the governor's mansion and hundreds—no, a *thousand* times as long. Its form is a bladelike edifice, cleaving the sky in two. It is not merely a splinter; it shatters the clouds and re-forms the pale blue around it. The Imperial capital is beautiful and terrifying.

The shuttle dips lower, decelerating as it draws near to one facet of the Splinter. A black landing pad materializes, sliding out from the main structure as they approach. The shuttle lands on it with a mechanical sigh, settling before a wall as dark and as gleaming as volcanic glass. Enitan stares as the barrier slips away to reveal a large shadowed tunnel. The pad turns slowly and draws back into the passageway, taking them with it.

The ramp hisses open and thuds against another obsidian disk. Enitan unbuckles herself, secures her satchel, and strides out. Sentinels loom at her sides, their hands pressed close to their weapons as if she might suddenly flee or attack. Enitan nearly scoffs as the disk begins to drift upward into a tube; she has nowhere to run.

The lift comes to a gentle halt, its walls melt away into the floor, and Enitan finds herself standing in the very center of a colossal, vaulted hall. The whole chamber is as black as the vacuum of space, with only a few flickering lamps to break the darkness. Massive stone faces line the ceiling, exquisitely rendered eyes glaring down at her. Unease worms its way into her gut, and she hugs her arms to herself. Koriko is a lush, open world; the expansive domed sky and surrounding swamp are visible no matter where one stands. Here, there is only the void. The palace feels far too much like a monument to be anyone's home.

A man in the gray of the Imperator's household staff rushes out from the shadows, scuttling toward them; his eyes widen as he takes in their disheveled appearance. "Where's Radan?"

The official, Enitan assumes. He never shared his name. Not that he had any real reason to.

"Dead," says one of the sentinels. "We were ambushed by pirates in the belt."

"While you were flying?" The stranger scrunches his nose. The silvery lamplight gives his pale features a gruesome cast, turning each wrinkle and fold of his grimace into a jagged chasm.

"Master Radan wanted to stop at Lagash. For dinner."

"Well." The servant shrugs, his mouth warping into an odd little smile. "It isn't as if he cannot be replaced. You're dismissed."

The sentinels bow and march away, swallowed by the darkness.

Then, like a bloodmaw turning on its prey, the servant spins to face Enitan. "I'm Guiyin, Her Imperial Majesty's head seneschal," he says in startlingly smooth Korikesian. "And you, I presume, are the provincial emissary."

Enitan blinks at him. "I'm hardly an emissary, but yes."

Guiyin pulls a small pouch from his jacket. "You're a woman, correct? Do you understand how the Imperial gender presentation system works?"

"Yes on both counts."

He pulls a dark blue brooch from his pouch and hands it to her. On Koriko, it's considered polite to simply ask what pronouns other people use. In Vaalbara, everyone wears enamel pins.

"All right, what am I?" he asks.

Enitan breathes out through her nose, glancing at his rust-orange pin. "A man."

"Correct." Guiyin extends a withered arm. "Allow me to take your bag."

"Thank you for offering," says Enitan, her grip around the strap tightening, "but it's quite light."

Guiyin clasps his gloved hands behind his back. "You Korikese *are* remarkably strong."

Enitan presses her lips together. "It's not over ten kilograms."

He looks her over and lifts a finger to point at the bruise on her cheek. "A village scuffle." It doesn't sound like a question.

"No. The pirates."

The seneschal's face contorts again into that strange smile. He gestures toward a circular door at her right. "The Imperator has selected your host herself."

"I'm honored."

"I think you'll be very pleased," continues Guiyin, ushering her through the door and down a dark, winding corridor. "Countess Deora Edwan is an amateur cultural anthropologist. I'm certain you'll have much to discuss . . ."

Enitan tunes him out. She can't fathom why he's running through this little script with her. No one, not even Enitan herself, cares if she'll be *pleased*. Assuming her people don't immediately declare their independence and she survives the night, all she cares about is rescuing Xiang.

Guiyin is in the middle of reciting a list of titles she's permitted to call the countess by when her mind snags on something. He just said she's an "amateur cultural anthropologist."

Oh, Ancestors, no.

"Pardon?" Guiyin turns to her, brows furrowed, and Enitan belatedly realizes she said that last bit out loud.

"Did you say that Deora is a cultural anthropologist?"

"Yes, *Her Ladyship* is."

Dread seeps into Enitan's stomach. *"Wonderful."*

A chime sounds from Guiyin's pocket. He pulls out his communicator and immediately frowns. "Oh."

Enitan tries to look over his shoulder at whatever's come in for him, nerves already prickling. "What is it?"

"They want to bring you in for questioning."

Her heart skips a beat. "When?" The word comes out as a whisper.

"Now." Guiyin turns on his heel and sets off in another direction. "Come along."

Enitan follows; her surroundings fade into a dark blur around her, her focus narrowing on the man ahead. Guiyin brings her to a door guarded by two sentinels.

"I'll be waiting for you right here," he says, taking her bag. His grin widens but still doesn't reach his eyes.

His words are a cold comfort as the sentinels all but shove her through the door. The chamber is strange, fashioned of pale-white stone that appears almost translucent in some places. It's like standing within the end of a selenite bar. While the floor fits only a tiny table with two stiff chairs, the ceiling appears infinitely high. The effect is very disconcerting. Enitan supposes she'll have to get used to that here.

A man with olive skin and auburn hair occupies the chair facing her. Though he's traded his uniform for a plain, sharply cut suit, he has the ramrod-straight posture of a born and bred sentinel. This is no standard interrogation. If it were, there'd be an official examiner here. The man in front of her does not have the mien of a person fond of asking questions and picking apart the answers. He looks as if he'd like nothing more than to put a dissection gun in her face.

"Sit," he barks.

Enitan sits, her mind racing. She feels like she's about to heave up half her digestive system.

He doesn't even bother introducing himself. "Normally, I like to stay out of these things," he says, "but this is personal. I myself trained some of the fine sentinels we lost today." His hazel eyes are sharper than any blade. "Now they're mincemeat, because of *you*." There's a world of derision in that one word.

Enitan lowers her gaze to the table, saying nothing. She doesn't know if she's even capable of speech at this point. It's probably for the best; the less she says, the better.

"Is your name Enitan Ijebu?"

The question takes her aback, startling her out of silence. "I—"

She swallows thickly, nearly choking on her own saliva as she finally notices the datapad in his left hand. The only reason he'd ask for an answer he already knows would be to calibrate a polygraphic field. He needs a standard of her biometrics so the machine, wherever it's hidden, can detect her lies. Enitan draws in a deep breath, attempting to center herself. She tells herself that this is just practice—she read once that the best spies never lie; they simply tell the truth everyone wants to hear.

"Yes, it is. Sir," she forces out.

"Are you twenty-five years old?"

"Yes, sir."

"Are you prepared to answer my questions, whatever the consequences may be?" There's a cruel hint of mirth around his mouth.

No point in lying. "No, sir."

His lips curl the rest of the way into a smirk. "Nevertheless, you'll answer."

The unspoken threat hangs in the air like a blade above her neck.

Enitan nods stiffly, clenching her hands under the table so she doesn't start rubbing them up and down her arms. Yet another nervous tic she'll have to learn to master.

"Why did the ship stop at Lagash before it reached the Splinter?"

"The official we were flying with—Radan?—wanted fresh food."

"Yes, Radan," the sentinel confirms impatiently. "So you set down, and then the pirates immediately attacked?"

Enitan shakes her head, nearly collapsing with relief. She tries to keep herself from falling back into the chair. If he'd asked her who exactly had attacked the shuttle, she would've been carrion.

"Use your words," he snaps.

Enitan flinches. "Radan sent almost all of the sentinels out to forage. He ordered the last one to . . . to air me."

Bitterness slides down her throat at the cold flash of amusement in the sentinel's eyes. In all her years, she has yet to meet a full-blooded Vaalbaran who never once laughed at her.

"And then?" he demands.

"He came out of the ship and told me to go help the sentinels. And that's when . . . when they came. They shot off his head."

His gaze flicks to the datapad's screen. It remains a placid gray. "How many?"

Enitan thinks back to the outpost, forcing back memories she's already begun to suppress. "Six."

"Did they wear anything that could be used to identify them?"

"I—I don't know, sir."

A touch of rage colors his tone. "You don't know?"

Her tongue feels as heavy as a stone in her mouth. "They wore rags."

"Did they speak to you?"

Oh, how she wishes she had a mirror, to check for any betraying changes in her expression. "Yes, sir."

"In what language? What did they say?"

"They spoke Orin." At first, anyway. She pauses for half a heartbeat to consider her next words; an omission isn't a lie. "Their leader told me to hold up my hands."

If the sentinel caught her brief delay, he doesn't show it. "Did you respond verbally at any time?"

"Yes."

His brows shoot up. "What did you say?" His voice is as dark and cold as the water beneath a frozen lake.

"I asked them not to kill the sentinel too." She said far more than that, of course, but he hasn't asked. Yet.

The disbelief in the sentinel's eyes is as clear as day. "Repeat that."

An omission is not a lie. An omission is not a lie. Enitan recites the words over and over in her head as he glares at his datapad. "I asked them not to kill the sentinel."

His frown deepens with every passing second. "And what happened after that?"

Enitan skips the ensuing conversation she had with Lwin and hopes it doesn't show on her face. Or on the datapad. "They shot me in the face. And then I woke up."

"Did they say anything about their motives? Anything that might hint at why they attacked this particular ship and killed Radan?"

She considers each word of her response carefully before she speaks. "I can think of only one reason why pirates might attack a ship in one of your largest mining outposts."

He stares at her, unblinking. If her heart speeds up any more, she's certain it'll burst.

"You had just landed; they attacked before you could retrieve a single kilogram of metal."

"Perhaps they took us out to clear the way for their escape?" Enitan asks.

"They didn't touch the vaults," he says lowly, after a long moment. "And there were no casualties beyond Radan and my sentinels. If raiding the station was their goal, they barely tried." He lets those statements hang in the air between them. "Perhaps they're the worst pirates in the system. Or perhaps they were operatives hunting Radan. And yet, they left *you* alive." He narrows his eyes slightly.

Enitan makes herself as small as she can. "Sir, this is the first time

I've ever left Koriko's skydome." She doesn't have to feign the exhaustion and fear in her voice. "If Radan was their target and they weren't pirates, then I have no idea what exactly he did to anger them."

The sentinel growls something about useless savages before heaving a great sigh. "*Fine.* Is there anything more you think I should know?"

She swallows a mad bark of laughter. She wished he knew *less.* "No, sir." *A thousand times no.*

"Do you have any intentions, in any way, shape, or form, to bring harm to the Empire?"

Her stomach twists at the blunt force of the question, but she doesn't even have to consider her response. "No." All she wants is to rescue Xiang.

For a long time, there is no expression on the sentinel's face. He just looks at her in utter silence again, the anger and cruelty that once stained his rough features slipping away.

"I don't trust you," he says, just as Enitan's breathing begins to calm. "I don't trust any of you. But that's all. For now." He flicks a hand at her. "Get out of my sight."

Enitan stands as if her chair has suddenly caught on fire. She walks out the door as quickly as she can without running. Guiyin, waiting just outside as promised, ceases his pacing. She must look haunted, because she thinks she sees concern cross his expression.

"Don't mind Ivar," Guiyin says, as if he didn't just deliver her to him like trussed-up prey to a predator. "He just cares deeply about his subordinates."

He hands back her bag, which now seems too heavy to bear. She slumps under the weight of it before hooking both arms under.

"Come along!" he says brightly, ignoring her brief struggle.

They finally reach the countess's apartments, a suite of rooms tucked away in the upper southern wing of the palace—which, Guiyin informs Enitan, occupies the top hundred stories of the Splinter. The seneschal presses his hands to the shimmering black screen-surface of the doors.

"Your Grace, the provincial emissary has arrived."

"Just a moment!" calls a flawless soprano.

The doors slide open, the countess steps out, and Enitan sheds an internal tear. She barely registers Guiyin bowing and slipping away.

"Fantastic, is it not?" Deora's smile stretches into a blinding white grin as she hikes up her grass skirt, a monstrosity of reeds and sedge. "My cultural advisors spent weeks preparing this." She puffs up with pride, her porcelain face flushed pink with excitement. "I always strive for authenticity." She says the last bit in Korikesian.

She looks and sounds very much like the Vaalbaran tourists that sometimes pop up in Ijebu. The visitors spend their vacations marveling at the natives' primitive arboreal lifestyle, trying on traditional Korikese dress and chortling at one another as they don the dyed fabrics.

"Pardon?" Enitan forces out. Deora's accent is so terrible it takes her a few moments to decipher what the countess is saying.

"The skirt," Deora says, her brilliant smile faltering before she purses her lips. "Am I speaking too fast?"

"You're not," says Enitan, in Orin. She stares at the loops and loops of beads braided through the getup. She's never seen ornamentation like that. Korikese stopped wearing everyday grass garb a couple hundred years ago. Now it's only worn on the most important holidays. And even the most elaborate never looked so ostentatious. "May I inquire as to the occasion?"

Deora laughs, waving Enitan inside. When she speaks, she continues to do so in Korikesian: "Ojuyori Day, silly!" She lets out a sorrowful sigh. "I'm so sorry you had to miss it. But I've had a traditional feast prepared for you."

No one has celebrated Ojuyori in decades because the Empire

invaded the week before. It is now a day of somber remembrance. If her circumstances were even slightly different, Enitan would berate the other woman. But Deora is a noble—and the minder the Imperator has assigned her. She probably means well, and Enitan can't afford to make an enemy so soon. She forces her lips into something resembling a smile.

"Thank you. I'm honored." She allows herself to briefly grit her teeth together as she bends to pull off her boots.

"Oh, we don't do that here." Deora stops her. "The entire Splinter is sanitary, so there's no need to take off your shoes."

"Koriko isn't *unsanitary*," Enitan blurts out. "Removing our shoes is more culture than necessity." But she keeps her sandals on.

When she turns, Deora gasps. "You're hurt! What happened to you?"

Enitan is too tired for this. "A village scuffle."

Deora claps her turquoise-gloved hands together, finally switching back to her native tongue: "God, my friends are going to just *love* you." She spins on a slippered heel. "Follow me!"

Enitan follows the countess into a spacious chamber carved from the same light-devouring rock as the rest of the palace. Painted scrolls hang from the walls, nearly touching the woven mats lining the floor. There is a wealth of art here, almost certainly stolen during the first Imperial raids on Koriko. That or Deora had these replicated, which feels nearly as bad.

The noblewoman strides across the room and lays a hand against the bed. It's a sumptuous thing, with four spindly posters that look like they might snap under the weight of the canopy. And with Enitan's luck, probably while she's sleeping under it.

"This is called a 'bed,'" says Deora.

Enitan smothers a frown. "We have beds on Koriko." It's only that she finds them uncomfortably soft. So did Xiang.

Does.

Some grain of emotion must surface on her face, because Deora draws near and pats her shoulder.

"Don't worry," consoles the countess, and Enitan flinches. "The monks were excellent teachers. You speak Orin very well for a Korikese."

Enitan breaks eye contact, fidgeting in her boots. Her fluency is the least of her concerns. "Thank you."

"But I'd appreciate it if you spoke only in your native tongue. I need the practice."

Enitan shakes her head, smiling tightly. "No, you speak flawlessly."

Deora purses her lips. "You're not what I expected."

"Is that so?" Enitan lifts her brows. It's ironic, as Deora is exactly what *she* anticipated.

"Yes, but I don't think you'll like Vaalbara at all."

She'd be surprised if she did, what with a death sentence hanging over her. "Why is that?"

"Because," Deora snaps, appearing suddenly frustrated, "the Empire has barely any culture. Or at least ours isn't as"—she pauses to wet her lips, apparently searching for the right word—"as colorful as yours. That's why I've devoted myself to studying the Korikese way of life, as you can see." She gestures expansively at all her looted treasure.

"How admirable," Enitan says, at a loss for words. She doesn't know whether to despise or pity this woman. Both, perhaps.

Deora takes Enitan's arm in hers. "You've traveled a long way. You must be ravenous."

They have dinner in an adjoining room. Deora wasn't exaggerating; spread out on a length of black damask is a full traditional feast, complete with pounded root vegetables and melon soup. There's even steamed bean pudding served in the traditional style, sprinkled with black salt and wrapped in thick leaves. The countess makes Enitan sit at the head of the table and serves her first, heaping food onto a thin gold plate.

"This looks magnificent," Enitan says, swallowing down her shock. She's not lying. She surveys the meal, salivating. And then it occurs to her where it must have come from. "You have a Korikese chef, then?"

Deora lifts her chin, pride flashing in her eyes. "I made this all myself." She lowers herself gracefully into a chair and begins shoveling curried grain into her mouth.

And because it's been niggling at the back of her mind, Enitan asks, "And the mats and scrolls?"

"Them too." A chagrined blush sweeps across Deora's face. "They're not very good, are they? I'm a better cook than artisan."

"I thought they were made on Koriko," Enitan admits, barely repressing the sour note in her voice. She picks up her fork.

Deora's lips curl into yet another grin, and Enitan wonders how her face isn't worn out. The countess sets aside her plate and reaches for a bowl of fermented greens. Astonished, Enitan watches her inhale it. That's the spiciest dish she knows of. Xiang made it for her, only once. The meal hadn't gone well for either of them.

Reluctantly but thoroughly impressed, Enitan turns to her own food. She wonders, amused, whether she might actually grow to like the countess—assuming that she survives long enough, and that Deora manages to tone down . . . everything.

Enitan reaches over to the tea bowl at her left and swirls it. The vessel is beautiful polished wood overlaid with silver. She squints; there's a small shimmering shape inlaid into the bottom. Unfortunately, the bowl's craftsmanship doesn't make up for the cold, bitter contents. It's theehma, and not even decent theehma. Enitan nearly chokes trying not to spit it out. It appears that for all her efforts and obvious wealth, the countess is unable to acquire proper Korikese tea. Resisting the urge to grimace, Enitan downs half the drink in one agonizing swallow.

"Back on Koriko," she begins, licking her lips, "I'm . . . I was a tea specialist."

Deora tilts her head. "I thought you were the provincial scribe. Wasn't there a whole scandal—"

"Tea-making was just a hobby." This time, Enitan's smile is almost genuine. "I actually brought a few of my own blends from home, if you'd like to try."

"Oh, I'd love to." The countess's eyes twinkle with excitement. "How much do you have?"

"Enough for all your friends." Enitan gulps down the rest of that awful Vaalbaran tea and peers into the cup.

There at the bottom is an inlaid vebweaver, the Korikese symbol of stories—and of deceit. She smirks, folding her hands together. The Ancestors have always been forthright, after all.

SEVEN

Enitan meets Deora's friends in one of the palace's many public drawing rooms. Seated cross-legged on a cushion, she sprinkles a handful of tea leaves into a clay teapot while the row of aristocrats before her clap their gloved hands in excitement.

It isn't long before she realizes that they're barbarians too. Or rather, their families were, hundreds of years ago, when their homelands were new Imperial provinces much like Koriko. As she surveys them, smiling politely, her mind slips back to the lessons slapped into her when she was still in crèche. When their peoples were assimilated into the Empire, they were allowed to retain much of their own cultures, albeit slathered over with the usual Vaalbaran adornment. Judging by garb alone, she can match about half of them to the various inner territories of the Empire.

And if they swapped those jewel-encrusted clothes for Korikese tunics, they could probably stroll through Ijebu without anyone the wiser. As long as they kept their mouths shut, anyway. Enitan tries hard not to dwell on the reverse—that if she hadn't already been introduced as the uncivilized hostage, her fluency in Orin and an ostentatious suit would be more than enough for her to pass as a born-and-bred Vaalbaran.

In these nobles, Enitan sees her people's future. A few centuries from now, Koriko will become as much a part of Vaalbara as any other region. As unholy tongues, Korikesian and Akyesi will fade from the fabric of history. Children will one day be taught Orin, monks will be selected from the populace, and scores of former savages will be recruited into the Imperial interior's foremost universities. They'll be integrated into the Empire, each person all but indistinguishable from a citizen whose family had been Vaalbaran since the nation's birth. Her home will be consumed completely. And she is powerless to stop it, just as she is powerless to stop the flood of anger and sorrow and dread crashing through her. The bitter emotions roil in her like poison and rise up her throat, threatening to spill out of her mouth.

Air rattles in Enitan's lungs as she takes a deep breath. The flood withers into a trickle as she pours the tea into each of the tiny glass bowls arranged on the tray before her. She tries not to think about how she's sacrificing a quarter of her precious blend for this gathering. Though she'd happily give up a hand, never mind the rest of her stock, if she knew it would buy her some useful information about Xiang.

Deora leans forward on her pile of silk pillows, closing her eyes and inhaling deeply. "That smells wonderful," she says, her words echoing up to the vaulted ceiling.

"Thank you," Enitan says demurely.

She's crafted a special blend for the occasion. The uhie base is one of her strongest teas, oxidized and roasted to generate a robust flavor and wine-red hue. To bring out its subtler notes, she's added a few pinches of a softer black tea.

Archduke Yehana Ta-Ji, Deora's best friend and a second cousin of the last Imperator, sighs appreciatively.

They make a striking pair. His features are dark, thin, and chiseled; hers are pale, round, and soft. He prefers deep colors; she wears only light ones. He's quiet and soft-spoken; she can't go a few minutes without opening her mouth.

Enitan picks up the tray with one hand and stands. One by one, she raises the bowls and pours the still-steaming tea into a row of even daintier glasses, lifting her arms as high as she can to incorporate as much air as possible. The archduke's full mouth curves fractionally as he watches thick, sweet-swelling foam accumulate over the tea.

Most of the others aren't nearly as highborn as he is; some of them come from merely wealthy families that the previous Imperator elevated in the last few years of his reign. Enitan sees how they all but cower before the archduke and thinks of how her own people will be expected to do the same, even once incorporated. Although dismissed as a lowly heathen, she hasn't yet been ordered to bow before anyone here. Better to stand a savage than kneel a noble, in her opinion.

Enitan crouches to stir in sugar and repeats the process, pouring the frothy drink back into the teapot. A faintly malty aroma fills the room, rich and warm and utterly at odds with the feelings twisting in her chest. Her people should not be made to wait hundreds of years to be seen as human, and she for one has no desire for her home to become yet another fragment of the ravenous Empire. But she came here to save Xiang, not the whole of Koriko. And so she does what she had Deora arrange this charade for in the first place: she listens.

A proper Korikese tea ceremony can go on for as long as three hours. Enitan told Deora it could take at least four. After the third frothing, the patricians finally tire of watching her fiddle with the tea and start chatting. Enitan shifts restlessly as the nobles discuss absolutely inane things at first—Yehana's new interest in embroidery, the handsome curator Deora met last week. Her patience begins to thin during a heated conversation about the finale of some period drama they're all obsessed with. Struggling to quash her rising irritation, Enitan re-froths tea as the conversation slowly turns to matters of actual import. Baronet Neneto recounts the tale of how the Supreme Abbot's nephew got outrageously drunk and went on a "spirit journey" to go "find himself," and then, finally, *finally*, they begin gossiping about the new Imperator.

"So," Marchioness Zumas drawls, leaning toward the archduke, "what's her name?"

"You know I can't tell you," the archduke says. He practically drips with hauteur as he reaches over to the platter of fragrant, lightly fried sprouts.

The other aristocrats let out a collective cry of outrage and begin to pester him—politely. Enitan learns that an Imperator's name officially becomes a personal possession once they're crowned, along with their likeness. Images of the emperors are tightly controlled, and only the closest of friends and relatives may use their name in public. Everyone else calls the Imperator things like "Your Imperial Majesty." Or just "God."

After a few minutes of relentless badgering, the archduke lifts silk-gloved hands in defeat. "All right, all right! Her name is Menkhet."

"Menkhet. *Menkhet*." The baronet rolls the name around in their mouth, flopping onto their back. "Now tell us why your cousin *actually* named her his heir. Honestly, I'd never even *heard* of her before the coronation. And they've already wiped every picture of her from the network."

The archduke shrugs, but there's an edge to his gaze. "She's a brilliant commander, second only to Obara."

Enitan freezes.

"Really?" The baronet rolls onto their stomach with a snort. They plant their elbows on the polished floor, their chin cupped in their palms. "But she only joined the military just over three years ago. And she's led less than a dozen raids."

"Each was extraordinarily successful," the archduke replies, his back straightening.

No one looks convinced, least of all the baronet, but the archduke's posture makes it clear this part of the conversation is over. However, not everyone is as eager to drop the subject of the new Imperator entirely.

"Do you know when she'll return from Esnaa?" asks the marchioness, painfully tentative.

The archduke relaxes again, and Enitan notices then that the other patricians had all but stopped breathing. "She'll be back tomorrow morning."

"Imagine that," says the marchioness. "God herself goes on bi-monthly pilgrimages."

When the archduke chortles, the others laugh with him, albeit a bit stiffly.

The marchioness turns to the baronet. "Isn't your brother a priest at the temple?"

"And he won't let me forget it," the baronet huffs, snatching up a particularly crisped sprout. "I can't believe he'll be meeting the Imperator before I do."

Although Vaalbaran law permits its former provinces to retain their traditional belief systems, all religions are subservient to the Church. For some reason, the new Imperator's been leaving the Splinter to visit faraway places of worship, and Enitan doubts it's to pay respects. She has to find out why.

She looks down at her work and frowns. If she adds any more sugar, the tea will be unpalatable, so she pours it out into yet another set of glassware for the last time.

Deora, who's been mostly silent throughout all of this, glances over. "It's ready?"

"It is, my lady," Enitan replies demurely. She takes the final tray with her when she rises, and hands out three minuscule cups to each of the nobles. When she returns to her own seat, she gestures at the left glass in her own row. "The first cup is bitter, representing the hardships of growing up. The second is strong but sweet, signifying adult life, the fruit of honest labor, close friendships, and first loves." She sucks in a breath, remembering when Ajana did this for her. She shoves away a wave of sorrow and points at the final glass. "And the third is mostly sugar, symbolic of the pure embrace of the Ancestors."

Ordinarily, there'd be a few moments of silent reflection between each round of tea, but when Enitan looks up from her little speech, the aristocrats' cups are empty.

"God, that's good." The archduke turns to Deora, smiling contentedly. "So much work for so little product, though. You'll lend me your savage, won't you?"

Enitan nearly spits out her tea. Visiting nobles on Koriko are one thing. This is something else entirely.

But she cannot show anger. She *cannot*. If she loses her temper, they'll see her as a threat, a danger. She is aware that when these patricians call her a savage, they do so almost fondly, in the same tone one uses when discussing a pet. She cannot afford to let them think of her as a savage in truth, no matter how much she itches to do something that might prove them right. She must be docile and slow-witted and *trained*, or she will die and Xiang will suffer for it; she can't save them from a prison cell. She can destroy the nobles later. She looks up just in time to see irritation flash across the countess's face, only for her to wipe it away before the archduke notices.

Deora meets Enitan's eyes, an apologetic cast to her features. "If she'd like to entertain you another time, she is absolutely free to do so."

The archduke chuckles as if she's told a particularly clever joke. "Yes, of course."

The baronet gives Enitan a considering look. "Is it true that Korikese people take small doses of opiates every morning to commune with their dead . . . Ancestors?" They grin. "That's the proper term, yes?"

Enitan's left eye twitches. She's never been the most devout, but the Ancestors are still her forebears. Her past family. The disrespect stings worse than a venintail's strike.

"Do I seem intoxicated to you?" she asks.

The baronet rolls their eyes. "But you're not *really* Korikese; of course you don't follow all of the, ah, rituals."

"I *am* Korikese," Enitan says flatly.

Deora's awkward smile vanishes entirely. The marchioness snickers behind a gloved hand.

The baronet stares at Enitan. "Watch your tone. All I mean to say is that you're not *Korikese*. You're not—"

A chime sounds and they glance down at the holowatch around their left wrist. The baronet spits out a curse, jumping to their feet. "I'm late for a meeting with the governor."

The marchioness smirks. "In trouble again?"

"Not for long, friends. Not for long," the baronet replies with a wink. They turn toward the doors, but not before bowing to the archduke.

The archduke heaves a sigh and rises, the silver-gold satin of his robe rustling over the floor. "My father wants me to join him for the evening mass, so I must also bid you farewell."

The archduke's departure signifies the end of what Enitan judges to be a fairly successful if infuriating social engagement. The marchioness hugs Deora goodbye and heads out another pair of doors.

As soon as she's gone, the countess's chin drops a little. "I—I'm sorry about them."

"It's all right," Enitan says, waving a hand.

"It's *not* all right," Deora says fiercely. "I was like them, too, once. I mean, not quite as horrendous. But . . ."

Enitan looks over at her. Full of surprises, this one. "But it's different when the savages you're insulting turn out to be not nearly as savage as you anticipated," she says, finishing the countess's sentence for her.

Deora's mouth twists, seemingly in embarrassment.

Enitan is a bit nonplussed by this streak of sympathy, but she's not going to look a gift osoosohoof in the mouth. It's probably just occurred to Deora that she and her friends have spent most of their lives as enti-tled nobles whose most demanding activity is mocking anyone less well off than they are.

Then again, if she's as good an anthropologist as she seems to be, she must know how complex Korikese society is, how rich the culture. Maybe it's not only the past day and a half of interacting with an actual Korikese person that has undone over two decades of lies for her. And yet . . . something about this feels a little off.

Enitan's second degree was in psycho-philosophy, but she hardly needed it to know that the mind is a wonderful, terrible thing. It under-stands what it wants to and discards the rest. As demonstrated so per-fectly by the nobles, most Vaalbarans would never recognize her humanity, no matter how obvious. The Empire measures the develop-ment of a people by their ability to dominate others. It's a flimsy, paper-thin metric. Any true scholar of Koriko would see this, and Deora is the closest thing to a genuinely respectful Imperial academic Enitan has met. If the countess was on the precipice of revelation, this gather-ing must have finally pushed her over the edge. Enitan brushes away her initial prickle of unease.

As if to confirm her theory, the countess's gaze sinks to her gloved fingers. She laces them together over her lap. "This certainly isn't an excuse, but Yehana's been . . . ill at ease since the coronation. His family lost a great deal of power with the change. Their dynasty still techni-cally reigns, of course, but not their blood. And the rumors . . ."

Enitan shifts closer, trying to mold her expression into a concerned one. "What rumors?"

Deora's expression turns wry. "No one just *becomes* Imperator like that. And Menkhet showed up out of nowhere, without a title or wealth or anything that might explain why she's in power."

Enitan folds her arms. "If I'm not mistaken, commoners have been known to ascend to the throne."

"Not after only three years in the military." Deora snorts, shaking her head. "No matter how *brilliant* of a commander they might be." She spreads her hands. "There are whispers that Menkhet was Princess Sunnetah's secret wife, and that the Imperator sought to honor his late daughter by further elevating her spouse. By all accounts, they were simply very good friends, but . . ."

"But every rumor is woven with a thread of truth."

Deora looks mildly impressed. "Indeed. Yehana wasn't next in line, but he and Sun were quite close." She shrugs. "The idea that she could have married without telling him stings, I suppose. Even if it's not true, I think the very suggestion is dredging up memories of the more bitter parts of their friendship." She reaches down and picks up her final glass of tea, surprising Enitan. She closes her eyes for a moment and then sips it. "Sun kept secrets from everyone."

Enitan gives a slight nod, though she's nearly giddy with excitement. She may be no closer to finding Xiang, but the foundations of her plans have been laid. She moves to pack up Deora's tea set, but the countess waves her off. "Absolutely not. I can wash my own dishes."

Enitan watches the noblewoman stack the tiny glass cups and almost smiles. It seems she was indeed wrong in her initial impression of the countess.

As they head back to Deora's apartments, Enitan turns to her and says, "You know, you're not what I expected either."

◆

Enitan turns on the sonic shower, then carefully sets the holoprojector on the bathroom floor and activates it. She steps back and kneels over the cool tiles, willing her breathing back to normal.

After a full minute of anxious waiting, the High Consul's face materializes before her. "I wasn't expecting to hear back from you so soon."

Enitan can barely hear them over the loud hum of the shower's vibrations. And hopefully, neither can Deora. "Sir," she whispers, "I've gained information that may be of interest to you."

The High Consul arches a brow. "Already?"

"I came prepared." She straightens. "I conducted a full tea ceremony for a group of nobles, including an archduke. It didn't take long for them to start gossiping."

The High Consul looks pleased. "So, what did you learn?"

"The new Imperator—Menkhet—has enjoyed a meteoric rise to power, precipitated, supposedly, by only three successful years of service in the military."

"We know." Their eyes narrow in what looks to Enitan like anticipation.

Enitan bends forward slightly, weighed down by their stare. She feels like an ekuwhisker under the gaze of a prowling wurahawk. "Well, no one quite believes that. I'm not sure if you can use this—"

"All information can be wielded."

Enitan lets out a small, nervous laugh. "There's a rumor Menkhet was the secret wife of the late princess. If I remember correctly, Sunnetah was torn in half at the Siege of Ilesa."

The High Consul looks thoughtful. "Yes, she was. And is there any truth to the rumor?"

"I'm not certain. Yet." Enitan leans forward. "What I do know is that Menkhet leaves the Splinter every two months to go on a pilgrimage to a new regional temple."

"Why?"

Enitan shrugs. "Surely not out of piety." She stiffens suddenly. "Perhaps she's imprisoned my people in the temples."

The High Consul gives her a sympathetic look. "Perhaps. Whatever the reason, you must uncover it." A corner of their mouth lifts into a cutting half smile. "Excellent work, Enitan."

They vanish, the holoprojector's silvery beam slipping back into the disk. Enitan peers at the large marble tub. Now that she's left the shower on, bathing again later would raise suspicion. After a moment of hesitation, she peels off her tunic and steps in. She sits on the cool stone, letting the finely tuned ultrasonic waves vibrate sweat and grime off her skin. And then, releasing a shuddering breath, she draws up her knees and drops her head into her hands.

She has never been so alone. Xiang and Ajana made up the whole of her world. And now . . .

Now she has only the gaping emptiness their loss has left behind. Enitan rocks back and forth as the impossibility of her mission presses down on her shoulders. Saving her sibling. Avenging her once-lover and closest friend. She tries to remember how to breathe, but her brain won't cooperate, too focused on how much of a fool she is. Her own skin feels too heavy around her, too tight and too hot.

What possibly made her think she could do this? She's no spy. She's no warrior or diplomat. She's nothing more than a scribe who knows a little about tea. Ancestors, she wants to claw at her own flesh.

In desperation, she flings out an arm and switches the shower to its water setting. The cold splash over her back does the trick, shocking her from her panic. She drags in choking mouthfuls of air, shivering uncontrollably. She slumps against the side of the tub as the screeching fear in her head flows out of her in a great tide.

Then she sniffles, shakes herself, and pushes back from the marble. She reaches for the fragments of her broken resolve, puts them back together piece by bloody piece, and drags it all back inside herself. She wasn't there for Ajana. But she has a chance with Xiang.

She must hold fast to this and never let go. A scribe who knows a little about tea will have to suffice.

EIGHT

Enitan rises with the sun for the first time in her life. It's a strange thing, marking her days by the revolution of a planet rather than the light-dark cycle of a skydome. She'll adjust. This near to the center of the system, the star's brightness makes waking up in the mornings easy. Evenings are harder; the lack of a visual shield and the addition of Vaalbara's own moons means that it never truly gets dark. She yawns, swings her legs over the side of the monstrous bed, and pads over to the balcony. When she was in the approaching ship, the Splinter's crystalline facets appeared perfectly smooth. Now that she's inside the colossal structure, it's clear that the Imperial city's walls are pockmarked with windows, balustrades, and stationary landing pads.

The doors leading to the balcony slide open at her approach, and Enitan steps barefoot out into an unbroken stretch of sky. Directly above, the Splinter's pinnacle vanishes into the clouds, an onyx poignard plunged into an atmosphere adorned with fading white flecks of light. She's still getting used to seeing stars at night, rather than during the day period. Acclimating to the gaping lack of a bright-orange gas giant is a little harder; she's caught unawares by the empty space where Jilessa should be every other time she looks out a window.

She grips the banister and peers down, where pale mist churns over a jagged outcrop of stone far below. Vaalbara began as a citadel, a single city clutching the knifelike rock somewhere below where the Splinter is now. Its people were once destitute raiders, stealing crops and cloth from their neighbors before they realized that conquering villages and demanding tribute was easier than invading every year. Enitan can't imagine it, can't conceive of any sane people scratching out a life in that frigid gray wasteland. It seems that escaping to the skies did nothing for their madness, for those ancestral Vaalbarans built equally monochrome settlements to live in.

The thick haze swirls, revealing the glinting edge of a particularly sharp bit of stone. Before the exodus to the clouds, Vaalbarans used to tear their enemies' heads from their bodies and stick them on stakes. Now executions primarily consist of throwing people right out of the Splinter. In some places on its predetermined flight path, the Imperial city nearly grazes the planet; Enitan wonders if some optimistic war captives thought they'd survive the fall only to be skewered the moment they dropped below the mist.

Something moves at the very edge of her peripheral vision. Enitan turns, leaning as far out over the balustrade as she dares. There's a long, straight line of shuttles, maybe fifty, all the same elegant shade of black. After a moment, she realizes it must be the new Imperator and her retinue, returning from her pilgrimage. There are hundreds of people in that slow, serpentine train—sentinels, religious representatives, entertainers, and an army of servants.

Despite the inlaid heaters pumping hot air up from the balcony's floor, Enitan is lightly dressed and has little hair to protect herself from the cold. When a chilly gust of wind runs its frozen fingers over her head and shoulders, she shivers so violently her bones rattle. Already beginning to sneeze, she wraps her borrowed sleeping robe tighter around herself and retreats back into the warmth of her room.

She's halfway to her bed when a knock sounds at the doors. Deora's excited face appears over the seamless steel, and Enitan presses her palm to the metal. When the doors slide open, the countess greets her with a brilliant smile.

"You've been *summoned*," Deora informs Enitan, making her voice go deep and gravelly at the end.

Enitan suppresses a grumble. She wasn't anticipating the news of her tea services to spread so quickly. "By whom?"

"Why, God herself!" Deora takes hold of Enitan's shoulders and shakes her, bouncing up and down on the balls of her feet.

"Pardon?" Enitan chokes out, her voice strained.

Instead of answering, the countess drags her out of the bedroom, down the hall, and into the foyer. Standing in the exact center of a woven rug is a man: short; hair tied up in a simple braid; polished, pinkish features; a certain dignified grace to his posture. He wears the dark gray of the Imperator's household; the only color on him is a garnet brooch and his orange pin.

"Her Imperial Majesty the Imperator requests your presence in an hour," he says.

As polite as the words sound, Enitan knows full well that it's not a request. "I'm honored," she manages.

The servant turns to Deora. "I trust you'll ensure she's presentable, my lady."

"I shall." As soon as the man's gone, she whips around to face Enitan, clasping her gloved hands together in unrestrained glee. "What clothes did you bring with you? A beaded collar? A traditional cap? An ancestral jacket?"

"I'll show you," Enitan says flatly.

Her old reservations about Deora begin to resurface. Enitan's culture is not some shallow source of entertainment for a spoiled noblewoman, but it's not as if she can scold Deora—no matter how much she would like to. In these moments, the countess genuinely seems to believe that the world is *for* her—that all its richness exists for her personal pleasure. Or at least, she acts like it. As far as Vaalbaran think-ing goes, it doesn't seem to be truly nefarious, but it still sets Enitan on edge. Enitan weighs this against her recent, more forgiving assessment of the aristocrat.

Deora follows her back into her room, whereupon Enitan carefully pulls her formal robe from her satchel. It's a flowing, wide-sleeved gar-ment, cut from warm yellow cloth and intricately embroidered with synthetic gold thread.

"God, that's beautiful," Deora breathes out, reaching over to grasp a handful of cloth before Enitan can stop her.

She's never cared much about clothes, but Xiang picked this out for her for the first time they attended the Festival of Ten Thousand Stars as siblings. According to them, the robe brings out the coppery under-tones of her ochre-brown skin (and almost compensates for her dull personality). Again she swallows her irritation at Deora and makes her-self ready. She pulls on the robe and borrows a hair clipper from the noblewoman, cropping her dark, tightly coiled hair as close to her skull as possible. When the countess scampers off to fetch alcohol to ease both their nerves, Enitan hides the poignard under the mattress, next to the projector disk. Then she knocks back the amber drink Deora brings her, slips on Ajana's ring for good luck, and paces around the room.

"If the Imperator just wanted tea, she would've had that man ask for it," Enitan thinks aloud, pacing back and forth. She turns to Deora. "She's not about to murder me, is she?"

The countess purses her lips. "I don't think she's killed anyone since she left active service."

"And how long ago was that?"

"Two weeks ago."

Ancestors, she really shouldn't have had that liquor. Enitan is on the verge of throwing up when the doors chime—the servant has re-turned. Tossing one last desperate look back at Deora, Enitan follows him out of the apartments and down a dizzying series of winding corridors. They step into a tubelift and shoot up fifty stories, stopping every so often to be scanned by hovering cameras and patted down by sentinels in full armor. After a final security check, they step off at the personal residence of arguably the most powerful person on the planet. Enitan finds herself tugging at the ends of her sleeves as the doors slide open. When she doesn't move fast enough, the servant yanks her through into a long, polished passageway.

"When you meet the Imperator, you will prostrate yourself, touch your head to the ground twice, and remain bowed until Her Imperial Majesty commands you to rise. When she dismisses you, you will genuflect, stand, and exit backward with your head bowed. You will not turn your back toward the Imperator." He narrows his gray eyes at her. "You will address the Imperator as Your Imperial Majesty, Your Supreme Holiness, Eternal Mother, or God Almighty and All-Knowing. Do I make myself clear?"

Enitan nods curtly, trying to concentrate on not tripping over her own feet. She expected she'd be ordered to bend the knee one day, and here that day is. The servant half shoves her through another pair of shimmering doors, and they come to a stop before a final portal.

"Do not speak unless spoken to," he growls at her, pressing a hand to the doors' screen-surface. "Do not move unless commanded. Do not *breathe* unless ordered to."

"I assume you don't mean that last part literally."

His smile is all teeth. "Oh, I do."

The doors open and Enitan steps through. The first thing she notices is that the Imperator isn't there. For one terrifying moment she suspects she's walked right into a trap, but if the Imperator wanted her dead, she could've just had her defenestrated instead of bringing her all the way up to her chambers. So Enitan looks around.

The room is surprisingly small, paneled with a lattice of black stone. And even though the dark marble of the floor has been buffed into a painfully bright mirror, Enitan's sure that this is as close to cozy as the palace gets. Two shelves stand facing each other, carved into opposing walls. Enitan steps over to get a better look at the colorful items stacked within one of them. They're religious souvenirs, bought from the shrines and churches and mosques scattered all throughout Vaalbara. Their sale is a widespread practice; clerics of all kinds peddle them as physical benedictions to finance costly temple repairs.

Enitan picks up one of the pieces, dark wood carved whimsically into a head with four silver-painted faces: laughing, weeping, screaming, and . . . the last one she's uncertain about. Is it dead or meditating? Or perhaps just sleeping.

"That's my favorite one too," says a voice behind her.

Enitan whirls in alarm, dropping the carving in the process. "Ancestors!"

The Imperator laughs like she's a normal person, though the sound is a bit rusty, as if from disuse. Enitan takes her in. She's tall and sturdily built, with military-grade posture and arms corded with muscle. Her face is moon-shaped and bronze, with thick dark brows. Intricate jet-black braids spill down her back. She wears shockingly simple black garb, thin muslin travel clothing and soft slippers. But what strikes Enitan the most are her eyes. They're darker than dark; they swallow light like a singularity.

"Don't feel inclined to bow," says the Imperator, reaching down to pick up the carving. She dusts it off on her tunic before setting it back on the proper shelf.

Enitan struggles to get her breathing under control. She doesn't worship or even really respect the Imperator. She doesn't consider herself part of the Empire. No, she hates it with every fiber of her being, resents everything it has done to her people and all it stands for. This woman is not her god. The Imperator possesses none of her allegiance.

It's just that Enitan is terrified of her. It's too much power all wrapped up into one person. The High Consul's whims, at least, are limited by their position. This woman's are not.

Enitan drops to her knees so hard she nearly dislocates them. "Forgive me."

The Imperator huffs, steps forward, and extends a black-gloved hand. The urge to scramble back hits Enitan like a blast from a dissection gun, but she holds herself perfectly still, her heart feeling like it's about to burst out of her rib cage. For a moment she's certain the Imperator's about to strangle her, but then she waves her fingers, and Enitan understands she's offering to help her up. Enitan takes the Imperator's hand and finds herself hauled to her feet as if she were made of paper.

"I meant it. Don't feel inclined to bow." The Imperator gestures to the door on the opposite wall. "I apologize for the delay; I got a bit lost finding the right room."

That's right—she's new here too.

"Your Imperial Holiness—"

"My name is Menkhet." Her voice is soft and deep, like the echo of an echo. "And you're Enitan, if I'm pronouncing that correctly."

Enitan nods, unable to scrounge up a verbal response.

The Imperator regards her coolly. "Have you had breakfast yet?"

Not comprehending, Enitan says nothing.

"It's a simple question."

"I haven't, Your Supreme—"

"Menkhet. My name is *Menkhet*," the Imperator corrects firmly. "Follow me."

The Imperator leads Enitan into a chamber identical to the first, save for a mosaic of the Vaalbaran flag on the floor. The banner doubles as a map of the planet, though it doesn't even bother to include Koriko, worlds away as the habitat is. At the center lies the supercontinent for which the whole planet is named, Gondwana, accompanied by a spattering of minuscule islands. The entire thing is Imperial black, with the border between Vaalbara and Ominira mysteriously absent. It is the vision of the Empire the First God-Emperor promised, vast and unbroken. The Imperator strides over all of it, headed straight toward a table laden with steaming food.

Enitan pauses at the doorway. They're the only ones there. The Imperator might be a supremely skilled warrior, but it still seems wildly foolish to leave her alone with a stranger, especially a barbarian from as-yet-untamed lands. If Enitan believed she had even a percent of a chance of taking the God-Emperor down, she'd leap at her right now, consequences be damned. But she has a sibling to save, so she does nothing. Besides, on second thought, just because she can't see the guards doesn't mean that they're not there. Perhaps the new monarch is simply discreet. Or this is a trap.

The Imperator seats herself and looks pointedly over at Enitan. "Well, don't just stand there."

She sounds like Ajana. So imperious, but so casual in the exercise of her power. This shocks Enitan so much, she moves without thinking.

"This is all plant derived, by the way," says the Imperator, gesturing at the spread with an onyx-encrusted fork. "And it tastes awful, because I'm allergic to everything decent." Her voice drops, almost conspiratorially. "The Imperial physicians can't figure out how to help me. I think they're taking their sweet time so I keep paying them, but they're trying my patience. Eventually, I'm just going to throw them out of the Splinter and replace them."

A joke? Enitan swallows. "Your—"

The Imperator cuts her off with a glare.

Enitan isn't going to call her by her name. "I believe you might have been given incorrect information. I'm not an emissary." Under the table, her fingers curl into fists. "I'm only your quasi-political hostage. And according to the laws of your Empire, I don't qualify as a person, so I don't understand why you're being so polite."

"I didn't come up with those so-called laws, and I didn't ask for you to be brought to Vaalbara. I quite honestly don't want you here any more than you want to be."

There's something about the Imperator that makes Enitan feel . . . not at ease, certainly. But it makes her want to be straightforward. Whatever it is, Enitan finds herself asking outright: "Are you going to send me back?"

The Imperator doesn't even blink. She puts her fork down and selects a pair of silver-tipped chopsticks. "As with many things, I'm discovering, that's beyond my abilities."

Enitan almost sighs in relief. As much as she'd love to flee this gilded cage, she knows she won't have a chance of finding Xiang all the way from Koriko. And then she draws back, startled, because the God of over half this world's population just admitted that there are things she cannot do.

"You've been here for two days now," says the Imperator, selecting a cube of protein paste. "What do you think you know about me?" After a second, she adds, "You may speak your mind without fear of repercussion."

Somehow, Enitan doubts that. She licks her lips. She could heap flattery, but the Imperator grew up without immense wealth or a title, so she probably won't appreciate adulation. Enitan decides to go with her gut and be honest. This will be no different from reporting back to the High Consul, only she'll be far more discreet. Because if the Imperator decides she doesn't like what she hears, she could just drive those chopsticks into Enitan's throat and call for someone to toss her out the window. She is not completely certain the Imperator was joking about her doctors. Enitan forces in a breath.

"I think you're a very talented military commander who somehow won the old Imperator's respect after only three years of service."

"Those are all facts." The Imperator waves an impatient hand. Then she cocks her head. "*Somehow?* You must have picked up something interesting. You will tell me."

"I heard that you were very close with the late Princess Sunnetah, and that her father sought to honor that . . . friendship." Enitan swallows thickly. "I'm sorry for your loss."

The Imperator snorts, though there's a hardness in her eyes now. "It *was* a friendship. What else do you know?"

Enitan opens her mouth, and then something clicks. She's begun to weave a tapestry of rumors and whispers, and here before her is the center of it all. This is a perfect opportunity to pull at threads, see what snaps and what holds firm. "I think, perhaps, you never wanted to rule," she says. She's speculating, but based on the Imperator's disregard for Imperial conduct, she figures it's as good a guess as any. If she coveted power, she would be reveling in all the trappings of it— including proper etiquette. "I think you just wanted to serve the Empire, not command the whole of it."

The hardness bleeds from the Imperator's eyes into the rest of her face. "What else? Use your imagination, if need be."

Enitan grips the arms of her chair, her palms going clammy.

The Imperator flicks an impatient hand. "*Speak.*"

"I think you're surrounded by people who covet the power foisted upon you." Enitan's brain is screaming at her to shut up. "And I think those people have the means to take it."

"You've met Yehana, then." It's not a question. The Imperator sits back, folding her hands over her stomach. "He's a spoiled child in a man's body. He poses no threat to me."

Oh, this is *wonderful*. The Imperator has just presented her with the opportunity to sow dissent on a silver platter. And Enitan can't resist. Forget plucking at tiny threads. She's going to stir the whole pot, as they say in Ijebu. She wagers that whatever floats to the top will be fascinating.

"What of the rest of his family?" Enitan points out, cocking her head. "Surely they're not all as infantile as he."

"They're on my side. They wouldn't be trying to make a war hero—" The Imperator cuts herself off.

"A war hero out of you, otherwise?" Enitan keeps her expression impassive, wrestling with the urge to touch her face to check. "So not everyone desires peace, then."

"You're a slippery one, aren't you?" The Imperator shakes her head wryly. "It's a good thing you're my—what did you call it?— quasipolitical hostage."

Enitan shrugs, feigning nonchalance. "In any conflict, there are only ever two sides. Those who want peace, and those who do not."

This is stuff they taught in crèche. If the Imperator's learning it for the first time, Vaalbara is more than a little bit doomed. Or perhaps not, if this Imperator isn't actually pulling the strings, as Enitan is beginning to suspect.

But the Imperator only smiles. "You're forgetting the most dangerous side of all: those whose plans extend beyond the conflict entirely. There are those for whom a war is the least of their concerns, those who are perfectly happy with either concord or carnage so long as their plots are furthered. You obviously haven't read anything by the great Keita. You're missing out."

Enitan reaches forward, picks up a pair of chopsticks, and selects a ball of shredded and fried vegetable matter. "May I be frank?"

The Imperator quirks a brow. "Haven't you already been?"

"You're being maneuvered into a game you can't win." Enitan chews thoughtfully, forces herself to swallow. "If you wage war on Ominira and conquer the rest of the planet, the old Imperator's kin will take credit as the family that appointed you Imperator in the first place. You'll owe them for helping cement your power after the war ends—if it does—and they'll hold that over your head for the rest of your life." She picks up a protein cube, words continuing to spill from her mouth. "And if anything goes wrong, you'll be the scapegoat. Vaalbara might pride itself on its impartiality when it comes to *proper* citizens seeking advancement, but it's obvious to anyone paying attention that the Empire is nevertheless run by aristocrats. If you lose, they'll blame it on your common blood and oust you, if not assassinate you outright."

The Imperator says nothing, her mouth clamped shut, her entire body going tense. *Shit.* Enitan knows she's gone too far, that she's overplayed her hand. From her fear sprouts a burning anger, flooding her veins and sinking into her chest. She's nearly breathless with it, suffocated and simmering like she's been heaped with hot coals. She's furious at herself for her stupidity, but much of her ire is at the Imperator—at the woman who now represents everything wrong with the world. She may be baseborn and newly crowned, yes, but she's still the head of the most powerful autocracy Gondwana's ever seen.

"Those are dangerous claims," the Imperator says slowly, "for which you have no evidence."

Enitan gulps. "I—"

"*No.* I'm speaking now. I may be new to rulership, but I've lived in the Splinter half my life. You've been here for forty-eight hours," she snarls. "You're not an emissary. You're not Vaalbaran. And you're certainly not my advisor. Your file shows that you haven't even taken a single class in politics." It's a near echo of the words Enitan snarled at herself in the tub. The Imperator plants her hands on the table and stares at Enitan, examining her for a long, tense moment. "Who the fuck do you think you are?"

Enitan's tongue is dry. She forces herself to answer anyway. "You asked me to speak my mind."

The sound that comes out of the Imperator's mouth is close to, but not quite, laughter. "You're dismissed."

Enitan quickly rises to her feet. "Your Imperial Majesty." She aims the title like an arrow, and from the look on the Imperator's face, it strikes true.

"Get. *Out.*"

Well, at least she's not dead. Enitan genuflects, stands, and exits with her head bowed. She does not turn her back toward the Imperator.

◆

Enitan finds Deora lying in wait for her in the antechamber of her apartments.

"How was it?" The countess leaps up from the couch and links their arms together. "What's she like?"

Enitan steers them toward her room. "Interesting, on both counts."

"In a good way or in a bad way?" Deora tugs on her sleeve.

"I'm not sure yet."

"Come on, you have to give me *details*."

"It was boring," Enitan says carefully, disentangling herself from the countess. She's learned her lesson about discretion from her visit with the Imperator.

"That's it?" Deora whines.

"I think she just wanted to observe a savage outside of its natural habitat," Enitan says as pointedly as she can.

Deora's face falls. She looks at her boots, evidently chagrined. "I'm sorry things didn't go well."

"As am I," Enitan says. Except she's absolutely not. She has more information than she knows what to do with.

She doesn't report in once Deora leaves, though. The High Consul could be wrong about the holoprojector's invisibility from scanners. No cloak is perfect. If the Imperator somehow suspects she's an informant for the Republic, the clever thing to do would be to plant false information and lay a trap. So Enitan decides to wait and see what happens. The Empire renewing their war of conquest immediately after signing a peace treaty sounds too obvious to be true. Only when Enitan is personally convinced will she contact the High Consul.

And though the Imperator seems little more than a figurehead, a single half-hour conversation is hardly enough proof. But none of that is truly important to Enitan. The Empire's endless squabble with the Republic is certainly a problem—just not hers.

All she cares about is finding Xiang and getting them home. Her interest in the Imperator does not extend beyond figuring out what role she's played in Xiang's disappearance. If she truly had nothing to do with the kidnapping, then Enitan will put their strange meeting out of her mind. If, however, the Imperator is behind Xiang's abduction, as the High Consul believes . . . well, emperors do not outlast their empires, and she's just discovered that Vaalbara is already on the precipice of eating itself raw. Enitan will see to it that the bloody job is finished.

NINE

The next morning, Deora hands Enitan a communicator. She left her old one at home; it isn't connected to the Imperial network and would've been useless in the Vaalbaran interior.

"Half the Imperial Court wants you at their own soirée," the countess explains. "You'll need something to arrange your, ah, tea ceremony appointments. If you accept." But the pinched expression on her face suggests Enitan doesn't really have a choice in the matter. "Also, I've commissioned a few suits from the palace tailors. You'll have them in a week or so."

Enitan tries not to think too hard about how Deora obtained her measurements and thanks her. She pockets the communicator and plops down on a nearby divan. She watches the countess slip on her outer robe and grab a datapad.

"Where are you off to?"

Deora's eyes sparkle. "I volunteer at the Imperial Museum of Anthropology. We're organizing a brand-new exhibit of the Statues of Ruya-Tesh."

"Sounds interesting."

"Understatement of the century! The statues depict a number of past Imperators having visions of the First God-Emperor. Over the centuries, she's called upon them to wage war on neighboring tribes or grant Imperial pardons, that sort of thing."

Not for the first time, Enitan is struck by the vast differences between Vaalbaran religion and that of her own people. The Ancestors are everything the God-Emperors are not—benevolent spectators to be called upon for spiritual support, rather than living deities apotheosized the moment they take the throne.

Deora is still talking. "The First God-Emperor is remembered primarily as a great conqueror, but she was a champion of peace as well. And since her death, she's saved as many people as she condemned. And . . . wait, you were just being polite, weren't you?"

Enitan says nothing. Somehow, "great conqueror" and "champion of peace" don't fit together well in her mind.

Deora points to the communicator. "If you want food, you can order some. There's also a map on there, if you'd like to explore the Splinter."

Enitan sits up, eyes going wide. "I'm not confined to your apartments?"

Deora snorts, grabbing her boots. "You're a hostage, not a prisoner. In the Splinter, that means you may come and go as you please." She grimaces sympathetically. "Where would you even go, if you tried to run away? We're floating kilometers aboveground, and the shuttles are impossible to hijack."

Enitan nods, but she's not relieved in the slightest. All this freedom means is that they'll be watching her. She's not certain who *they* are, exactly, but she doubts anyone expects a savage hostage to remain well-behaved. They probably *want* her to make some grave mistake so they can justify a mass execution back home. She's never quite understood this—Vaalbara's judgement of an entire group with more differences than similarities, all based on the actions of a single member.

Deora pulls on her boots, waves goodbye, and bustles out the door, leaving Enitan alone with her thoughts. And her new communicator.

It's flat and ovoid, far more comfortable to hold than her chunky rectangular one at home. Xiang always teased her about how outdated it was. This model feels out of place in her hands.

Enitan swipes through the applications. There's a holomap downloaded, as Deora promised, along with an instant messaging function. The countess was right—there are already dozens of invitations, sent from all manner of officials and aristocrats. She accepts them all, and the communicator drops them neatly into her calendar. She makes a mental note to steal some of Deora's awful theehma leaf stock to replace her own for the vast majority of these. It's not as if any Vaalbaran is going to notice the difference.

She decides to spend the afternoon exploring the Splinter. She has no gatherings to perform at today, and she's not going to miraculously uncover Xiang's whereabouts without leaving this suite. She checks that the poignard and disk are well hidden. Then she snatches up her satchel, slips on her boots, and steps out into the corridor.

The palace is a silent maze of empty, shadowed hallways. Most of the aristocrats have already gone down to the city proper in the bottom three-quarters of the Splinter. Some probably have actual work to do— overseeing family businesses or volunteering like Deora. Most, Enitan supposes, are out for fancy social engagements.

There's a sentinel or servant in almost every passageway, but they largely ignore her and go about their work. A few simply watch her make her way through the palace, posture tense, as if expecting her to commit a heinous crime any second. She imagines they'd get along swimmingly with Stijena.

It's only a matter of time before one of them stops her. She's just exiting a tubelift when a servant woman with platinum-blond hair asks her if she's lost. When Enitan shows her the map she's following on her communicator, the servant asks her point-blank what she's up to.

"Dismantling the entire Empire, obviously," Enitan tells her, keeping her expression completely serious. She steps past the woman, who is now gaping, and continues on her way.

She uncovers very little of interest; there's no one to squeeze information out of, and any doors that open for her—of which there are surprisingly many—lead to vacant public spaces for the aristocracy. She's about to give up and go back to Deora's rooms when she comes across a vast mosaic.

It's impossible to miss. The copper and iron tiles have been polished to a wet gleam; the light they reflect cuts through the endless black of the palace like a knife. And it's colossal, dominating all seventy square meters of the wall it lies over. A cursory glance reveals that it's a map of Vaalbara, a massive waxing gibbous shape taking up the eastern half of Gondwana. Ominira, by comparison, is a waning crescent to the west.

But closer inspection reveals that the mosaic is so much more—it depicts the *origin* of the Empire. One of Enitan's first-year professors had told her that Vaalbara's greatest invention wasn't the monoliths, or dissection guns, or anything that came after its formation. No, the Empire's greatest invention was itself.

A thousand silver lines crisscross the map, recording the displacement of conquered tribes and clans. After each victory, the Empire forcibly uprooted indigenous populations, shifting them around to fulfill its various needs. This also served to break the people's bonds with their homelands and sever loyalties among local groups.

Fist-sized hemispheres of silver mark the settlements that surrendered immediately, with tiny engraved script listing the local administrators who were allowed to remain as a reward for accepting the Empire with open arms. Golden rays symbolize the myriad religions of each village or city, all of which were allowed to flourish as long as the faiths' leaders acknowledged the supremacy of the God-Emperor.

And in the center of it all is the Imperial capital, constructed centuries ago at the exact nexus of the region's largest trade network. From this vantage point, the Empire has long controlled the flow of food, technology, and precious metals across half the continent. Eventually, the proud, free settlements that had not yet fallen were starved of resources. In the end, they were forced to bow to Vaalbara to survive.

Enitan is striding over to inspect another part of the map when a shadow at the edge of her blind spot shifts. Someone's watching her.

She forces her posture to relax, unease creeping over her skin. She takes a few steps toward the nearest exit, and the shadow shifts again. Whoever it is isn't just watching her—they've been following her. But for how long?

Enitan had suspected she'd be monitored; she should've been more vigilant. She mutters a string of curses under her breath as she considers her options. She can make a run for it, but then her shadow will simply resume tailing her the next day as soon as she leaves Deora's apartments. She could retrace her steps and confront them, but they might well be armed. Something between the two, then. She sets off at a brisk pace, and sure enough, a blurred shape vanishes from her periphery.

She opens the holomap and navigates her way to the palace's hanging gardens, a four-tiered alabaster complex in the center of a massive domed space. According to the communicator's helpful virtual assistant, this is one of the few structures in the Splinter that isn't constructed from entirely black materials. (There are also the interrogation chambers, of course.) Expectedly, the space is packed, mostly with monks and their attendants. Unexpectedly, there isn't a single tree or shrub. Just the complex itself, only darkness visible between its glowing white columns.

Still, there's a steady stream of people flowing into the gardens. She's relatively safe here, surrounded by hundreds of potential witnesses. A group of monks pays her little mind as she follows them in, though a few do stop to glare or pointedly raise a brow. And from the prickling sensation running up her spine, she's certain she's being followed again. She crosses the threshold, looks up, and very nearly laughs. The infamous hanging gardens of Vaalbara—she should have known.

There isn't so much as a vine. There are, however, thousands of jeweled skulls, suspended from various lengths of silver cord. Row upon row of glinting eyes peer down at her: a king's ransom in black star diopside, all cabochon-cut for roundness. The white asterisms at their centers shine like pale pupils. This is the part of the story untold by the mosaic map. Surrendered cities that later rebelled were massacred, often by conflagration. And when villages didn't just roll over, the Empire made good use of terror and siege tactics. Impalement, flaying, death by a thousand cuts. One of the early Imperators, an avid historian, decided to resurrect the ancient Homeworld practice of scaphism, whereby victims were slathered in sugar and trapped between two small boats, one vessel sealed over the other with holes cut out to expose the head, hands, and feet. Then the captive was left to fester. Eventually, they'd be devoured alive by insects and vermin. There are many, many narratives of past Imperators' so-called strict understanding of justice. Including right here, rendered in bone and diopside.

Enitan shivers and tears her gaze away from the skulls, to no avail. She can still feel them staring at her. But this is part of her plan, and she's not about to abandon it because of a little disquiet. She grabs her communicator and makes a show of scrolling through an article about the garden. Apparently, the skulls above are exclusively those of warriors or chieftains. Vaalbaran generals made a habit of saving and bringing back—willingly or no—doctors, scholars, engineers, and artisans from the bloodshed, simultaneously depriving conquered peoples of healthcare, knowledge, and culture while enriching the Empire's. She counts to a hundred and then pivots on her heel. There, just behind a column, is her shadow. She's certain of it—they're draped in a cape, for Ancestors' sake. It's dark orange and as simple as a monk's frock. She looks first for their gender brooch, but there isn't one. Which makes sense. If she were going to trail someone, she wouldn't wear any identifying markers either. The shadow cast by the hood of their cape covers much of their face.

Enitan watches the figure stiffen as they realize she's onto them. Well, that answers quite a few questions. They're probably not a professional, or they would play it off and go about their business. And they likely wouldn't be wearing that cloak in the first place. They could still be dangerous, though.

She begins walking toward them, hands clenched at her sides. They take a step back. She walks faster. The shadow swings around and dashes out of the gardens. Enitan curses and runs after them. The monks shout and scramble away, giving her a wide berth. She won't chase the figure down some dark corridor, but if she can catch up to them while still in public, perhaps she can get them to talk to her.

A sentinel steps right into her path, so suddenly she nearly crashes into him.

"Emissary," says someone right behind her.

She knows that voice. Gritting her teeth, Enitan turns around to face the Imperator, who's flanked by a pair of sentinels in full laminar armor. People prostrate themselves as soon as they notice her, dropping like felled trees. The Imperator's deep-black eyes now resemble shards of ice. It's a jarring shift from the woman Enitan met yesterday, though there was never any softness in her face.

"Come with me," she orders, curt and demanding, and turns on her heel. "I'd like a cup of tea."

After a moment, Enitan follows. She'd like to pursue her shadow, but what choice does she have? The Imperator leads her out of the hanging gardens, down a dim hallway, and up a tubelift. Several silent minutes later, the sentinels peel off and they're back in the Imperial residence. Enitan follows the Imperator into the chamber where she first attempted to stir dissent—and failed miserably. Or perhaps not, since she's back here.

"Sit," the Imperator tells her, and she does. "I realize that I was perhaps . . . discourteous yesterday." Enitan catches the unhappy flex of her jaw. "You were only being honest. I was irritated because there was, I admit, a seed of truth in what you said. I apologize."

Enitan stares at her, trying not to let her surprise show. "I . . . accept your apology."

The Imperator reaches into the center of the table, where a bottle of spiced cider lies. "It is my understanding that you will attend a number of private engagements in the coming days." She fills two shallow porcelain bowls and holds one out.

Enitan accepts the proffered cider but doesn't drink. "I am honored that so many of your illustrious subjects have taken an interest in Korikese tea ceremony."

"Hmm. Somehow I doubt that you're *honored*," the Imperator says casually. "Are you aware that many of your hosts number among the most politically influential nobles in Vaalbara, and are thus potential threats to my reign?"

Enitan considers playing the fool but thinks better of it. "The thought had occurred to me."

The Imperator's mouth twitches into a slight smirk. "Most citizens know of the scandal that allowed you to learn Orin, but many would be surprised to learn you're fluent in it, and they'd need a fair bit of convincing to believe it. The rest will assume a savage like yourself couldn't possibly understand the intricacies of the Imperial Court." She pins Enitan with a pointed stare. "So I'm certain they'll say all sorts of interesting things around you."

Oh, Ancestors. Enitan swallows. "You want me to spy for you."

"Of course not. You'd act as more of an . . . informal advisor."

The words leap from Enitan's mouth before she can stop them: "That's worse!"

The Imperator's answering laugh is probably intended to be reassuring. It's not. "I don't need you to report to me regularly. But occasionally, I will call for your opinion on certain matters, with the expectation that your opinion is informed by what you learn during your engagements."

Enitan bites the inside of her cheek. There's no way she can spy for both the High Consul and the Imperator and keep her head in the end. Nor does she wish to serve the Empire in any way, shape, or form, even if she finds this Imperator to be reasonable and perhaps even well-meaning. "You must have an entire network of spies at your disposal."

The Imperator lifts her hands before dropping them with a sigh. "I do. But sneaking them into the small private gatherings of possible enemies has proven . . . difficult." She takes a sip of cider. "I live in an echo chamber of stone and silver, Enitan. My hope is that you, as a newcomer, will notice what my agents and I cannot. Fill in the gaps, so to speak."

"May I speak openly once more, then?"

"From now on, always."

"As you pointed out yesterday," Enitan says, "I'm unqualified to advise you. But most importantly, my loyalty is to my own people. To be perfectly frank, I have every right to hate you."

"That's what I'm counting on. Unlike most of my court, I know exactly where you stand. There is an ancient Homeworld saying: better the devil you know than the devil you don't." She pauses. "Perhaps I'll even change your mind about me."

Enitan, who neither knows nor cares what a devil is, frowns. The Imperator knows less than nothing about her. "Your army set Koriko ablaze and subjugated its people for sport."

The Imperator stiffens, her shoulders rising. If Enitan didn't know better, she'd say the woman looks *offended*. "First of all, I was a child when that happened. And I wasn't even in Vaalbara. Second, I didn't say I could change your mind about the whole Empire."

"Nevertheless," Enitan says, "I stand to gain nothing from helping you." She knows she's playing a treacherous game here. But she's no longer so terrified of this woman, and she knows that agreeing too readily to the arrangement will only prove how little her worth is. She can tell the Imperator doesn't want another sycophant. She wants someone brave enough to see the truth for what it is and tell it to her.

"I disagree." The Imperator leans forward. "I will relinquish Koriko if you help me survive the next year on the throne."

Enitan isn't sure she's just heard correctly. In the space of a second, she can feel the racing of her heart in her ears, reverberating up from her ribs. "You would so willingly give up the Jewel of Vaalbara?"

The Imperator snorts. The title is an old joke; Koriko is a tin trophy hundreds of millions of kilometers away from everything and everyone that matters on Gondwana. The last God-Emperor once jokingly offered to free Enitan's homeland if it paid "reparations" equal to 80 percent of its gross domestic product, an impossible task since Korikese people have never really used Vaalbaran currency.

"I mean no offense," the Imperator drawls, "but your moon isn't worth my life. Besides, Koriko could bring more to my Empire as a willing ally than a chunk of bitterly occupied rock."

"What about the rest of the Empire?"

"We're not talking about the rest of the Empire. The other provinces are far too intertwined with us. They're Vaalbaran. In fact, quite a few descendants of former colonies are, I suppose, your oppressors now."

Enitan has already seen ample proof of this; she thinks back to Deora's friends. She wants to ask another question, wants to pull at the glittering threads the Imperator is dangling in front of her, but manages to hold back. "Less than twenty-four hours ago, you told me you couldn't even send me back home."

The Imperator smiles serenely, but it doesn't quite reach her eyes. "Yes, because my power isn't well established. *Yet*. Once I deal with certain threats and cement my reign, I'll be able to do whatever I want. That includes giving up Koriko and providing its people restitution."

Enitan should really start making a list of all the promises the leaders of the planet's two greatest powers have given her. She doesn't quite trust the High Consul to actually save Xiang and herself if it becomes inconvenient, and she trusts the Imperator even less. But the influence she'll have with the Imperator's ear will be unimaginable, and if somehow she does keep her word, Enitan's people will be free.

This conversation has made her certain that the woman before her has nothing to do with the abductions. Whoever's kidnapping Korikese is powerful enough to do as they please and get away with it, and certainly wouldn't need the aid of their own hostage. This *could* be an elaborate trap to ensnare the High Consul. But Enitan suspects that if the Imperator knew about that arrangement, then she'd already be dead. From what she knows, the Imperator is a soldier at her core; she doesn't seem like the sort to relish in overcomplicated political machinations.

Enitan's master plan to save Xiang is minuscule compared with the intrigues of an entire Empire. All she wants to do is find them and get out, and this will help her accomplish that. Even if the Imperator is lying through her teeth about Koriko.

"Well?" prompts the Imperator.

Enitan folds her arms. "All right."

The Imperator arches a brow. "I thought it'd be harder to convince you."

"All I have to do is offer my honest opinion?" Enitan shrugs. "That seems like a small price to pay for a chance at Koriko regaining its independence." She doubts there's a high survival rate for people who refuse God-Emperors anyway. "But I have a question."

The Imperator narrows her eyes. "Ask."

"Why did you ever want to meet with me in the first place?"

"Oh." Her face melts swiftly. "I just thought you might be . . . interesting."

Enitan immediately interprets *interesting* as *useful*. And just like that, she's become the enemy's new weapon.

TEN

Enitan contacts the High Consul the next day, reporting everything save the Imperator's offer to free Koriko. She doesn't want them thinking her loyalty might be compromised. And while the Imperator's promise is far greater than the Consul's, it is also far less likely to be kept.

When she finally finishes her account, the High Consul just tells her to tread lightly, especially now that she has a shadow.

In any case, Enitan's shadow doesn't follow her to her first engagement—as far as she can tell. It's a formal reception to celebrate the investiture of a young earl, now the governor of a highly prized region in the Imperial interior. Half the guests are close friends who were simultaneously promoted to advantageous positions. The rest are aristocrats invited only because propriety demanded it.

Enitan arrives at the earl's apartments just as the soirée begins and sets herself up in the parlor as agreed. The noble himself stops by as she tosses a few spoonfuls of tea into a pot Deora gifted her. The blend she'll be serving tonight is a strong black uhie heavily diluted with Vaalbaran stock. It won't be nearly as good as a pure blend, but she can't risk running out of her personal stash so soon.

Her host's first words to her are: "You Korikese *do* have names, don't you?"

The question is so ridiculous she almost laughs. "We do. I'm Enitan."

"Eneetan," he says. "*Eneetan*. Funny name."

"Please accept my most humble congratulations for your new position," she says, emphasizing Orin vowels the way she imagines *he* imagines a proper savage would. "I understand that it is a great honor."

"This is fascinating," he remarks, his gaze flickering over the tea ceremony accoutrements she's brought. He looks up at her with an expression that makes it clear *fascinating* isn't the word he really meant. "You froth the tea by hand? Why don't you use a machine?"

Enitan's mask cracks, irritation flickering in her chest. Five aristocrats have already badgered her about the inefficiency of Korikese tea ceremony. It's funny how Vaalbara's obsession with doing work by hand conveniently seems to apply to everyone but nobles. "Tradition, my lord."

"Well," says the earl, planting his hands on his hips, "I suppose not all cultures can be quite as refined as Vaalbara's."

Enitan barely restrains herself from pointing out that Koriko is *technically* part of the Empire—though she personally would rather fling herself out of the Splinter than identify as Vaalbaran. But whether she's technically Vaalbaran or not, the people she is serving tea to will call for her blood at the faintest whiff of opposition. Her goal here is to win them over, to make them feel comfortable enough to loosen their lips around her.

"It is a shame," Enitan agrees, shaking her head mournfully. "But perhaps by the Imperator's grace, the light of progress will shine upon my people."

The earl lifts a brow. She overdid it. Enitan curses inwardly, mentally kicking herself for good measure.

But then he guffaws and smiles at her. "How adorable." He pauses to survey her; she pretends not to notice. "I must admit, you're the first Korikese I've met. I'm surprised. I didn't expect you to be quite so . . . well trained." He reaches over without warning.

Enitan goes very still. A hot prickle swells under her skin as his fingertips brush over her jaw and down to her chin.

"Very good." He pats her cheek, before retracting his hand and wiping his fingers on his embroidered coat.

Enitan tries to keep her trembling at bay. Her hands hidden by the sleeves of her formal robe, she clenches her fists in a sorry attempt to redirect some of her disgust and fury. "Thank you, my lord," she manages.

He nods graciously and goes on his way. Few others speak to her, instead swinging by her table to snatch up a cup of tea. This gives Enitan almost uninterrupted freedom to observe court drama flourishing in its natural habitat. Which she does, as soon as she regains control of her breathing. The promoted nobles eventually separate themselves from the less fortunate partygoers. The snubbed aristocrats spend much of the occasion in the corners, complaining about the sociopolitical vicissitudes accompanying the change in Imperator. Nothing Enitan overhears from either party is exactly what she'd call scintillating. Most of it is balderdash and bluster, until one very inebriated viscount climbs up on a table.

"Friends!" he calls out. "I have a . . . a toast!" He belches, the fist pressed to his mouth doing nothing to muffle the sound. "Saevak! You've always been my favorite cousin," he begins, squinting as he scans the crowd for the earl. When the nobleman steps forward, his expression blank save for a lukewarm smile, the viscount lets out a gurgling cackle.

"Reryn," Saevak hisses. "Get down. *Please*."

"I'm only going to wish you luck," replies Reryn, slapping away his cousin's entreating hands. "I promise. This isn't like at Grandfather's funeral."

An alcohol-fueled chuckle rolls through the assembled nobles, and Saevak's pale face goes fire red.

"Saevak." Reryn pauses for suspense. "I know you're not a religious man, not given over to spirituality in the least." He grins. "And let's hope that you're wrong about the existence of an afterlife, may Grandfather find peace."

The chuckle grows into a chortle.

Saevak lunges for his errant relative. "Reryn, *please*."

The viscount somehow dodges, despite his quickly degrading balance. "But you may want to reconsider your atheism, cousin." He raises his goblet in a wobbly toast. Wine sloshes out of the cup and onto Saevak's coiffed brown hair. The earl lets out a tiny shriek, but Reryn continues. "I had the pleasure of meeting the Imperator before her coronation, and . . ." He trails off, smiling. "Well, you may want to start praying."

A jest, obviously, because God and the Imperator are the same person. Cackling now.

"*Cousin!*" The earl looks as if on the verge of tears, and the wave of schadenfreude that hits Enitan nearly bowls her over.

"All right, all right." Reryn hops off the table. "But let's just say that only God knows how you'll survive this Imperator's reign. How *any* of us will."

And the room erupts into screaming laughter. Enitan doesn't have enough background information to fully appreciate the joke, but she nearly joins them. This all but confirms her suspicions. No noble fond of breathing would ever insult an Imperator with real power, or even laugh at such an offense. They certainly wouldn't find the idea of an atheist earl so funny, given that apostasy is tantamount to treason. Only a quarter of the aristocrats here are actually inebriated enough to lose their senses; if the Imperator were truly dangerous, they'd be quaking in their satin slippers.

Enitan's judgement of the Imperator is a fragile one; she's only been here at court for a few days, after all. But these patricians grew up in the Splinter; they see only strength and the lack of it. Most of the nobles must have personally met the Imperator by now. A few moments are all they'd need to evaluate her. And the results of that assessment are made painfully clear by their cackling.

The earl, though, must only now be realizing this. Enitan watches with relish as abject horror dawns on his face. She can't imagine the Imperator ever favoring him enough to appoint him governor of a bucket of vomit, let alone a prized region. Perhaps he made some sort of arrangement with her. If so, he might have sacrificed a great deal to obtain the title and lands handed to him. But power bestowed by a figurehead isn't real power at all.

This also means that the Imperator is certainly not in any position to free Koriko from Vaalbara's crushing grip. Enitan doubts the God-Emperor ever will be, even once those "certain threats" are handled (which she also finds unlikely in this case). Still, Enitan will enjoy whatever influence she'll have as the Imperator's advisor. And she can enjoy this moment. She catches the earl's gaze and grins, baring all her teeth. Holding his stare, she lifts a glass of inefficiently made tea in a small, silent toast.

◆

If the Imperator isn't in power, then who is?

Enitan spends the rest of the week in search of an answer to this question, flitting from gala to function to fête. To her growing disappointment, the nobles, dignitaries, and abbots she serves are almost entirely uninformative. While a few of the conversations she eavesdrops on seem like they might lead somewhere interesting, most of the aristocrats she encounters are the ones with enough free time on their hands to throw soirées—though they're some of the most politically important Imperials in the Splinter, they don't actually *do* much themselves. Even if she weren't rooting around for the barest scraps of intel, they're the blandest people she's ever observed. Occasionally, one of them will suggest a new game or contest to amuse themselves with, but her hosts' creativity is evanescent at best. At least none of them are as terrible as the earl. As the days drag into weeks, she begins to think he's the worst of the bunch. She finds out just how wrong she is during a gathering on one of the palace's upper floors.

The host, Duke Banurra, is an amateur archaeologist fond of hosting academics from the Imperial University of Opuroth. His interests include eugenics; transhumanism; and, according to Deora, leering at naked statues. Once a month he invites a number of distinguished professors to his apartments and pledges vast amounts of funding to the ones who affirm his beliefs.

Enitan knows it's going to be horrible the moment she walks through the door and into Banurra's chambers, which are stuffed with Korikese relics that actually *are* stolen. After a handful of parties, she's mostly gotten used to Vaalbaran aristocracy. She's normally ignored at best and treated as an exotic entertainment at worst, like a never-before-seen species on display in a menagerie. It's clear that this evening it'll be the latter—awful on every level, but she'll survive. Their ignorance works to her advantage anyway. Perhaps the duke will divulge something besides his "deep appreciation for sensuous art."

Enitan is frothing tea when the duke, lounging on a silk-smothered couch, mentions the ruins of a ziggurat he's discovered just to the west of the Vaalbaran-Ominirish border. Enitan actually read an article about the expedition a few days ago, when she looked up the duke to gauge how much internal screaming she'd be doing.

The duke sips at his rum. "As I said, I just don't believe the locals could've built those ruins." His hand glitters when he tips the cup to his lips; each finger sports an ancient Korikese wedding band. Enitan wonders if he's aware of the significance behind each carnelian ring.

One of the guests, a woman with dark hair and darker eyes, leans forward. If Enitan remembers correctly, she's a visiting lecturer from a slightly less prestigious school than Opuroth. "My lord, there's actually quite a bit of evidence supporting the theory that the ruins were built by a, um, nomadic pre-Empire group."

"Really!" The duke lifts his brows, as pleased as a pointy-eared mossicat. "Once again, my instincts are correct."

Enitan struggles not to roll her eyes. Even on the other side of the system, everyone on Koriko knows Ominira's Ancestors built ziggurats as a precursor to their now-beloved pyramids.

"I can prepare a dossier on those findings," says the scholar, subtly straightening her posture, "and perhaps even expand upon them, with a little financial support. My lord."

"Of course!" The duke snatches her glass from her gloved hands and fills it to the brim with rum. "Consider it done. I look forward to seeing what you dig up. Ha!"

Enitan clamps her teeth together and arranges the finished cups of tea on a tray. When she stands to distribute them, the duke's blond head swivels around, his gaze latching on to her.

"Come over here," he demands, beckoning her with crooked, heavily ringed fingers.

Though every fiber of her being tells her not to, Enitan takes a single halting step toward him.

"As the resident expert on Korikese ritual practices," he drawls, "can you speak to the accuracy of my latest acquisition?" He extends a silver-bound arm, gesturing at a cluster of obsidian, bronze, and marble bodies. The limbs are so entangled it's difficult to discern where one form begins and another ends.

I hope you catch on fire, Enitan thinks, fury trickling down the back of her throat. *I hope your lungs are ripped out and sprinkled with salt. I hope you fall into a bloodmaw den covered in sugar.* She lowers her eyes demurely. "I'm afraid several artistic liberties were taken."

"Oh?" He moistens his lips, utterly unabashed. His eyes glitter dangerously, desire and demand glinting in the aquamarine of his irises. "My personal study proves otherwise."

As the assembled guests scrounge up a bit of uncomfortable laughter, Enitan looks down at him. She imagines dumping the tea on him and bashing his skull in with the tray. "Festival dances aren't . . . orgies, my lord. They're just dances."

"But it's a known fact that you Korikese are more, ah, *energetic* than we Vaalbarans are," he tells her, his tone so patronizing it stings. "There must be some way you manage your excess vitality." He smiles, showing off nearly all thirty-two of his perfectly white, perfectly straight teeth. Saliva shimmers over the enamel, the sharp curves of his canines illuminated by handwrought lanterns. "Perhaps you'd care to demonstrate for us. Or just me."

Silence falls, and Enitan freezes. She hears nothing but the rasp of her own breathing, the hot rush of blood in her ears.

She's no stranger to this particular stereotype. The myth of her people's uncontrollable promiscuity stems from the nascent Empire's first encounter with Koriko after the Sundering. Vaalbara sprouted from a frigid waste, and Koriko took root in the engineered warmth of a tropical habitat. Unaccustomed to the requirements of such a clime, Vaalbaran explorers mistook partial nudity for depravity. This is well-known in her community. She's even joked about it herself a few times. But she is a stranger to whatever this is. Enitan has no idea how to respond.

"Better not," says the visiting lecturer, breaking the quiet. "You might catch something, my lord."

The duke snorts, rakes his gaze down Enitan once more, and turns back to his rum.

Enitan looks over at the scholar, whose narrow, sharp face reminds her of an unsheathed blade. She feels sick. Her communicator chimes in her pocket. Numbly, she puts down the tray, fishes out the device, and stares at the screen. It's from Deora. She has to read the message twice before the black squiggles resolve into words. Something about the hilarious thing her new assistant did today.

"Forgive me," Enitan says. Her throat feels like it's closing up, but somehow she manages to keep her voice perfectly flat. "I'm afraid I have another engagement."

The duke shrugs, waving a dismissive hand at her. Enitan turns, drags herself through the foyer, and steps out the door. She leaves the dishes behind, along with most of her composure.

It's too much. Humiliation and cruelty hammered into dual knives that slide into her gut. If not for Xiang and Ajana, Enitan would wish to crumble into smoke and dissipate into the air. She breaks down in the corridor, collapsing against the wall. She brings her arm to her mouth and screams into the fabric. Most of the sound is muffled.

She stays like this for a long time.

ELEVEN

Enitan cancels her appointments the next day. She spent about ten minutes trying to come up with an excuse. She knew she couldn't tell the nobles she was sick; they'd just start a rumor that she's a carrier for some vile swamp contagion, never mind that there are vaccines on Koriko. And she certainly couldn't say the truth, which is that whenever she sits still for too long, she feels the duke's leering gaze crawling over her like slick worms burrowing under her skin. In the end, she made up a severe allergy and took the day off.

Before she can head out of the countess's apartments, though, her host accosts her.

"Good morning!" Deora grabs her by the arm and tugs her away from the door.

"I thought you'd gone off to do . . . museum work," says Enitan, swallowing down her surprise. She rarely sees Deora these days, though every once in a while, the countess will go all out and they'll devour whatever feast she's whipped up.

"I told the head anthropologist I'd be late. Said I was helping out a friend." She finally drags Enitan into the living room and waves her hands at a pile of clothes.

"Ah," says Enitan. "The suits."

Each is meticulously wrapped in synthetic tissue paper and bound with silk ribbon. Enitan smothers a sigh. She couldn't care less about her new wardrobe, especially after the events of yesterday. But Deora looks so hopeful and excited, Enitan resists the urge to shove past her and take the day for herself.

There are twelve outfits in total, ranging from pajamas to lounge-wear to a samite dress suit she's supposed to wear at formal functions held by the Imperator. They're all jewel tones: ruby and sapphire and emerald. There are even matching shoes. With her new gender pin and the enclosed matching gloves, she'll be indistinguishable from a proper Vaalbaran citizen. Now that she considers it, if she ever needs to sneak around incognito, she'll have the perfect disguise. Each garment, she notices, is edged in goldwork and black pearls.

"How much did these cost?" Enitan begins folding the suit back up. The fabric is softer than a cloud. "I can't pay you back." Her hosts never compensate her, and she never bothers to ask. While payment wouldn't be an issue for most, a number of them would balk at paying a Korikese for what they likely think she owes them anyway, especially given her status as political prisoner. The currency chits she brought from home wouldn't cover a single glove here.

"A lot." Deora's smile stretches. "And these aren't even the suits I asked for. I didn't think goldwork was your style. Too gaudy."

Actually, as far as precious metals go, she prefers gold. Enitan crosses her arms and lifts a brow. "So who are they from?"

"They appear to have been paid for by a mysterious someone." Deora clasps her hands together. "You have an aristocratic admirer."

Enitan stares at the countess, unamused. She hopes it's that innoc-uous, as unlikely as that is. The nobles here seem precisely as romanti-cally interested in her as she is in them, with the exception of the duke. Though *romantic* doesn't exactly describe his proposition.

Though the High Consul might be able to pull such strings in order to better prepare her for her assignment, it would be risky, and they would have informed her beforehand. Her brain comes up with the horrible notion that the garments might be lined with a topical poison. But though she'd never call the Imperials frugal, she can't imagine any of them spending so much just to kill her. An assassin would probably be cheaper.

She rubs at her eyes before she continues folding the clothes. She has little use for them at the moment.

"Wait, you aren't going to wear them?" Deora's lips almost tremble.

"Ah, no." Enitan stacks up the bundles. "I have to wear my tunics for engagements." She has a role to play here, and traditional Korikese garments have become her costume.

"Oh." Deora grimaces, as if she understands. "Fools, the lot of them. You know, you could probably tell them a burlap sack is sacred attire, and they'd believe you."

The countess has taken to ridiculing her fellow nobles about fetishizing Korikese traditions. Enitan can't tell if the irony amuses or annoys her. Does Deora really believe her own particular brand of commodification is special somehow?

"I wouldn't be surprised," is all Enitan says.

Deora sighs. Then she perks up, her smile returning in full force. "But you don't have any parties today, right?"

Enitan presses her lips together. She'd rather wear her regular tunic; she won't have many other opportunities to don her normal clothes without having to perform in them. She wants to be comfortable, for once. But she'd rather stew in a stiff suit than explain how she feels to the countess.

"All right," she acquiesces.

She carries her new clothes into her room and comes out in the brightest outfit, a warm yellow suit that almost reminds her of home. She runs a hand over the painstakingly embroidered cloth, a sudden bolt of longing coursing through her.

"You look amazing!" Deora makes her spin around. "How about some jewelry? I have a pair of silver chains—"

"No, thank you." Enitan steps around the countess and almost runs out the door.

She decides to spend the day exploring, picking up where she left off when she first arrived. Much of the palace is still empty. Over the week, she's learned that while there are a couple of floors where high-ranked or favored nobles like Deora live, most of Vaalbara's aristocracy reside in estates in the Imperial city below. A few powerful but somewhat out-of-favor nobles reside in their own monoliths. Enitan's prints allow her access to a number of vaulted common spaces, but most of the offices, chapels, and storerooms are barred to her.

She does find the main library and an adjacent church, both of which are open to all the denizens of the palace. They're almost the same size, and their design is indistinguishable. Thin, dark stone pillars stretch up the walls, pressed so close to each other as to be unsettling. They look like clamoring arms, reaching for something precious across the ceiling. Curtains with night-black cassiterite sewn into them hang between the columns, falling over triangular windows like drooping eyelids. She finds herself alone in both buildings, or at least it seems like she is.

In the library, Enitan crouches down to inspect a tome about the Sundering. No expense was spared in its craftsmanship; its pages are real eyrus sedge paper, either smuggled in from Ominira or purchased before the war. The authors hail from two different schools of thought. One takes a spiritual approach, claiming that the soul of Gondwana rejected its human colonists for their hubris. The other is a firm atheist, asserting the environmental inevitability of the catastrophic event that drove nearly all of humanity to extinction. To Enitan's mild surprise, both agree that the species should never have left faraway Homeworld, ravaged as it was. They bemoan that civilization was forced to begin anew, resulting in the loss of information and culture and the rise of a movement denying the existence of Homeworld altogether. She's halfway through the fifth chapter when the air changes. It feels heavier. There's someone here with her.

Enitan rises slowly to her feet and turns to face her shadow, finding them draped in the same cape as yesterday. Before they slide back, she gets a good look at their eyes, gray and lined with kohl. The two of them are utterly alone. If her shadow decides to slit her throat, there's no one to stop them. A shiver ripples down her arms and legs.

"The hood isn't very subtle, you know." But perhaps that's the point. No one fears someone who tries to look inconspicuous and fails spectacularly at it. Enitan grips the book, wondering just how hard she'd be able to strike her shadow with it. "What do you want from me?" She keeps her tone even, gentle.

"The truth." Their voice is incredibly deep. "Do you love the Empire?"

An assassin would stab her and be done with it. A Vaalbaran operative would never ask her such a question outside of an interrogation chamber; the patriotism of anyone under Imperial surveillance is probably suspect to begin with. Enitan lets out a breath. A nosy noble, then? Yet another Imperial with a strange interest in her opinions?

"Did you buy all those clothes?" she asks.

"Clothes?" They cock their head, visibly confused. "No. Please answer the question."

Enitan crosses her arms. "Of course I do. I am, by law, a citizen of the Empire. It's my home. Technically speaking."

Her answer seems to please them; the darkness under the hood shifts. Are they smiling?

Enitan slips a hand into her pocket. There's an emergency call button on her communicator. "What else do you want?"

"Don't do that," the shadow warns sharply, lifting their gloved hands. "I'm not here to hurt you." They tilt their head. "Any sentinels you summon are more likely to arrest you than they are me."

So they're not the bumbling fool she thought they were. That whole show in the gardens was just to ensure she noticed them. If not for the Imperator, she definitely would've followed them, and they would've been having this conversation much earlier. The ease with which she's been manipulated frightens her. "Tell me what you want."

"Your help."

She almost laughs. "No."

They stiffen as if slapped. "You don't even know who I am. Or whom I serve."

Oh, Ancestors. Could they be an agent of a third party—the islands, even?—come to recruit her as an informant? "I don't care," she says. She bends and shoves the Sundering tome back into its spot. "Are you going to keep following me?"

They shake their head. "You've made your position clear."

"Well, thank you." She turns toward the doors. "Good luck with whatever you're trying to do."

"Likewise, Enitan. Your tread will have to be more careful than mine if you're looking to survive this."

She spins back, panic knotting her gut, but they're gone. She spends the next hour worrying about what her shadow knows, and another telling herself if they were attempting to blackmail her, they would've already made that clear. But she can't afford to waste her time agonizing over setbacks, warnings from mysterious strangers, or her fear of sinister dukes—she needs to be gathering intel to find Xiang and help Ominira. She needs to move.

She wanders for another hour, and it's almost time for dinner when she finds a dusty stairwell and stumbles into an area that shouldn't exist. On her holomap it's between the seventh and eighth stories, illustrated as a slightly thicker floor. All the windows have been plastered or boarded over, so it's far too dark to see within. All she can discern from the shadows are piles of broken-down shelves and what looks like a stack of outdated datapads. The tiling is terribly uneven, and when she takes a step inside, glass crunches beneath her feet. The probability she'll get lost or hurt is too high for her to simply waltz in.

She'll investigate tomorrow.

◆

"How was your day?" Deora asks during supper, right before popping a bird into her mouth.

"Pardon?" Enitan didn't hear her; she was too busy gaping at the evening's main course: a golden platter of small iyebirds, roasted whole and meant to be eaten as such—head, feet, and all.

Deora daintily spits the larger bones into a lace napkin. "How was your day?"

"Fine." Enitan accepts the plate Deora hands her and looks down, trying not to grimace. "Are you certain these weren't real animals? I won't tell anyone."

Deora chuckles, reaching for another bird. "I'm sure." In Vaalbara, the concept of murder applies to not only humans, but all animals.

Korikese have always been strict pescatarians, so when the Empire outlawed the consumption of meat, little changed. Enitan and her people simply swapped fish for beans and nuts. But evidently, Imperials have perfected everything down to the art of plant-derived flesh and bone. The very tiny, very convincing bird-shaped piles of fake meat remind her of the time a former classmate got outrageously drunk and tried to fight a bloodmaw with a blowtorch. They brought his remains back in little smoking lumps.

Enitan picks up a "bird" by the head. They're supposed to be swallowed feetfirst. It smells entirely different from her poor peer, but she's so put off by its appearance she can't bring herself to try it.

"You don't like it?" Deora asks, eyes wide and watery.

"I had a big lunch." Enitan pushes aside her plate and folds her hands in her lap. "I found an old floor that wasn't on the map today."

"I'm not surprised. The palace is *massive*. We need perhaps half the space, so sometimes whole levels fall into disuse." The countess crunches down on yet another bird, juice dripping down her chin. "And we can't exactly bulldoze the floors we don't need. Eventually, they're just sealed up." She chews exactly twenty times. "Normally, all the accesses are locked, though. Find anything interesting?"

"Not yet." Enitan takes a piece of yellow flatbread from the platter beside the flesh heap. She tears off a corner and pops it into her mouth. It's slightly spongy and quite sour. It'd probably pair very well with the fake meat, but she's still a bit nauseated. "How was your day?"

"Oh, fantastic." Deora cleans sauce off her hands with a perfumed wipe. "The museum got a couple of new figurines from a private collection." She smiles, almost ruefully. "They're not Korikese. They're pre-Sundering, actually."

"You jest."

"Nope!" She pours herself a chalice of juice and refills Enitan's goblet. "And Banurra wasn't even there to ogle them." An excited gleam fills her eye. "Oh, before I forget! I'm putting on a little fundraiser event for the museum tonight, and you're invited."

It's not like she has plans; she canceled them all. "I'd be honored," replies Enitan, and she almost means it. "Will there be food?"

"Of course." Deora sits back in her seat, smiling contentedly. "Though not nearly as good as mine."

Enitan has observed many of Deora's weaknesses, but cooking is not one of them. She still has to admit, if begrudgingly, that the traditional feast Deora cooked in those early days was truly impressive. The amount of time and effort spent perfecting each dish must have been immense. The countess is obsessed with Korikese "authenticity."

She observes Deora closely. "I realize I've never asked, what first interested you in Koriko?"

Deora's eyes grow wide. They glitter as brightly as the crystal chandelier above the table. "It's a bit of a long story."

Enitan laughs as she fills her plate with side dishes. "I have time."

Deora claps her hands with glee, scooting to the edge of her chair. "Well! Funnily enough, I actually didn't care—or think, really—about anywhere beyond Vaalbara until I was in my late teens. All I knew was that there was the Empire, and what would eventually become the Empire, so what was the point of learning about other places if they were going to be absorbed anyway?"

The ease with which she says these words is brutal. As if no one bled, suffered, and died to make them true. Enitan can barely breathe in the face of such blissful ignorance. How nice it must be not to fear for one's life, family, and home every waking second.

Deora must take Enitan's stunned silence for rapt attention, because her excitement only swells. "But then I got caught up in a bit of a scandal—what can I say, the heart wants what it wants!—and everyone involved agreed that it was best if we all disappeared from court for a while, at least until the whispers cooled down. My family has always been one of the Church's top donors, so my parents used their connections to squeeze me into a missionary program on—surprise!—Koriko."

Enitan is not surprised, actually. She could name a dozen rich Vaalbarans just like the countess here, who flew into her home for a month or so to study abroad or help the monks indoctrinate her people. They each thought themselves admirably impressive, and were so very eager to run home and brag about how worldly and virtuous they were. None of them were quite as high-ranking as Deora, though.

"I was only supposed to stay out there for a few weeks," Deora continues, "but . . . Enitan, you have to understand, everything in Vaalbara is so utilitarian, especially in the central monoliths I grew up in. Going from the cold, sanitized austerity of the Splinter to the wild beauty of Koriko . . ." She closes her eyes and fills her lungs as if breathing for the first time. "It was just magical. I fell in love. I spent four whole years doing humanitarian work in a dozen communities before my parents finally strong-armed me into coming back. But I never let go of Koriko; I can't." She reaches out toward Enitan, who nearly flinches. "Your home has a hold on me, my friend. It's your birthplace, but it's my place of rebirth."

Enitan can't speak, but Deora evidently doesn't need a response. The countess lets them sink into what she clearly thinks is awed silence. Deora may not be a raging bigot, but she's so shockingly unaware of how heavily Vaalbara's hand rests upon Koriko. How beaten down and crushed Enitan's people have been. And for what? The communities of Koriko have so much to offer the system: art, medicine, biotechnology, and even—for the purely materialistic—abundant natural resources, besides rare-earth minerals. But the Empire, beyond a few bored, insensitive nobles like the one across the table, has touched almost none of it. Most of Vaalbara, students and volunteer missionaries aside, remains intensely xenophobic.

She understands on some level why the Empire's constantly attacking the Republic. There's history there. At the height of its power, Ominira swallowed up all the fertile land on Gondwana, starving extorting Vaalbara when it was young and feeble. Their thousand-year grudge might be stupid, but at least she *understands* it. What she doesn't comprehend is why the previous Imperator would conquer Koriko for his own pleasure and keep it, seemingly for no other reason than because he could.

◆

Enitan stares up at the entrance to the gala. There's a replica of a Korikese nature arch built into it, a traditional curved gate placed before protected land, meant to symbolize the transition from the outside world to the sanctity of what lies just beyond. Enitan can't help but feel that here, it marks the exact opposite.

Forcing her lips into a smile, she strides under the gate behind a group of wealthy museum donors. Electronic lanterns wash the vast chamber in gold, spilling artificial light like oil across the polished black floor. Diamond-shaped windows fitted with silver-stained glass further illuminate the space and the people within.

Noble patrons scurry about like glittering insects. The heavy incense wafting throughout the hall is not quite enough to conceal the acrid stench of greed. All this indulgence, all at the expense of everyone else. And the worst luxury is that none of them will ever have to admit it.

Anger builds in Enitan's stomach as she steps further into the chamber, ears filling with the babble of pampered voices punctuated by polite, tittering laughter. She never expected Deora to see the error of *all* her ways, but neither did she expect *this*. Glass display cases of artifacts from conquered states stand at neat intervals along the tiled ground, many of them Korikese. She watches the aristocrats circle them like ravenous bloodmaws catching a scent. There are delicate stringed instruments overlaid with jade, countless ornaments of crystal and amber, hundreds of Ancestor statues clearly stolen from community shrines.

And yet, despite the overflowing displays, Enitan can already hear excited whispers about what new items will be presented when the Empire finally gets around to taking over the islands. She almost wishes she could be surprised. But no. Vaalbaran avarice is a vast, hungry sea, its never-ending waves always lapping at yet-unbroken lands.

Enitan stomps over to get a closer look, nearly crashing into a servant. Hordes of attendants are flooding in now, circling with gilded platters of food: baked fruit soaked in wine, steamed nuts, fried balls of black grain, stir-fried vegetables pierced with silver toothpicks, tarts and cakes sticky with spiced syrup. Even if Enitan weren't disgusted by all this, she's still too full from dinner to partake; the idea of so much as touching one of the delicacies makes her stomach churn even more.

Deora strides in, draped in a traditional Korikese robe. It's appliquéd with a flowing grass pattern, the kind that would only be worn at a birthing ceremony. The garment is fashioned not out of natural materials, as is custom, but out of synthetic fabric that sparkles unnaturally. But what unnerves Enitan more than the dress is the hush that settles over the room. She clearly recalls the countess saying that she merely *volunteered* at the museum.

"Friends, thank you so much for coming. The Imperial Museum of Anthropology is eternally grateful for your continued support," she says, beaming as she hands a three-legged goblet off to a server. He and the others bow out of the room. "I won't keep you in suspense. Please take your seats, and we'll begin the bidding."

As Deora ascends a podium of layered obsidian, the courtiers scrabble for the brilliant crimson seats below her. One woman jostles Enitan as she hurries by. She whirls around with a snarl, fingers flying up as if to slap whoever got in her way. Her unsteady gaze falls upon Enitan, whose own eyes notice the empty goblet in the woman's right hand.

"You—"

"Why don't you go find your seat, madam," cuts in a voice behind her, as clear and deep as a spring lake. "You wouldn't want someone else to take it."

The woman gives her a look colder than a glacier. She spits out a curse before twisting on her heel. Enitan turns around to face her rescuer. A short, stocky man smooths out the creases of his purple tunic.

"Enitan Ijebu?"

She nods. "The very same. And you are, my lord?"

"Jeong. And I'm not quite a lord." He picks at one of the gold-threaded birds soaring up his right sleeve. Two nest just below the heavy brocade collar. "You look absolutely furious."

Enitan blinks at him, taken off guard. "I am not."

Jeong snorts as Deora opens a case of ancient teacups for her gasping audience. He waves a hand at her face. "Your expression says otherwise."

With some effort, Enitan forces her features to relax.

"Five!" shouts a man.

"Five thousand?" Enitan asks.

Jeong looks upon the proceedings with profound disinterest. "Five million," he tells her, his tone flatter than a table. "Rumor has it you're living with Countess Edwan."

"Ancestors, you lot must be starved of entertainment." Enitan takes a moment to study his face.

He has broad cheekbones and tawny skin, and his eyes are large and brown, accentuated with scarlet at the edges. He leans in slightly and lifts an eyebrow at her. "Like what you see?"

Enitan snorts, though she can't quite tell if he's joking. "Yes, but not like *that*."

Jeong laughs softly and leans back against a nearby wall. He flicks a hand at Deora. "We interned at the museum together when we were younger. She really fell in love with the work. Now she's overseeing all the artifact loans and putting together the biggest events."

"Nostalgia, then?" Enitan asks, smirking a little. "Is that why you're here? Or is it her?"

Jeong rolls his eyes. "Neither."

Deora takes a pristine white length of cloth in hand and uses it to pick up a crystal dagger of Korikese origin, obviously looted. The blade is so thin it's translucent. As Deora waves it around theatrically, the triangular slice of her face behind the knife ripples as if underwater.

"See the hilt? It's inlaid with real human metacarpal," she says, beaming. "Let's start the bidding at ten."

Enitan's stomach curdles. Her shoulders knot up with the effort of staying still, of keeping her back straight under the weight of Deora's words. The dagger isn't a weapon; those are Ancestor bones preserved in its hilt. That knife is a sacred, priceless relic, and they're haggling over it like it's just another exotic bauble. Does the countess even know what she's saying? What she's doing? She must—she's educated; she's an adult. But of course, she was schooled and sculpted in the heart of the Empire.

A man lifts a blue-gloved hand. Diamond rings shimmer over his fingers. "Fifty."

Deora positively glows. "I said *ten*, Your Holiness."

The man chuckles. "Yes, but I don't want to be here all night, my lady. I'm simply attempting to avoid wasting everyone's time."

Enitan leans forward, trying to get a better look at him. The man's eyes are like two black beads stuck into the paper-white dough of his face.

"Who's that?" she asks.

"The abbot of Bireen," says Jeong. "Sacha Surui. He comes to every auction and always leaves with something."

Enitan recognizes the name of the diocese but not the man; she read an article about the appointment of a new abbot in the Imperial interior a few days ago.

Another hand lifts, this one gloved in a purple so deep it could almost be Imperial black. Scandalous indeed. Typically only servants of the Church are permitted to don anything so daringly dark. "Sixty."

Enitan can't see his face, but she recognizes the voice.

"And that's Archduke Ta-Ji," Jeong supplies.

"Oh, I know."

His eyes widen, just a little. "You're acquainted?"

Enitan weighs a dozen possible responses. "Unfortunately."

Up ahead, Deora's smile has shockingly vanished, despite the profitable turn of events. "My lord. I'm so very pleased to see you here."

After quite a bit of cohabitation, Enitan knows the countess's voice well enough to catch the sliver of hesitation, as if she's unused to addressing the archduke this way. Or perhaps unwilling. Aren't they best friends? But court etiquette cares little for closeness, especially in formal settings such as this.

"Not as pleased as I am to be here, my lady," the archduke says smoothly. He flaps an insouciant hand at the abbot. "So, Your Holiness, are you going to let me have the toothpick or not?"

"I think not," the abbot replies. "A hundred."

If Enitan didn't know better, she'd say Deora is smirking at the archduke. "Well, my lord?"

"Eh." The archduke flops back into his plush seat. "I already have a few daggers. I'll win the next trinket."

And on it goes.

"You know, Korikese scholars have to request stuff like this from Vaalbara," Enitan finds herself saying. "The sentinels were ordered to plunder as much as they could carry and burn the rest."

"Surprisingly, I know the history," Jeong says tightly.

"Do you?"

"Yes. They were given orders to destroy as much of the past as possible so that Koriko would only have a future—a Vaalbaran one. One cannot miss what they do not remember." He sounds so angry. Hurt, even. He makes the sacking sound inexplicably personal.

"If not for old times' sake or an old infatuation, why *are* you here? You're not buying."

"My family keeps me locked up in their estate, lest I embarrass them," Jeong says. His voice takes on an even sharper edge. "So when they say I can attend even something like this, I try to make the most of it."

"So you're a hostage, like me," she jokes.

He doesn't smile. "Something like that." He looks over at her. "Everyone knows this already, so I suppose there's no harm telling you that I was born in the traditional way, as our people do."

Enitan blinks at him, taken aback. "*Our* people?"

"Yes. I'm half-Korikese. My father was from Dakwu Community."

Enitan grimaces, a sour taste on her tongue. Dakwu conceded to Vaalbara's might with minimal resistance because its headman believed that annexation was inevitable—that his people needed to become Vaalbaran to survive at all. As a reward, the Empire treats Dakwu with a lenience resented by all the other communities.

"And how exactly did his son end up in the Splinter?" she says, in Korikesian. But when he looks at her with an abashed, confused expression, she repeats the question in Orin.

"He participated in the governor program to produce provincial rulers. But the circumstances of my birth dishonor me."

Realization hits Enitan. She can only stare at him. Only one man from Dakwu was chosen for the program. "You're Jeong Uloyiso. Obara's son," she says, the words squeezing through her tightening throat.

Obara Uloyiso, the greatest general Vaalbara has ever known and the worst monster the Empire ever spawned. Obara Uloyiso, the woman who ordered the mass execution of all suspected Korikese rebels when Enitan was a child. She can't bring herself to offer condolences for his mother's sudden passing several months ago. She'd celebrated, albeit discreetly, with the rest of the communities when the news reached them.

When Enitan was very young, Ijebu's headwoman sent all of the community's children on a camping trip to the southern marsh for a few weeks. They didn't return until three months had passed. That was before she was reassigned to Xiang. Her siblings at the time had made her life a living hell during the trip. None of the children understood what was going on, and her brothers' confusion soon became fear, and then anger. Which they'd both taken out on her.

In an interview months after the atrocity, Obara joked that she'd kicked the communities hard so they'd be grateful to be slapped later.

Enitan feels a chill down to her bones. She turns and stalks over to the closest balustrade. Jeong follows her.

"It's a shame they didn't let you be a governor," she whispers. Her tongue feels heavy in her mouth. "Then you could burn it all down from the inside." The words fly out before she can catch them.

Enitan squeezes her eyes shut as panic seizes her lungs. Ancestors, hasn't she learned *anything* from her meetings with the Imperator? Even if he's not a spy with a completely fabricated backstory, he could've been brainwashed into Vaalbara's most loyal defender.

But Jeong only gives her a pitying look. "Why burn something down when you could rebuild it?"

"Vaalbara can't be rebuilt."

"It must be," he says. "We need them so we can heal. Together."

Bitterness slides down into Enitan's twisting stomach. He means this. He really believes it. The earnestness of his words is tattooed on his kind, trusting face. Vaalbara is so much like a contagion, it hurts. What the Empire does to conquered territory and bodies is nothing compared with its infection of conquered minds. If Vaalbara gets its way, her people will forget the chains wound around their throats, the shackles clamped around their ankles. The Empire will no longer need its sentinels; Korikese will *want* Vaalbaran rule, its technology and its riches, and most of all its guiding hand. They will beg for the burden.

"Vaalbara will never let you rise high enough to make that dream a reality," is all she says.

Jeong shakes his head emphatically. "The governor program was a terrible plan, but there was a kernel of a good idea in it," he continues.

"We were supposed to be interpreters, a bridge between our people and Vaalbara. Korikese in blood, but Vaalbaran in culture."

Enitan releases a sharp breath from her nose as Ajana's face surfaces into her mind. "Look at me, at what's become of our home, and tell me exactly how well you think that turned out."

"As I said, a terrible plan. But—"

Enitan interrupts him with a hollow laugh. "You can worship the Imperator as much as you want. You can go to every church on the planet, kneel before every statue, and kiss her gilded feet a thousand times each—"

"I don't worship the Imperator."

Well, at least he's not a *complete* lost cause. Enitan surges on. "You can learn their language better than an Imperial scholar. You can even praise their brutality. But you will *never* be one of them."

"Is that what you think of me?" Jeong chokes out. "Is that what you think I want? I have as much choice in this as you do. Am I not allowed to try to make the best of my situation?"

The heat rising up Enitan's throat cools as quickly as it boiled; fresh guilt pricks at her.

"I'm sorry," she says, because she has no idea what else to say.

She's had enough of all this. She wrenches her gaze from Jeong and shoves past now-tipsy flocks of nobles. But before she can step through the arch, a hand closes around her upper arm, yanking her back.

Enitan yelps, whirling around halfway before she's stopped by a hard chest. "I thought I was clear—"

But it's not her shadow. It's the sentinel that interrogated her the day she arrived, Ivar. He drags her in close, bringing his lips to her ear.

"I knew I was right not to trust you," he snarls. "I don't know what you have planned, or what you're doing, but already you've won the Imperator's favor."

"That's just gossip—"

Enitan bites back a cry of pain as his grip tightens mercilessly. No one's even turning to look at her. Of course not.

"Know this. The Imperator's grace is not a shield. Someone could stab you right now, and of course our God would punish them." She almost feels him smile against her skin. She certainly smells the alcohol on his breath. "If they were caught, that is. And it's not as if she can't find herself another Korikese whore."

And with that, he lets her go. By the time Enitan turns around fully, he's gone.

She presses back against the wall and struggles to breathe.

◆

Enitan takes a very long, very hot bath that night. She forgot to shower yesterday after the duke's party. That evening swept by in a colorless blur; she remembers nothing between collapsing in the corridor and falling into bed. The water is cold by the time she drags herself out and bundles herself into a towel. Dripping a wet trail across the carpets, she pads over to the closet, a circular recess built into the wall.

She riffles through her clothes and considers her immediate next moves. In the end, there's only one option. Ivar is a liability of the highest order. He may not have anything on her now, but she can't have him snooping around until he does. She has to get him out of the way.

But how?

At long last she finds her new sleepwear, a set of soft cobalt-blue pajamas. When she unfolds the shirt, a tiny alabaster box falls out of the sleeve. She slips on the pants and buttons up the top, taking the box with her to the bed.

Inside are five carnelian rings. The duke's rings. The gemstones are almost as dark as the blood flecking them.

TWELVE

Enitan stands waist-deep in a massive vat filled with tea leaves. The fragrance is overwhelming, filling her lungs like cold perfume. She can't breathe. She can't speak. Something ignites in her chest, burning her up from the inside. She is fire, conflagration. Tears pour from her eyes in a boiling-hot torrent. A hand shoots up out of the roiling tea. Blood-caked fingers wrap around her shoulder.

Her mouth flies open, only for her cry to be cut off by a burning gush of water. She sinks to her knees, dragged down by agony and this inhuman grip.

"Look at me," gurgles a voice. It's achingly familiar. "Look. At. Me."

"I can't," Enitan sobs, squeezing her eyes shut. "I'm so sorry, I can't."

But her head cants down anyway, her eyes cracking open. There's a face just below the surface of the tea.

"You're failing me, sister."

Enitan jerks awake, a scream catching in her throat. That voice, that arm . . . that was Xiang. And they're right. She is failing them.

Oh, Ancestors. She slides her trembling hands down her sweaty face.

She stumbles out of bed and grabs her communicator. When she activates it, the map of the Splinter comes to life. Right—the abandoned level. Exploring it could be a brief distraction from all the horror, just so she can resume her mission with as few night terrors as possible.

Enitan sets out, armed with a lightrod she purloined from Deora, her satchel, a holosheet, and an electronic brush. She takes Ajana's poignard with her, almost as an afterthought. The duke's bloodied rings seemed less like a threat than some sort of terrible gift. But she's not taking any chances. A sentinel on their way home found the duke's body in one of the private tea rooms on his floor. Enitan only knows the meager details sent out to every communicator in the palace, but apparently they've ruled it a suicide. Even if the assassin isn't out to get her, they know who she is, and they know what happened at that gathering. They've been watching her. They got into her chambers somehow, and that's dangerous enough.

A part of her is certain the killer isn't her shadow, though. It wasn't that they didn't seem deadly. They just didn't seem like the sort of person who'd slaughter a man and then gift her his bloodied jewelry, like a mossicat dropping a dead rodent at the feet of their human companion. In any case, she takes the poignard.

She doesn't make much progress. She stops every twenty steps to scratch shallow marks into the walls so she doesn't get hopelessly lost. The thought of starving to death in the darkness isn't an attractive one. And she brought the holosheet and brush for a reason—she's making a map, though she's not certain if she'll ever return here. As she wanders farther, she becomes increasingly sure she won't. There's almost nothing that pulls her attention, just defunct tubelifts that don't go anywhere and dusty apartments and dilapidated common spaces. This floor is like every other floor in the palace, except full of refuse: cracked holoportraits of frowning people, torn slippers, love letters so dry-rotted she can't make out the sweet nothings. She doesn't stop drawing the map, though. The walls are already pockmarked and gouged out; in some places it's nigh impossible to tell her knife marks from the surrounding wear and tear.

There's so much more unexplored area, she gives up after a few hours and navigates her way back out. She returns to Deora's apartments and lies on her back, staring up at the dark ceiling. She has no engagements for the second day in a row. Out of respect for the duke's rank, if not the man himself, all recreational gatherings in the Splinter have been canceled.

Enitan briefly considers turning in the rings before common sense kicks in. Everyone will assume she either stole them off the corpse's fingers or killed the duke herself, especially after what happened the other night. But she's not foolish enough to keep them either. She flushes them down the toilet and lobs the box off the balcony.

She spends the rest of the day in silence. Propriety demanded that Deora, as the duke's closest colleague, attend his funeral. Enitan is thereby left to her own devices. She pokes around the apartment and comes across a room whose function seems solely to be to store spare copies of all the countess's fancy technology, including a stack of holo-projectors. Enitan runs a finger over them and finds them coated in a faint layer of dust. They haven't been used in weeks, if not months. She grabs her own projector and slips the disk into the bottom half—where better to hide something than in plain sight? As for the poignard, it'll hardly blend in with Deora's paring knives. It stays under her mattress.

Enitan scans the rest of the chamber's contents and pulls a datapad off the shelves. She rifles through the downloaded collection until she finds an anthology of pre-Empire folktales. She's halfway through a story about a clever marcroaker with two skins—one of them human—when her communicator chimes. It's an invitation to serve at a funeral party that evening.

She flinches when she cackles, startled by her own laughter. She begins typing out a curt refusal. But then her eyes fall on the sender, and a shiver runs up her spine and down her arms. She doesn't recognize the first name, and a last hasn't been provided. But the coat of arms is unmistakable. It was carved onto every flat surface of the governor's mansion in Ijebu.

The host is Ajana's mother.

◆

The duchess's personal monolith is currently flying a few hundred kilometers away from the Splinter. At first, Enitan considers declining anyway. She's still a hostage, and the likelihood that the Imperator is going to let her cavort around Vaalbara to serve tea is a small one. She could try to negotiate a day out, but she already has precious little to barter.

Before she can do anything, a missive sent straight to her communicator informs her that she's received special dispensation from the Imperator to attend the gathering. Enitan yanks on her formal tunic, and an hour later, a shuttle arrives for her at the same station she first landed on.

Enitan boards with nothing but the clothes on her back and her tea set. The pilot takes them over a stretch of shattered land. Craters and canyons and calderas mar much of the region, as if a fusillade of giant fists struck the planet's crust. Alluvial fans embroidered with dark vegetation unfold between ridges of steeply inclined strata. And all of it, from the highest mountain to the deepest ravine, is smothered in fog. For a moment, she can see the edge of a massive silver lake, but then that bright glimmer of water slips beyond the horizon.

The duchess's monolith is twice as large as Ajana's but still nowhere near the size of the Splinter. Where the Imperial capital is mind-breaking, the mansion is merely astounding; it is a splinter to the Splinter's spear. The shuttle lands and Enitan steps out. A waiting tubelift carries her into a plainly furnished atrium. When she looks up, she sees a sliver of the swiftly darkening sky. It reclines rich and velvet above her head, so close but so achingly far.

Belatedly, she notices a lone woman standing off to the side, draped in white mourning silks. She looks stretched past the point of slenderness, her bones pulled so far they might snap in half at any moment. Even so, Enitan's breath lodges in her throat. The woman's resemblance to Ajana is unmistakable. And incredibly painful.

Enitan sucks in air and bows. "My lady," she rasps, "thank you for your invitation."

The duchess says nothing. She just looks straight at Enitan, her gaze so sharp it goes through her.

"I knew it," the duchess says, finally severing the silence. "Ajana was right about you."

Grief clenches around Enitan's heart. Her mouth opens and closes for several moments; she's too stunned to form words. The duchess knows about her, about *them*.

The duchess folds her arms and turns toward a brilliantly lit hallway. "Come with me."

Enitan stumbles after her, anxiety sweeping up her spine. "Ajana . . . spoke to you about me?" she sputters.

"She wrote me a letter." Her dark eyes flash. "In case she did something foolish and died."

Enitan's gaze falls to her feet. "I—I'm so sorry."

"So am I." Her face softens. "But not because she died for you. I only wish I'd known her better."

"You're not angry?" Enitan asks, though what she really means is *You don't want me dead?*

The duchess laughs, her shoulders jerking as if the small movement is almost too much for her. "They wouldn't let me see her once they took her out of the artificial womb. But it seemed like she had grown into a talented young woman. And a halfway decent governor, as far as they go."

The duchess presses her palm to an octagonal door and it slides open, revealing a room shaped like an upturned vase. Wide, round walls taper toward the polished floor, capped by a square skylight. A breeze snakes through the open windows, rustling the potted plants arranged throughout the space.

Enitan places her tea set on a low table. "How many guests will you be hosting, my lady?"

"Just one." She lifts a hand as if in benediction. Light glinting off her heavy, ruby-studded cuffs, she gestures at the sunken couch at the center of the chamber. "Please."

Enitan joins the duchess on the soft cushions. The noblewoman sticks her hands under her hair and pulls it out from behind her back, letting her elaborate braids hang over the couch. "I'm not going to waste your time or mine. I brought you here to warn you."

Enitan stares at her for three full breaths. "About what?"

"Things in the Empire have a way of getting lost and staying that way." The duchess lifts her legs onto the low table before them, stretching her toes. "You came here to look for something. You won't find it. Or *them*."

Enitan sits perfectly still for a few seconds, far colder than she has any right to be, even with the breeze. "Why are you telling me this?"

A soft, heavy sigh. "Better a bitter truth than a sweet lie."

"There is a way." Enitan clenches her fists so tightly that her nails almost draw blood. "There is always a way. If my people are being abducted, not killed, then I will find out where they're being taken, and—"

There's that look again. The light in the duchess's eyes is harsh, almost dangerous. "If you survive this ordeal, you will do so as someone very different."

"Then I'm willing to change. For Xiang, I'm willing to do anything." It's the first time she's spoken their name aloud in days. She doesn't know this woman, but she feels she can trust her. Besides, the duchess clearly knows enough to destroy her anyway. Her sibling's name isn't going to change that.

The duchess takes Enitan's limp hand in hers. "You look tired."

"I am," she says honestly, her eyes burning with unshed tears. "I'm no closer to finding Xiang than when I arrived. I'm tired of swallowing my emotions. Tired of serving people who hate me."

"Only equals can truly despise each other." The duchess grimaces. "And as far as my fellow nobles are concerned, we are unmatched."

Enitan clenches her jaw, scrubbing at her face with both hands. "Well, I hate *them*."

"And just as you cannot love another without loving yourself, you cannot truly despise another without despising some part of yourself."

"*Enough* with the wulushit," Enitan snaps. Then she forces her mouth shut so hard she nearly breaks a tooth. Ordinarily, she would *never* speak that way to an elder. It's just that Ajana used to share startlingly similar platitudes all the time, and that would always be Enitan's response.

The duchess raises her eyebrows. *Ancestors.* Enitan feels like her tongue just crumbled to dust in her mouth, and now she's choking down the remains. "I—"

The duchess cuts her off with a howl, and it takes Enitan a moment to realize she's laughing not at her, but *with* her. She's so startled, she starts laughing too.

But when the duchess's cackling winds down, there's something in her face that makes Enitan flinch. "Never do that again."

"Forgive me," Enitan says, sobering immediately. "I know that was completely inappropriate, and I—"

"No, not that. It *is* wulushit." Her gaze is firm, neither kind nor cruel. "But you must not weep. You *cannot.* Your enemies will drink your tears like wine. Vaalbara feeds on suffering, and my kind are no different."

Enitan lets out a long, slow breath.

The duchess's gaze slants away, her attention narrowing on something outside the nearest window, just out of Enitan's field of vision. "Allow me to give you another piece of advice. If you're going to align yourself with anyone in court, don't make it the Imperator."

Enitan marvels at how swiftly rumors spread among the nobles. And that's when it comes to her: the solution to the problem of Ivar. Knowledge is power—perhaps false knowledge most of all. She doesn't have to get rid of him. She can let the aristocracy do it for her.

Enitan smiles as she meets the duchess's gaze again. "Are you saying I should pledge my allegiance to you instead?"

"Oh, God no." The duchess shudders, scandalized. "Just speaking from experience—I served as a minor advisor to the last Imperator for less than a year. He never once saw me in person and ignored almost everything I said to him." She sighs. "I just want you to understand that there is a difference between the appearance of power and the real thing."

"I know full well she's a figurehead," Enitan says, shrugging. "But I have no idea who holds the leash. And neither, I suspect, does the Imperator."

"I wouldn't be surprised if that was the case." The duchess's lips thin into a sharp line. "Most of our Imperators do little more than warm the throne."

Enitan folds her arms. Perhaps her ire at the last Imperator is best directed elsewhere, then. A thought begins to form at the back of her mind.

"How long has there been another power behind the throne?"

The duchess arches a brow. "Oh, a simple question with a simple answer."

Enitan lifts her gaze to the sky at the noblewoman's sarcasm. "In your opinion."

"Perhaps it began with Psamtik the Unlikely." When Enitan looks at her blankly the duchess adds, "About four Imperators ago."

An ice-cold clarity comes over Enitan as it all clicks together.

Most of our Imperators do little more than warm the throne.

"A shadow council," Enitan whispers, staring right at the duchess.

"Pardon?"

"Have you met the new Imperator?"

"No," says the duchess, a smile starting in her eyes and spreading to her lips.

"I really do think that she doesn't know who's pulling the strings. If a bunch of sniveling aristocrats showed up in person and tried telling her what to do, she'd just laugh in their faces." Enitan presses her hands together, fingertips against fingertips. "What if there's a cabal of seemingly unimportant nobles that the Imperator never meets?"

"It seems improbable that such a council could have survived over four reigns," the duchess says, tilting her head. Then she lights up. "Unless they regularly placed outsiders on the throne when there was no suitable living heir, which they'd take measures to arrange, one way or the other." Her eyes are gleaming now. "I always thought the rumors about Princess Sunnetah's secret marriage rang hollow."

Enitan taps her fingers to her chin, deep in thought. "But how does the council control the Imperator once they're on the throne?"

"Simple." The duchess is fully grinning now. "The image of the Empire's strength takes precedence over all else. The council can pull strings from behind the scenes, doing whatever they please through the application of clever gossip and well-placed funding, and the Imperator is forced to go along with it to save face. And certainly there would be an unspoken understanding that a recalcitrant Imperator doesn't remain Imperator long. Or alive, for that matter."

Enitan frowns. "I can't imagine any leader letting an anonymous group yank their chain around and smiling through the indignity."

"Of course you can't," the duchess replies. "You're Korikese. Perhaps Vaalbaran in name now, but Korikese in your heart." She gives another pained shrug. "Your communities are held together by things greater than appearances."

After a moment, Enitan says, "What should I call you?"

"My name, of course. Zuhura." She takes Enitan's hand again. "It's been a pleasure."

Enitan smiles. "And an honor."

On the way back to the Splinter, it dawns on her how little she understood Ajana. She assumed that because half of Ajana's blood was deemed savage, the Empire would never embrace her. She was barely Vaalbaran enough to rule, and just Korikese enough to be one of them. The Imperials had designed Ajana so that the people of Koriko would accept her just enough: a ruler less alien than an Imperial, but not so much so that the moon's loyalty would be hers alone. And so Enitan had been certain that there would only ever be one place in the world for her companion. But she was so, so wrong. Zuhura is far from the sneering aristocrat she imagined. Ajana would have been loved here.

And without Enitan, she would be alive.

THIRTEEN

After returning to the capital, Enitan resumes her tea services. Her noble hosts continue to be noble only in name, though this time their moral bankruptcy works in her favor. They're all too happy to water the rumors she seeds like weeds across the fertile gardens of the Splinter.

"My lord, if you're looking for someone new and interesting to add to your game table, I hear there's a high-ranking sentinel who might be interested," Enitan suggests to a marquess.

Suddenly, there's a sentinel running around the capital who's secretly an incurable gambler. Enitan has no way of knowing if the marquess actually ended up making inquiries, but she doesn't really care. She has work to do.

"Did you hear?" she asks, pouring tea for an influential abbot. "That sentinel everyone's talking about is drowning in debt. Forgive me for saying so, but I believe his money would have been better spent supporting the Church. I served as a scribe myself, back on Koriko."

The abbot wants to know the sentinel's name.

Enitan smiles.

"They say Ivar took considerable bribes from Ominirish mafia bosses to pay off the loan sharks," Enitan informs Deora over dinner one day. "Outlandish, isn't it?"

By now, this is one of the milder accusations. The countess just shakes her head sadly and says as much.

"Whatever the truth, the man is utterly ruined," she says. "He's been discharged from service and more or less banished from the Splinter."

"How unfortunate," says Enitan. "Can you pass the bread?"

She's been eating dinner with Deora regularly now, which would be enjoyable if not for the museum gala the other night. Enitan was always skeptical that they could become close, given the vast differences between them. Whenever she looks at the countess's face these days, all she can see is the sparkling, gloriously ignorant grin Deora wore while selling off her people's relics.

At night, Enitan rolls around in her too-soft bed and tries to force herself to sleep. She's rarely successful. She stalks the palace with her fists shaking inside her sleeves, furious at her lack of progress locating Xiang. She's finding herself increasingly caught up in the vicissitudes of Vaalbaran politics instead, most of them inane. Her clandestine meeting with Zuhura certainly hasn't helped things. The more she learns, the less sense the world makes, each discovery only raising new questions. Enitan spends most of her evenings on the balcony, staring up at a sky that has no answers for her. She has no idea what to do. She is lost.

And then, when nearly a month has passed since her arrival, everything changes again. The day begins just as any other. Enitan drags herself out of bed and spends a few moments in front of the mirror, polishing her mask of perfect, subservient serenity. Dark circles have formed under her eyes, and they're not going anywhere. She almost asks Deora for cosmetics she can pancake on to hide her fatigue, but decides against it. Let them think her weak and broken.

In the afternoon, Enitan serves tea at a merchant's birthday party. He's no aristocrat, but he loaned so much money to the last Imperator, it appears he bought the right to act as one. He lives only two levels below the Imperator's residence, just six suites from Archduke Ta-Ji himself. Enitan grits her teeth together when a servant ushers her into the merchant's chambers: the rooms are beautiful, and it annoys her no small amount that she finds them so.

There are slender, twisting columns and vivid stained-glass windows, recessed carvings of churning oceans and rolling deserts. Unlike those of most of her patrons, his home is bare of the typical spoils of war—it is a spoil of war in and of itself, purchased entirely through the merchant's lucrative sponsorship of Vaalbaran expansion efforts. She's just put a pot of water on to boil when the servant returns with the merchant himself. She struggles not to frown when he appears. He's the loveliest person she's ever seen.

His skin is midnight black, perfectly complemented by the indigo satin of his jacket. His hair, bound into locs that reach his waist, is threaded with delicate strands of tiny teardrop pearls. He beams at Enitan, and it is a slow, gentle thing.

"It's a pleasure to finally meet you, Enitan," he says. "Though I regret the circumstances."

"The pleasure is all mine, sir." She bows, donning a polite, smiling mask.

"Somehow I doubt that." He laughs, and even that is exquisite.

It's not that Enitan is attracted to him; that much is certain. But whenever she finds a Vaalbaran beautiful, she's confused in the same way she'd be if a herd of wulubison were trampling her and she found herself thinking one was cute. It's irrational and makes her irritated with herself. This palace is a nest of rukhvipers, and here she is, admiring one's scales.

But that is the danger, isn't it? The duality of Vaalbara, of all empires: the open, generous palm, and the closed, hard-knuckled fist. Half of the Empire is tart wine and jeweled maps and paper books. The rest is spilt blood and charred bone. It doesn't matter how different those halves are. They still form the whole: that which seduces and that which destroys.

There was once a time when Enitan envied the Empire. Why couldn't her own people have built castles in the sky? Why couldn't they have forged their own great nation, so that everyone in the system feared and honored them in equal measure? Why couldn't they be civilized? Why couldn't they be *Vaalbaran*?

And then she'd grown older, wiser. She'd stopped thinking about how uncivilized her own people were and more about what "civilization" meant in the first place. She saw that the monoliths were resources ripped from the planet, built by laborers who'd been forced to choose between swinging hammers and starving. The Imperators' enlightening hands were gluttonous claws, cleaving benefits from death and decay. To Vaalbara, civilization meant empire, and empire, Enitan realized, despite the best efforts of her imported teachers, meant one thing.

Pain.

The merchant yanks her from her thoughts when he gestures excitedly to the servant, a large man with bronze hair. "Savik here will take care of the tea. My companions and I would appreciate your company."

He extends an arm and Enitan takes it, dread curdling in her gut. She imagines this will be much like what happened with the duke, but that the torture of their attentions will last even longer, and with a thin veneer of courtesy. The merchant leads her through a pair of screens filigreed with thick-petaled inablossoms. Lounging on mounds of plush cushions is a circle of aristocrats, each adorned with pearls and precious crimson coral. A sea theme, then? The silver thread of the merchant's cuff scrapes along her skin when he pulls away, only to guide her to her own heap of pillows.

"Friends and family," he says, gloved hands on her shoulders, "this is Lady Enitan of Koriko, a close personal *friend* of the Imperator."

Ah.

So this is what this is. She's not sure whether she should laugh or curse. Quite a few people saw the Imperator call her in the hanging gardens. The encounter was formal, and the Imperator was nothing but commanding. But if Enitan has learned anything, it's that by the time palace gossip makes its rounds, the story is unrecognizable. She was counting on that very phenomenon when laying the groundwork for Ivar's downfall. She almost wants to ask what the merchant thinks happened after the gardens. The way he's just emphasized *friend* dissuades her.

Well, she certainly won't correct his erroneous assumption. Her entire life—especially now—Enitan has been forced to subsist upon the barest morsels of respect from Vaalbarans. She'll wring out what little she can from this.

But the conversation that follows isn't the session of ass-kissing she expects (and almost hoped for). They ask her about her home. The people, the food, the culture. It irks her a bit to be treated once again as though she represents the entirety of Koriko, but it's not like she hasn't thought of individual Vaalbarans any differently. (Zuhura, of course, is a recent exception.) The conversation tilts toward the treacherous during their fifth serving of tea—Savik knows what he's doing—when the merchant's sister asks Enitan about the old language of her people.

Korikesian isn't outlawed, but before Ajana, schoolteachers would smack children across the knuckles when they answered questions in anything but Akyesi. Everyone still speaks Korikesian at home, and sentinels only glare at those who do so elsewhere. But this woman didn't ask about something factual, like Korikesian's use of click consonants. She's basically asked Enitan if she resents the Empire for forcing her people to learn a tongue meant to subjugate them. Whether her loyalty to her home is greater than her fear of the Empire. And, judging by their near-salivating looks of curiosity, how her supposed *friendship* with the Imperator plays into it all.

Enitan puts down her tea. "I understand the reasons behind the creation of Akyesi. But it's caused far more problems than anything else. For the Church, anyway."

The merchant and his sister both chuckle. Even years after the scandal, the Linguists' Coalition still criticizes the Church's pragmatic interpretation of the Black Codex, Vaalbara's most sacred text, in petty acts of ongoing revenge. Most recently, the Coalition called for a complete rewrite of doctrine, citing the Church's flawed understanding of the social context within which the thirty-fifth chapter of the Codex was written. Nothing will come of it—the thirty-fifth chapter is hideously outdated no matter the translation, as it concerns itself with simple agricultural matters Vaalbara hasn't paid an iota of attention to since they took to the skies, let alone the stars. But the Linguists' warnings will be seen for what they are.

"In any case," Enitan continues, "I trust the Imperator's judgement on whether Akyesi should continue to be taught in Korikese schools." Of course, if the Imperator actually relinquishes the moon, her opinion on what language the people speak won't matter.

"About the Imperator's judgement." One of the merchant's university friends gawks openly at her, as if she's the lone representative not only for her people but for all of the Imperator's secrets. "Do you know what Her Imperial Majesty intends to do about Iëre?"

Enitan purses her lips. Iëre is one of the many islands hugging the Vaalbaran coast. This is the first time she's heard of it by name outside of a class. Even when the nobles at Deora's auction were slavering over the idea of new loot from the archipelago, they didn't bother discussing the individual islands. In Vaalbara, they're mostly thought of as a single entity, rather than a network of vastly different polities.

"She hasn't spoken of it to me," Enitan says.

"Well, something has to be done," they say, voice low. "They've closed down all the trading routes! And if Iëre refuses to pay tribute for another month, then a lot of people are going to consider invading the island themselves." By *a lot of people*, they clearly mean themself.

Enitan finds everyone looking at her pointedly, making it very clear she should bring the issue up with the Imperator. *Ah, there it is.* "I'll speak of it to Menkhet—I mean, the Imperator."

Her easy usage of the Imperator's name has its intended effect. Eyes wide and reverent, the merchant takes her hands in his. "You have my gratitude, Lady Enitan. I'll be sure to repay the favor."

Favor. How gentle a word to describe Imperial forces thrashing fear back into a proud people. But Enitan simply returns the merchant's brilliant grin with a tight smile. She's about to say something hollow and meaningless when Savik pops his head in.

"The other guests are here, sir," he announces, and two seconds later, the merchant's suite is packed with over forty people.

Apparently, the party has only just begun. And from the look of it, Enitan guesses she's not the only person the merchant's trying to win over. Among the guests are new members of the tripartite parliament, minor nobles, and a man the merchant tells her is the Supreme Abbot's favorite nephew. The merchant drags Enitan into a hug, kisses her on both cheeks, and then goes off to schmooze. His friends and family tell her how wonderful it was to meet her before scampering off to join him.

Since Savik has gone right back to brewing, and she's pretty sure no one will care or even notice if the tea is authentically frothed, Enitan wanders the crowd, hoping she'll pick up some valuable information. It doesn't take long for nearly everyone to get abominably drunk. Some servants distribute chalices of wine, whiskey, and brandy. Others just hand out bottles.

The seconds become minutes and the minutes become hours. The sun has tumbled below the horizon by the time Enitan decides she's sick of getting dragged into heated debates about how many pet marcroakers is too many. She's wading through a woozy lake of people when she stumbles over a woman napping in the middle of the hall, and finds herself in a small chapel. There are only two people there, a nobleman and the captain of the merchant's best planet-bound ship. They're both incredibly inebriated.

"Can we sit down?" the nobleman mumbles, an arm braced against the porcelain face of a minor provincial god.

"Absolutely not," replies the captain. "Sitting is really . . . really . . . bad for you."

Enitan sighs, rubbing at her forehead and turning to go. All she wants to do now is sleep.

"But about your aunt . . . she's just—" the captain says, cutting herself off as she regains her balance. "She's just a magistrate. No offense."

"None taken," the nobleman slurs. "Th-that's actually why they wanted her. Contacted her right after the duke's funeral." He hiccups.

Banurra's funeral? Enitan freezes.

The captain pops open a can of beer with a cartoon bloodmaw on the front. "Sure."

"No, really." The nobleman licks his lips, slumping against the wall. "Another of their members went missing a few days before."

And these are the words that make Enitan cram herself between a gilded carving and the wall, close enough to hear but just out of sight. The world melts away as she listens.

The captain hiccups. "They don't have a name?"

"Nah," says the nobleman, tipping down his bottle and shaking out the last few drops. "She wouldn't tell me. But I call them the Hidden Ones. Pretty cool, right?"

"Oh my God, Cahiyr," the captain snaps, suddenly furious. She shoves her can into his chest. "Will you s-stop with the lies?"

"I'm not lying!" He drops his bottle, and it bounces on the wooden floor before rolling away. "I swear to God."

"You know what?" she snarls. "Maybe your new best friend will be more gullible." She shoves him away and turns on her heel.

Cahiyr chases his friend out of the chapel, leaving Enitan shivering with excitement. She was right; there *is* a shadow council. It makes perfect sense that such an entity would recruit a low-ranking magistrate—no one will suspect her of pulling the strings. And now that Enitan knows for certain, she will find them. And she will wring their blood from their bodies, if that's what it takes to find Xiang. A smile touches her lips as she shoves her way out of the party. At last, she has somewhere to begin: a name.

Cahiyr.

◆

That night, Enitan contacts the High Consul after nearly three weeks of silence.

"So what are you going to do now?" they ask, once she's finished.

Enitan draws back from the holoprojector. "I thought you might tell me."

"You're not an Ominirish agent. I won't tell you to *do* anything." They steeple their hands. "As I understand it, our agreement is that you will continue to supply the Republic with information until you find your sibling, upon which we will retrieve you both. Nothing more and nothing less."

The message is clear: she's on her own. Enitan bites her lip. "And what happens after that?"

"That's also entirely your decision. You'd both be welcome to apply for citizenship in Ominira."

Up until now, her only goal has been to find Xiang. She never considered what might happen after that. She curses herself for not demanding citizenship as a fail-safe, or at least protection in exchange for serving the High Consul. The fact that they haven't offered both drops a seed of doubt into her stomach. *Welcome to apply.* As she examines the High Consul's perfectly blank expression, she grows certain that any request of hers or Xiang's will be denied. Enitan's not surprised. She's not naive enough to think she's anything but a tool to the High Consul, to be disposed of as soon as she's outlived her usefulness. She and her sibling will become Vaalbara's most-wanted fugitives, and it's hardly as if the Republic ever stepped in to help Koriko before.

"All right." She rubs at her face with a tired hand. "I'll start looking into the magistrate, then."

The High Consul's smile is a polite one, their eyes hollow. Enitan reaches over, turns off the holoprojector, and tucks it into her pocket. She buries her head in her hands. Ancestors, what is she going to do?

Her worrying is cut short by her communicator chiming in her other pocket.

It's the Imperator.

◆

Led by her communicator, Enitan makes her way toward the palace's central church. She passes shuffling groups of imams, ministers, rabbis, holy elders, priests, clerics, and monks; none pay her much attention. Their number increases steadily as she goes on, and so do their voices—they chant sutras and whisper prayers, sing hymns and murmur blessings. Enitan eventually reaches a massive circular door guarded by a pair of sentinels. They both place a hand against the screen-surface. Hidden scanners read their prints through their gloves, and the door slides open, revealing a featureless hall capped by yet another guarded door.

She walks through the second door and finds herself in a cavernous chamber, a colossal icosahedron filled with nothing but shadows. And at the center of it, seated on a dais, is the Imperator. Enitan's palms go damp when she sees the silver battle-axe in her hands. The Imperator glances up at her, a grim set to her mouth.

After a moment, she returns to her current task: scraping a black whetstone against the fan-shaped blade of her weapon. "Don't worry, this isn't for you. I promise." Her words reverberate up to the ceiling, which stretches impossibly high above them. Enitan notes that two full breaths pass before the echo returns to them. The church is vast.

The Imperator's word or no, Enitan's not taking chances. She stays right where she is, clasping her hands behind her back. "So . . . how has your day been?"

The Imperator's snort is half humor and half surprise. "It was fine. I held an audience for the people to bring me their grievances." She puts the whetstone aside and holds up the axe to the meager light, inspecting the gleaming edge. "Except no one came to complain, since the survival rate for those who have in the past has traditionally been low." Her smile is unnerving, a blend of menacing mirth and amicable threat.

But Enitan will not be intimidated. She gestures at the axe now lying across the Imperator's thighs. "Don't you have servants to do that for you? Or something more . . . high-tech?"

The Imperator slides the whetstone against the silver-plated steel, muscles flexing under the scarred skin of her arm. There are neat, pale slashes and dark starbursts and jagged white gashes. "I've always done this myself. And this is the axe I received when I was crowned, handed down from Imperator to Imperator since the founding of the Empire."

"May I ask, Imperator, whom the axe is for?"

"Him." The Imperator slings the axe over her shoulder, stands, and steps aside.

Ancestors. A few meters behind her is a bald man lying peaceably on a white-veined slab of black marble. As a supposed member of the Vaalbaran Empire, she's read about ritual sacrifices before. She never thought she'd be brought to witness one. She knows being invited to such a sacred ceremony by God herself is a heavenly gift, the greatest of honors. Still, she hazards a quick glance at the exit.

The sacrifice turns to look at her, mouth curved into a heavily anesthetized smile. "Hello," he murmurs. "I've heard a lot about you."

"All good things, I hope," replies Enitan, wiping her sweaty hands on her pants. She forces herself to inhale. She looks up at the Imperator, who's walking around the dais. "What's the occasion?"

That she knows what's coming does not make her feel any less ill when the Imperator lifts her weapon, gripping the handle with both hands.

"We're going to war."

Enitan doesn't turn away when the axe falls.

FOURTEEN

War.

Her world should have screeched to a halt.

But it doesn't, not at first. Not until the Imperator sits her down in a clean, spacious drawing room and says, "There will only be a few legions. But they're . . . they're your people. I'm sorry." Her gaze drops to the floor. "Everyone who's been kidnapped."

And then a great and terrible sorrow rips through Enitan, sinks its teeth deep into her bones and scrapes out the marrow. She barely recalls the first time the Empire invaded her home. She was too young to remember or to understand. Besides, the Empire wasn't much of a presence in her life until she was nearly an adult. After the last Imperator ripped open Koriko and tore out its entrails, he was relatively content to sit back and watch the *savages* suffer. Conquest for sport, plain and simple. She sees that now. Nearly a decade passed before Vaalbara finally took over in truth.

But Enitan does remember the helmets. Smooth, round shells. Gleaming faceplates. She remembers her own visage, the perfect reflection of a blank-faced girl trapped within a shining visor. And now she imagines her own people, their faces behind those shining metal masks. She imagines Xiang, their eyes obscured by a sheet of curved polycarbonate, their hands curled tight around a shockstaff.

"They would never fight for Vaalbara. Not willingly," Enitan says. She's shaking, her breath coming fast.

The Imperator is perched on the very edge of a divan, her legs crossed. She's as far away from Enitan as her fourth private drawing room allows, almost as if she's afraid of her. Her posture is as taut as an ancient Homeworld bowstring.

"There's a sort of . . . brainwashing," says the Imperator. "But not quite. It's more of an intensive conditioning." She falters abruptly. "I—I don't know if it's possible to undo. I'm sorry, Enitan."

Stomach acid creeps up her throat, the horror of what she's just learned twisting her insides. "Why?"

"Iëre is a lesser target than Ominira. The treaty with the Republic only protects, well, the Republic. Everything else, including the island nations, is fair game." Her mouth contorts into a pained expression.

"What a way of saying you're going to use an entire country as target practice for your new legions," Enitan snarls, though self-preservation keeps her voice quiet. "Legions kidnapped from Koriko, my *home*, and brainwashed into a sentinel army."

"Actually," says the Imperator, very softly, "some of them were taken from the Republic too."

Enitan glowers at her. "So you knew about the kidnappings." She's not wholly surprised. If the Imperator could be forced into war, she could be forced into anything, reluctant or not.

"Most Vaalbarans do."

"*What?*"

"The majority of my people don't know what happens to the victims, or why they're being taken." The Imperator's gaze falls to her feet. "The purpose always varies. But the disappearance of people in enemy or . . . recently acquired lands is part of our history. They accept it as an ugly truth and assume it is necessary for the preservation of the Empire. But even in the closest of company, it's taboo to speak of."

Despair ripples through Enitan until she goes numb. "Did our government know too?"

Ajana was right.

"I'm sorry."

The apology brings white-hot rage into Enitan's veins, and for half a second everything goes red.

"Stop apologizing," she snaps. And then, softer: "Listen. We can save Iëre, along with my people." It is then that something terrible occurs to her. "Unless . . . unless that's not what you want."

"Vaalbara has finally ended a thousand-year conflict!" The Imperator slams her hands down on the table between them. "I will not be the one to restart it."

"Then why are you doing this?"

"Because, I—"

"I know about the shadow council." Enitan watches the Imperator's face carefully, but there's nothing, not even a flicker of surprise. "We can find them, take them down. We can stop this from happening." Ajana *cannot* have died for nothing.

"Please, enlighten me as to how you'd go about doing that," the Imperator says, crossing her arms. "I've never even been able to identify a single member of the council, much less met them. There's no way for us to—"

"I have a name. There must be some sort of intermediary, a chain of command—"

"No. All I get is letters." The Imperator holds up a hand when Enitan straightens. "But they're paper and ink. Untraceable."

"We'll figure something out," Enitan says, then grimaces at having used *we*, despite every cell in her body warning her against a true alliance. Such a pact would require genuine trust. "We need a plan."

"A plan?" The Imperator shakes her head. "No."

"*No?*"

"We're too late. The invasion begins tomorrow."

The words shock Enitan into silence. The Imperator sighs helplessly. But she's *not* helpless. Her power may be in name alone, but even that is far greater than what Enitan has. And if Xiang ends up on the front lines, she will truly have nothing. Do they even remember her?

Enitan sits back in her chair, her hands braced against the armrests and her feet planted on the floor. Her teeth sink into her tongue, barely managing to stop the scream racing up her throat. Vaalbara's decimation of her life is finally complete. It has wrung her country dry of its blood and carved out every dream and aspiration from her people. As ever, they were not content with Korikese bodies. They had to take their minds, too. Now Xiang is in the Empire's clutches, and they could kill or be killed tomorrow. Enitan thought there was more time.

The Imperator is spinning excuses now, saying how she didn't plan the invasion. It doesn't matter. She knew it was going to happen and did nothing to stop it. The righteous indignation of Enitan's youth returns in full force, flaring up as a pure and blazing fury.

She flinches when the Imperator's hand settles on the back of her chair, distressingly close to her shoulder. "Did they take someone you know? Perhaps I can get them out."

"No." Enitan doesn't trust the Imperator enough to tell her about Xiang. If things fall apart even further, she has no doubt that the woman will use her sibling against her. And even if Enitan could somehow slip away with the person who's nothing to the Empire but everything to her, there are hundreds of others just like Xiang. Hundreds lost to their families, only to be forcibly conscripted and sacrificed in a needless war.

"I'm doing what I can, Enitan." The Imperator retracts her hand and crosses the room. "I'm going to free Koriko. Please trust in that, if not in me."

Enitan somehow manages not to laugh aloud. She swallows her bitterness, crossing her arms over her chest instead. "Menkhet, wait."

The Imperator stills, her jet-ringed hand nearly pressed against the door.

Enitan pushes herself to her feet. "I'm coming with you."

"Why?"

"Because I need to see what they've done to my people." *To Xiang*. And as soon as she gathers all the intel she can, she'll report straight to the Consul.

"All right."

Enitan blinks. "Really? You'll let me?"

The Imperator bows her head. "I really am sorry, Enitan." And then she's gone.

Enitan returns to her chambers that night to prepare for war.

FIFTEEN

Enitan leans over the balcony railing, watching the burnished gold sky drip sunlight over the ocean far below. What a beautiful day for bloodshed.

She's at the end of a corridor in one of the Imperator's terrestrial warships, a monolith about a quarter of the Splinter's size. The Imperial flagship is somewhere between the capital and the Vaalbaran-Ominirish border; the Empire needs only a crumb of its full might for what's to come.

Bells begin to chime, their soft, tinkling song riding a chill breeze. Enitan drags her hand over the banister of sleek metal and carved stone. She presses a fingertip to the snout of a tiny bloodmaw cavorting in a field of blossoms.

"I almost didn't hear you," she says, her breath puffing white in the cold, salty air.

The Imperator joins her on the balcony. She moves in near silence, her presence more like a shadow than the commanding weight befitting a monarch. Enitan wonders if this is due to modesty or simply a habit drilled into her during her army service.

Enitan turns to find the Imperator looking at her with a strange mixture of caution and remorse. "Come with me."

She turns and Enitan follows. They enter a hemispherical chamber with hexagonal screens floating over the walls and ceiling. A throne sits in the very center of the space: a huge, triangular block of unbroken obsidian.

The Imperator looks like she was born to sit in it. Her uniform is the standard Vaalbaran military cut, but is fashioned from pure-black cloth with platinum trimmings. Two rows of minuscule onyx buttons, probably ornamental, slash diagonally across her chest. But instead of sitting, she leans over the throne and presses a hand to an inlaid scanner.

"This is my observation room," the Imperator tells Enitan flatly. Several screens drift together into a seamless display and flash to life, revealing a vast swath of ocean. Black dots skim over the dark waves, and the screens magnify them automatically.

Warcraft. Thousands of them.

The last thing Enitan wants to do is watch the Empire rain fire and brimstone from above. She wants to be on the ground with Xiang. She may not have a concrete plan, but she'll certainly have better chances retrieving them there than up here.

"Let me go down with you," she says, in a carefully neutral tone. "Please."

"No," the Imperator says in a voice that brooks no argument. She waves her hand, and a man melts out from the shadows. "This is Fenris, captain of my honor guard. He'll be making sure you stay put."

He's not wearing a helmet, though he might as well be. His splotchy red face is completely blank, a mask Enitan is sure outclasses anything she herself has been able to produce.

"Sit," the Imperator commands her, though there's a little regret in her eyes. "This will be over soon. If something happens, I've had my personal com-code added to your contacts."

With no other choice, Enitan does as she's told. The second the doors slide shut behind the Imperator, the captain's mask slips away. He scowls at her, eyes dragging over her clothes. She's wearing the simplest of her Vaalbaran suits, a burnt-orange piece edged in red brocade. His scowl turns upward into a smirk.

"I know," Enitan says, and he stiffens, as if he expected her to remain silent and still under his scrutiny. "A savage in finery is still a savage."

"You're not a savage, my lady."

"No," she agrees, a strange coldness crystallizing in her chest. "And the rest of my people?" If there's anything she's learned in the past few weeks, it's that her perfect behavior and surprising influence in the Splinter has made her *special* in the eyes of the nobles. An exception among her people, rather than emblematic of them as usual. Bigotry is a downward-flowing river: new information and experiences might divert its course or chisel it into streams, but its water will always flow in the same direction.

"Well, not all of them," says the captain, shrugging. "I've been to Koriko myself. In many ways, you're much like us."

Enitan ignores his patronizing. She knows he intends it as a compliment, which is even worse. She busies herself turning over his actual words. Vaalbarans only travel to Koriko for one of three reasons. They're posted there either as sentinels or as monks, both to serve the will of the God-Emperor in their own way. Or they're tourists like Deora. The man before her is by no stretch of the imagination a holy man, and she can't imagine him as a frivolous sightseer with more money than sense. And if he's a member of the Imperial honor guard, he'd never be stationed to serve as a lowly enforcer. No, he was ordered by someone very high up to sojourn to Koriko. Possibly the shadow council (which she has taken to simply calling the Council, as she disagrees with Cahiyr on how good "the Hidden Ones" sounds). Perhaps the order even came through the Imperator. Enitan keeps her eyes trained on the screens, her face as serene as possible despite the quickening of her heart. This Fenris was involved in the Korikese kidnappings.

Perhaps even Xiang's.

She considers confronting him outright, but she holds her tongue for now. She can't be certain whether his loyalties are with the Council or his God. If it's the former, he might not suspect she's spying for the Imperator, but she's sitting on the God-Emperor's throne in her surveillance room, after all. And if he suspects she knows something she shouldn't and decides to attack her, she knows this day will be her last. She is weaponless, and he has a foot and perhaps fifty kilos on her.

"The Imperator tells me that the troops are new," Enitan says quietly, watching the first warcraft dip toward a brilliant crimson speck. Ière is famous for its bountiful red flora. "Is there any chance they'll lose?" She turns toward the sentinel with wide eyes, pouring desperate concern into her voice. It's only half acting; she's terrified for her sibling. "Could Menkhet get hurt?"

It works. The sentinel's mask is back, but now there's a cruel gleam in his eye. *Perfect.* Let him think her loyalty to her kin and country shallower than a rumored romance. Let him think her a traitor at heart, only proud and self-righteous until her beloved Imperator is in danger. She'll face the consequences later, once he reports back to his friends and the whispers burst like a flame doused in oil. During Enitan's brief, intermittent romance with Ajana, she received mildly preferential treatment from Imperials, but everyone in the Splinter is an aristocrat; they will not be as easily removed as a trigger-happy sentinel. The Imperator has just enough power over her court that lower-ranked nobles have mostly kept their mouths shut about the matter, while sycophants like the merchant have tried pandering. But high-ranked aristocrats can and do say whatever they please, whenever they please. They treat her accordingly.

Enitan forces her gaze back to the screens, pressing her lips together and making a show of gripping the throne's armrests. The warcraft descend as one, two rows settling down on a ribbon of black-sand beach. She waits for him to reply, drawing as much fear into her face as she can. After a month of hiding all emotions, forcing them out is hard.

"These regiments may be new, but they're not untested, my lady," he says finally, and the honorific sounds distinctly mocking on his tongue. "They've been training for years, and I oversaw some of their instruction myself. You have nothing to fear."

"Oh, thank God," Enitan breathes out, just loud enough for him to hear. And she means it, if not the religiosity. If the kidnapped legions require years of training, then the Imperator was wrong. Xiang probably won't be on the battlefield today. They're safe. Or as safe as they can be, with their mind being hollowed out and their body shaped for violence.

The new sentinels pour from the warcraft the second the doors slide open. They tramp out across the island in perfect lockstep. Something tightens in Enitan's stomach as she watches them flood the island, a wave of steel and synthetic fiber and sinew. It's very possible—certain, even—that she's met at least a few of them. She hasn't kept in touch with anyone from university; her whole graduating class could've been abducted and she'd never have known. She scans the marching troops, searching for any idiosyncrasy that might hint at the person under each helmet. It's hopeless.

A chime sounds in the sentinel's pocket. "Pardon me." He turns away, communicator in hand.

The second he's out, Enitan rushes over and presses her right ear to the doors.

". . . Third Sister," he's saying. "You're not jesting, are you?"

She can't hear whoever he's speaking to, but the other person talks for a long time before the sentinel opens his mouth again. "Yes. Yes. Of course I am. She—no, she won't be a problem."

The doors fly open before she can scramble back to the throne. The sentinel looks down at her, his green eyes razor-sharp. Every muscle in Enitan's body tenses as she shrinks beneath his glare.

"You stupid little beast," he snarls. "How long have you been plotting to kill her?"

He must mean the Imperator. Enitan steps back, putting as much space between them as possible. Her tongue feels like it's made of stone, but she forces it to form words anyway. "I haven't—I wouldn't—"

"A convincing act," he snarls, spittle flecking her face. "The endless tea brewing, the harlotry—though I'm sure that last bit's genuine. But you're not much of an assassin, are you?"

"I'm *not* an assassin," Enitan gasps. Adrenaline screams through her muscles as her mind races frantically. There's nowhere to flee, and she can't fight him. "I—"

His hand swings out, whiplash-quick, and grabs her by the collar. "Whoever sent you must be truly desperate. Hiding the Third Sister under your mattress?"

"Third Sister?" Enitan kicks at his legs even as he lifts her above the ground. Her fingers pry uselessly at his. "Who—oh no." *Ajana's poignard.* They've searched her rooms. Thank the Ancestors she hid her holoprojector elsewhere. "It was a gift—"

The sentinel punches her. There's a sickening crunch as his fist smashes the cartilage of her nose. Enitan wheezes in agony, releasing his other hand. She brings her fingers to her face, and when she pulls them away, they're covered in blood.

"It was a *gift*," she hisses. "I didn't know—"

When he punches her again, she swallows the cry of pain. Her teeth sink into the inside of her cheek, and she goes limp in his grip.

"You'll die for this," he hisses, and his free hand reaches up to wrap around her throat. He's not quite strangling her, not yet. The pressure of his fingers on her trachea is just enough to hurt.

"Please." She claws at his wrist, but it's useless. Her heart thrashes like a trapped rukhviper in her chest. "I—" Her breaths turn to gurgles as his grip tightens incrementally.

"You'll be fortunate," he whispers, his voice soft, "if all the Imperator does is toss you from the Splinter. You'll die for this."

"Actually," says a congenial voice, "I haven't quite decided. Put her down, Fenris."

The captain drops her. She lands hard on her knees, nearly face-planting onto the floor. She drags in a breath, her throat sore and aching. When she looks up, the Imperator is seated in the throne, fingers drumming idly on the armrests. Her mouth is bent into a friendly smile, but that good humor doesn't reach her eyes. There's not so much as a hair out of place. She looks nothing like a woman who has just returned from battle. It occurs to Enitan then that the Imperator is beautiful. It pains her little to admit it; it's simply a fact. *Jilessa is red-orange-gold, theehma is a poor excuse for tea, the God-Emperor is beautiful.* The realization comes upon her without warning, and frankly, at a bad time.

Behind her, on the screens, sentinels march out of a village with curved turquoise roofs. In a single smooth motion, hands reach up to their helmets and activate thermal vision. They spread out into a V formation and begin to wade through a field of waist-high, bloodred grass.

"Well?" the Imperator says, in that same dangerously pleasant tone. "I'm waiting for an explanation as to why you were choking our emissary."

The captain drops slowly to the floor. He bends over his folded knees. Only when his forehead touches the black tile does he speak. "The Third Sister was found in her room, Your Imperial Majesty. We believe she's an assassin."

The Imperator arches a brow. "*We?* Who ordered the search, and who ordered you to harm her?"

"Minister Sornoi," says the captain. "And the emissary—the emissary resisted arrest. She fought back."

"Before or after you had your hands around her throat?"

"I—"

"Get out," the Imperator snaps. She's still seated on her throne, and the captain is a tall man, much taller than even she is. But she looks down at him regardless. "*You'll* be fortunate if all I do is toss *you* from the Splinter."

"Your Imperial Majesty." The captain picks his head up from the tile. "She could be dangerous. I cannot leave you alone with—"

"I'm not going to tell you again, Fenris." To Enitan she says, "Are you all right?"

The only sound that comes out of Enitan's mouth is a horrible rasp.

"Nod if you need immediate medical attention."

Enitan shakes her head.

"Nod if you're an assassin."

She shakes her head again.

Menkhet—no, *the Imperator*, Enitan firmly corrects herself—pauses. "I believe you. Or, at least, I believe that if you wanted to kill me, you're not stupid enough to attempt doing it with a measly dagger." She reclines further into her throne. "I've chosen to save your life today, but I want you to understand something. Our interests may align for now, but they are not the same. At the end of the day, I am a servant of the Empire before all else. You're a nominal citizen, but if I am forced to choose between you and the lives of even two good Vaalbarans, I have to choose them. Have I made myself clear?"

This is all to be expected, and of course Enitan wants honesty from her. She knows she's nothing more than another implement in the Imperator's toolbox, and far more replaceable than most . . . so why does the admission sting? She gives a slow nod and stands, waving a hand at the screens around them. If the Imperator's back, the conquest of Iëre must be nearing its end, but all she can see and hear are lines of sentinels striding around silent blue-roofed settlements or uninhabited wilderness.

"Oh, the invasion?" The Imperator glances over her shoulder with disinterest, watching a sentinel step out from a flower shop, a hand on his gun.

He looks around, his shoulders tense. "Come on out," he barks.

After a moment, the shopkeeper steps out into the paved street. There are deep shadows under their eyes. They lean against the pale stucco wall.

"Where are the militias?" the sentinel demands.

The shopkeeper brushes a pollen-coated hand over the front of their apron. "Like we told you, they're gone."

The sentinel grips his gun.

"Demobilized," says the shopkeeper, hands up and trembling.

"Get back inside," snaps the sentinel. He looks to one of his comrades, who's turning full circle in the middle of the street, looking for an enemy that isn't there.

"Isn't it obvious?" The Imperator's smile is as sharp as cut glass. "We've won."

SIXTEEN

The Imperator grabs the poignard as soon as they get back to the Splinter. She takes Enitan right up to one of the many chambers of her residence. It appears the whole room is dedicated to housing personal plunder, though the contents are far from Deora's cultural artifacts or the museum's priceless treasures.

"The Third Sister," she says, sliding her finger along the blade, "is the weapon that was used to kill Kuzatta the Seventeenth." Her gaze latches on to Enitan's.

"You're looking at me like you expected me to know that," Enitan rasps. Speaking no longer hurts, but her voice still hasn't completely recovered. "I have no idea who that is."

The Imperator's eyes widen. "But he died only nine years ago! It was the shock of the decade. Kuzatta the Seventeenth served in the last Imperator's parliament."

"Do you know who Moremi Ajasoro is?"

"I'm afraid I don't."

Enitan widens her eyes dramatically. "She's only the most famous Korikese folk hero!" She drops the act. "You see? I don't expect you to know random pieces of my people's history."

"Oh. Fine, you're right." The Imperator holds the poignard aloft. Light tessellates across the room as the glinting blade cuts through the air. "Kuzatta was petty and corrupt and generally one of our worst politicians. One of the commoners he well and truly screwed over forged a trio of knives—the Three Sisters—and set out for vengeance. The rest of the story isn't important, but the commoner was forced to give up the first two poignards along the way and used the third to cut out Kuzatta's heart."

"Fascinating," Enitan deadpans, resisting the urge to scratch at her newly reset nose.

"It is. The commoner managed to get away, but was then himself mysteriously murdered, and the Third Sister went missing. It's now a popular symbol of justice." She twirls the poignard in her fingers. "There have been a dozen copycat assassinations since, each involving a replica poignard." She brings the knife down hard, and the blade sinks into the table's dull surface. "Speaking of replicas, my oh-so-accomplished intelligence team was wrong. This is a fake, though an excellent one."

"How do you know?"

The Imperator picks up an unglazed teapot from the shelf nearest her, turning it this way and that. Enitan recognizes it as eleyisha, a porous Gondwanan clay known for soaking up flavor. With repeated use, a glossy patina forms, and the legend goes that on the thousandth pour, hot water goes in and tea comes out.

"Because I have the original," she finally says.

"How?"

"I took it from the assassin himself, just before I killed him. After Kuzatta, he kept delivering his particular brand of vigilante justice. Ended up killing a bunch of civilians to cover his tracks." She smiles wistfully, placing the teapot back on its shelf. "Taking him down was my very first mission as commander."

Enitan feels like she should've seen that coming. "How many replicas are there?"

"Tens of thousands at least. There's an arms producer who manufactures *only* Third Sisters." The Imperator screws up her eyes at a box full of enameled combs. "I can't believe I took these," she mutters.

"So your agents found an extremely common replica knife in my room and assumed I, a scribe, was going to try to murder you, a seasoned commander, with it, based on the story behind the weapon?"

"I'd say hiding a weapon as a hostage doesn't look very good, especially if you need a permit to possess such a weapon on Koriko. A permit you do not have."

"For the twentieth time, it was a funerary gift. I couldn't leave it at home, and I didn't want your people confiscating it."

"I understand that," says the Imperator. "But . . ."

"But I'm Korikese," Enitan finishes.

"You could hold a particularly sharp stylus, and my people would start sweating."

"So what now?"

The Imperator waves a hand at the poignard, still embedded deep in the wood. "You can have that back." She turns and sits, plopping down on a large black-lacquered medicine chest with tarnished brass handles. "A funerary gift? Who would bequeath you a thing like this?"

"A . . . a friend." Had it been merely a keepsake to Ajana, or did the Third Sister mean something more? Had Ajana tried to push back against the Empire in ways Enitan never noticed? Had she wanted her to do the same? Perhaps Ajana had involved her mother—

Oh.

The duchess had known about the shadow council all long. Which meant, at some point, that she must have warned Ajana. Ajana must also have sent word to her mother to find Enitan. But what had she wanted Enitan to do?

Enitan looks down, smothering her emotions before they can emerge on her face, whatever they may be. She can ponder these questions later, when the Imperator isn't observing her every move. Her gaze latches on to the smooth wood below. The table is so plain it sticks out from the rest of the objects stored here, even as simple or worn down as they are. It's a scuffed wooden piece without a single carving to embellish it.

The Imperator follows her eyes. "I took it from an Ominirish furniture store on one of my first raids as an up-and-coming commander." She sighs. "To the victor go the spoils, I suppose."

" 'Victor.' That's a nice way of putting it," Enitan says.

The Imperator shrugs, albeit a little stiffly, and says nothing.

"What made you want to keep it?" Enitan asks.

"Those raids were mostly ceremonial." The Imperator sighs. "But it still would've looked odd if I'd taken nothing."

" 'Ceremonial'? I'm sure the Ominirish you murdered would beg to differ."

"I didn't kill anyone. The only lives I've personally ended have been those of ritual sacrifices. All of whom, let me remind you, are volunteers. Or murderers who would've gone on to take many other innocent lives if I hadn't ended theirs."

"Oh, is that so?" Enitan grabs her communicator and opens an old article she read a few days ago. *"In recent news, Commander Menkhet Ta-Miu of the Fourteenth Section, Thirty-Second Battalion, Nineteenth Legion of the Seventh Holy Fleet, has been awarded the Golden Fly, the Empire's most prestigious military honor. This comes after her last raid on the island of Iëre, where she earned the epithets 'the Slaughterer' and 'She Who Massacres,' among many others."*

The Imperator freezes. And then her sculpted features take on a theatrically wounded expression. "That's propaganda. *I* didn't hurt anyone. The soldiers under my command did. And on my predecessor's orders, not mine. I was only there to supervise." She looks away. "I know better than to try defending myself, but we were raised to believe that what we were doing was good and just—if our God-Emperor said we should plunder and pillage, then who were we to disagree? And if you didn't obey his will, then someone else would. They'd get silver and military honors, and you'd be imprisoned for disobedience. Or worse."

That sounded like an attempted defense to Enitan. "Fine. What happened out there today?"

"Like I told you, we won."

Enitan tells herself that smacking the Imperator upside the head is probably a bad idea. "I watched most of it. Granted, I was preoccupied," she says, rubbing her throat, "but I didn't see or hear a single weapon go off. It seemed like the troops just landed and declared Iëre yours." She narrows her eyes. "In fact, I didn't see a single Iëreii outside, except for that shopkeeper. They were all huddled up in their homes."

"Yes, very strange," says the Imperator.

"Okay, one other question," says Enitan. "When did you warn the Iëreii about the invasion?"

The Imperator gives Enitan a careful sidelong glance. "Who told you?"

"I had my suspicions." Enitan runs a finger across the table. It comes away free of even a speck of dust. "You've just confirmed them."

In reality, the High Consul told her last night. When Enitan contacted them and recounted everything she'd seen, they informed her that the Iëreii Prime Minister had begged them for help a week ago, only to tell them half an hour later that whoever had warned her had convinced her to surrender. The invasion had been entirely bloodless.

The Imperator scowls at her.

"It makes perfect sense," Enitan says, allowing herself a smirk. "I did a little late-night reading; apparently, it's an unforgivable dishonor in Vaalbara to attack a surrendered foe. As long as they don't take up arms, they can't be touched. You get your undisputed victory, no one dies, and the Council has to figure out another way to test their new forces, buying you more time."

The scowl deepens. "How obvious was it?"

"Not very, I think." Enitan reaches past the poignard and selects a flower-shaped cake from the plate at the center of the table. "I doubt anyone would suspect someone dubbed *the Slaughterer* of sabotaging their own war." Her teeth sink into the crispy layers of the confection. She barely manages not to spit it right out. "Ancestors, this tastes awful."

"I told you I'm allergic to everything decent."

"There are drugs you can take," Enitan chokes out. "No one should live like this."

"Oh, I agree wholeheartedly. But I'm allergic to the treatments."

"Have you tried berraleaf?" Enitan asks. "It contains the only known antihistamine without any recorded side effects. I used to give it to—" She cuts herself off abruptly.

The Imperator lifts her brows.

"To someone with really bad allergies, though I've never seen a case as bad as yours." She stands, her palms growing damp. "It tastes amazing in black uhie tea."

"How have I not heard of this before?"

"It's Korikese." Enitan yanks the poignard out of the table and turns toward the door. "Anyway, if you get someone to acquire it for you, I'll make you a cup. Please excuse me. I'm going out to find some real food."

◆

Enitan does eat, because she really is hungry. She raids Deora's conserver and throws her dishes in the sink, where someone will come by to clean them later. But as soon as that's done, she changes into her church frock. She slides the poignard into her boot and heads for the honor guards' apartments on the second story. She has access to all levels of the palace; it's the doors that are the problem. Not today, though.

The Imperator demoted Fenris from captain of her honor guard to a common sentinel, soon to be sent to the least desirable post in the Empire. His chambers are being cleaned out for his replacement. Enitan knows from experience that Imperial scribes will handle any sensitive documents; when the local abbot got himself fired, she was accidentally assigned to organize his files with the rest of the scribes. Unfortunately for her curiosity, the error was fixed before she went anywhere near the inner church.

In her official frock, no one will question her presence as long as she keeps her head down. She'll slip in with the rest of the scribes she knows will be pouring in and out of the former captain's rooms. She'll grab as many documents as she can and split from the group when she gets the chance. Enitan has no idea when Xiang's training will be complete and they'll be formally assigned to a battalion, but she's not going to wait around for that to happen.

She takes a tubelift down to the second level of the palace, schooling her features into a servile mask. When the doors slide open, she wipes her sweaty hands on the frock and steps out. At the end of the hallway is an open door. That must be it. But there's not a single scribe or servant. Perhaps she's early.

Or perhaps this is a trap.

Heart stuttering under her ribs, Enitan makes her way down the passage. If this is truly a lure, ensnaring her will be child's play. But better to spring the trap now and face the consequences.

She creeps over the threshold, shoulders hunched and tense. A quick scan of the room reveals nothing but covered furniture and four doors, all closed but for one. She can see the edge of a sumptuous bed.

"Hello?" Enitan calls.

When nothing happens, she pulls the poignard from her boot. It may not be the real Third Sister, but it'll cut just as deep. She slinks through the open door and slips on a pool of blood. She slams into the floor and flops painfully onto her back, unable to find purchase on the slippery wood. Something hits her aching nose, runs down her chin, and spatters onto her frock. More blood, barely visible on the near-black fabric. She looks up to meet the former captain Fenris's glassy eyes.

There's a scimitar through his chest, pinning him to the wall like he's an insect in a display case. Rivulets of blood flow down the blade and over the hilt onto her head. Just above his paper-pale face is an empty sword mount.

Enitan sits there for a moment, too shocked to scream. Too shocked to do anything. But then her self-preservation instincts kick in, and she forces herself to her feet. She needs to leave immediately—she's a sitting paangfowl here.

Panic surges through her as she tucks the poignard back into her boot, wrings out as much of the blood from her clothes as possible, and stumbles out the door. The hallway—thank the Ancestors—is still empty. Most of the guards must be at the new captain's swearing-in. She jumps into the tubelift and makes her way back to Deora's apartments. There are a few people in the corridors, but they don't even glance at her. Even if most of the palace residents weren't already used to her wandering around, she's well camouflaged in her frock.

Once safely inside, Enitan rips off her clothes and throws them in the washer, one of the few personal machines in the palace. The countess, apparently, demanded it after a servant ruined one of her grass skirts. Ten minutes later during the second rinse cycle, Deora walks into the laundry room. She looks at the washer, which is in essence a very large, very transparent glass ball. She drops her basket. Beaded shawls spill over the floor.

"That's . . . a lot of blood," she says.

Enitan would ignore her if silence under these circumstances wouldn't be so suspicious. "I have a very heavy flow," she says.

Deora looks at her, eyes wide as moons. "How are you up and doing chores right now? You should be in hypovolemic shock!"

Enitan simply closes her eyes and says, "I hydrate."

SEVENTEEN

"The former captain's demise will be hidden from the public. It'd cause too much unrest, and I already have a headache," the Imperator says the next morning over breakfast in her chambers. "Banurra's death was entertainment for the nobles, but the graphic murder of a formerly high-ranking sentinel means none of them are safe." She sips at her uhie-berraleaf tea. "Damn. This is amazing."

"I know," says Enitan. She breathes in the fragrant, woody notes of the brew, which glows dark gold in their amber cups. The color is the exact hue of Jilessa through the skydome in the evening, just before the world begins to darken for the night period.

This is by far the highest-quality tea she's ever set eyes on, let alone tasted. It must have cost a fortune, although Enitan supposes money is no object for the God-Emperor. The leaves were plucked from the very mother plant from which all other uhie bushes descend, then treated for half a century through a hundred-stage process that's been said to drive tea specialists mad. One step even involves the help of jenelocusts, a species of short-horned insects whose nibbling speeds along the oxidizing process.

The result is, in a word, exquisite—rich and velvety, with sweet hints of molasses and stone fruit. It is said that the ancient Korikese philosopher Xawirias leapt into a canyon after a single sip, knowing he'd never experience such pleasure again. According to the pupil that had been accompanying him, he'd wanted to die at his happiest.

"How long until the berraleaf kicks in?" asks the Imperator.

"Give it an hour, just to be safe." Enitan pushes the bowl of hetar-nuts the Imperator's been ogling out of reach. "Do you know who killed Fenris?"

"Well, I'm pretty sure it wasn't you," the Imperator says, noncha-lantly refilling her teacup. "Though I am curious as to why you snuck into his chambers."

Enitan nearly chokes on her tea. "How did you know?" she sputters.

The Imperator smirks. "You just told me."

Enitan huffs. "How obvious was it?"

"When the honor guard discovered him, they found blood smeared all over the place." The Imperator takes another sip of tea. There's a brilliant gleam in her eyes that Enitan missed when they first met. "Anyone skilled enough to impale Fenris with his own scimitar proba-bly wouldn't have slipped in the blood and then glided around in it. There *could* have been a struggle—the death blow wasn't a clean one, and he had multiple other wounds—but I found a single footprint that was slightly smaller than the others."

Enitan's heart flops around in her chest like a fish out of water. "Shit," she whispers.

"Don't worry, I got rid of it," says the Imperator. "You're welcome."

"Thanks," Enitan says quietly. "I snuck in because . . . well, he told me he'd been to Koriko. I thought maybe he'd taken part in what's been happening to my people." She looks down at her cup. "Even if it's too late, knowing still helps."

"You're aware that what you were doing was unbelievably danger-ous, right?" The Imperator's lacquer-over-onyx eyes search Enitan's. Enitan tries to avoid her gaze, lest she betray or discover something she doesn't want to. "That man lost his position because of what he did to you—I'm betting he wouldn't exactly have been a friendly source of information. And what if the Council found you? Why didn't you come to me first?"

"Do I really need to answer that?"

The Imperator sits back. "Look, I know a little wariness is healthy. But if we're going to be working together against the Council, you're going to need to trust me. You need to trust that I know the limits of my position, and that I won't stab you in the back. At least not without giving you fair warning. There's a difference between betraying you and choosing to protect my people above all else."

"Okay," says Enitan, giving a half-hearted shrug.

A frustrated sigh. "That sounded more like giving up than actual acceptance." She reaches for the nuts, only for Enitan to smack her hand away.

"Is there a suspect?" Enitan asks. "Besides me."

The Imperator lets her sloppy deflection slide with a huff. "More than just a suspect." Then she lunges for the bowl of hetarnuts. She grabs a handful before Enitan can stop her again. "A system-wide scan found that the surveillance network monitoring the abducted soldiers was tampered with yesterday, set on a loop overlapping with the approximate time of Fenris's death. Last night, my anonymous overlords sent down the order to torture the soldiers until someone confessed, but before anyone got hurt one of them came forward. They admitted to everything. Said they broke their conditioning weeks ago during a training simulation. It was the one where you have to burn down a hut with a family inside. Apparently, they'd been plotting revenge on Fenris, who commanded the squad that kidnapped them, ever since they left Koriko." She places a single hetarnut in her mouth and chews mechanically. "They're going to be executed this afternoon."

The world grinds to a halt. "What did you say?" Enitan whispers. The sharp edge of the table jabs into her stomach as she leans forward.

The Imperator doesn't repeat herself. She eats another hetarnut.

Enitan keeps her face still despite the adrenaline tearing through her. "The simulation—you said they had to burn down a hut?"

The Imperator nods once before her attention returns to her snack.

"Did you try to save them?" Enitan asks, the Imperator's words ringing in her ears. Her limbs have gone wobbly, and staying upright has become all but impossible.

"Of course I did," the Imperator snaps, her face hardening. "But they *begged* for death, rather than having their mind hollowed out completely. I'm surprised they were even given a choice. Old Vaalbaran respect, perhaps, for a warrior—"

"I want to see them," Enitan says, very slowly.

"At the execution?"

"No. As soon as possible. They should see a friendly face before the end." Under the table, her fingernails dig into her knees. "Please, Menkhet."

"I've noticed," says the Imperator with a quick, wistful smile, "you only call me by my name when you want something."

Enitan grinds her teeth together. She knows offending the God-Emperor of Vaalbara is a dangerous risk to take, but she can't let fear silence her, especially now. "Does it really bother you?"

"No. I'm using you too, as I've made clear. If I were a better person, I'd relinquish Koriko *without* demanding your help first." She reaches for the hetarnut bowl again, and this time Enitan doesn't attempt to stop her. "And . . . it's better to hear your name from someone who doesn't mean it than never at all."

"How can you *mean* a name?" Enitan demands.

"Never mind." The Imperator picks up the bowl. "Let's go."

Enitan shoots to her feet without a word. The Imperator takes her down a narrow hall. It must be a private passageway; they encounter no nobles, monks, or scribes. Not even a servant. For a moment, Enitan wonders once more if the Imperator's finally going to throw her out a window. But then they turn toward a single glossy tubelift.

The transport deposits them at the end of a dimly lit corridor. Ink-scroll paintings hang between each door, depicting strange animals cavorting around flowing streams. Although much less colorful than Korikese art, their austerity is almost beautiful.

No. She snaps herself out of it. Everything in Vaalbara has a cost, including the beautiful things. *Especially* the beautiful things. She can't let herself forget that.

Enitan glances at the Imperator, who's watching her with a strange, furrowed expression. "This isn't the prison," she says.

"No. The dungeon is on the bottom level of the palace, and the prison for the rest of the Splinter is ninety floors down. These are my personal holding cells." The Imperator stops before an engraved copper door. She presses a hand against its screen-surface, and it whooshes open. "Come."

Enitan follows her into a richly appointed living room. There are more ink-scroll paintings here. A Homeworld tortoise whose shell forms the full moon. A great tufted kinukmane on a grassy rock, stretching in a show of feline grace. The Imperator knocks gently on a bronze door etched with all manner of flora and fauna.

"Xiang, there's someone here to see you," she says in Akyesi.

Their name is a swift punch to Enitan's gut. She almost collapses where she stands, her body unbalanced by surprise and her mind unable to trust what she's hearing. More than anything, she wants to believe it's her sibling behind that door. But if this is yet another disappointment, she doesn't know if she'll be able to go on.

"I don't want to see anyone," says a voice so small it dwarfs her.

Relief and joy wrap around Enitan like a warm blanket. It's *them.* The Imperator looks back at her and beckons.

"Can . . . can we have a moment alone?" Enitan chokes out, her mouth drier than the Uluaan desert to the north.

"Enitan, they broke their conditioning less than a month ago. They're still—"

Enitan surges forward before she can stop herself. She latches on to the Imperator's arm. "Please."

"It's not just them. You should probably take some time to process this."

"Menkhet," says Enitan, her voice breaking as her grip tightens. "Let me see them."

"Okay," says the Imperator, "but what's best for you, what's best for them, and what you want in this moment are three very different things. Don't forget that in there."

"I promise," Enitan lies through her teeth.

"All right." With a great sigh of defeat, the Imperator leaves the main chamber.

"Xiang," whispers Enitan, in Korikesian. "It's me."

The door flies open, and suddenly Enitan is enfolded in a pair of arms. She closes her eyes, embracing Xiang so tightly she worries for a moment that she might be hurting them. Tension and fear and panic slowly unknot themselves from around her heart. The sun has returned to her starless sky. For the first time in weeks, she feels whole again.

"I've missed you so much," Enitan whispers into their shoulder. She can feel the tears on her face; she doesn't bother to wipe them away. "When I saw the blood, I thought— I thought you might be dead."

Xiang pulls away, just enough to look at her. "I thought I'd never see you again— What happened to your nose?"

She stands there, unable to speak, unable to breathe. They look exhausted and beaten down, but the person before her is still Xiang, in every way that matters. Enitan almost passes out from relief.

Then reality slices into her happiness like a hatchet. Xiang's execution is fast approaching. There's no way she'll be able to get them out in time. If the Republic can't even keep a single uncompromised operative in the Splinter, sneaking in a team to extract them in eight hours is impossible. She wonders if the High Consul ever meant to hold up their end of the deal. She wonders if they were lying when they said they'd just discovered their own people had been taken.

"I'm going to get you out," she says anyway, gripping their hands tightly. Their palms are warm and callused. "Why did the Imperator bring you here?"

When Xiang speaks, their voice is heavy, anguish and anger cooled to ash. "She said I couldn't be in the dungeons, so she was going to put me somewhere more secure. Said she was going to take care of me herself. Enitan, I thought she was going to torture me." The sound they make is too brittle to be laughter. "But then she brought me here and apologized about fifty times for putting me in a perfectly nice room. She's strange." A thoughtful pause. "How are *you* here?"

"I volunteered," says Enitan. Xiang's dark eyes widen. "As a political prisoner. And I've agreed to spy for the Imperator. Not on Koriko, or even Ominira. On her own people." Enitan looks away, glancing back at the door to make sure it's still shut. "She's promised to relinquish Koriko if I help her survive the next year on the throne. I think she intends to follow through, but I can't be certain."

"Do you think she can help us get out of this?"

"I don't know," Enitan says. "She has enough trouble helping even herself. I believe she'll keep her word, but she hasn't made any promises about helping *us*. We might have to figure this out on our own."

"Like always," they say.

"Like always," Enitan agrees, pulling them into another tight hug. "I have to go. I'll be back. I promise."

Xiang's hold on her tightens. "Be careful."

She can feel the strength in their hands, the raw power beaten into them by Fenris and his accomplices. The man is lucky he's already dead.

"I will." Enitan takes one last look at them and walks out of their room. The door slides shut behind her, leaving her feeling like she's left most of herself behind.

When she exits into the hallway, the Imperator is leaning casually against the opposite wall, her arms crossed and a leg propped up against the stone behind her. "So," she drawls, "when are you going to try to break them out?"

She knew this was coming, from the moment the Imperator first called Xiang by their name. She holds up her hands in a conciliatory gesture. "Menkhet, I can explain—"

"Don't *Menkhet* me. Did you really think I wouldn't look you up?" the Imperator snaps, pushing herself off the wall. "Enitan Ijebu of Ijebu Community of Koriko Province. Scribe of the Holy Church of Vaalbara and tea entrepreneur. Twenty-five years old. Formerly the third sibling in a triplet pod unit. Current assigned bond-sister of Xiang Ijebu, who is soon to graduate and logged *missing*." She lets out a frustrated groan. "You are extremely lucky that the Council doesn't seem to oversee the details of their little project, or they'd have shot your shuttle down before it even docked." She turns sharply on her heel.

Enitan follows her into the tubelift, trying hard not to raise her voice as she says, "I had no choice. Xiang is my family."

"You don't understand," the Imperator hisses through gritted teeth. "The Council will stop at nothing—"

"No, *you* don't understand. Vaalbara has never taken a thing from you."

The Imperator doesn't respond for a long moment, her expression stoic. "How did you know it was Xiang?"

"The simulation you mentioned." Enitan slides down the wall of the tubelift. "Burning down a hut with a family inside. Perhaps your files didn't include this, but I'm not Xiang's first sibling either." She runs a hand over her head. "They won't talk about it much, but that was exactly what happened to their first family. The exercise must've triggered the memory and allowed them to overcome part of the brainwashing somehow."

The Imperator sits beside her. "What are you going to do now?"

Enitan keeps her eyes trained on the floor. "Can you help us?"

She counts seven breaths before the Imperator answers. "There is a line at which I risk more of Vaalbara's future helping you than I do abandoning you to fate. No matter my personal desires, I will not cross it. I'm sorry, Enitan. If anyone finds out I helped a sentenced Korikese sentinel escape, both my life and my plan for the Empire will be forfeit."

"No they won't," Enitan says, her voice much firmer than she feels. "The only ones who can truly threaten you are the Council, and I'll rid you of them. I'll even stay here as your *informal advisor* for the rest of my life. Whatever it takes."

The Imperator says nothing. When the tubelift's doors slide open, she stands and offers a hand. Enitan takes it and rises. She meets the other woman's eyes, holding them for just a heartbeat too long.

"The rest of your life," echoes the Imperator, her voice softer than a whisper. It is a question.

"Yes." Enitan's next breath leaves her numb. Part of her victory, a bright spark of joy, cools to an ember, then to smoke, as she promises, "The rest of my life."

The Imperator's hand tightens around Enitan's before she lets go.

EIGHTEEN

Menkhet will burn Xiang alive. Or rather, pretend to. Immolation is the most sacred of Vaalbaran sacrifices; even more private than the execution Enitan witnessed, it cannot be monitored or recorded. The ceremony is as follows: the reigning Imperator and the sacrifice walk into the inner sanctum of the palace temple. Hours later, the Imperator walks out, alone and speckled with the ash they themselves are supposed to scatter out a sacred window.

Enitan still can't bring herself to trust the Imperator completely. Fear trickles into her lungs every time she thinks about the cold, yawning emptiness of the sacrificial chamber. Every time she imagines great flames reflected on those oil-black walls. But it doesn't matter, because at this moment, the God-Emperor is her only ally. As far as she can tell, the High Consul's loyalty is to Ominira alone. There's little doubt that if aiding Enitan and her sibling presents even the possibility of provoking the Empire, the Consul's oath will evaporate. She can't blame them for prioritizing their own people.

She paces around Deora's apartments, her insides a sick tangle of nerves. The countess left for some fundraiser at the museum, leaving Enitan alone with all her fears. What if the Imperator caves to the looming threat of the Council? She doesn't really need Enitan. All she's managed to do thus far is come up with a single name, and he's not even one of the councilors.

News finally comes in the form of Guiyin, who brings her up to the Imperator's personal infirmary. Apparently, the sacrifice was insufficiently sedated and tried to attack her before they were killed. Now she'd like a cup of tea to calm her nerves. Servants usher Enitan through a series of circular doors, each flanked by a pair of sentinels. The last door is unguarded. She knocks on the smooth, dark screen-surface until the Imperator's face appears. She looks tired. She says nothing, merely nods once and vanishes as the door slides open. Enitan strides through.

Relief settles over her shoulders when she sees Xiang curled up on the bed, the Imperator seated beside them on a sumptuous black divan. Enitan drops down beside her sibling, who links their arms together.

"I've told them everything," the Imperator says.

After a moment of heavy silence, Xiang sighs. "So. What now?"

The Imperator's eyes widen. "You can speak Orin too?"

Xiang snorts, jerking a thumb at Enitan. "Of course. After living with this one for fifteen years?"

"Anyway," Enitan cuts in, "it's obviously not safe for them on Koriko."

"If they return home, they'll doubtlessly be hunted down," the Imperator agrees.

"But it's even less safe here," Enitan says, rubbing at her reddened eyes. She can't remember the last time she slept more than a few hours.

"For now," Xiang says quietly.

Enitan blinks at them.

"If we manage to get rid of the Council, we'll be fine." They wave a tired hand at the Imperator. "Menkhet's said I could stay here indefinitely."

Enitan looks over at her, eyes narrowed.

The Imperator nods. "They need to recover, with lots of rest and certainly therapy too. Who knows how long that'll take?"

Enitan takes Xiang's hand in hers. "How do you feel?"

They let out a quivering breath, a soft sound between a moan and a whimper. "I don't . . . remember much of what they did to me. But everything feels *thin*. Like the whole world is a piece of paper that could tear apart at any moment." That tiny ghost of a smile again. Part of Enitan's heart breaks off. "Therapy sounds good right about now."

"My best therapists are no strangers to secrecy," says the Imperator. "They're more loyal to me than my own sentinels." Something in her eyes makes Enitan think that the Imperator has made it very clear what the consequences of betrayal would be. "But even if they weren't, they're permanently hidden residents of the Imperial apartments. They're functionally invisible to the rest of the world, so our enemies are highly unlikely to be looking for them."

"So it's settled, then?" asks Xiang. "I'll stay here until I'm okay again. And in the meantime, I'll help you take down the Council."

"Absolutely not," Enitan and the Imperator say at the same time. They flinch and glance at each other.

"The Imperator and I will handle this," Enitan says, turning back to Xiang. "I'm not going to let you put yourself in harm's way—"

"They *broke* me, Enitan. Made me into one of their weapons. I want them to pay for that."

The Imperator sighs. "Revenge is a double-edged blade."

"Yes, thank you, Menkhet," drawls Xiang, glaring, "but a Vaalbaran maxim won't cut it here. Besides, everyone thinks I'm dead. I'd be the perfect spy."

Enitan rubs at the space between her eyebrows. "We'll discuss this later. For now, rest. *Heal*." She holds Xiang's hand just a bit tighter. "Promise me you'll stay here and won't go doing anything foolish."

"Shouldn't I be telling *you* that?" Xiang smirks. "I'm your elder, you know."

"In age alone, and only by a few months," Enitan retorts, slipping off the bed and onto her feet. "I have to go serve tea to a bunch of ass-holes now. I didn't have a credible excuse." She turns to the Imperator. "How do I get back up here?"

"Actually," the Imperator says, standing, "it'd probably be best if you didn't. The Korikese hostage, visiting the infirmary so soon after the unobserved sacrifice of a kidnapped Korikese soldier?" She holds up a hand when Enitan begins to scowl. "Let's give it a few weeks. Just for now."

"I don't think that's necessary," Enitan says. "Your bedroom is on this floor."

The Imperator's eyes narrow. "And why would that matter?"

Enitan shrugs. "Half the palace already thinks I'm your mistress." She doesn't miss the deep red that spreads up to the Imperator's ears.

Xiang coughs loudly.

"My bedroom," says the Imperator, quite stiffly, "is on the other side of this level, accessed by entirely different tubelifts. And between here and there are legions of servants and sentinels—"

"Fine," growls Enitan. She spins back around and yanks Xiang into a bone-crushing embrace. "You still haven't promised me you'd stay put."

Xiang crosses their arms. "I'll stay. At least until I'm better."

"Thank you."

"I have to go too." The Imperator holds out a datapad to Xiang. "I thought you might get bored, so I . . . downloaded a few books and dra-mas for you. I'll send the help we spoke of soon."

Xiang takes it from her. "Oh. Thanks."

Enitan pulls them in for another hug before forcing herself to let go. Then she follows the Imperator into the tubelift.

"Thank you," she says as soon as the transport closes around them.

"It's nothing I didn't promise," the Imperator answers, looking anywhere but at her.

"I don't recall you promising lodgings or therapy or entertainment. Your end of the deal was just to save their life." Enitan crosses her arms and looks away from the Imperator as well. "Thank you."

"Of course. They're your sibling," says Menkhet—Ancestors, *the Imperator*, as though it should matter to the God-Emperor how Enitan thinks of her. "But you're welcome." The tubelift slides open, and she steps out.

"I hope the event you're headed to isn't as terrible as the rest," she says. She turns, and they finally make eye contact. "You need to request a floor, you know."

She strides off, and when the tubelift closes again, Enitan presses her palm to the screen surface.

◆

The event is indeed as terrible as the rest, though this time her aristocratic hosts are the type that will barely even look at her. A servant instantly ushers her into a corner and grabs the serving tray as soon as it's full. Apparently, Duchess Huadija wants Enitan to be as unseen as possible. She wants to enjoy authentic Korikese tea, but certainly not the Korikese person required to make it. It doesn't help that Enitan's purported affair with the God-Emperor has made her this month's obsession in the Splinter, as Huadija isn't known for sharing the spotlight.

"You understand," the servant says, their pinched expression sufficiently apologetic.

"Of course," Enitan replies, and stays out of the way.

While the guests sip their tea, Enitan skims through one of the books downloaded onto her communicator. It's a collection of Homeworld poems, rescued from the ancient archives of one of the seeder ships. She's halfway through a string of haiku when the servant swings by again.

"You can go," they say. "No one will notice if you leave."

Enitan snorts and packs up her things. As soon as she's back in her room, she grabs the holoprojector and slips into the bathroom.

"We can extract you both in a week," says the High Consul, after Enitan's done talking.

"Actually . . ." Enitan laces her fingers together. "I'm going to stay in the capital."

Their lips pinch as if suppressing a yawn. Enitan suspects she woke them up; she has no idea what time it is in Ominira, but it must be late.

"Why?" they ask. They sound bored, but there's a curious glint in their eye.

Enitan fidgets for a moment. There's no getting around this. "The Imperator has asked me to spy for her, just as you did. But on her own people."

The High Consul doesn't so much as blink. "And you agreed to help her."

"Yes, and I will do so to the best of my ability unless it conflicts with our arrangement." Enitan forces herself not to break eye contact. "She has made certain promises regarding Koriko."

The High Consul's thin mouth twists as their eyes narrow. "Then why are you still talking to me?"

"I can't take her at her word," Enitan says. "And there's still the matter of Xiang."

The High Consul tilts their head. "I assume you still want me to take your sibling." Their tone is cool, distant.

"Not just yet," says Enitan. "They're recovering. In a few weeks, perhaps."

"I will make the arrangements."

"Thank you, sir." Enitan straightens. "I have a request."

The High Consul arches a brow. "Another?"

"I want you to make Xiang a citizen of Ominira. Koriko isn't safe."

"That's not part of our arrangement." They give her a sympathetic look that's just a shade too practiced. "Rescuing someone and harboring them are two very different things, Enitan."

She keeps her voice even. "I've gleaned information from you as well. Some of which the Imperator might find—"

"I hope you're not threatening me," the High Consul says with a poisonously sweet smile. "Because if you are, you won't live to regret it."

Ancestors, that was stupid. But she had to try. Her life means precious little if Xiang's ends. "Forgive me." Enitan ducks her head. "I would never betray you."

"I know." The High Consul lifts an arm, as if reaching for their own projector. "Sleep well, Enitan."

"Wait." She leans forward. "The Imperator wants peace just as much as you and I do. She could be a powerful ally to you."

Their face hardens. "I suggest you focus on your job and allow me to do mine. Menkhet was raised by Adehkonra himself. She's just as bloodthirsty as he is and his daughter *was*, if not more so. Don't speak of this again."

Enitan presses her lips together. "Yes, sir."

They nod to themself. "I can grant your sibling Republic citizenship if you complete a task for me."

Enitan sits up. "What is it?"

"Go down to the lower city. There's a tavern called the Tipsy Croaker—"

"Attractive name."

"Indeed. I need you to be there at precisely midnight to pick up a parcel."

"From whom? And then what?"

"It'll be obvious who you're meeting. You'll receive further instructions upon receipt." The High Consul steeples their fingers. "Do you accept?"

"I'm not sure I'll be allowed out of the palace," says Enitan.

"You don't have sentinels guarding you for a reason. They know you're aware that Koriko will pay the price if you step out of line. Besides, I doubt you have access to any of the hangar bays to make your escape from, or really anywhere else they don't want you to go. Your cage may be the size of a city, but it's still a cage."

Enitan presses her lips together. She's skeptical, but it's possible that no one cares if she goes down to the bowels of the Splinter. If she's murdered there, they'll just scrounge up another hostage. She has to try. She bids the High Consul a stiff farewell.

She looks up the exact location of the Tipsy Croaker before getting dressed. She pulls on her temple frock and slips on her sturdy boots. No one will wonder about a monk wandering around the lower levels. Vaalbara's vowed religious are known for sojourning to less fortunate neighborhoods across the Empire and scolding the denizens there for their debauchery. She packs the poignard and half her currency chits. They should cover a drink or two at least.

The sun sinks below the horizon as she makes her way to the palace's main tubelifts. She presses her hand to the side of the transport.

"Level 2,187," she orders. Nothing happens. Then she remembers. Each level is vast; she has to input a specific destination. "Tavern district."

She waits with bated breath while the capital's artificial intelligence inputs her request and charts a route that somehow won't smash her into the thousands of other speeding transports within the Splinter. Without warning, the tubelift slides horizontally, plummets down a few hundred stories, executes a quick left turn, and falls once more.

Enitan, only slightly ruffled, steps out into a cacophony of sound and scent. The hues here are similar to those of the palace, though the blacks are a bit bluer and the grays have a hint of green. The noise more than makes up for the still-monotonous color scheme. Sound echoes up from every corner, laughter and shouts and jarring music. Citizens run and stroll and dance, weaving themselves into a molten tapestry. And the smells: cheap, oily food and sweet, watered-down alcohol.

Enitan stumbles into the din, trying to force her face into the serene, pious guise of a monk who's just taken her vows. Experienced enough to think herself enlightened, but too young to know better. Huge windows along the cavernous outer wall of the Splinter light her way, showing off the sunset as it fans scarlet flames over the darkening sky. Enitan marvels for a moment at how much it's like—and yet unlike—Jilessa. Like a reflection in a warped mirror.

As Enitan moves farther away from the tubelifts and deeper into the lower level, the scenery changes. The establishments in the central plaza cater to sheltered nobles and rich tourists who want to spend the day pretending they're poor. They don't want to go too far, though. The streets are still clean, and the servers wear bright uniforms and brighter expressions. But as she continues on, the wide, polished passages taper into long, grasping fingers. Nooks and crannies become choked with grime and refuse like filthy fingernails, sizable puddles of fetid water pockmarking uneven paths.

Even as Enitan pulls the side of her hood over her nose, she commends the High Consul's ingenuity. These streets are the perfect rendezvous point. Everyone in the Splinter seems to pretend this part of the capital doesn't exist. Children swaddled in rags juggle cracked marbles for tossed change. Elders meander through the district, begging for food. The environmental support here is patchy at best, especially near the looming walls; scattered groups huddle around outdated heaters, shivering in the shadows. And these are all legal, acknowledged citizens of Vaalbara.

Enitan's eyes go wide as she takes in the destitution around her. The allied communities of Koriko seem a utopia by comparison. Or rather, they were, until Vaalbara invaded and forced her people to assimilate into its trade- and military-fueled economy, which was, of course, engineered to take for itself, no matter the fantasies of shared resources and reciprocity it feeds its subjects. The Imperial economy keeps those it parasitizes just comfortable enough to survive—though not so comfortable that they might challenge their betters—all while further enriching those at the top.

This was the goal for Koriko all along. Until the conquest, money was a foreign concept in the communities. Enitan pauses to hand a couple of skeletal children a few of her currency chits and goes on her way. She has to wonder whether a utopia so easily subjugated was ever a utopia at all. But what they had was better than *this*, at least.

The Tipsy Croaker, she discovers, is an apt name. The building resembles a plump amphibian that's fallen into a jug of wine, its sagging gray form supported by a crumbling excuse for a porch. A dying tree slouches in a cramped plot of dirt, its gnarled roots framed by soiled napkins and wrappers. Fading gray-green tiles from the clay roof lie shattered about the courtyard, lying in wait for an unsuspecting foot.

Enitan pushes through the entrance—there isn't even a door, just a beaded curtain—and into the tavern. A tall, wide woman with a face like sliced marble nods at her from the bar. Enitan walks over, her boots squelching on the sticky floor. She's here almost two hours early; now she regrets being so cautious.

"What'll it be, monk?" the woman demands, leaning over the counter on her elbows.

Enitan shoves a hand into her satchel, only to find her cash missing. Either she's been robbed, or she gave everything to those kids. Understandably, she's been distracted lately.

She looks up sheepishly. "I'm actually waiting for someone."

The woman wipes her hand on her top, a ratty shirt with a lewd phrase silk-screened on it. "Look, you gotta order something or get—"

"Sorry I'm late!" A tall woman slides onto the stool next to Enitan.

It takes a moment for Enitan to realize who she is. She's in brightly colored civilian dress. Her hair, combed out of its braids, wreathes her face in tight brown curls. And she's wearing amber contacts. Enitan's heart begins to pound. *Ancestors, is this a setup?* Her whole body tenses, ready to flee or fight. But if the Imperator has come here herself, she wants to talk. This also means she's been following Enitan, either via communicator or by another method.

"You know, you almost look like the Imperator," says the woman. "Maybe if you were in better shape."

"Thanks," says the Imperator, deadpan. She lifts a menu from the grimy counter. "We'll have the mushrooms. And also two leaf dumplings." She digs into a pocket and slaps down a handful of shiny new currency chits. She turns to Enitan. "Booth?"

Enitan grits her teeth and slides into a seat upholstered in patchy mud-green cloth. They're in a secluded spot, just out of sight and earshot of the handful of other patrons.

"So," drawls the Imperator, her gaze maundering the mostly empty room. "What are you doing here?"

"What are *you* doing here?" Enitan snaps. It's not like the God-Emperor can pull rank in disguise and with no backup in a place like this. "I can't believe you followed me."

"I asked you first."

The mushrooms arrive in a chipped ceramic bowl. A server with an oily mustache plants a small grill at the center of the table, along with a pair of wooden sticks.

Enitan uses her sleeve to wipe the grime off a piece of orange fungus before skewering it. "Well, I was about to drink myself to an early grave."

The Imperator selects her own mushroom. "Maybe you should've brought cash, then."

"Maybe the last Imperator shouldn't have taken over a country that places no value in little bits of metal and expected it to stick," Enitan retorts, her voice low. She grimaces inwardly; it's not her best comeback, considering she's still eating off the Imperator's suspect generosity. She pulls her skewer off the fire and blows on it. "Why did you follow me?"

The Imperator shrugs. "I saw you sneaking out of the palace. Thought you might be up to something interesting."

If Enitan weren't so stressed right now, she'd chuckle. "You're really that bored?" She nibbles at her mushroom. It's surprisingly good, salty and tangy and chewy.

"Yes." The Imperator huffs. "My former position as commander in the fleet has been filled, so I only see war plans once they're practically set in stone. And the Council has been pulling more heavily on its strings lately; I've had little more to do than sign documents these days."

"Oh, you poor thing," Enitan retorts, her words coming out as nearly a hiss.

The Imperator's answering smile is like a gilded scythe: beautiful from afar, deadly up close. "You know, you're rather hard on me, Enitan Ijebu."

Enitan pauses, not quite sure how to respond.

"You've been like that since the first day. It's refreshing," the Imperator says. "Everyone else is afraid to speak their mind around me."

Enitan wonders whether she ever truly feared the Imperator before her. She respects her, in a way, for what she's done with the mess she inherited. And Enitan will always owe her for saving Xiang—she has no regrets about committing her own life to secure her sibling a better chance at one.

The arrival of the leaf dumplings interrupts her introspection. While the Imperator's happily distracted with those, Enitan pulls her communicator out of her pocket. An hour and a half until she's supposed to pick up the parcel. Tapping her fingers against her jaw, she looks up at Menk—the Imperator. She has no idea how to get rid of her. But she might as well eat while she figures it out.

The leaf dumplings in Ijebu are far better, but these are decent. They're filled with shredded bean curd in a sweet huchroot sauce. Enitan munches at the crispy bits she's always loved. They almost taste like home. Almost.

"I hope that's temporary, for your sake." She waves a hand at the Imperator's dyed hair.

"Oh yeah." The Imperator chews, swallows. "It's just a spray. I'll wash it out tonight."

A thought occurs to Enitan. "Is this . . . what you looked like before you were crowned?" Cosmetic procedures are heavily restricted within the Empire. One of the rare uses is to change the appearance of the Imperators. Their hair and eyes are turned to the deepest of blacks, the same color as the First God-Emperor's.

"My hair has always been black. But yes, my eyes were like this. The surgery nearly killed me. They do it without anesthesia, you know."

Enitan lifts her brows. "And you call *us* barbaric."

"Enitan." The Imperator puts down her leaf dumpling with the utmost solemnity. "I have never called your people barbaric."

Enitan lifts her eyes to the grimy ceiling and shrugs, taking another bite of bean curd. "Okay."

"What Vaalbara has done to Koriko was and is unforgivable."

Another bite, larger now. "I'm aware," she says tightly.

The Imperator frowns. "Is that all you have to say?"

"Nope." Enitan plants her elbows on the table. "Congratulations on not being the absolute worst you could be. If you just turn around, I'll give you a pat on the back."

The Imperator's frown deepens into a scowl.

"I just watched you invade another country with an army of *my people*, who, let me remind you, were kidnapped and conditioned into serving the same monsters who razed our moon. I suppose you only like being held accountable when it's convenient and comfortable for you."

The Imperator shakes her head ruefully. "No, I'm sorry—"

"Please, stop apologizing," says Enitan, pulling her hands under the table and digging her fingernails into her palms, "and *prove* how sorry you are by keeping your promise."

The Imperator flinches as if she's been slapped. "You expect me to betray you. I thought we discussed this."

Enitan picks at a mushroom. "I can't afford not to suspect that."

When a server comes to take away their dishes, Enitan glances at her communicator once more. How quickly time flies when one least wants it to. Fifteen minutes until she meets whoever it is she's supposed to pick up the parcel from. She needs to get the Imperator out of here.

The Imperator looks away. "I'm going to get drinks." She slips out of the booth and heads to the bar, fingers flexing.

Enitan rubs at her eyes. A flicker of green. She jerks upright just as her caped shadow slides into the Imperator's seat. They're holding a tall glass of Triple Solar Eclipse, the bar's signature drink.

"You're early," Enitan says.

"You shouldn't have followed me." They lace their hands together over the table. "You can't stop this."

"*I* was sent here." An alarm goes off in her head. "I was told you had something for me."

They laugh, a harsh guffaw that holds no humor at all. "Oh, Spirits."

Spirits—they're Ominirish. "I thought you were a badly trained Vaalbaran spy." Now there's a full-blown mental siren going off.

"I thought you were just a hostage." They let out a long, slow breath. "Well, this complicates things."

"The High C—" She cuts herself off. "We've both been manipulated."

"It would seem so." They offer her a thin smile. "Nevertheless, I have a job to do."

"But why would they send me—"

Oh.

She shoots to her feet, frantically scanning the tavern. "Menkhet—"

The Republic spy grabs her wrist. She hisses in pain as they yank her arm and slam her down hard onto the table. Their hand clamps tightly over her mouth. *"Don't."*

"Let her go," says a lethally quiet voice, "and maybe I'll think about letting you live."

Enitan twists to face the Imperator. There's a festive tumbler in each of her hands.

The spy releases Enitan. "Forgive me." Their gaze lifts to the Imperator's enraged face. "The High Consul sends their regards."

They shove a hand into their cloak. Before the Imperator can even drop the glasses, the world erupts into flame.

◆

When Enitan comes to, she's choking. Dense, acrid smoke floods her mouth and lungs. Sound returns to her slowly, snaking through the horrible ringing in her ears, and then all at once. A klaxon begins to ring, its metallic screech reverberating in her skull. Dozens of people, perhaps more, are screaming. Weeping. Enitan hoped she'd never have to hear the sounds of people dying in every direction ever again.

She's flat on her back. Her eyes are closed. Her head is cradled in something soft and human. She forces in a breath, keeping her eyes firmly shut.

More noise. A familiar voice, barely audible. "Please don't die, please don't die, please—"

Enitan opens her eyes. There's blood and fire everywhere. "Fuck."

"Oh, thank God," says the God-Emperor, her soot-smothered head very close in Enitan's vision. "You're alive."

Enitan looks up. They're outside the tavern, under one of its roughly hewn windows. "How long have I been out?"

"No idea. I just came to."

Enitan's frock clings to her body, thick and wet and suffocating. She reaches down to pull it away from her skin, sucking in a breath when her hand comes away dripping red. The heavy pall of smoke and dust hanging over them has barely begun to dissipate. They can't have been out for more than an hour. Probably less.

Enitan shifts and groans, and it's only then that she realizes she's lying in the Imperator's lap. She tries to sit up, but a wave of agony hits her so hard she's forced to lie back again.

"You jumped in front of me," says the Imperator. There's a trickle of blood running down her face.

"Did I?" Enitan's face scrunches up. *Ancestors*, even that hurts. "That was stupid of me."

The Imperator chuckles, low and rusty and so very sad. "Yes, it was." Her voice rings very loudly in Enitan's ears.

"I'm glad you're not dead," says Enitan. Her skull feels like it might burst.

"I'm glad you're not dead either. And I'd like it to stay that way." The Imperator's arms slip out from under Enitan's head. "Move your arms so I can open your frock."

"You should at least buy me dinner first," says Enitan, unable to squeeze out a laugh. "Well, I suppose you did."

The Imperator's eyes are inflamed from the smoke. Or perhaps she's been crying, as unlikely as that seems. "I have basic medical training. Let me take a look at your wound." She holds up a portable medkit.

"You just carry that around with you?"

"Old habit from the front lines," the Imperator replies. She pops the kit open. "I'm pretty sure you have a concussion, but I can't do anything about that. I've called someone, but they won't be here for another half hour. We're pretty far from any decent hospitals."

"Figures," Enitan murmurs, raking her nails over the floor. "It's not as if peasants need proper medical care, right?"

A drop of the Imperator's blood lands on Enitan's face. The Imperator reaches down and brushes it away, her fingertips barely touching Enitan's skin. "I know. I'll work on that later. But for now, please move your arms to the side."

She does so, her breath coming in fast, shallow spurts. The Imperator reaches into her boot and pulls out a dagger. In a single quick upward motion, she slices the frock from the hem to the collar and pulls aside the crimson-soaked cloth. "Oh fuck," she says, which is the last thing Enitan wants to hear.

"Am I going to die?"

"There's quite a bit of blood."

"I could've told you that."

"It's far more blood than I expected."

"Well, fuck indeed."

"The blast threw you into a cabinet," says the Imperator. "There's a lot of glass."

"I suppose your basic medical training doesn't cover this?"

"Well, sort of." The Imperator lifts a hand and sweeps hair out of her eyes. The dark tangles are caked with sweat and ash. "But it's best not to move large lodged objects. They help keep severed vessels closed. If I mess with them, you'll probably bleed out."

"So I'll have to wait for your medic."

"I mean, I might be able to stitch up some of the other wounds." The Imperator rummages through the medkit. "Shit, there are only bandages in this one. I'm sorry."

"Stop." Enitan heaves a trembling sigh. She can almost feel the glass in her, slicing deeper with every desperate breath. "Stop. Apologizing."

Her people do not believe in the afterlife of the Vaalbarans, a neatly tiered system of heavens and hells. This must be the end. After this, only nothingness awaits her. Enitan tries to make peace with that. It's surprisingly easy. She feels weightless, unmoored. She lets her eyes fall closed for a few glorious seconds before forcing them open again.

"This isn't about Koriko. I put you in danger by coming here. I never should have—" Menkhet pinches her arm hard, but Enitan's senses are too dulled now to register pain. "Don't fall asleep, Enitan, please. Stay with me."

Enitan doesn't reply. Her eyes flutter closed, and she slips back into darkness.

NINETEEN

Enitan awakens in a cocoon of unfamiliar velvet quilts. She wiggles her toes and fingers, flexes her feet and hands, and works her way through her entire body. She feels almost no pain at all; either she's been given enough drugs to down a saber-toothed saljutiger, or she's been out for a while. Probably both. She sits up and looks around.

The chamber looks like it's been carved out from a single boulder of onyx. The walls are space-black and faceted, polished to a mirrored sheen. There's little decoration or furniture, only the gargantuan bed beneath her, a slender nightstand, and a plush black chair with a single occupant. It's the Imperator.

There are deep circles under her red-rimmed eyes and her face is ashen; her once-warm complexion looks more gray than brown. And yet, Enitan looks at her as if for the first time. Objectively, she knew the Imperator was captivating from the moment she met her—there's no debate to be had there. But now it is no longer just a fact, as it was at the end of the attack on Iëre. It is a feeling, and that makes it all the more terrifying. If only the world they lived in were different.

Enitan yawns, very loudly, and the Imperator starts, suddenly awake and blinking blearily at her. Her mouth curves into a concerned frown. Enitan has no idea what she herself looks like at the moment, but it can't be good, because the Imperator's worried expression deepens with each passing second.

Enitan shoves off the covers and scooches toward the edge of the bed.

"Get back under there," says the Imperator. Her voice, though sleep-roughened, brooks no argument. "You just came out of a healing pod."

There's only one healing pod in the entirety of Vaalbara: the Imperator's own. Enitan slips back under the quilts. "My pension doesn't cover that," she jokes.

"I saw a bite mark on your side," says the Imperator, combing a hand through her tangled braids, which are back to their normal light-sucking black. "Fifty-five tiny scars, according to the pod, so it was a qimafur. How in the world did you get one to maul you? They're such gentle creatures."

Enitan pulls the covers up to her chin. "It was a bloodmaw, not a qimafur."

The Imperator's face scrunches up in confusion. "A bloodmaw? What's that?"

The scars throb painfully, as if tugging on the memory pulls the frayed nerves with it. "It's what we call a qimafur when the sentinels have trained it."

The Imperator's posture stiffens. "What happened?"

There's a sarcastic answer on the tip of Enitan's tongue, but she holds back. "They thought I was part of a drug ring, or at least that's what they claimed after the fact. Followed me out of an alley and waited until we were alone—no witnesses—to sic their pets on me." She settles down on the heap of pillows behind her. "They're still cute, at least until they maul you."

The Imperator pushes herself up from her chair. She looks like she wants to strangle someone. "Give me their names."

Enitan snorts. "They're already gone. My . . . friend got rid of them while I was in the hospital." She struggles not to picture Ajana. She can't start crying right now.

"Friend?" The Imperator winces. "Ah." She sits down again, closing her eyes. "Listen. I think you should return to Koriko."

Enitan freezes. "Wait. I know I haven't made much progress, but—"

"That's not what I mean. Taking out the shadow councilors should never have been part of our agreement. You're a civilian, and not a Vaalbaran one by choice. This isn't your burden."

"It certainly is. And what would you do if you sent me back anyway—bring another hostage here to replace me?"

The Imperator's eyes are trained on the cuffs of her long sleeves, as if the black embroidery is the most fascinating thing she's ever seen. "I—when we came back, the physicians told me you might not make it."

"And?" prompts Enitan, with as much gentleness as she can muster. It isn't much.

"I don't want you to die."

"And I don't want any more of my people torn from their homes and brainwashed into a slave army. I have to stop this."

"I can deal with the Council on my own."

Enitan swallows a retort about the Imperator's shoddy track record. "There's no reason to. I'm right here."

"I'll still relinquish Koriko," says the Imperator. She lifts her head, her eyes finally meeting Enitan's. "I never once considered going back on my word, if that's what you're worried about."

"I'm not worried about that, not anymore," Enitan says honestly. "I trust you. And you should trust that *I* value my own life."

"I don't." The Imperator looks away again. "I don't trust that, Enitan. There's a shuttle coming for you and Xiang at dawn."

"Do you really think," Enitan says, voice low, "that the Council won't hunt us down? Koriko isn't free until they're gone, and neither are we."

As she says the words, something crystallizes in her heart. Saving Xiang and saving Koriko are one and the same. Her time in the Splinter has made that clear—what life would the two of them even be returning to? One where they're treated like criminals upon the very bones of their Ancestors? An occupied homeland can never be home for them.

Enitan thinks back to the last conversation she had with the High Consul, the one before they nearly got her killed. They'd refused to protect Xiang. She's done putting the survival of her family and her people in the hands of heads of state. No one can fix this for her, not even Menkhet.

Enitan forges on before the Imperator can interrupt her. "We were never safe. Not before all this, not even as children. Do you really think they'll let a political hostage and an escaped sentinel go free? With everything we've seen, everything we've done?"

"I told you before that I wouldn't protect you if doing so endangered my mission. I know now that I *can't* protect you, not here. But I can ensure your safety outside of the Splinter. I've personally selected members of my own honor guard to watch over you. Fenris was an outlier, I promise." The Imperator holds out her hands in a pleading gesture. "Please, believe me when I say I have your best interests at heart."

Enitan never thought she'd fight to remain at the heart of the empire that destroyed Koriko—the irony almost makes her laugh. "I do believe you. But I'm not leaving."

She must finish this. For Xiang, for Ajana, for her people. Enitan has long dreamed of the way things could be. And now, she can make that change happen herself. Even if she didn't fear for her life outside the Splinter, to run away now would be a betrayal of everything she's come to believe in. She didn't destroy Koriko. Saving it shouldn't be her burden. But there's no one else.

The Imperator opens her mouth. "But—"

"No." Enitan shakes her head. If she doesn't fight for Koriko's future, then she doesn't deserve one at all. This truth is in her core, solid as steel. "I'm not leaving, Menkhet. I have to finish this."

The Imperator's teeth are clenched so tightly, Enitan feels a sympathetic ache in her own jaw. "I wasn't *asking*. I am officially dismissing you," she says, her words so soft Enitan has to strain to catch them. "Don't make me drag you back to Koriko myself."

Enitan pinches the bridge of her nose. She's never liked being coddled—fussing over people has always been *her* job. She finally understands why Xiang complains so much when she does it. Frankly, she finds the Imperator's overly keen regard for her well-being supremely annoying. The Imperator's features harden into the expression she probably wears when she wants to intimidate the politicians and aristocrats of her court.

But Enitan is no politician, and she's certainly no aristocrat. "They tried to destroy my family. That probably doesn't mean much to you, Your Imperial Majesty. I may be but a lowly peasant, but I want to see their punishment through myself."

The Imperator's face closes in on itself. She draws in a deep, deliberate breath. "I don't think that's what you're really after."

Enitan drags herself off the bed, nearly toppling over. The Imperator surges forward in an attempt to help her. Enitan wrenches herself away from the woman's hands and grabs on to the bedpost. "You don't know *anything* about me."

"I don't have to." The Imperator glowers at her. "You're leaving tomorrow, Enitan." They stare at each other for what feels like full minutes before she breaks their gaze with a sigh. *"Fine."*

"Good." Enitan takes the opportunity to look at her surroundings. "Where exactly am I?"

"The private healing chamber in my apartments." Menkhet stands. "Do you need help getting back to Deora's suite?"

"I'll be fine." Enitan shoves herself off the bedpost. She's only a little light-headed. "Does Xiang know?"

"No, and I've taken measures to ensure that they won't. It's up to you if you want to tell your only family that you were nearly killed."

Enitan sighs. "What time is it?"

"Early morning." The Imperator tucks her hands into the pockets of her tunic and walks Enitan to one of two identical doors.

When she steps over the threshold, Enitan looks back with a half smile. "Thank you again, Menkhet."

The Imperator waves off her gratitude with a tired hand. "Yes, well. Repayment for saving my life, even if you *were* the one who almost got me killed."

Enitan slips away, and the door slides shut behind her. A tubelift deposits her near Deora's apartments, and she orders breakfast on her communicator as she walks. The countess is preparing for yet another museum gala and won't be back in time for supper tonight. Enitan is a few corridors away from her destination when the merchant she served appears in her path.

"Lady Enitan of Koriko!" he exclaims. "What a coincidence."

How long has he been following her? "How nice to see you again . . ." She's forgotten his name.

In the privacy of her own mind, she refers to almost everyone in the Splinter by their title or profession. It's different from how she sees the headwoman of Ijebu, for example, whose oath to protect Koriko describes her better than her own name. But in the Splinter, using titles helps her keep things in perspective. The last thing she wants to do is get attached to anyone here in any way, including the Imperator. *Especially* the Imperator. She makes sure to admonish herself every time she catches herself slipping up. Deora is one of very few exceptions. She may be obnoxious at times, but at least she's trying to be better, in her own way.

If the merchant notices Enitan trailing off awkwardly, he doesn't show it. "I'm happy to see you alive and well. No one would suspect you almost died last night!"

"Thank you?" If he knows about the incident, so must all of society.

"Coming from the Imperial residence, are you?" The merchant gives her a conspiratorial smirk.

Ancestors. "Yes." Enitan keeps walking.

He follows her. "My companions and I would like to thank you for Iëre."

She comes to such a sudden stop that he nearly crashes into her. "Excuse me?"

That suggestive look spreads like wildfire over the rest of his features. He wiggles his sculpted eyebrows at her. "Come now. Everyone knows it was you who finally convinced Her Imperial Majesty to knock some sense into those islanders."

Despite the frequent sneering and the occasional mocking remark, the rumors that she's the Imperator's secret lover are harmless. In fact, they've proven beneficial; hundreds of requests for her tea services pour in every day. But it's another thing entirely if people think she's making decisions for Vaalbara's precious God-Emperor. The last thing she wants is to be considered a serious threat.

She gives the merchant a stern frown. "I wouldn't say I have that kind of sway over the Imperator."

The merchant only laughs. "Lady Enitan, Marchioness Zumas saw the Imperator carry you into the palace herself."

Well, shit. Enitan is pretty sure that didn't happen, but by now she knows better than most how little the truth means in the palace. Especially when the ridiculously gossipy marchioness is involved. Correcting the merchant again will probably only encourage him, so she suffers through his retelling of fabricated events woven together by a string of aristocrats with too much time on their hands.

When they finally reach Deora's chambers, the merchant leans in close. "And I heard you threw yourself in front of the Imperator when the assassin attacked. How romantic."

Enitan steps into the countess's suite and presses her hand hard into a wall panel, slamming the door in his face.

◆

"How did you know she'd follow me?" Enitan keeps her voice low, though she'd really like to yell.

The High Consul folds their hands together. "I—"

"Don't lie to me," Enitan warns. "I spoke to your agent before they set off the bomb."

"I'm pleased to see you alive and well." The High Consul's tone is as patronizing as that of the worst nobles she's served.

Enitan considers her next words carefully. "How can you expect me to trust you now?" She can't send Xiang to the Republic, not after this.

They sigh. "It would have been foolish for us to reveal the identity of our agent. You needed plausible deniability—"

"You told me I'd be meeting someone for a drop-off," Enitan hisses. "Not luring the Imperator in unguarded so you could assassinate her."

"You have my most profuse apologies," says the High Consul, without an ounce of remorse in their voice.

For a moment, all Enitan registers is the low burbling of the bath beside her, which she's turned on as usual. This time she's trying the river setting. "Four civilians *died*."

"I don't see how that's your concern." The High Consul sounds supremely put out. "They would barely have blinked, had your life been the one taken."

"Am I supposed to find solace in that?" Enitan scoffs. "Your operative nearly took me with them."

"Please, allow me to make amends," the High Consul says. "I have a new proposition for you."

"And that is?" Enitan asks, despite the flat refusal already on the tip of her tongue.

"Kill the Imperator."

Enitan's blood freezes. "Pardon?"

If she gets caught, the honor guard won't simply kill her. They'll keep her alive for as long as they can. They'll torture every drop of information possible out of her. She doesn't even want to imagine the joy Fenris's type would take in interrogating her. Her torment would be eternal.

"Your reward will reflect the risk." The High Consul's head tips as they lean back in their seat. "War is on the horizon again, Enitan. We knew this treaty would only be temporary. When the Republic defeats the Empire a second time, we will restore independence to Koriko. Is that an acceptable offer?"

It would be, if she hadn't been promised the exact same thing for what seems like much less. Enitan crosses her arms, resisting the urge to point out that the Republic didn't actually win the first time. The God-Emperor had Ominira nearly beaten before he'd surrendered.

Enitan knows she should accept, if only to have insurance. If the Imperator backs out or something happens to her—though Enitan hopes it won't be at her own hand—she must secure her people's freedom some other way.

She nods, and the High Consul smiles. "Good. Gaining access won't be a problem. You've already done an excellent job of . . . ingratiating yourself." The pause is the worst part. "I'm certain it won't be much of a challenge. And we will, of course, retrieve Xiang if you are . . . detained."

"No, you won't. You never answered my question earlier. I cannot trust you with my family, given what you've just done. I know it was for your people, and I'd have done worse in your position." She shakes her head. "I'll make arrangements on my own for Xiang."

"Then I wish you the best of luck." The High Consul glances away. "We'll speak again soon."

"No, we won't."

Their eyes narrow into dangerous slits. "Pardon?"

"I will no longer inform you of matters within the Imperial Court. From today onward, this will be my last and only job for you."

"Enitan, you—"

She cuts them off. "If I kill the Imperator and they discover we've been chatting, Vaalbara will make the last war look like child's play. You will see in time if I succeed." She waits for their response, fingers flexing in her pockets.

"Watch out for yourself," says the High Consul slowly, their eyes glittering. "She finds you useful, not equal."

Enitan gives them the same smile she's given dozens of aristocrats. "You're no different, sir."

Without another word, she picks up the holoprojector and drops it into the bath.

TWENTY

Xiang sits up in bed when Enitan steps through the door the next day. "What's that?" they ask, gesturing at the ceramic bottle in her hands.

Enitan lets out a little huff of laughter at the spark of interest in her sibling's eyes. "It's kamadin," she says. "It's a bit like wine." She plucks out the enameled stopper and hands it to Xiang.

They hum a reply as they take a hesitant sip. "Fruity. Nice."

Enitan sits on the bed, the quilt wrinkling as she scoots closer. "Are you all right?"

"I—" Xiang stiffens, every visible muscle in their limbs tensing. She's never seen them coil up like this before. "I'm fine."

Enitan's heart twists in her chest. She reaches over and squeezes their hand. Their fingers remain limp and cold in hers. "Look, it's okay to not be okay." She crawls up the bed and sits beside them, lying back against the headboard.

Xiang shrugs, their shoulder gently bumping hers. They take another sip of wine. More of a gulp, really. Enitan begins to regret bringing it.

"They kept me and the others in this cold, dark chamber," Xiang says, when the bottle is half-empty. Their voice is distant. "No food, no water, no rest—alarms blared night and day, not that we had any sense of time. Sometimes they'd let bloodmaws loose on us." Their mouth screws up, as if trying to keep the words in. They come tumbling out anyway. "By the time they brought us in for conditioning, our bodies were beaten down and our minds were malleable as clay. But they were still *our* minds. They underestimated me, underestimated all of us. It was only a matter of time."

Enitan doesn't know what to say, so she says nothing. She lifts her other arm and wraps it around Xiang's shoulders.

"I hate how similar we are," they say.

They mean their people and the Vaalbarans. "I know. Me too."

The Imperator brought Xiang a couple of suits, all cut in the regional fashion. Disguised in silver embroidery, they look like any upper-middle-class Imperial. Enitan and Xiang were always taught that Vaalbarans were superior. But with the lies stripped away, the river between Koriko and its conqueror shrinks to a stream.

"Maybe if we were more different . . ." Xiang hands her the kamadin. "Then this would all make sense."

"All the things they say separate us don't really matter," Enitan adds, sampling the alcohol. The sweet, dark liquid scorches her throat as it goes down. She takes another, deeper sip. "There's never anything rational about cruelty."

"I can't sleep. I can't eat," Xiang whispers. "Whenever I close my eyes, I see the flames. I hear their screams." A tear swells at the corner of their eye, but they wipe it away with the edge of their sleeve before it falls. "Why can't they just let us *be*?"

Their hunched, broad shoulders shudder in the mirror at the foot of the bed. Their angular face is drawn, closed off. Their eyes and nose are red. Enitan's heart wrenches again, harder, as she watches tears roll down their cheeks. Xiang doesn't try wiping them away this time. She thinks back to the days when the provisional governor forced everyone in the community to attend her monthly addresses. He always spoke of the myriad gifts Vaalbara would bestow upon them. He spoke of civilization and ethics and humanity.

"I wish I knew." Enitan comforts as best she can, setting her gloved hands over Xiang's. The Empire has broken her sibling, and she's not certain they'll ever be able to heal completely. There is nothing civilized or ethical or humane about this. "I'm so sorry."

They sniffle, rubbing at their nose. "So am I."

Enitan searches their eyes for a glimmer of the old Xiang, the one who existed before their world fell apart. They're still there, she thinks. Just buried under a weight they should never have had to bear. She tilts her head down, touching their temple to her own. "We're going to fix this. I promise."

She almost believes it herself.

◆

The sun is sliding into the mist below by the time Enitan leaves Xiang. When she steps out of the Imperial infirmary, the Imperator's waiting for her. She leads Enitan to yet another of her private drawing rooms. Enitan notices for the first time that the Imperator always slows her long-legged gait to match her pace.

"I've been reading my predecessor's journals," says the Imperator, dropping into a cushioned seat. "I never understood why he treated your people as he did but still offered you the opportunity to earn full citizenship."

Enitan shrugs; this is common knowledge on Koriko. "It was an empty offer, nothing more. A distraction. He wanted my people to bleed ourselves dry trying to become Vaalbaran, even if we could never be in more than name. Better that than to have us shedding blood resisting him." The image of Xiang hunched over their practice exam books stabs into her like a knife.

"Yes." The Imperator averts her gaze. "But I didn't know that until now. I know you've told me to stop apologizing, but it's hard not to."

"Still. Don't." Apologies won't undo the annexation. Actions will.

"Okay." She fidgets for a moment. "I took the liberty of canceling all your appointments for the next four weeks."

"I don't need that long."

"You will." The Imperator looks away. "I have bad news."

Enitan waits.

"I've received plans for an invasion of Ominira in a year."

Ice water churns in Enitan's stomach. "I assume that entails the mass kidnapping of more of my people soon."

"Very soon. In slightly less than a month."

It's so much closer than she feared. Enitan sucks in a breath, the familiar embrace of anger constricting her chest.

"They're moving forward in part because of a small uprising on Koriko." The Imperator forges ahead before Enitan can interrupt. "Not in your community. In Lishtaqa. It began a few hours ago. And it's spreading."

"Is there actually an uprising?" asks Enitan. Her voice isn't nearly as strong as she'd like it. "Or a fabricated excuse for them to arrest and conscript all the suspected 'conspirators'?"

The Imperator looks impossibly sad. "I . . . I don't know."

Enitan's fists ball into the front of her tunic, nearly tearing the fabric in two. "So I have one month to kill them all?"

The Imperator crosses her arms, her eyes hardening. "There's no way you can take them out before this is underway, Enitan. They're powerful, protected. And we have no leads."

When Enitan looks up at the Imperator, something in her face makes the supreme ruler of Gondwana flinch.

"You could die."

"Only if you don't help me."

"I want them dead too." She sighs. "But something like this requires careful planning and flawless execution. And we don't have enough time."

Enitan stands. "I have an idea. I overheard a monk complain once about how hard it was to get Imperial permission to move into the palace. Do you actually give it, or does the Council?"

"It's one of the few duties they've left to me," replies the Imperator.

"So I imagine you have some sort of private record of everyone you've authorized to live here, with information on their relatives and whatever else is of note." Enitan leans forward. "I need you to find someone."

The Imperator makes a sound that proper etiquette would call lethally close to a snort. "Cahiyr's aunt, right? Her name is Erseydis. She lives in a monolith a few hours away by shuttle."

Enitan thinks of Ajana, of how terrifying her last few moments alive must have been. She looks the Imperator in the eye. "I think it's time we paid Erseydis a visit."

TWENTY-ONE

A pair of hands seizes Enitan's shoulders and rattles her from sleep that night. She jerks upward, a scream filling her throat, and a hand clamps down hard on her mouth. White teeth flash in a razor-sharp smile. Enitan claws at the gloved fingers, heart slamming against the cage of her ribs, until her attacker leans forward, light sliding across her face. It's the Imperator. Her iron grip matches the steel in her eyes, and neither softens until Enitan ceases her thrashing.

"What are you doing?" Enitan hisses.

"My spies tell me Erseydis has two new servants arriving in the morning." She releases Enitan and bends down. When she straightens, she's holding a forest-green uniform identical to her own. "If we leave now, we'll get there before them."

Enitan shoves off the covers and snatches the disguise out of the Imperator's hands.

"Sorry," the Imperator says, brushing back her newly burgundy hair. "But we won't get another opportunity like this."

"It's fine." She's been awoken in far worse ways, before Ajana. Getting shaken into consciousness is worlds better than getting the end of a shockstaff.

Without a word, Enitan pulls off her pajamas and starts dressing, yanking on the servant's uniform. When she turns around, she finds that the Imperator's brown face has turned maroon.

She snorts. She didn't know people could blush so deeply without passing out. "Right, probably improper by your standards. My apologies, Your Supreme Holiness."

"It's not—" The Imperator shakes her head. "Let's go."

The aircraft sits on the Imperator's private landing pad, back on her residential level. The ramp glides open at their approach, revealing a dark shape standing at the back. The figure steps out of the shadows and into the dim light of the waxing moon. It's a sandy-haired man in the neat gray of the Imperial staff. He's tall and broad, with ivory skin. He looks perfectly human, until his right eye begins to rotate horizontally in its socket and he doesn't so much as flinch. He's a synth.

"A pleasure to meet you," says Enitan, swallowing her surprise.

"Enitan Ijebu, the pleasure is mine. I'm Kulta, an agent of the Imperator." The synth smiles. "Please, don't worry about my eye. I'm affecting repairs as we speak."

"I thought synths were outlawed by the Church," Enitan blurts, following the Imperator back into the shuttle. There's no way that came out politely, and for a moment, Enitan's terrified she's more like the Vaalbaran nobles than she'd like to admit.

Kulta laughs humorlessly as he buckles himself into the pilot's seat. "We are. The primary Ominirish ambassador to Vaalbara, the man who commissioned us, didn't like our personalities. He wanted us torn apart for scraps, but our new Imperator spirited us away before we were deactivated. The only person who knows my craft-siblings and I are here is her. And now you."

"Wouldn't you be the perfect spy out in the Splinter, then?" Enitan tightens her own belt. "Or perhaps assassin?"

"My craft-siblings and I don't blink, eat, or breathe," replies Kulta. "You would have noticed eventually. My creators made me this way on purpose. In Ominira, crafting a synth that's indistinguishable from humans is a crime punishable by death. We've made quite a few modifications, but there's only so much that can be done."

"And as far as killing anyone," says the Imperator, "all synths are programmed to be unable to cause lasting harm."

Many of us didn't want that fiddled with," Kulta adds.

"What about human operatives?" asks Enitan.

Kulta laughs, swiveling his seat around to face them.

"The Council controls my official spy network," says the Imperator. She turns to Kulta and nods.

The synth's face goes perfectly blank for a moment. "Autopilot activated."

The shuttle purrs like a mossicat and leaps into the air. Enitan almost yelps as the sudden force of the takeoff shoves her into the plush cushioning of her seat.

When the Splinter is little more than a speck, Kulta reaches into the pocket of his robes and produces a pair of delicate silver collars. "Shall I tell her, Menkhet?"

"No, I'll do it." The Imperator takes the collars and gives Enitan an agonized look. "So, ah, Xiang isn't actually the first Korikese sentinel to break conditioning. They're just the first to get away with it long enough to do real damage."

"So we won't be impersonating *servants*, then." Enitan struggles to keep her breath steady. "Are those shock collars?"

"Yes," the Imperator says, her voice gentle. "No longer functional, of course."

Enitan forces her gaze away, narrowing as much of her focus as possible onto the shifting landscape beyond the window. An ocean of fog has washed over the broken earth, craggy mountains jutting from the roiling white like islands. "How many of my people are enslaved to your nobles?"

The Imperator's eyes cast downward. "A few hundred."

"I don't understand," Enitan whispers. "I thought slavery was one of the Great Sins."

The Empire never made its conquered toil in factories, in fields, or inside asteroid mines for a reason. (The ones who were considered sufficiently law-abiding, at least.) Even if Vaalbarans didn't think Korikese too unskilled for even the simplest of labor, their culture forbids them from forcing work upon other free souls. In the Empire, one's own labor is honored above all else. But once again, that rule doesn't seem to apply to nobles.

"It is." The Imperator looks away. "Or it should be."

Enitan turns around, takes a collar from the Imperator, and fastens it around her neck. She says nothing for the rest of the trip.

◆

The magistrate's monolith home, Emgai, is about twenty times smaller than the Splinter. It houses approximately forty thousand people. Though the shuttle has only just begun its approach, Enitan knows already that the architecture inside the floating city will be a mixture of round and triangular shapes. Emgai's seven-faceted surface gives it away as a Yyita-era monolith. Enitan knows far more about Imperial architecture during the reign of Imperator Yyita than she ever wanted to. Despite her best efforts, some of the facts Xiang spent hours reciting before their exams wormed their way into her brain.

Just as the shuttle touches down on the magistrate's landing pad, Kulta hands Enitan two small glass vials: one tinted blue, the other a milky white. Enitan mumbles her thanks, and the ramp extends to reveal a short man in the same dark green she and the Imperator are wearing.

Enitan expected a flood of anguish to overcome her upon seeing one of her people like this. She feels the absence of emotion instead, a deep, soulless void where she knows empathy should be. She feels utterly empty.

The man's round, lined face is completely blank. "I'm Iris. Follow me," he says in a hushed tone. "You will be prepared for inspection."

He leads them through three doors and down four different passageways. Each hall is expansive and brilliantly lit, with ornate foliate designs running over the tiled ground. The floor is entirely devoid of people, which makes sense; a magistrate wouldn't want to be caught smuggling kidnapped Korikese into her apartments. The layout is similar enough to the upper levels of the Splinter, though the inhabitants are cut from what a palace resident would consider lesser cloth. This tier of the monolith is home to judges, officials, and the like. The top floor of Emgai is the abode of the local earl.

Iris waves them into what appears to be the servants' quarters: rickety bunk beds in stacks of four; threadbare curtains; and a peeling paper screen, behind which is a toilet, a sink, and a row of towels.

The door grinds open as Iris hands them their washcloths (for which, he warns them, there will be no replacements). A tall woman strides in, her dark eyes wide with hollow amusement. Her uniform is the same as Enitan's, save for the gray circle over her chest.

"I'm Lavender, Miss Erseydis's attendant." She laughs suddenly, her voice high and wild. "Welcome to the highest tier of hell."

There's a grim set to Iris's mouth. "Lavender . . ."

"Well, it's true." Lavender leans against a bunk. "You should have hidden your freedom better. You're going to wish you were sentinels again."

"Lavender!"

She throws her arms out, and now Enitan notices the red around her eyes. "What? They're going to find out soon enough."

"She might hear you."

Lavender snickers. "As if she'd ever come all the way down here."

"Can you just . . ." Iris looks as if he's on the brink of tears; his lower lip trembles. "I'm going to get Rose."

Lavender lets out a shaky breath. "I'm sorry. I don't mean to scare you. But you should know what awaits you."

"How scared should we be, exactly?" Enitan asks in Korikesian.

"Don't—don't do that." Her mouth is a small, tight line. "If anyone hears you speak that, you're done."

"I assume you don't mean dismissed," says the Imperator.

"Well, that," replies Lavender. "And then dead."

Iris returns with a slender-faced person in tow. "This is Rose."

Rose scratches at their short, spiky black hair. "She'll rename you after a Homeworld flower, if you haven't figured that out already." They squint at Enitan and the Imperator with dark-brown eyes. "You got your washcloths?"

Enitan nods.

"Well, you better get cleaned up." Rose rolls up their sleeves. "You'll be naked for inspection."

The Imperator takes a full step backward. "What?"

"Erseydis wants us . . . pristine." They cross the room and pull a small box out from under their pillow. "You'll get used to it. Also, if you have any scars or blemishes, you should tell me. I'll cover them up for you." They open the box, revealing an assortment of liquid concealers.

The door opens suddenly, and a man rushes in. There are three gray circles on his uniform. He glances at Enitan and the Imperator. "This will have to wait," he says. "Apparently, Erseydis has invited this archduke and some friends over for dinner. I have to run to the market, so I need one of you to bring up her breakfast."

"I'll do it," says Enitan.

"I wasn't talking to you," he says. "You got off the shuttle—what, seven minutes ago?"

"It's just delivering her food, right?"

"If only," says the man. His lips curve into a tiny grin that makes the hairs on the back of Enitan's neck stand at attention. "I'm Cyani. I've been here the longest." He turns to Iris. "Go get—"

"I said I'll do it," says Enitan. "What's she going to do to me?"

"There's no way to know," says Lavender, a note of warning in her voice. "She's grown erratic lately, and she's the worst in the mornings."

The Imperator crosses her arms. "For example?"

Rose holds out their left hand. At the center of their palm is a reddish-purple spot, puckered at the edges. "She made me stick a needle through my hand a week ago."

"She threw her boiling-hot tea at me yesterday," Iris adds, his voice sharp. "I can show you the burns if you need proof."

The Imperator shoots Enitan a concerned glance.

Enitan bites the inside of her cheek. There's nothing to worry about; the magistrate will be dead before she does anything to her. "Well, that's all the more reason for me to get my turn over with."

Cyani frowns. "She's not going to like that. She hasn't checked you over yet."

"She has a serious hangover," says Lavender. "In the state she's in, she might not even notice."

"She mixes us up anyway," adds Rose. They squint at Enitan. "I can't tell if you're clever or just lucky."

"Fine, if you're so eager to be abused, you can do it." Cyani sighs heavily. "Come with me."

Enitan throws one last look at the Imperator before following Cyani out the door. He leads her silently up a short flight of uneven stairs and to a faintly scratched door. She waits for it to slide open.

When she waves her hand at it, Cyani laughs before reaching to grab a knob. Enitan stiffens in embarrassment as he pushes her into a hot, cramped kitchen.

"Hey, Carnation," Cyani calls. "I brought one of the new ones. She wants to take Erseydis breakfast."

A deathly pale man steps into the light, his skin nearly as white as the cloud of steam flowing around him. Breath catches in Enitan's throat; she recognizes him immediately. He's her eldest brother. Or rather, *was* her brother before the headwoman reassigned her to Xiang. His muscular form has withered to skin and bone, and his once-flowing curls have been shaved down to the scalp. But there's no mistaking the harsh lines of his jaw, the green eyes somehow still bright with mischief. His name was Saban. *Is* Saban.

She never much liked him. After she moved, they spoke only two times via communicator before they both decided to stop pretending they were fond of each other. But the realization that his home and freedom have been torn from him still hits her like a punch to the gut.

"Do you have a death wish?" Saban arches a brow at her.

Enitan can't muster up any words. She shrugs stiffly. He doesn't recognize her. Sorrow and guilt and anger and relief twine together inside her.

Saban raises his eyes to the ceiling. "Ancestors, I'm surprised they let you live. You're a bit damaged, aren't you?"

Enitan blinks at him, a familiar pinch of irritation returning speech to her. "Excuse me?"

Cyani taps his temple. "What they take from you during conditioning, you don't always get back." He gives Saban a flat look. "Don't be an asshole." To Enitan he says, far more kindly than he's been to her the entire morning, "You'll be fine. Our people are good at adapting."

Saban huffs, stacking covered, hand-painted plates onto an enamel tray. "Sorry," he says. "I didn't mean— I'm like you. I remember very little from before." He leans over and spits into the cup of tea.

"It's fine." Enitan forces a smile as she takes the tray from him. Her gaze drifts to the dishes. "Is that the Bowl of Ogenias? I thought it was destroyed in the massacre."

Saban lets out a mirthless chuckle. "No. The sentinels might have shot the old headman and burned his housepod down, but they took the Bowl first."

Enitan's grip tightens around the handles of the tray. She wants to throw the whole thing onto the floor, break every beautiful stolen object in the Empire. Even the destruction of her own people's treasures would be better than this.

"Don't worry," Saban drawls. "She only has it on loan, from the Imperial Museum."

"Yes, that makes all the difference," she mutters under her breath.

"Go up the staircase on the right. Her bedroom is the second door on the left." He walks over and opens the door for her. He lays a hand softly on her shoulder as she steps out. "Sometimes it gets better."

Enitan says nothing and leaves, tamping down the emotions welling up within her. She pauses halfway up the staircase to pour some of the blue vial's contents over each dish. The last few drops go into the tea. The magistrate's door glides silently open at her approach.

"Lavender," the magistrate says, scribbling something on a datapad with a slender stylus, "if the tea's too cold, I'll have to hurt you again."

Enitan sets the tray down on her desk and steps away. She waits for the magistrate to take a sip before she speaks. "I checked it myself, miss."

The magistrate looks up at her, the delicate quartz flowers in her hair shivering at the sudden movement. She's beautiful, technically. But while the pretty merchant in the Splinter is a harmless fool, this woman is anything but. She is cruel and certainly clever, or she wouldn't have been inducted into the Council. Enitan finds everything about her revolting, from her rippling silver-blue dress to her dainty freckled nose.

The magistrate puts down her stylus. "Who are you?"

"Your new slave," Enitan replies.

"I don't like that word." The magistrate frowns, piercing a bright-red berry with her fork. "I prefer to call you servants."

Enitan snorts. Terminology is what she balks at? "Call us whatever you want, miss. We've been kidnapped from our homes, brainwashed, and forced to serve you."

"Obviously not very well." The magistrate chews and swallows. "I think I'll have to discipline you." She reaches into the desk and pulls out a small tear-shaped device. She presses the button at the center. When nothing happens, she presses it again, harder. "You're not Korikese, are you?" She slowly rises to her feet.

"I am." In a single smooth motion, Enitan reaches down into her boot and pulls the poignard free. "Sit down, miss."

The magistrate returns to her seat, glaring up at Enitan with an impressive amount of contempt. "Who's paying you?"

"No one," Enitan says, stepping around the desk. "I'm doing this for my people."

The magistrate cocks her head, blinking. "What did the Imperator promise you?"

Enitan narrows her eyes. "If you don't mind, *I'll* be the one asking questions."

"And yet." The magistrate's attention returns to her breakfast. "I'll never understand the obsession of Imperators with savages." She selects a slice of sughfruit. "The last one had quite a soft spot for Koriko."

"We have very different understandings of that phrase," Enitan says.

"Of course we do." The magistrate is staring at her now, dabbing clumsily at the juice running down her chin. "We tell our armies that it is our divine right to spread the seeds of the Empire wherever we wish, but you and I both know that's wulushit. It's that you barbarians aren't able to see beyond the quotidian minutiae of your shallow lives. You eat and you breed and you do your tribal dances. You're incapable of understanding much else, including the glorious purpose of Vaalbara. I suppose your parochial little mind can't grasp that you Korikese simply can't govern yourselves. You need us to tell you what to do. And yet you call us tyrants."

Jeong's words resurface in her consciousness. *We need them.*

Enitan falters, unease twisting in her gut as the accusations piled up in her mouth dissolve. "You're not going to deny it, then? That you're one of the powers behind the throne?"

"If you're here, then you already know." Her tone is that of an adult speaking to a very slow child. "So what is it you want? Money?"

Enitan adjusts her grip on the poignard. "Tell me the others' names."

"You'll just have to kill me." The magistrate's smile drips with condescension. "I'll die before I betray them." Her smirk falters when she tips forward in her chair. She looks over at the half-finished meal on the desk, sweat beading on her forehead. Her mouth slackens as she realizes what Enitan has done. "Poison?"

Enitan holds up the white vial. "The antidote. Tell me what I want, and it's yours."

"We should have killed you all," the magistrate snarls. "You Korikese are nothing. No, worse than that. You're parasites."

Enitan takes a deep breath. Then another. When the heat behind her eyes cools, she lifts the poignard to the magistrate's throat. "I'd rather not hurt you more than I have to."

The magistrate tries to stand and fails. Her knees give out, and she crumples to the floor. Enitan crouches beside her, watching her alabaster skin grow nearly translucent.

"You don't have to die," Enitan tells her. "Just give me what I've asked for."

"Savage bitch," she snarls.

Enitan sits back, her mouth twisting. "This poison doesn't kill."

It doesn't take long for the toxin to begin its true work. The rest of the color drains from the magistrate's face as the pain settles in, flaring in her stomach and bursting outward as it's designed to. Kulta chose well.

"I order . . . ," the magistrate gasps out, her fingers clawing desperately at the embroidered rug. Her voice jumps in pitch. "I order you—just end it . . ." Her veins lie in stark relief on the white canvas of her face.

"Names, miss."

"Oh God." Tears coalesce over the swollen inner rims of the magistrate's eyelids. Her gasping turns into shallow gurgling.

"Your nephew, Cahiyr, has already told me everything," Enitan lies. "All I need you to do is confirm a few things for me. I suggest you tell the truth." She taps the edge of the poignard to the magistrate's pallid cheek. "Because if your information doesn't match, I'll have to pay him another visit."

Enitan knows that if the magistrate were in her right mind, she'd probably see through this paper-thin lie. Enitan knows this woman told her idiot nephew almost nothing at all; he said as much in the merchant's chapel. But the magistrate's nerves have been set alight. It appears she can barely breathe, let alone consider the truth of what Enitan has said.

"There are th-three of us." A fit of violent coughs rack her body. "There were four, but t-two died . . . Banurra, he . . ." She stops to hack up blood.

"I know, you're his replacement," Enitan snaps. "Give me the names of the others."

"I only . . . I only know the identity of one other," she chokes out. "It's a safety measure, and I—"

Enitan grits her teeth together. "What's their name?"

"Vidra," she wheezes. "Vidra Ingilazar. Now please . . ." She reaches for the white vial, her whole arm trembling.

Enitan hands it over and watches the magistrate drain the opaque contents. Her eyes glaze over within moments. Then, with a final, shuddering gasp, she dies. As her soul leaves her body, a torrent of raw emotion pours into Enitan's. She's never killed anyone before. Horror and sorrow and disgust—at herself, at what she's done, at the body, at *everything*—fill her lungs, suffocating her. She can't draw enough air to scream, let alone breathe.

She cannot bear this.

Enitan stumbles to her feet and slumps against the wall. She slips twice before getting herself fully upright again. The twelve steps that carry her across the room take more strength than she has left. As the door slides open, she tips forward into waiting arms.

"Is it done?" the Imperator asks, leaning her against the wall like a plank of wood.

"It was so easy," Enitan whispers, breath hitching in her throat. She ducks her head; she has no idea what expression she's wearing.

The Imperator hesitates before placing her arm, very lightly, around Enitan. Her other hand falls softly on Enitan's elbow, the touch so delicate it's as if she thinks the other woman is made of glass.

"How do you live with this?" Enitan rasps, leaning into the contact without quite meaning to.

The Imperator pulls her closer, tucking Enitan's head under her chin. "I don't know."

"Does it ever get better?"

The Imperator draws back and bends just a little, looking Enitan in the eye. "I like to believe that it will."

TWENTY-TWO

Enitan drifts in and out of sleep. It's not quite the anxious tossing and turning she expected, but her slumber is still far from peaceful. A few hours before dawn, she gives up trying to rest and clambers out of bed. She finds herself on the balcony, staring down at the rustling forest hundreds of meters below. A vast gray river snakes through the woods, bifurcated by a tall hill a few kilometers upstream. Enitan squints; there's an uneven black shape atop the hill, some ancient fortress from a bygone era. She checks her communicator, pulling up the Splinter's automatically generated travelogue. The ruins apparently served as an Imperial palace when the heart of the Empire was still on land.

The sun rises pale and white over the horizon, illuminating a sky of curdling gray. Thunder rumbles, and the lightning that flashes soon after is barely bright enough to cut through the ashen sky. The weather complements Enitan's mood perfectly. She returns to her bed as the steady drizzle outside swells into a full storm. The floor heaters on the balcony protect her from the chill but do precious little for the rain.

Killing someone is easy. Living with it, as she's discovering, is hard. What she feels isn't guilt, exactly. The magistrate deserved to die. If anything, Enitan is angry—angry that she has to murder to free her people. And she will have to do it again and again, because her enemy knows nothing of compromise, peace, or empathy. The weight of that terrible responsibility presses down on her like a blanket of wet wulu-fleece.

Her communicator chimes with her morning alarm. Groaning, she rolls out from under the covers once more and gets dressed in silence. She has yet to see Deora again, and she's dreading the inevitable moment she will. Twelve minutes later, she finds Xiang seated on the infirmary's couch, their morning meal spread out on the low table before them. They're watching the news on the holoscreen the Imperator had installed.

"Good morning." Xiang yawns, handing her a mug of spiced, double-caffeinated tea.

"It's not, but thanks." Enitan settles down onto the couch.

"That's . . . rather graphic."

"Pardon?"

Xiang tilts their head at the screen. Laid side by side are three images of the magistrate's corpse. Blood—more than Enitan remembers—runs from her ears, eyes, nose, and mouth. Enitan sets down her tea and lifts her arm. The screen's motion sensors register the movement and the volume increases by four levels.

". . . *Magistrate Erseydis Batorva was found dead in her apartments last night. After reviewing the evidence and discovering vast debts, the local authorities have ruled her death a suicide.*" The anchor's visage pops back up on the screen, her blue eyes grave. Enitan recognizes her face immediately, if not her name; as a prominent resident of the Imperial city, she's been invited to a handful of gatherings. "*Although she was a relatively minor official, this is the nation's third self-inflicted death by a politician or noble since the signing of the Treaty of Ilesa.*" The holoimager zooms in on her face. "*Could there be a link, or are these tragedies a mere coincidence?*"

Xiang pulls a plate of dainty fruit fritters onto their lap. "Was that your doing?"

Enitan arches a brow. "How'd you guess?"

"Menkhet said you missed breakfast yesterday because you wanted to sleep in. You *never* sleep in." Xiang squints at her. "You should've helped her come up with something more believable."

Enitan drops a dollop of spicy blue sauce into her soup. "I'm sorry I didn't tell you. I didn't want you to worry."

"Don't be sorry." Xiang drains their tea and grins at her. "Just let me help with the next one."

Enitan swallows a spoonful of sweet, peppery broth. "No."

"But—"

"It's too dangerous. You're still healing." She recoils inwardly, hating how much she sounds like Menkhet—

Ancestors, how hard is it to remember a title? she rebukes herself. *She's the Imperator.*

"The therapists say I'm fine."

"You're still not back to normal."

"There's no such thing as normal anymore." Xiang crosses their arms. "I asked, and they've all said my treatment is basically over."

Enitan frowns. "Basically?"

"In a few days, I might even be ready to fight—"

"We're not fighting anyone," Enitan snaps. "We're eliminating the shadow councilors, quickly and quietly. We're not running around challenging them to honor duels."

Another anchor's voice fills the room. *"We've just received a startling update from the head of Emgai's sentinel force. Servants' quarters have been found in the magistrate's residence. They appear well used, but the staff are nowhere to be found. Could it be that this seemingly simple suicide was, in fact, murder?"*

"Nice bit of alliteration there," says Xiang. "Where are the, ah, *servants*?"

"The Imperator's 'holding cells.' They're receiving treatment too." Enitan refills both of their mugs. "We said they could return to Koriko if they wished, but they chose not to, obviously. Until it's safe." *When the Council is gone.*

She's about to turn off the news when a blurry video fills the holoscreen. It's obviously a Korikese community, what with its stacked rings, lush surroundings, and a glowing slice of Jilessa behind the skydome, but she's not certain which.

She turns to Xiang. "Is that Lishtaqa?"

"No, that's Tamoko." They point at the housepods. "The roofs are all peaked and a bit curled at the tips. Their master architect said she was inspired by burning leaves."

"That's nice," says Enitan, her palms growing sweaty. "Why is a Splinter reporter on Koriko?"

Xiang laughs. "Stop worrying. It's part of the big news stations' new cultural program—they send a representative to communities to show how 'rustic' they are."

But then the video dips dramatically, shooting below the tiled, gently sloping roof of a pre-conquest temple, and proves them wrong. It's utter chaos. Crowds of snarling Korikese pour from their housepods and spill out into the streets. There's fire everywhere.

Enitan lurches forward for a better look when she sees that the horde is decked out in flowing ceremonial robes and armed with ritual daggers and swords. The words on their lips are in Akyesi. This riot is orchestrated wulushit, obvious to any actual Korikese person. But then again, this fake rebellion isn't for the benefit of Koriko.

"These Korikese villages have been trading goods for generations. But now it's evident they've been sharing more than tribal drums and

ritualistic carvings." A third anchor folds her hands together over her desk. *"The rioting and looting in Lishtaqa have spread to nearby Tamoko. Now, I understand it's unkind to call the provincials savages, but . . . God, this is barbaric!"* She trembles as she stares into the camera, visibly holding in laughter.

"Rioting? *Looters?"* Xiang exclaims. "I thought it was a full-fledged revolution!"

Enitan's gut twists. Ancestors, she wants to punch something. "Revolutions are organized and often merited. No one in the Empire thinks our people are capable of anything but senseless crime." Now the sentinels can round up any innocent Korikese they want, in addition to anyone desperate or foolish enough to actually try joining the rebels.

Enitan freezes when her own face flashes onto the screen.

"Any Splinter residents who want their own authentic Korikese tea ceremonies should make arrangements with Enitan Ijebu, the political prisoner from Koriko, as soon as possible," the anchor continues. *"Because if this disturbance spreads any farther, her skills may not be enough to save her from the Imperator's axe."*

Audible laughter this time. The holoimager swivels to focus on an anchor back in the Splinter. *"Actually, Joagna, if there's any truth to recent court gossip, her other skills just might—"*

Xiang turns off the holoscreen with a flick of their wrist. They turn to her, taking her hand in theirs. "Are you okay?"

Not in the slightest. "I'm fine—" Her communicator chimes, a gentle reminder from Kulta. "Shit." She crams three fritters into her mouth and pulls Xiang into a hug. "I'm late. I'll see you later."

They hug her back just as tightly. "You need to take care of yourself too."

Enitan forces a smile back at them before she heads out. The door slides softly shut behind her.

◆

The Three Virtuous Columns of Vaalbara are simple: constant innova-
tion, excellent infrastructure, and efficient administration. The words
are inscribed along the doorway of Her Imperial Highness Princess
Sunnetah Kiniun's sepulcher. The Columns aren't very poetic, but they
did once help Vaalbara consume three-quarters of the planet, and lay
claim to the rest of the system besides.

The princess's final resting place lies at the edge of the palace's
middle floor. The hallway leading up to the internal tomb glitters. Between a dark stone floor and a ceiling of silver lights are walls of fine
white quartz. Every ten paces, the Vaalbaran flag stands at attention,
black and ancient. Millions have died beneath that piece of cloth, and if
the Council succeeds in their plan, so will countless more. Titanium and
steel sconces cradle blue flames, dragging flickering shadows from the
flags and casting them down the length of the passage.

The doors slide open at Enitan's approach; the sepulcher is open to
all. The chamber is huge, the ceiling stretching nearly as high as the
church's. On the right side, a single massive window reveals a vast cross
section of sky. The weather remains terrible; curling banks of cumulo-
nimbus clouds dominate the glass. The entire left wall is a waterfall
rushing down into a thin pool bordering the bottom, then into a series
of slender recesses. Each slice is a black abyss; the water rushes through
the rest of the Splinter via smaller water fixtures. At the bottom of the
city, it coalesces once more into a waterfall, misting into oblivion somewhere far above the land.

And at the center is the princess herself, her coffin housed at the
heart of a thirty-meter statue. Her gargantuan feet are planted firmly
upon a shimmering sunburst, an old but unforgotten symbol of the early
Ominirish Republic. She wears a flowing black robe, a thousand square
meters of obsidian and onyx and jet. On her head, resting within a mag-

nificent cloud of carved hair, is a crown of tektite and black opal. The platinum points shine like spear tips. At the center is a red diamond the size of a skull, so dark its facets only glint with color as one moves.

Sunnetah's pleased eyes gaze downward over all those who have gathered to pay respects. The plaque at her feet decrees her many titles: she is the Lady of Flame and Blood, the Protector of the Old Lands, the Great Storm of the One Sea, Sole Child of Imperator Adehkonra the Great.

Or is the look on her carved face one of scorn? A pride so deep it might as well be disdain for everyone who did not have the honor of being her? There is a point at which the line between regard for oneself and contempt for all else blurs into nothingness. For the Vaalbaran princess, that line would have been more nebulous than for most.

"We all loved her," says a familiar voice, concerningly close. "She exemplified everything an Imperator should be. Everything Vaalbara *could* be."

Unlike me, she doesn't say, but Enitan hears the words nevertheless.

It startles her how brittle the woman sounds, as if she's a column of sand that might crumble apart if pushed too hard. She feels a twinge of sympathy for the Imperator, one she immediately sweeps away. The Imperator is just that—the *Imperator*, the monarch of the most successful empire in human history. (If success is measured in lives snuffed out and lands taken, at least.) Even though her power is, at present, mostly nominal, she certainly doesn't need Enitan's pity.

"I was never meant to become God-Emperor, you know that." She says her title almost hesitantly, as if she still doesn't quite believe it's hers. As if she doesn't want it.

Enitan doesn't bother disagreeing. The princess, their God made flesh, and now made stone and gem above them—*she* was made for the throne.

No. The throne was made for *her*.

Enitan's gaze slides over the statue, to where Sunnetah gestures with a massive, many-layered stone sleeve at what appears to be a celestial entourage. Rendered in silver mosaic behind her, the princess's otherworldly handmaidens have giant pearls for eyes and quartz shards for teeth. "The Seven Daughters," murmurs the voice. "The followers of the southern regional god Asett. The statue is made in her image. As far as deities go, Sun always liked Asett more than her father."

Enitan finally turns to face her. "And where is the old Imperator now?" she asks. "I heard he was journeying through the wilds as a wandering hermit or something."

"Who knows? Adehkonra was always eccentric." The shift of the Imperator's shoulders is more of a nervous jerk than a nonchalant shrug. "How are you doing?"

Enitan waves a tired hand. "I'm as fine as I can be, given the circumstances. You?"

The Imperator chuckles sympathetically. "I imagine I'm coping a bit better."

She leads Enitan over to a row of thick satin cushions and settles down on one.

"The massive debt was a nice touch," Enitan tells her, just as Kulta materializes before them. Perhaps someone will try to link Erseydis to Ominira too.

The synth smiles as the hidden door slides shut behind him. His expression freezes for a moment, and Enitan hears the click of a heavy lock. "Actually, that was the Council's doing. I hacked the late magistrate's accounts, and it appears all her debts are to entities that don't exist. A part of her cover, I assume." He drops down on a cushion. "Radan, the official who brought you here—what was his excuse for landing in the middle of nowhere?"

"He said he wanted fresh food and sent most of the sentinels out to forage." Enitan shrugs, trying to affect as nonchalant an air as possible. But her pulse is ringing in her ears. If the Imperator realizes that she met with the High Consul . . . "It seemed odd at the time, but I had more pressing personal concerns to worry about."

Kulta's hands form a pyramid over his lap. "Well, as it turns out, Radan occasionally moonlighted as a drug mule." He pulls apart his hands, and a light flashes in the center of one palm—a holographic projector inlaid into his skin. A rotating shape unfurls over his fingers, a three-dimensional image of two men in a pavilion, the official and a bearded man in a fitted coat. "After a little digging, my youngest craft-brother discovered that Radan had been skimming for at least a decade. It appears that his boss found out. The little evidence we were able to scrounge up suggests that the brigands who ambushed the shuttle were in fact assassins."

Enitan isn't about to correct him. She leans forward. "How does Vidra fit into this?"

"He's the boss," says the Imperator. "A minor noble and a media magnate by profession. I've been trying to have him arrested for thousands of other crimes, but the Council warned me off. Said there was too much of a spotlight on him—he's a famous patron of the arts. Massive donations to almost every cultural center in the Empire." She lifts her hands in an exasperated gesture. "Now I know why. He's one of them."

"Vidra's going to be meeting with an up-and-coming drug manufacturer named Dennach in a few days to finalize a new deal," Kulta says. "My craft-siblings and I aren't yet sure what, but it involves a new form of skeyroot." He holds a small cloth bag out to Enitan.

She takes it and pulls it open. Inside is a spoonful of glittering black dust. "Poison?"

"In its current quantity," replies Kulta. "It's Shimmer, chemically enhanced powdered skeyroot. It's an extremely potent euphoriant in small doses. In larger ones . . ."

Enitan hands the pouch back to him. "I know it would be suspicious if we used the poison I gave Erseydis, but why drugs?"

"It's well-known that Vidra himself is a recovering addict. He's been actually quite open about it." Kulta tucks the Shimmer into his pocket. "It won't be hard to push the story that he relapsed and over-dosed."

Enitan stares at him, her mouth going dry.

The Imperator leans forward. "If you don't feel comfortable—"

"He deserves it." This man had a hand in kidnapping Xiang and murdering Ajana.

The Imperator nods. "He does."

"There's one more thing," says Kulta. "Because of the nature of this meeting, Menkhet and I will both be able to accompany you."

Enitan arches a brow.

"It's a party," says the Imperator. "Unfortunately, I won't be able to kill Vidra myself, since I'll be attending formally."

Kulta cants his head toward her. "Enitan, I'd be more than happy to do this alone. I hacked my pacifist module years ago—"

"No." Enitan straightens. "Even if this weren't personal, it would be fitting for him to die by a Korikese hand. But my face was all over the news this morning—I'm not sure I'll be able to carry this through either."

"Not to worry. The party isn't your standard soirée." Kulta crosses his arms. "It's a masquerade."

◆

Enitan is a few corridors away from Deora's apartments when she hears footsteps coming toward her from up ahead. They're fast and hard, accompanied by the telltale click of armor. A sentinel. She stops in her tracks, then turns on her heel and—

A gauntleted hand slams into her jaw. Enitan lands flat on her back, head spinning. She brings a trembling hand to her cheek. The entire left side of her face roars in pain. Something might be broken. Once her vision clears, she looks up at her attacker—no, *attackers*. There's a sentinel behind her too.

"Go ahead and scream," growls the sentinel that hit her. One hand is placed lightly on his holster. The other grips a shockstaff. "See what happens."

Her mouth goes dry. She knows that voice.

Ivar.

Fuck.

"On your feet," barks the second sentinel.

Enitan wobbles upright, wincing. "What are you doing?"

"I'm just making good on my promise," says Ivar. "You should have heeded me when I warned you."

Of course he's back. Getting rid of him for good couldn't have been so easy. And now she'll pay for her hubris with her life. But first, she wants to know how he managed to worm his way back into the Splinter.

"Who—who's helping you?" Not her most eloquent, but she can barely think through the pain.

Ivar laughs, low and dangerous. "Someone who agrees you have far too much influence at court. Someone who sees you for the threat you are."

The Council? It has to be. Who else could have snuck a disgraced sentinel back into the most highly guarded city in the system?

"What happens now?"

"What happens now is we take you somewhere dark and quiet," murmurs Ivar, deadly soft. He presses the muzzle of his dissection gun to the middle of her back. "I've been wanting you dead for some time, Enitan. I know it was you who cost me everything. And now I'm going to repay the favor, and then some. But I'll take my time."

So he knows nothing about the plot to kill Vidra, or he'd threaten to rip the whole story out of her. Then she hears the rest of what he's said, and her relief evaporates. But she's not going to die without a fight. Her shaking hands curl into fists.

"Move," orders Ivar, punctuating the command with a jab of the gun.

Enitan does as he bids. She leaps at the second sentinel, tackling her before she can rip out her gun. Ivar aims his weapon. Fires. He misses. The blast skims Enitan's shoulder and catches the struggling sentinel just under the edge of her helmet. Enitan goes unnaturally still, every part of her body on fire. She stares down at the woman for a split second. The fact that her head is still attached to her body means Ivar has the gun set to stun. Switching it to its lethal mode will take precious seconds. Seconds she will not give him.

Enitan flies to her feet and launches herself at Ivar. He shoves his gun back into its holster with a rapid string of curses and flips out the hidden blade of his shockstaff. He swings the weapon at her. Enitan swerves and dodges, barely. The serrated edge whistles past her ear. She doesn't escape the second blow, however. The blade slices across her hip.

Enitan can't help it. She cries out. She staggers, falling to one knee. The agony lancing through her flesh is unbearable. But she's already decided she won't go lying down. Ivar lifts the shockstaff for the killing blow. Enitan's hip roars in protest, but she forces herself up again. She throws out an arm. Grabs the end of the shockstaff. The force of the impact rattles her bones, nearly dislocating her shoulder, but she hangs on.

Her other hand shoots out to grab the gun. She shoves her arm up and pulls the trigger, firing wildly. Ivar knees her in the gut, knocking the air out of her. Stars explode across her vision, but the pain only hones her focus. She will not let herself die. There is more at stake here than her own life.

She keeps shooting, the blasts bursting against the ceiling. Ivar is screaming. She is screaming. She can't hold on for much longer.

Ivar wrenches his staff from her grip, slamming her against the wall. Enitan slides down and hits the floor with a dull thud. Her teeth sink into her tongue. Blood gushes into her mouth. Ivar raises the bladed edge once more. She tries to scramble back, but her limbs won't obey her. There's nowhere to go anyway. Enitan can barely draw air into her burning lungs. There's not enough breath left over to cry, let alone beg for her life.

"This is the end, Enitan," he says.

"You're right," says another voice.

And then the blood-slick curve of an axe goes through the center of his chest. Ivar gasps wetly, his shockstaff falling harmlessly at Enitan's feet. He gurgles desperately as the woman behind him plants a boot against his tailbone to kick him off her weapon. He crumples like a puppet with its strings cut. Enitan forces her head up, blood still dribbling from her mouth.

There stands the Imperator, axe in hand and tunic flecked with crimson. "Oh, Enitan."

Kulta appears from around the corner, medkit in hand. With methodical efficiency, he lifts Enitan's shirt and presses a regenerative bandage capsule to her hip. Mesh flows over the gash, covering the wound and stopping the flow of blood. He pries open her mouth and sticks in a healing tab to keep her tongue together. Once everyone's confident she won't hemorrhage to death, they help her stand.

Luckily, Deora is away for the night again and the hallways are clear, so they put her to bed in the countess's chambers. The Imperator paces back and forth at the foot of the bed while Kulta checks over Enitan's bandages for the thousandth time. "This shouldn't have happened."

"Obviously," Enitan mumbles lowly. The word doesn't really get around the tab. She resists the urge to spit it out. It's as bitter as the deepest Vaalbaran hell.

The Imperator looks over at her. Her expression is as smooth as glass, but something dark burns in her eyes. *Oh.* Enitan knows now what brought down that axe: pure, unbridled rage.

"I'm going to assign guards to you," says the Imperator. "You can't refuse." Her tone is soft, but Enitan hears the subtle edge to it, a dagger sheathed in velvet.

"Like Fenris, who nearly choked me to death?" Enitan asks. "Absolutely not."

That's what she means to say, anyway. The noises she's making barely sound like words, even to herself. Kulta starts to translate, but the Imperator cuts him off, gesturing impatiently at the synth. "Him or one of his siblings."

"No. I don't want to attract more attention than I already do," Enitan says. "This attack was revenge for the downfall he thought I orchestrated." No matter that he's right. "Don't confirm the rumor that I have too much influence over you."

The Imperator mutters something that sounds vaguely like "not just a rumor," but Enitan is still regaining all her senses.

"You got lucky tonight," says the God-Emperor. "Like you did with the bomb, in case you've forgotten. What'll you do if this happens again?" By now she's more or less looming over Enitan.

"I can take care of myself. I almost took down two highly trained sentinels alone today."

"Almost?" the Imperator snaps. When Enitan doesn't respond, she sighs and straightens, sweeping two loose braids behind her ear. "Tell me what you need."

"I . . ."

Her injuries aren't the problem. She's bruised and beaten, but she'll heal even without the pod. She's suffered enough by now to know that the worst wounds don't bleed. The real damage is the target on her back. She could be murdered anywhere, at any moment. She's been aware of the fragility of her own life for as long as she can remember, but this is the closest encounter she's had with death. The bloodmaws and shockstaffs of her youth, and even Fenris half-strangling her, pale in comparison to Ivar's blade at her throat. She can still *feel* his bloodlust, and he just as easily could have succeeded.

"I don't need anything right now," Enitan grits out, "other than for us to finish what we've started." Her eyes sting, but she refuses to cry. She sucks in a shuddering breath instead. "Don't tell Xiang about this. Please."

For a moment the Imperator looks ready to argue. But then she lowers her head. "Fine. We'll proceed as planned and hope for the best. But for now, try to get some sleep."

After everything, Enitan doesn't need to be told twice.

TWENTY-THREE

Enitan has always been horrendous at Sanctuary, which is completely fine. It's a ridiculous game anyway—she's always preferred Beyond. Unlike Sanctuary, winning a game of Beyond relies on more than random chance and guesswork.

"I win," says Xiang, for the fifth time. They drop their tiny green orb on the game board's final square.

"You cheated," says Enitan, baselessly.

Xiang laughs. "No, you're just terrible at this."

"Because it's stupid," she huffs, even as she fights back a grin.

"Of course." Her sibling shakes their head, tutting. "That's the point. Sanctuary *is* stupid. It's supposed to be pure fun. If you stopped trying to calculate the angle at which you throw the dice and the force with which you work the spinner, you probably wouldn't lose all the time." They pluck up her blue orb from its spot several squares behind theirs and drop it into the center of the holoboard, which takes the form of a volcano erupting in a fit of glowing magma.

"We're playing Beyond now." Enitan reaches over to the holo-projector. An array of game boards appear and disappear as she slides through the offerings. "Time to put you in your place."

"You can try," Xiang retorts, "but Katun's taught me a few tricks."

"We'll see," Enitan says. "Who's Katun?"

"I am," says a low-pitched voice.

Enitan whirls around and flies out of her chair. "Who are you? How did you get in here?"

"I'm Katun, as I've just informed you," the speaker replies. His topaz-blue eyes are bright with amusement. "I'm one of Kulta's craft-siblings." He tilts his shaggy head at Xiang. "And your sibling's . . . friend."

Enitan looks from Katun to Xiang and back. A wide grin stretches over her sibling's face. She crosses her arms. "When did you two meet?"

Katun arches a heavy brow. "You're protective, aren't you?"

"That's an understatement," Xiang mutters. "We met a few days ago, while you were off poisoning people."

Enitan ignores them, glaring at the synth. "I need to speak to you, Katun. *Privately.*"

Xiang frowns. "Enitan—"

"Just a quick word," she insists.

Katun heaves a huge sigh. "Very well. We can talk on the way to the Imperial residence. We've just been summoned." He gestures to Enitan's blinking communicator.

Enitan glances at it, then drags Xiang into a quick hug. "I'll see you later."

She follows Katun to a horizontally sliding tubelift. As soon as the transport slides shut around them, she turns to the synth.

"Xiang is sensitive. They get hurt easily. And I want you to know that if you break their heart, I'll murder you."

Katun folds his arms. "They're stronger than you think. But in any case, I'm not sure if Xiang feels the way I do."

"I know my sibling." Enitan stares hard at Katun. "I've seen that look on their face only once before, and you are *not* a fresh slice of om-vuutberry pie."

When the tubelift opens, she follows him through a winding hallway and into the Imperator's seventh private drawing room.

Katun glances over at the Imperator, who's sitting on a divan munching on a large orange pepper. "Did you steal that from my garden?"

"Yes," says the Imperator, looking down. "Sorry."

"I was planning to make soup with that!"

"I said I was sorry!" says the Imperator. She takes another large bite. "I'll get you a new one."

"Don't bother," Katun says, agitated. "You're well aware that no one else grows zhoprika correctly. Hydroponics are wonderfully efficient in a monolith, but the flavor's always off."

Enitan thinks back to her own tea leaves, which she cultivated herself for similar reasons. "Who's the soup for?" she asks, recalling now that synths aren't physically able to consume food.

Katun shrugs, already heading for the door. But Enitan catches the look on his face—he probably doesn't have the ability to blush, or he'd be a bright red. So he's cooking for Xiang, then.

"Back to the infirmary?" she asks.

Katun pauses, his left foot hovering over the threshold. "Perhaps."

"You're lucky it's so difficult to kill a synth," Enitan mutters under her breath.

Katun, of course, hears her. He simply laughs and steps the rest of the way out.

"What happened?" asks the Imperator.

Enitan flops down beside her on the divan. "He and Xiang have taken a . . . liking to each other. I'm not sure how to deal with it."

The Imperator pulls another, smaller pepper from her pocket, looking amused. "Aren't they older than you?"

"So?" Enitan sinks back into the pillows, resisting the urge to bite her nails. "This has never happened before. I thought romance just wasn't for them, honestly."

"Okay, well, perhaps you shouldn't meddle in this," says the Imperator, very gently. "Love is like an inablossom; the most beautiful grow wild and free, without a hand to guide them."

"But I'm their sister; it's my job to meddle."

The Imperator just shrugs, crunching away on the second pepper.

"That's a beautiful quote about the inablossom, by the way," Enitan says. She supposes a few Vaalbaran maxims have merit. "Where's it from?"

"Myself."

Enitan snorts. "And what would you know of love?"

"You'd be surprised." The Imperator smiles wistfully.

Enitan wonders again about her rumored marriage to Princess Sunnetah, but can't quite bring herself to ask about it. The thought is cut short when Kulta comes in and dumps two tightly bound men onto the floor like sacks of grain.

The Imperator jumps up from the divan and crouches down to peer at the unconscious pair, shifting to rest an arm on her knee.

"Is one of these Vidra?" Enitan asks, bending over to get a good look too.

Kulta shakes his head. "Nope. These are Dennach's men." The Imperator pokes one in the side with the toe of her boot. "He only ever sends representatives in his stead. Coward."

One of his craft-siblings, a synth with dark eyes and a thin nose, rolls in a nondescript black suitcase. "Finally found their belongings. Their getup for the masquerade is in here, including their masks."

The Imperator nods at him. "Good work, Kadek."

A third synth strides through the sliding doors. The Imperator stands, turning to the newcomer. "Kiran, any sign they're onto us?"

"They don't suspect a thing." She pulls a pair of communicators from her coat and waves them. "I've been texting Dennach. He says Vidra will be wearing a dark-blue suit and a silver mask. Finding him will be part of the challenge."

The Imperator turns to Enitan and Kulta. "It's almost time."

◆

Grand Duke Paavli, the host of the masquerade, lives in a private monolith, which he brings right up to the Splinter's proverbial doorstep. Enitan watches the massive structure drift ever closer from her balcony, anxiety and anticipation swelling with every crossed kilometer.

The monolith is wider than it is tall; it looks less like a proper monolith and more like a very large brick. Eventually, it blocks out her entire view, coming to a slow stop a hundred or so meters away. A bundle of tubelifts extends like outstretched fingers from one featureless side and sinks into the Splinter as if the Imperial capital were made of water.

Beside Enitan, Kulta pushes himself off his chair and onto his feet. "Let's go."

They step out into the main hallway and go up a tubelift. Enitan follows the synth past a slow, chatty procession of lesser nobles and notable officials and through a pair of nondescript doors. When the last door slides open at Kulta's touch, Enitan finds herself in one of the tubelifts bridging the two monoliths.

Though appearing perfectly black from her balcony, the walls and ceiling of the passage are transparent from the inside. Bloody light pours in from a particularly red sunset, pooling over the seamless obsidian floor. She and Kulta, disguised in jeweled masks and stolen suits, make their way toward the other side.

"The grand duke's abode was once a prison," Kulta says, apropos of nothing.

"You mean like the Splinter is now?" says Enitan.

Kulta's voice drops low. "The Splinter is a cage for those the Council wants to keep close." He points ahead. "This was where they sent those they wanted out of the way. A better fate than a knife in the gut, I suppose." A knowing smile takes form beneath his mask. "But there are knives everywhere, along with people to wield them."

When they reach the other end, the doors slide open and they step out into a vast chamber. Enitan stiffens as Kulta pulls her into a crush of silk-smothered, heavily perfumed people. She feels like a painted target: her suit is a brilliant shade of gold, and her mask, which covers her entire face, a matching yellow.

Though, now that she looks around, her outfit is almost boring compared with the outrageously ostentatious fashions on display. Highborn Vaalbarans make their way across the polished floor, their bodies sparkling with gems. Performers in sleek costumes dance and sing on levitating black platforms. Gold and silver dust shimmers in the air. Enitan swallows thickly. She may as well have just stepped into another world. Gone is the minimalism of the Imperial capital; the room is stuffed with priceless art and furniture, amassed and arranged by someone with clearly more money than taste.

Kulta takes her arm again. "I don't have enough data on Vidra to locate him with my sensors alone," he whispers into Enitan's ear. "We'll have to find him the hard way."

Enitan scans the chamber. She turns, visually combing through the surrounding aristocrats. Her gaze hooks on the Imperator, who is only a few meters away. Despite her mask, there's no mistaking her. She stands by a miniature pond, a tall glass vase filled with floating plants and vibrant aquatic life. The Imperator bends a stem to sniff the flower crowning it. She's traded her usual light-consuming black for a streamlined suit the color of the evening sky. Faceted black opals are woven through her braids, glittering at the slightest movement.

Enitan sees that she's not the only person who's recognized the God-Emperor. A man in emerald-green samite sidles up to her, joining the crowd of sycophants mewling around her like mossikittens.

"Your Imperial Majesty," he slurs, wiping his mouth with a malachite-encrusted sleeve as he bows clumsily.

Enitan grimaces. She knows that voice, that face. It's Viscount Reryn, the cousin of one of the earls she served. Ancestors, he's wasted.

The Imperator sighs. "The entire point of a masquerade, Reryn, is to pretend we're not who we are."

"My deepest apologies." The viscount dips his head, supporting himself on a marble statue. He looks around blearily. "Where's your savage?"

One of the sycophants titters before another cuts him off with an elbow to the side.

The Imperator straightens, pulling herself to her full height. "What did you just say?" she asks with a lethal softness.

"Your savage," he repeats, oblivious. "Left her leashed at home, did you?"

For a moment, the Imperator says nothing. Then she whirls around to face a short, sturdy woman in a brown suit who seems to have materialized at her side out of nowhere. Clearly a sentinel, waiting for her orders. Enitan notes the dissection gun at her hip.

"Lakis, get him out of my sight," the Imperator says.

Reryn jerks back, knocking over a potted wasulily. "What—?"

The Imperator cuts him off. "You are no longer a viscount. And that means the property granted to you as such is reclaimed by the crown as well."

Lakis grabs Reryn by the shoulder, stunning him with her gun before he can make a scene. Enitan watches him get dragged off, only for Kulta to step in front of her, interrupting her entertainment.

"I thought you weren't one for palace drama."

Enitan snorts. "I'm not."

Kulta peers at her. "Are you all right? You're still—"

"Kulta." Enitan brushes him off. "I'm fine. Come on, let's look around."

Night falls by the time they finally find Vidra. Enitan spots him sprawled on a low couch, hidden in plain sight. Just as Dennach inadvertently informed Kiran, he's wearing a formfitting suit of sea-blue silk. The shade complements his complexion, a pale brown the color of desert sand. His delicate silver mask covers his eyes and wraps around to the back of his head, leaving uncovered most of a slender nose and a sharp jawline. His mouth seems permanently frozen into a blinding smile. Beside him slouches a tall young man with a sharp black undercut. He looks to be much younger than Enitan, though the mask makes certainty impossible. If she had to guess, she'd say he's somewhere around eighteen. His youth makes her uncomfortable; she knows that anyone with Vidra might die as well if things go wrong.

Enitan turns to Kulta. "Who's that?" she whispers.

"His son, Taavir." Kulta frowns. "All Dennach said was that he'd be bringing his personal assistant."

Enitan's already heading toward the pair. "Let's just get this over with."

The magnate stands when he sees them, his lips stretching to reveal even more perfect white teeth. He taps his son on the shoulder and they close the remaining distance. Enitan and Kulta bow simultaneously.

"Good evening, sir," says Enitan, her gloves growing damp with nervous sweat.

He peers down at them, gesturing for them to rise. "What are your thoughts on Enheduanna's latest work?"

"*The Exaltation of Inanna* . . ." Kulta pauses. "It's extraordinary."

"I never thought she'd be able to re-create the beauty of *The Tem-*

ple Hymns," adds Enitan. She stands perfectly still, waiting with bated breath for some indication that they've said all the correct words.

The magnate frowns. "I've been here for two hours."

"Forgive us," says Enitan. "Dennach wanted us to, ah, cut a few ties on our way here."

The magnate snorts. "I hope he pays you two enough."

"Before we forget, he would like to reiterate his most profuse apologies," says Kulta. "He wishes he could have been here to meet you himself."

"I completely understand." His voice drips with sarcasm. "We'll talk somewhere more private. Please, follow me."

He leads them through a discreet doorway, down a short hallway, and into a small chamber. Enitan wonders whether the man is friends with the grand duke or has simply paid someone off for the privacy.

A large window reveals the full moon, a pale lamp throwing silvery light over the world. A circular couch dominates the space, a round table at its center. On the table are four cups and a sizable bottle of whiskey.

"I do apologize for the haste," he drawls as soon as the door slides shut behind them. He lowers himself onto the couch and crosses his legs. "The uprising in Lishtaqa has made it *impossible* to send in new associates."

His son sits beside him. "After everything we did for the wretches," Taavir sneers in a low, thin voice. He speaks with the tone of a man who believes he knows all there is to know. "Vaalbara ushered their communities into the future, asking for nearly nothing in return. Koriko deserves this."

There's a seasoned sort of wrath to his little speech. As Enitan joins them on the couch, she wonders how many times he's given it. Is it all just for show, or does he truly believe this?

"They deserve this and more," Enitan agrees, folding her arms. "Dennach wants to move as quickly as possible."

"Last we talked, he sounded quite hesitant."

"He's come around," Kulta says. "He understands that this is nec-essary for the good of the Empire."

Vidra spits out a laugh. "And for the good of his purse." He leans forward, clapping a hand on his son's bony shoulder. "But on to busi-ness. My son here has come up with a new plan for getting Shimmer onto Koriko."

Taavir smiles anxiously, and Enitan sees that he's clutching a copy of the Black Codex. "I got the idea from the Book of Sekhmet."

Enitan sits up. The monk who taught her Orin made her memorize the Codex's first seven books. "That details the First God-Emperor's de-feat of the Hekau-Khasut tribes."

The son puffs up like an iyebird. "I see you know your scripture. But do you recall *how* she conquered them?"

Enitan's stomach constricts painfully. Whatever their scheme is, it can't be good; the first Imperator's war with the tribes cost millions of lives. "She knew the tribes' depravity knew no bounds. With her forces shrunken and starving, she fled a week before the barbarian solstice celebration and left the great city of Hewwara undefended. The pursu-ing tribes massacred the citizens and set the High Library of Djehuty ablaze. But before leaving, they raided the city's stores for the coming festivities. Little did they know, the God-Emperor had every grain, every fruit, every drop of wine poisoned. On the day of the solstice, she watched, hidden, as the savages fell, one by one, onto the scorched stone of her ruined city. Their blood put out the flames, if I remember correctly."

"You remember well enough," says the son. "The Korikese don't have a solstice celebration, but they *do* have a great number of similar festivals."

Kulta crosses his arms. "I imagine most events will be put on hold while the Imperator deals with the local agitators."

The magnate smirks. "I have sources that say the insurgents carry out certain initiation rites for new recruits."

Enitan's heart skips a beat as she realizes what their plan is.

"We're going to offer Shimmer to the rebels free of charge. A gift to celebrate their cause and rally for freedom." That perfect, shining grin again. "I've already formed inroads. It seems everyone in the real rebel army could use something to look forward to. A bit of relief."

They plan to flood the communities with Shimmer, then begin charging exorbitant rates once addiction settles in. A blinding rage takes hold of Enitan, and she has to fight to keep her fingers from balling into fists as he settles back into the couch, looking terribly smug.

The son pulls a datachip from between the pages of the Black Codex and holds it out. "I've drafted a formal plan." His casual eagerness belies the destruction on that chip. He knows that the stench of rotting bodies in the fallout will never reach his nose.

Willing her hand not to shake, Enitan accepts it and tucks it into her pocket.

"Dennach will look over your terms and revert to you," Kulta says, offering her a cup of whiskey.

Enitan blinks in surprise before taking it. She didn't even see the synth pour it.

"With luck," says the magnate, accepting his own cup, "in a decade the savages will be too dead or drugged to care about what's to come."

It takes Enitan nearly everything to keep her voice steady. She holds her drink aloft. "A toast, sir."

"Can I have a glass?" whines the son, staring at the remaining whiskey. "It's *my* plan we're toasting to."

"You're too young, my boy," replies Vidra with an indulgent smile, meeting the others in the toast. "When you're older, perhaps."

Taavir sits back and sulks, but he says nothing. Enitan notices that the magnate waits for Kulta and her to sip before he partakes of his drink. It doesn't matter, though. She saw Kulta's thumb slip along the edge of the cup, seemingly by accident, as he poured Vidra's whiskey. Minuscule mechanisms under his artificial skin have already deposited a lethal amount of Shimmer.

The magnate looks over at his son. He sighs, smiling indulgently. "Fine. One sip. *One*."

Enitan nearly chokes as Taavir quickly drains the rest of the drink. She forces herself not to look over at Kulta, whose posture has straightened by a nearly undetectable measure.

It isn't long before the symptoms appear. Both their breathing grows shallow. Their pupils dilate, consuming their irises. Their throats then begin to turn blue. Enitan stares at the boy, mouth agape. This was not the plan.

"What have you done?" the magnate gasps out, tipping forward on his seat.

He falls into the table and tumbles onto the floor. His son slides down the couch, gasping fruitlessly.

"Only what is necessary." Enitan bends over Vidra, her hands trembling. "We know who you are, Lord Ingilazar. That you're one of them." She keeps her gaze on him, struggling to tamp down her horror at what she and Kulta have just done. "What I don't know are the names of the last members of your group."

"Why would I tell you anything?" he snarls. "You've already killed me."

"Listen to me, Vidra." Enitan crouches down beside him. "Your son can survive this. We'll call for a medic. I have no desire for the death of a child on my conscience."

He tries to spit at her, but the saliva only dribbles down his cheek.

"So you'll let your son suffer for your crimes, then?"

The magnate twists onto his side, looking up at his dying boy.

Enitan takes hold of his shoulder. "He doesn't have much time."

He closes his eyes. "Meayng. That's . . . the only name I know."

Kulta drops down at Enitan's side. "Meayng died months ago. Shuttle accident," he whispers.

"Shit." Enitan looks back down at the magnate. "Haven't you replaced them?"

"We *did*, with Erseydis. Banurra's death accelerated her ascension, though it'll be months before a candidate is confirmed to take her place."

"You must have code names," snaps Kulta. *"Tell us."*

"We call ourselves the . . . Nlamiraan."

Enitan has heard this word before; it's the Vaalbaran name for the largest planet in their solar system, a gas giant orbiting between Jilessa and the asteroid belt. "Go on."

"We are named after its moons. Meayng, and then Erseydis . . . was Isatho. Banurra . . . was Isheen." He shudders. "I . . . am Ishlaat."

"And the final two?" Kulta demands. "Isamu and Ishamsa?"

"There is no Isamu," the magnate chokes out. "There are only ever four of us."

"That doesn't make sense," snarls Kulta. "You must have an odd number—"

"Every vote is unanimous, or we do nothing at all." He grits his teeth together. "You know, we didn't suspect . . . foul play until Erseydis died. Banurra was always . . . vulnerable. He felt too much. We believed he really did . . . what they said he did. But Erseydis—she was made of iron." Then his arm shoots out, faster than it has any right to. He grabs Enitan's wrist. "That's everything I know. Save him."

Enitan wrenches her arm out of his clammy grip. She turns to Kulta, forcing herself to speak. "I assume you've already summoned a medic."

The synth gives Enitan a long, hard look. "He'll be a witness."

All of Enitan's anger and hatred crystallizes in that moment. "Kulta," she snaps. "Call for a medic."

"We can't risk it."

"*Kulta.*"

"We *can't.*"

Enitan turns back to the magnate. It feels like it takes a century for her to face him. "I . . . I'm sorry."

"You . . . promised . . . ," he cries, tears welling over blank, defeated eyes. "Please, my son . . ."

Enitan ducks her head. "I'm so sorry."

An agonized gurgle escapes the son's lips. Vidra is bawling now, forced to watch his only child die during his last moments.

Enitan scrabbles upright and staggers over to the window, commanding it open with a flick of her wrist.

Kulta surges forward. "You're not about to jump, are you?"

Enitan's skin feels overly tight, like a robe three sizes too small. The desire to tear it all off trickles into her mind like sickly-sweet poison.

"No. I just— I just need air." She rubs her hands up and down her arms, and when that doesn't suffice, she starts scratching, digging her nails into her skin until they draw blood. She presses herself to the windowsill, shivering violently as a cold burst of wind drags itself across her face, turning the sweat on her skin clammy. "We had to do it," she grits out. "You were right. You heard what they were going to do. Xiang won't be safe until they're all dead, and neither will Koriko. They *had* to die."

The words ring true but hollow as she says them. She wraps her bloodied arms tightly around her middle, humming a loud, discordant tune. But even that cannot drown out the sound of the magnate's and his son's gasps, which are growing shallower by the second.

"Enitan—"

"I know."

When she turns back around, father and son are dead.

"We need to go," says Kulta with terrible softness. "Now."

Enitan collects herself, shoving down all her roiling remorse and self-disgust, and follows Kulta through the door, leaving behind two bodies that she desperately wishes could be her last.

TWENTY-FOUR

"It's such a tragedy." Deora passes Enitan a shallow bowl of homemade nut paste. They're having breakfast in the countess's bedroom. "Taavir was only nineteen. Practically a child."

Neither of them are much older, and Enitan feels like she has an eternity left to live, no matter how often she puts her life at risk. She sips at her drink—half tea and, unbeknownst to her host, half vodka. "Did you know him?"

Deora blows on a spoonful of pepper soup. "He spent all his free time at the museum. Used to follow me around and badger me with questions." She shakes her head mournfully. "God, I can't believe he's really gone."

Enitan puts down her cup to cover up any shaking. She spent last night tossing in bed, and the caffeine and alcohol certainly aren't helping. Try as she might, she just can't reconcile herself to the cold fact that saving countless lives means ending even a few. Her calm facade is tearing at the seams.

"I'm sorry," Enitan manages to say. "Are you all right?"

Deora drags in a breath. "I'll be fine. I have an appointment with my therapist on this floor later today." She looks thoughtfully at Enitan. "You should give her a call, set something up."

"How would I pay?" Healthcare is free on Koriko, but she has no idea how it works in the Empire.

Deora laughs. "You wouldn't, of course! All Vaalbarans have the right to seek and receive free counseling."

Enitan drains the rest of her drink. "I'm not technically a Vaalbaran citizen. And even if I were, I'm not sure any therapist here would quite understand my situation."

Deora's face falls. "Enitan, I'm sorry."

"It's not your fault." Yet another futile beg-pardon; hiding her exasperation is easier said than done.

"Well, it's just . . ." Her painted lips quiver. "I hope you're all right after what happened at the masquerade."

Enitan's mouth goes dry.

Deora's eyes shimmer with unshed tears. "I heard about Viscount Reryn. Well, *former* viscount. And I need you to know I stand with you. I would never—" She takes a deep breath. "I know I caused you pain during the museum gala. I didn't know there would be Korikese relics. I told my assistants to recall the artifacts purchased from your homeland so we could figure out a better purpose for them, but I must've been too late. If I had known, I would never have sold those objects, but it's not a simple matter of just taking them back. You understand."

Enitan can't stop herself. "Deora, I don't think those objects were purchased," she says, as gently as possible. "No Korikese would even think of selling them."

Deora sniffles, shaking her head. "I don't know how to say this, but you're wrong. I have the papers to prove the exchanges; you can look them over yourself if you'd like."

Enitan clenches her hands. She's not going to let this go. "That dagger you auctioned off is an Ancestor relic."

The tears don't fall from the countess's eyes when she narrows them; they remain sparkling on her lashes. "I know that."

Enitan forges onward, despite the danger she can feel pouring into the room. "Korikese artifacts belong in the communities."

"As long as they aren't sold, fine," says Deora, her voice a little tight. "But if they are, a museum is where they rightfully belong. I shouldn't have auctioned the pieces, but my hands were tied. Beyond that, we'll have to agree to disagree."

"I suppose," Enitan forces out.

But now Deora isn't ready to drop the subject. "What would you have had me do? Give them back after spending the museum's funds on them?" She throws up her hands. "If we set that precedent, then we'd have to keep doing it, and then we'd have nothing! Is that your vision?"

"No, I—"

But Deora isn't listening anymore. "Don't you want people to appreciate Korikese art? If those relics of yours were back in the communities, how would people be able to see them?" She tuts sadly, as if at a misbehaving child. "It would be selfish to not share the communities with the world."

Enitan gives up. Arguing will get her nowhere but a dungeon, and the countess seems all too ready to escalate the conversation. "You're right. I'm sorry."

Deora's mouth opens as if to rant some more. But then she sighs. "Oh, you don't have to apologize. It's fine, you just weren't thinking about the big picture," she says, tapping a gloved finger against her own temple.

Enitan has had enough. She's too busy, exhausted, and—right now—frustrated to patiently walk Deora through her people's history and right to their own artifacts. She's not here to serve as a live-in cultural tutor. She wipes her mouth with only slightly unsteady fingers and stands.

"Thanks for breakfast. I have to go."

When she reaches over to collect her dishes, Deora waves her off, flicking away her tears with her other hand. "I'll take care of those. Another tea service?"

Enitan nods. "Ever since that news segment about the . . . rioting in Lishtaqa and Tamoko, the requests have been pouring in."

"Well, the Imperator won't harm you," says Deora quietly. "So you don't have to worry."

Enitan debates telling the countess that the supposed rioting is more than enough reason to worry. Even if she weren't in danger of being killed, the rest of her people are. She considers admitting to Deora that she's not actually having an affair with the Imperator. But in the end, Enitan does neither of these things. She bids the countess goodbye and leaves.

When she reaches the Imperial infirmary, she raises her hand to the door. Nothing happens. She tries again, pressing her fingertips harder against the smooth screen-surface. Again, nothing. A black box with white script pops up on the door, informing her that the current occupant has barred all entry.

"Katun," Enitan snarls, "you'd better not be in there."

No response. Cursing, she punches in the emergency override code she made the Imperator give her.

Enitan's body turns to stone when the door slides open. There's blood everywhere, drenching the dark bedsheets and dripping onto the polished stone floor. Two of Menkhet's physicians sit propped up against the walls, their heads blown off by what can only have been a dissection gun. Another lies flat on the floor, disconnected from a sliced-off arm reaching toward the destroyed panic button. And at the center of the carnage is her sibling, covered in blood on their bed.

"Xiang!" Enitan chokes out, throwing herself at them. She takes their cold, limp hands in hers. "Xiang, please. You can't—you can't leave me. *Please.*"

Her breath catches in her throat. She feels like she'll plummet straight down through the bottom of the Splinter, through the clouds right onto the rocks below. The person she cares most about in the universe lies lifeless before her.

Then Xiang lets out a ragged gasp, blood flecking their lips, and looks up at her, their eyes wide and filled with tears.

"Enitan," they whisper.

She almost collapses to the ground in overwhelmed relief. Her lungs pull in air, and she lets out a happy sob. And then bright, hot rage flares up. "Who did this to you?"

Xiang lifts a bloody, shaking arm, pointing over Enitan's shoulder. "*Him.*"

Enitan whirls around, a tremor rippling over every inch of her skin. There, behind the brocaded black curtains, she catches a shiver of movement. Before she can say anything, a man steps out.

His ash-blond hair hangs in a lank curtain around his pallid features. The hatred and derision in his eyes is staggering, even after all these months in the Splinter.

Enitan shoves a hand into her pocket, only to find it empty. Ancestors, she left her communicator in her room. She looks up at the assassin, but he hasn't moved. They stare at each other for a long, silent moment.

"Who sent you?" she demands. "What do you want?"

"A friend of Vidra's." The words are a low growl. "You've caught the attention of the Nlamiraan. And as for what I want . . ." A thin, nasty grin spreads across his face.

Enitan has never been more terrified in her life. Despite her best efforts, her voice cracks when she speaks. "If you kill us, the Imperator will hunt you down." She steps directly between the assassin and Xiang. "They had nothing to do with it."

His smile goes even wider. There is no trace of humanity there, only the promise of a painful death. "That matters little to me. But that's enough talking." And then he pulls a dissection gun from the folds of his suit and aims it at Xiang.

Adrenaline floods Enitan. She launches herself at the assassin before he can fire and knocks him to the floor. She grabs the gun and twists as hard as she can, breaking the finger caught inside the trigger guard. The resulting scream is deafening. She tries to wrench the gun from his broken grip, but he jerks his arm wildly, flinging the weapon away. The gun slides across the floor, far from both of their reaches.

She needs to get him away from Xiang. Blood pounding in her ears, Enitan shoves herself off him and scrambles desperately toward the attached drawing room. The assassin catches her just as she darts across the threshold, grabbing her wrist with his uninjured hand and slamming her into the doorframe. Blood bursts over her face as her nose breaks again.

His other hand swings into her abdomen, his bony fist driving deep into her gut and knocking the wind out of her. Enitan crumples to the floor, gasping in pain. She still hasn't recovered from Ivar's attack. The assassin kicks her in the side, and she goes limp.

Enitan hears Xiang call for her, their voice distorted as if they were underwater. The assassin swivels around and steps toward them.

No. He won't lay another hand on her sibling. Enitan forces herself up, every muscle roaring in protest. She lunges, throwing her shoulder into his back. He goes down with a groan but doesn't stay there for long.

He comes at her with a horrible roar, arms outstretched. But she has just enough time to finally pull the poignard from her boot. He twists away at the last second, and the blade flies past his chest instead of sinking between his ribs. Then he punches her in the side of the head. As he beats her again and again, her vision fills with stars.

When her sight returns, he has the poignard. He charges forward, aiming it directly at her heart. Enitan throws herself back. The blade slices through the air and slashes across her raised arm. She hisses as blood flows from her skin. He strikes again. Enitan kicks out wildly. Her heel drives into his elbow. He screams as his arm snaps the wrong way, the poignard slipping from his fingers. She dives for it. But before she can grab it and slit his throat, his hands grip hers.

"You're all vermin," he snarls at her, shoving her onto her back. "We were fools to try to refine you. Vaalbara should have put you out of your misery instead of letting you breed in that filthy lunar swamp."

Enitan writhes on the stone, trying to throw him off as his hands close around her throat. He's too strong. Her lungs scream for air that isn't coming as she flings her arm out, reaching for the fallen poignard. Her vision has begun to go dark when finally, finally, she finds it. Her fingers slip along the slick blade, drawing even more blood, before they close around the hilt.

With every scrap of strength she has left, Enitan drives the poignard into his neck. The assassin gasps, his eyes bulging with shock. His grip around her throat tightens, as if he might finish strangling her even with the blade buried in his flesh. But his blood is already gushing over her face, over the tiles. His fingers soon grow slack, and she kicks him off.

This time, when he falls to the floor, he stays there.

Enitan finds the second, hidden panic button and slams her fist into it. Then everything goes dark.

TWENTY-FIVE

Enitan considers cutting her mission short, while she and Xiang both still have their lives. She considers telling the Imperator that she's just a scribe and tea specialist, that she should never have agreed to spy on the court. That Enitan should never have asked to kill anyone.

When she closes her eyes at night, curled up beside Xiang, all she ever sees is the magnate's son—practically a boy. A horrible boy who would have grown into a worse man, but still. He was too young to die, especially like that, clawing at his own swollen throat.

And whenever she wakes up, covered in cold sweat and trembling, she wrestles with the impulse to flee. In a thousand years, perhaps the descendants of her people will look back at history and speak of how strong and resilient their forebears must have been to have survived the Empire. Perhaps they will speak of how they suffered under Vaalbara's boot with their honor intact. But Enitan reaches the same conclusion every time temptation arises. She wants more than mere survival. She wants to *live*. She wants her people to live. And she stopped caring about her honor the moment she thought Xiang had truly been taken from her. If she hadn't come up to check on them just then . . .

There's only one shadow councilor left. She cannot turn back now, not after all the blood and tears and sweat she's shed to get this far. Not when Ishamsa—the last of the Nlamiraan—almost certainly knows of Enitan's involvement. What they must have uncovered to track Xiang here is enough to destroy them all. The enemy knows the Imperator is moving against them, which means time is short. Enitan must find Ishamsa and end them before they end her.

After the incident, the synths discovered a number of devices on the assassin, but they were unable to find a single contact.

Xiang is still sleeping when Enitan tiptoes out of the infirmary that morning. Three days have passed since the assassination attempt, but the haunted look she sees reflected in her sibling's eyes has only deepened. Now, though, their face is a tranquil, slumbering mask. If only she could give them that peace in waking hours. One day, maybe. She meets Kulta and the Imperator in an informal dining room where the lacquered walls and furniture reflect everything. Nothing is hidden; here, even the shadows have eyes.

But Enitan's hunger outweighs her discomfort when she sees the food. Breakfast has been laid out: marinated vegetables, bean pudding, and scarlet grain boiled in sweet hetarnut milk. There's also a glass pot of black uhie tea, triple brewed to produce dangerous levels of caffeine. It's flavored with delicate flower petals and oil cold-pressed from a variety of Korikese citruses. It's all food she would have eaten at home. Enitan raises her brow.

The Imperator pushes aside a thick stack of holosheets, each projecting hundreds of scrolling lines. She gestures at the empty chair across from her. "How are your wounds?"

Enitan sits, a hand lifting of its own accord to press against her ribs. There's a bruise there, purplish black and sending pain coursing through her chest whenever she breathes too deeply. Regenerative bandages do wonders for superficial wounds, but internal injuries still take ages to heal. "I'm fine."

Kulta makes a disbelieving noise from where he sits on a nearby couch. He's flipping through news segments on a holoprojector.

"I hope you have an appetite," says the Imperator.

"Oh, there's no need to hope." Enitan drops her elbows on the table and digs in, starting with a slice of grilled fruit. She waves a hand at the decadent meal between them. "What's all this for?"

The Imperator pours them both a cup of tea. "Xiang says you're homesick—"

"You spoke to Xiang about me?"

"I was worried." She frowns. "I was in the middle territories when it happened. I tried calling you."

Enitan didn't even realize the Imperator had left the Splinter. It would explain why she was spared the usual fretful looming. She shrugs. "I was probably sleeping," she lies. She just didn't feel like having the God-Emperor fuss over her directly after being swarmed with physicians.

While she's a bit annoyed that Xiang took the liberty of divulging feelings not intended for the Imperator's ears, she does appreciate this gesture. She *is* homesick. She longs for the crimson-gold glow of Jilessa spilling over the roof of her housepod, the rustling of salofeathers in the trees, her own stars. On Gondwana, they wink slowly into existence, flashing jewels sewn one by one into the fabric of the sky. On Koriko, when the skydome enters its transparent mode during the day period, they are simply there.

And the food is excellent. As good as Deora's, which is nearly as good as the best stuff Enitan has eaten on Koriko. Not that she'd ever admit it aloud.

Kulta looks over at her. "I'll be your guard until this mission is over."

Enitan stiffens. "But—"

"This isn't up for negotiation," the Imperator says, frustration edging into her voice. "I went against my better judgement and listened to you after Ivar. I'm not making the same mistake again."

"If anyone here needs more security, it's Xiang," Enitan says firmly.

"They have guards assigned, too, of course."

Kulta rises from the couch. The synth bows deeply, the first sign of reverence Enitan has seen from him. "We'll keep them safe, Menkhet."

"I know." The Imperator sits back and pulls a holosheet from the middle of the stack at her side. Enitan serves herself a little bean pudding and attempts to read the tiny script on the other side of the holosheet. She doesn't recognize the language; the characters are fat and blocky, quite different from the sloping syllabary of Korikesian or the intricate hieroglyphics of Orin.

"What's that?"

"Nothing interesting," replies the Imperator.

Enitan doesn't believe her but refrains from prodding. "You know, the Nlamiraan had no idea they were being killed off until Erseydis."

The Imperator doesn't look up from the holosheet. She waves a finger, and the words fly by a little faster. "Whoever took out the first ones must have known what they were doing."

Enitan has long suspected that the Imperator was involved in Banurra's demise. Who else would gift her an entire wardrobe just to conceal a dead man's jewelry? She's had a gut feeling about the God-Emperor for some time, but now she's certain.

Enitan watches her pull an electronic seal from her pocket and affix the Imperial sigil onto another holosheet before looking up.

"So, what do we do now?" Enitan asks.

"It's simple," says Kulta. "We have to get to Ishamsa before they come after you. My craft-siblings and I will continue to scour the worldnet for information, but we've found few leads." He sighs. "For now, the final councilor has the advantage. They must know for certain that you're working against them, Menkhet."

Enitan massages her temples. "I'm confirmed for a dozen events this week, and there's no acceptable reason I can give for excusing myself. But perhaps I can make something useful of them. The first is tonight."

The Imperator gapes at her. "Look at the condition you're in!"

"But no one else can know I'm hurt," Enitan says. "I have to keep up appearances. I promise, I'm fine."

Kulta folds his arms. "In the meantime, it's possible they haven't connected you to Vidra's death. But if one assassin found Xiang, we have to assume others are coming."

Of course they are. Enitan's been trying not to think about it. She drops her head into her hands, the appetite she somehow managed to summon evaporating.

"Listen," the Imperator says. "The rest of Kulta's siblings will be watching over Xiang at all hours. I swear to you, this time I'll keep them safe."

"If your only trusted forces are with them, who will protect *you*?" Enitan asks softly.

An emotion flickers across the Imperator's eyes, too quickly for Enitan to decipher what it is. The God-Emperor waves her hand in dismissal. "There's no need to worry about me. I'll be fine."

◆

"Can you wait outside for a moment?" Enitan asks Kulta, who's dutifully followed her to the infirmary.

Enitan presses her hand to the door. When it opens, she finds Xiang watching a drama with Katun. She immediately recognizes the whiny voice of the secondary villain—she used to mock the actor with Ajana. They're watching the adaptation of *The Matchbreaker*, a fantasy romance novel that came out eons ago. Enitan and Ajana used to binge the same trashy drama together, which throws Enitan so much for a moment she isn't even annoyed at how close the pair is. Then her instincts kick in again, along with her irritation.

"Mukuta dies in the last episode," she says. "And the Matchbreaker and Khutulun get together right after the funeral."

Xiang stares at her, horrified. "You'd better be lying."

"We'll see." Enitan points at Katun in his dark-gray uniform. "You. Out." Of course *he's* volunteered to keep an eye on Xiang.

The synth pushes himself off the bed, but not before planting a quick kiss on Xiang's temple. "I'll be right outside. We can discuss the new security features this evening."

Enitan glares at him, tapping a foot against the floor..

When the door slides shut behind him, she plops herself down on the comforter beside Xiang, who crosses their arms with a frown.

"You don't have to be so mean to him."

"I'm not!" exclaims Enitan. "This is me at my nicest."

Xiang arches a brow.

She sighs. "Fine. I'll go a little easier on him."

"Thank you." Xiang settles back onto the pillows. "Saban and the others are moving to the Imperator's vacation home this evening for their own safety. Just until we rid the world of the Nlamiraan." They glance away, just for a moment. "The monolith, Alta, was a gift from Sunnetah, back when the Imperator was a commander in her fleet—"

Enitan narrows her eyes. "Why are you telling me this?"

Xiang's mouth thins into a hard line. "I spoke with the Imperator. She said you're safer without having to worry about someone. And she's right. I'm going with them."

Enitan frowns at her sibling. "Are you serious?"

"I've made up by mind." They sigh, rubbing at the spot between their brows. "I'm sorry."

She opens her mouth to argue, but she knows the Imperator is right. Xiang needs to get out of the Splinter. All Enitan has ever wanted was for her sibling to be safe, so why does this make her feel so awful? Perhaps it's that, even after a fortnight of trying to convince them to stay out of the bloodshed, she still can't believe they want to run from all this entirely.

It's true that even with its number whittled down to one, the threat the Nlamiraan presents is great. And the last councilor knows Xiang is alive, even their identity. Enitan will not let the last good thing in her life be swallowed by the Empire. Even if that means letting them go. She knows that the chances of them both surviving this are extremely low.

"Come with us." Xiang reaches out to take her hand. "You're in just as much danger as I am."

Enitan draws back, stunned for a moment. "I wish I were, if only to keep Ishamsa's eyes off you." She laughs humorlessly. "But I can't go now. Not before this is over."

"Enitan." Their fingers tighten around hers. "It's not your responsibility to right every wrong in the world. Menkhet can handle this."

Enitan shakes her head, thinks back to the fight she had with the Imperator after she nearly died for the first time. "I have the chance to really change something for us." She pulls them into a hug. "We can have a home again, Xiang."

Enitan stands to leave before her willpower snaps and she changes her mind. She fights back tears as she heads for the door. Just before she walks through, she pauses. "I'll see you soon. And please, be safe. I can't lose you again."

She can hear the soft smile in Xiang's voice when they say, "Likewise, little sister."

The door slides open. Enitan leaves without looking back.

◆

She doesn't join the Imperator at the landing pad that evening to wish Xiang goodbye. A treacherous part of her mind hisses that she'll sorely regret not seeing them one last time. But if Xiang asks her to leave with them again, she might not have the strength to say no. And if everything goes as planned, Xiang will be back here in a week, which is how long Enitan estimates it will take to find and assassinate the last shadow councilor. Or for the shadow councilor to find her. Surprisingly, none of the members of the Nlamiraan she's met are the type to flee and hide. They're all power hungry, vicious, and decisive. And the accelerated sentinel program is set to begin in a handful of days. Either way, this will be over soon.

At around the time the shuttle departs for Alta, Enitan heads to her first engagement with Kulta in tow. The synth is decked out in a full set of sentinel armor, disguised as an Imperial escort. The helmet covers his entire face, so the fact that he doesn't blink or breathe won't be a problem. At this point, the threat of a Nlamiraan assassin is greater than the danger of a disgruntled noble. Even if Enitan had the energy, she wouldn't have argued when the Imperator insisted upon assigning her a bodyguard.

The host, Count Azhuros, is a spindly man with bushy eyebrows and a grating personality. He ushers Enitan and Kulta into his apartments with a series of grandiose gestures. The guests have already arrived, nearly an hour earlier than the count told her they would. They turn to regard her with a patronizing fascination. Enitan sighs inwardly, bracing herself for a barrage of questions about her relationship with the Imperator.

"Well, Korikese," the count says, far louder than necessary, "demonstrate your craft."

Even after all this time, her hackles still rise at an order to perform like this, as if she's someone's trained pet. She swallows her irritation and gets to work. She's pleasantly surprised when the guests don't ask her a thing about the Imperator. That curdles quickly when they ask her about the unrest on Koriko instead.

The guests seem to be operating under the assumption that she's closely tied to the people responsible for the so-called rioting.

"There must be *something* you can tell us," insists the count, after she assures him for the tenth time that no, not all Korikese know each other.

"My lord, I can assure you I haven't the slightest idea what's going on," Enitan says, just barely keeping her voice level. "I'm limited to communication within the Splinter."

"Well, this is disappointing," the count huffs.

Enitan agrees; Ishamsa is certainly nowhere near this crowd.

"It's a good thing your services are free," the count tells her. "I'd demand my credits back otherwise."

Kulta steps up to Enitan's side before she hurls an insult back at him. He leans over to whisper in her ear. "Menkhet wants to talk."

Enitan looks up at the synth, panic immediately thrumming in her blood. "Why? Has something happened to . . . ?" They both know she can't say Xiang's name aloud.

Kulta shakes his head. "No, they're fine. They just changed their mind."

"*What?*" They seemed so sure just that morning.

Kulta straightens and faces Azhuros. "The Imperator has requested her presence, so I'm afraid today's service must be cut short." His hand falls on Enitan's shoulder. He steers her gently toward the door. "Enjoy your evening."

The count grumbles something undoubtedly rude, but it's not as if he can do anything more.

"Is this the Imperator's doing?" Enitan demands, walking briskly toward the nearest tubelift. Letting her sibling make the choice was hard, but she thought they'd finally found relative safety.

Kulta shrugs. "You can ask Xiang yourself soon enough."

The tubelift carries them silently up to the Imperial residence, but there's ringing in Enitan's ears. She stomps down the corridor leading to the Imperator's informal dining room, anger building with each step.

The doors slide open at her approach. The Imperator and Xiang are having supper.

Enitan rushes over to her sibling's side. "You didn't leave?"

"Well, the shuttle did take off." Xiang daintily wipes their mouth with an embroidered napkin as Enitan pulls them in for a hug. "I just made it turn around."

Enitan levels a withering stare at the God of Vaalbara. "What did you say to them?"

"Nothing much, really."

"That's a lie. They were ready to leave," Enitan says. She turns back to Xiang. "You should have gone."

"It's not my fault you weren't there to stop me." They give a dramatic sniffle. "You didn't even come to say goodbye."

Enitan leans against the table. "I knew I'd end up on that shuttle with you if I did. Why did you change your mind?" she asks, since the Imperator's lips seem sealed on the subject.

"We're stronger together," Xiang says simply as they serve themself a sliver of fake fish. "And I have an idea."

TWENTY-SIX

"The chest piece is surprisingly flexible," says Xiang, pulling on their new helmet.

Enitan frowns. Like Kulta, they're indistinguishable from another sentinel in the armor. This is too close to a version of what the Nlamiraan wanted: a faceless warrior trapped in a body not their own. Seeing Xiang dressed in armor plucks at every nerve in her body. And she's already been on edge since Xiang shared their plan.

"I don't like this," she says again. The new arrangements don't allow for Kulta and Katun to escort them. They're on their own.

Xiang paces around the room. "It's our best option. I'll be hidden in plain sight, and we'll be there to protect each other." They stride over to a shelf of energy weapons. "How many events do you have today?"

Enitan's frown deepens. "Three. The first is in half an hour."

Xiang pulls a dissection gun from the shelf and attaches it to the magnetic holster at their hip. Enitan reaches over and lifts a shockstaff from the wall. It's surprisingly light. The blunt end of the weapon felt so much heavier when being struck by it. She hands the staff to her sibling.

As they take the tubelift down to her first engagement of the day, unease brews in Enitan's stomach. Out here in the open, they're both extremely vulnerable, although she supposes once they're among nobles, there'll be a layer of relative safety. And she can't cancel all her appointments without arousing serious suspicion, so she might as well use these as reconnaissance. Still, she's unhappy at potentially putting Xiang directly in harm's way.

Fear curdles in her gut as she leads Xiang across a wide atrium with high windows. All it would take is two good shots from a dissection rifle to end them both. To her relief, however, they reach the suite of the event's host—Admiral Qinnalt, a war hero to Vaalbarans and a terrorist to Korikese—unharmed.

A bolt of anxiety shoots through Enitan when the door flies open before she can even knock.

"Oh, look!" The admiral turns toward her guests. "It's the Imperator's pet."

There it is. Beneath her usual plastered-on agreeable smile, Enitan curses all of them via the Ancestors she knows by name. She sets a pot of water to boil and pulls out her last tea tin. Its contents are more theehma than uhie now, considering how many times she's topped off her original stock.

"I must know," says the admiral, draping her lanky form over her plush cinnabar-colored couch. "Did the Imperator assign you a sentinel to protect you from her enemies or to keep you from straying? I know you Korikese are *insatiable.*"

When she speaks, Enitan keeps her face and voice studiously deadpan. "I can't claim to know Her Imperial Majesty's mind."

The admiral smirks. "Only her body, then?"

Xiang stiffens beside her and takes a half step forward. Enitan grabs them by the arm and shoots them a sharp look. Giving the admiral a taste of the suffering she's heaped on Koriko isn't worth it, not when they can get a far more lasting revenge by freeing their home. Xiang moves back, but Enitan can tell they're still staring hard at the admiral, who is laughing obliviously with her friends.

"Well?" snaps the admiral, turning to them with a flare of impatience. "I told everyone I'd have God's plaything at my party, but that doesn't mean much if no one sees you." She flicks a gloved hand at her. "Go show yourself."

Enitan nods, too nervous about their safety again to focus on her anger. Xiang follows her out of the foyer and down a wide hallway stuffed with classical Imperial art. Two monks glare at her with an acidic mix of disgust and rage, but this is hardly the most hostile behavior she's seen since she entered the Splinter. Then a third appears, glancing at her in alarm and elbowing his brethren away.

All too familiar warning bells go off in Enitan's head, but she forces her body to relax. She's being paranoid. They're *monks*, for Ancestors' sake. Like Stijena back home, they're harmless.

"How can you tolerate this?" Xiang whispers. They don't sound accusatory, just shocked and sad. "Serving tea to these monsters and smiling through the abuse."

"We've got bigger problems to fret about than their derision," Enitan replies, ignoring the wide-eyed stare of a member of Parliament. Her communicator chimes, and she pulls it out of her pocket—it's an encrypted message from the Imperator. Her mouth goes dry as she unlocks it. She says in a low voice, "The uprising has been quelled. Looks like the Nlamiraan's operations are still moving forward."

A short colonel sidles up to Enitan, sweeping wavy black hair behind her ear. "Lo and behold." Her breath reeks of wine. It's only midday. "Qinnalt isn't full of it after all!" She sticks out a hand to touch Enitan's hair. "Are styles this short common back on Koriko?"

Xiang grabs her wrist before she can make contact. "Please keep your hands to yourself."

The colonel lets out a harsh laugh. "Oho! Right, she's private property, hmm?" She smirks before stepping away from Enitan.

"I'm going to tell Menkhet about her," Xiang growls.

"Again, we have more important things to worry about." She puts a hand on their armored elbow. "If the rebellion has been crushed, then Ishamsa already has everything—every*one*—they need for their army, even with the rest of the Nlamiraan gone."

Xiang nods. "We have two days to find them, then."

Enitan swallows tightly, the muscles of her throat contracting painfully. "Why?"

"The formal conditioning program can take as little as two days," Xiang says, their voice tight. "Breaking free of the brainwashing isn't impossible, obviously, but it's not easy. We have to stop Ishamsa before they even start the process on their final wave of captive soldiers."

Yoraq was the true name of the man Erseydis had called her most senior "servant," Cyani. The words he spoke to Enitan back then echo in her head. *What they take from you during conditioning, you don't always get back.* How many others are already too far gone?

"Let's just leave," Enitan whispers. "No one here is of any interest anyway."

Xiang follows her back toward the foyer. When the admiral runs up to stop them, they snap, "The Imperator has summoned her. If you want to complain, petition Her Imperial Majesty."

The admiral practically scurries away. Enitan and Xiang stride through the sliding door into the hallway. They're halfway to the nearest tubelift when the trio of monks step into their path.

"Enitan!" Xiang yells. "Get back."

Two of them pull dissection guns from their robes while a third draws out a wickedly curved knife. The first two turn on Xiang, guns cocked and aimed. The knife wielder stalks toward Enitan.

"Who sent you?" she hisses, backing away. Panic coils around her heart like a slyythfang, its venom a heady mix of adrenaline and fear.

"You'll find out soon enough," says the monk. "Come with us and you won't get hurt."

It's obvious now that these monks aren't trained fighters. If they were, the trio would've gotten far closer to them before revealing their weapons. Even Enitan knows that in an ambush, surprise is key.

"And the sentinel?" she demands, keeping her voice as even as she can.

He glances over at his fellow monks. "Why do you care?"

Enitan doesn't answer. She charges at the first monk as Xiang fires off two shots at the others, stunning one. She barrels into the man, throwing them both to the ground. She doesn't attempt to wrestle the knife from him; fingers take months to regenerate. Instead, she pins his thrashing arm to the ground, struggling to keep the rest of him down with a knee on his chest.

A stray shot slices deep into the wall by her head.

"Watch it!" Enitan yells.

"Sorry!" Xiang calls from over their shoulder, gasping.

The monk gives up trying to buck her off and wrenches his arm from her grip, releasing the knife. The weapon clatters onto the marble floor. He surges upward, driving his shoulder into Enitan's chest. She falls off him and scrambles away as he takes hold of the knife. He rushes toward her, the blade held high.

But before he can deal a lethal blow, the third monk runs in between them. He opens the nearest window with a sweep of his hand. He glances at Enitan's attacker for one searing second, then throws himself out, condemning himself to a bloody death kilometers below.

"Florus!" the knife wielder screams. "No!"

The second monk, half recovered from the stun blast, darts after the first. He's not as quick. He falls in neat little slices at Enitan's feet. Her sibling is standing a few paces behind her, their dissection gun, now set to lethal, smoking in their grip.

Xiang pivots so that the firearm is now pointed at the last monk's head. "Drop the knife."

It clatters to the floor.

◆

Xiang shoves the man into a tubelift, wrists bound.

His lips peel back into a grimace. "Where are you beasts taking me?"

Enitan ignores him, pressing her hand against the screen-surface of the transport.

The monk wriggles around, glaring up at Xiang. "You traitor," he hisses. "How could you side with the savage over your own?"

A strange crackling sound comes through the helmet's speaker. It takes Enitan a moment to realize Xiang is laughing. They grip the monk a little tighter. When the tubelift slides open, they steer him through the door. "Well, you attacked me first."

"If you're going to kill me, just do it," whispers the monk, going slack.

Enitan falters, nearly stumbling. Even though he's just tried to kill her, ending him would feel wrong. He may be a bigoted fool, but he's just a pawn, and that's cost him two of his people. He was probably fed lies about her before being sent on this mission.

She crosses her arms. "We're not planning to kill you."

"Just get it over with," he chokes out. "Know that God will avenge me. She will condemn you to an eternity of suffering."

Any compassion for him suddenly evaporates. "That's funny," she says instead, pressing her fingerprints into the final door.

It slides open. The Imperator turns around.

When Xiang lets the monk go, he drops to the ground immediately, his knees hitting the tile with what sounds like a painful crack. He folds over onto his elbows and presses his forehead to the glistening floor.

"I suggest you start talking," says the Imperator, "while you still have a tongue with which to do it."

"Forgive me, Your Supreme Holiness, but I had to," the monk gasps out, his voice catching in his throat. "She's a threat to your safety."

"I disagree," says the Imperator.

"Of course your word is true and perfect," the monk says. "And of course it is our sacred burden as Vaalbarans to aid the poor wretches of this world, for without us to guide them, their souls would fester and rot beneath the weight of their sin." He's trembling now. "They know not what they do. How could they, with their shrunken minds? But she and her kind are dangerous."

"I hope, for your sake," the Imperator growls, her voice like thunder, "that the next words out of your mouth are a very good explanation for why you tried to abduct my friend."

"She's a spy, Your Supreme Holiness." The monk pushes himself up onto his elbows. "She was sent to ensnare you by the treacherous High Consul, seducing you just as she seduced the traitorous governor of Koriko Province."

Ajana.

Enitan freezes, her heart pounding so hard she can't hear his next words. She forces herself not to turn to look at Xiang.

The monk stops speaking. For a horribly long moment, the Imperator says nothing. Then she cocks her head at him. "Who told you that?"

The monk hesitates. His gaze flits frantically about the room before falling to the ground.

The Imperator narrows her eyes. *"Speak."*

"We were told our actions were in your best interest, Your Supreme Holiness," the monk whines.

"How dare you presume to know my best interest," the Imperator says quietly.

It's as if she roared in his face. The man wilts like a malnourished plant.

"It was the abbot of Bireen," he whispers.

Enitan recognizes the name—he's the man who always shows up to museum galas to bid on Korikese artifacts. "Sacha Surui?"

"You will refer to His Holiness with the proper address," the monk snarls.

"The very same," the Imperator says, ignoring him. "Sacha is the Supreme Abbot's ex-husband."

"He still holds influence over them," says Enitan, recalling a tidbit of gossip she overheard a few weeks ago. "Possibly blackmail."

Xiang crosses their arms. "Why did Sacha tell you to kidnap Enitan?"

"We . . . we were supposed to hold her hostage so we could set a trap for her sibling."

And the Imperator, no doubt, though the abbot would certainly have omitted that part.

The Imperator arches a brow. " 'Her sibling'?"

"Yes, Your Supreme Holiness. A rogue auxiliary sentinel. The abbot told us of your plan to use the Korikese to crush Ominira." The monk sits up, a fire burning in his eyes. "The savage Xiang Ijebu turned traitor and went missing from the new army forces. They are responsible for all the deaths these past few months. Banurra, Fenris, Erseydis, Vidra and his son. None of them were accidents or suicides or whatever nonsense the news stations are peddling." He falters now, gaze flicking from the Imperator to Enitan and then settling upon Xiang. "Abbot Surui has been attempting to hunt them down, but the Imperial spies he sent have vanished without a trace. He has selected only the most loyal among the Holy Order to replace them."

There it is. The abbot is Ishamsa, the last of the shadow councilors. Enitan looks over at the Imperator; she has no doubt that the synths are responsible for the vanished spies.

The Imperator clasps her hands behind her back. "Where is he now?"

The monk doesn't even hesitate. He truly believes the woman before him is divine. "He and many of my devout siblings are positioned on the abandoned floor between the seventh and eighth stories."

If so, they are in hiding, which means she was wrong about Ishamsa; the man *is* craven. She curses herself for exploring the floor no further.

"Sacha is not acting on my orders," says the Imperator, very quietly. "In fact, he's been working *against* my best interest all this time."

"I've begun to suspect that just now, Your Supreme Holiness."

The Imperator snorts. "You should've reported him when he told you to hide out on an abandoned level with him."

The monk prostrates himself for a second time. "Please, have mercy on me."

"I don't blame you for this," the Imperator says. "But I also can't let you run off and warn Sacha, inadvertently or not." She turns halfway around. "Kazu, restrain him."

From the shadows, a hulking shape emerges. An eight-foot-tall synth steps into the light.

"Enitan and Xiang, this is Kulta's little sibling," says the Imperator. "Kazu, this is Enitan and Xiang."

The monk sputters. "The traitor sentinel serves you?"

The Imperator regards him with cold eyes. "Xiang is their own master." To Kazu she says, "Take him to my holding cells. We'll deal with him later."

The Imperator stalks off toward another door.

"Where are you going?" Enitan asks, rushing to catch up with her.

"We can't wait for Sacha to realize his monks have failed," says the Imperator, striding into her armory. "We have to find him immediately, before he can escape." She pulls her axe off the wall and offers a dissection gun to Enitan. "I assume you'll be coming even if I ask you not to."

Enitan accepts the gun. "So you're learning."

TWENTY-SEVEN

With a swipe of her finger, the Imperator rotates the three-dimensional projection before her. The abandoned story between the seventh and eighth levels, color coded and rendered in exquisite detail, spins so that its holographic entrance now faces Kulta. All twenty of the synth's craft-siblings stand in rows behind him.

"I have no idea which of my honor guard and the Splinter's sentinel force are loyal to the Nlamiraan," says the Imperator, "so we have to do this alone." She expands the entrance and looks up at the synths. "The level is one massive, near-perfect square, with a corridor running around the outer edges. Kulta will take half of you around the corridor to secure all the exits. No one gets in, no one gets out. The rest of you will come with Enitan, Xiang, and me. According to our little monk friend, Sacha's underlings are all in the central area of the level, save for the ones currently prowling the palace. There are about a hundred sentinels under his direct control. I'm going to announce myself to Sacha's monks, since most of them are unaware that they're not acting on my orders." She crosses her arms. "Now, I'm hoping that the majority will turn on Sacha, but I anticipate a number of them are going to try to make a run for it or, worse, attack us. In the case of the former, Kulta and his group will handle them. And if the latter happens, the rest of you will arrest them first, as well as any sentinels we find. Try not to kill anyone." She closes the holomap with a brisk sweep of her hand.

"If everything goes to shit, our priority is Sacha. We can let everyone else slip through our fingers if it comes to it, but he's going down. Understand?"

The synths all nod at once.

"Any questions? Objections?"

"No, sir," the synths say in unison.

"Good. Let's go."

They all head toward the exit of the war room, but before Enitan can follow Kulta out, the Imperator steps up to her side. She opens her mouth, hesitates, and closes it again. "Just . . . be careful." Before Enitan can reply, she gives a tight smile and rushes to the head of the group. Enitan follows Xiang into one of the secured tubelifts, which drops them off on the eighth floor. From there, they creep down a flight of emergency stairs and up to the main entrance of the story, the same one Enitan came across weeks ago.

The Imperator gives the signal, sweeping a flat hand into the swirling darkness, before darting over the threshold. Kulta's squad splits off a few steps in, and Enitan increases her pace to close the gap. The abandoned story is as quiet as she remembers, but much colder; its temperature regulation system must have been removed. At least this area, which she never came across in her wanderings, has a little more light; the burning blue sky peeks out from between boarded-up windows, and dust motes dance around in the narrow golden beams.

Xiang, now in the same simple protective garb as Enitan, exchanges grins with her as they round a corner. She feels strangely calm. It's as if her soul has left her body; she moves through the passages like she's being pulled by invisible strings. In a few minutes, this will all be over. The last of the Nlamiraan will be eradicated, and her people will be free. It's so much more than she could have hoped for the day she arrived at the Splinter.

It's when they reach the chosen entrance to the central area that

Enitan's peace shatters. Every muscle in her body tenses as two synths step forward to pry open the rusted doors. Shouts echo as the craft-siblings pour in, the Imperator at their head. Enitan follows them, pulse quickening and a hand slipping down to the gun holstered at her hip.

The huge chamber looks like it might've had a past life as an auditorium or ballroom. Lightrods hanging from the walls and silvery lamps scattered over the floor illuminate dozens of stricken faces: Sacha's monks, frozen in fear. Enitan swivels and spots the Imperator climbing onto a huge block of stone at the other end of the room—a stage.

"Friends," the Imperator calls out. "I mean you no harm. I know that you are all loyal citizens of Vaalbara and faithful servants of the Church. Abbot Sacha Surui has deceived you. He is an enemy of the Empire, and I need your help to apprehend him."

None of the monks attack Enitan or the synths—a massive relief, though Enitan isn't surprised. Like the monks who ambushed her and Xiang, these aren't trained warriors. And even if they haven't figured out that the squads flanking the Imperator are made up of synths, there's no way anyone could miss that they're armed to the teeth. Half the monks make a run for it, scrambling toward the exits where Kulta and the others are waiting. The rest fall wailing and useless onto their knees, begging their God for forgiveness or mercy or death. Enitan watches the Imperator bark out inaudible orders to the nearest synth.

"Your Imperial Holiness, he's running away!" screams a monk, pointing at a rapidly retreating figure in rich cobalt.

Enitan springs into action, racing for the abbot. Xiang and the synths fly after her.

Katun fires off a warning shot, speeding past Enitan. "Halt!" he yells. "Halt in the name of your God-Emperor!"

The abbot doesn't oblige. He flings himself through an ancient door, which slams shut just as Kiran reaches it, nearly slicing off her nose. Enitan and Xiang catch up to her, panting hard. They both curse when they see the door. There's no screen-surface to hack or override, only a manual lock.

Kiran pulls a thin electronic tool from her pocket and sticks it into the lock. "From what I can tell, the mechanism is ancient," she says, fiddling with the pick. "None of us have the training for models like this. It's going to take a while."

The Imperator joins them, frowning deeply. "Get started. If it doesn't work, we can always wait him out. He can't stay in there forever."

"I'm detecting an outgoing signal," says Kiran, pressing a hand to her temple. "Shit. He's calling for his sentinels."

Enitan's hand tightens around her gun—in the chaos, she forgot about them. "Where are they? Why aren't they here?"

"They must have been sent to your chambers, Menkhet." Kiran clenches her jaw. "To kill you."

The Imperator's brows practically disappear into her hairline. "Well, good thing we're here."

"We can take them," says Katun, cocking his gun.

"And let Sacha sneak away in the bedlam?" The Imperator shakes her head. "No, we need to get him now."

"I can do it," says Xiang. "Maybe."

Enitan stares at them before understanding. "Your friends back home."

Xiang takes the pick from Kiran's outstretched hand. "The sentinels used models like these on storehouses so we couldn't hack them." They kneel and get to work, a familiar look of concentration settling over their features.

Enitan stands stiffly beside them, ears straining for the telltale march of armored boots or the modulated growl of voices through a helmet.

"They're coming," says Kiran, shifting into a battle stance. "Kulta and the others should be able to hold them off for a little while, but . . ."

"Shit, shit, shit," says Xiang. Their hands are shaking as they continue working the lock.

"How much longer?" asks Enitan.

"I don't think I can—" There's a loud click as the door slides open with a whine. "It worked!"

The Imperator pats Xiang on the shoulder. Enitan grimaces when Katun leans down and lands a big kiss on their cheek. She's about to say something when someone screams outside. The cry is quickly swallowed by the screech of dozens of dissection guns.

"Go," the Imperator yells. "Now!"

The group bursts into the room, and Kiran shuts the door behind them. A long corridor stretches ahead, all of the doors closed—all of them with standard locks, to her relief. Enitan's heart beats faster with each step she takes down the passage, synths opening entryways as they go. They're nearly at the end of the corridor when they find the abbot.

He's pressed against the back wall of the second-to-last room, a dissection gun gripped tightly in his hands. He chuckles ruefully when the Imperator steps in. "Never in a thousand years would I suspect our God of colluding with savages to destroy her own Empire."

"Put down the gun," orders the Imperator. "It's over. You're outnumbered. The monks have learned of your deception, and those who have not yet been captured soon will be."

"Congratulations, Your Supreme Holiness," snaps the abbot. He drops the gun and folds his hands, the picture—if not the reality—of demure surrender as he sinks into a deep bow. "You should kill me, then." His face is perfectly smooth, but his voice is flinty. He won't go down easily.

"No, I don't think so," says the Imperator. "Not yet, anyway."

"You want information? I'd die before telling you a thing." He looks around the room, pure loathing in his eyes. A sneer crawls over his face when his gaze latches on to Enitan. "The others wanted a Korikese hostage. I tried to convince them not to take you," he says. "Tradition, they insisted. They didn't understand that certain tactics only work on *people*, not you abominations—"

The Imperator backhands him. He topples onto the floor, blood dripping from a split lip. She bends down over him, her serene face inches from his. "You will give me the names of every last person working under the Nlamiraan," she says, her tone icy as a glacier.

Without warning, the abbot yanks a dagger from his robes and swings it toward her. "Never!"

In the space of a few seconds, the Imperator grabs his wrist, snatches the knife, and stabs it through his hand, pinning it to the floor. With no small amount of satisfaction, Enitan recognizes that the dagger is the same one the abbot obtained at the auction.

The Imperator sighs. "You won't die before you give me what I want, Sacha. I'll make sure of that."

The abbot gapes at his impaled hand, mouth gasping and eyes bulging. His other hand, trembling and sweaty and pale, lifts toward the handle of the knife. The Imperator grabs his wrist before he can pull out the blade and breaks three of his fingers in one quick motion. This time, he screams.

"Names, Sacha." Her voice is impossibly level.

He whimpers, nostrils flaring.

The Imperator's grip tightens around the broken appendages.

The abbot gives a terrified moan. "All right, I'll do it," he wails. "Whatever you want, just please—please . . ."

"Now that wasn't so hard, was it?" the Imperator says. She yanks out the knife and stands.

The abbot cries out as blood gushes from his hand onto the dusty floor.

The Imperator turns to Katun. "Take him to the interrogation room. Use whatever methods necessary to get those names, then pull up those records and arrest all of them. If it turns out Sacha here has missed anyone when you question them, make him sorely regret that he did." She pauses at the door, frowning. "What's the situation outside?"

Kiran touches her temple. "Kulta and the others have restrained the arriving sentinels, with the help of most of the monks."

"Excellent." The Imperator wipes her hand on her tunic. "I'm scheduled to hold court this evening, so I'll see all of you later."

She strides out, leaving the abbot a twitching mess on the floor. Xiang takes Enitan's hand in theirs, a question in their eyes.

She takes a long, deep breath to steady her heart. "I'm fine." More than, actually.

They've won.

◆

Along with a long list of names, the abbot supplies the locations of every holding facility the abducted Korikese have been trapped in. Kulta departs the Splinter with all but one of his craft-siblings; Xiang is off with Katun somewhere, celebrating as they should. For a few hours, at least, the only company Enitan has is her own.

With the rescue of her kidnapped people and the capture of the shadow councilors' underlings, the blight of the Nlamiraan will be finally purged from the system. The members of the shadow council are either dead or rotting in prison. Their followers will be brought to justice. And the therapists who facilitated Xiang's recovery are finalizing a treatment program for the Korikese sentinels.

Enitan's work, for now, is over.

She finds herself wandering the halls, meandering down twisting corridors and through vast, open rooms. An hour passes before she realizes that she's following a sound, small and burbling and barely audible over the background hum of the Splinter. As her feet carry her closer to the origin, the noise resolves into the Imperial anthem. Enitan stops in the middle of the passageway, brow knitted. The song is bright, uplifting. Cheerful. The last time she heard it, it sounded like death. Though perhaps that's because it was drowned out by gunshots and screaming.

She eventually finds the source: the palace's tertiary audience room. That's right—the Imperator said she was holding court. There are no doors to the chamber, so Enitan steps right in, joining the dense crowd of people already inside. It seems the Imperator was being over-dramatic about the low survival rate of complainants.

She looks around, her fingers twining together as a sudden wave of unease washes over her. The walls, towering stretches of darkened, gold-flecked steel, sport black banners and torches filled with real flame. The floor is a massive slab of inky stone, seamless and perfectly even. A length of black silk runs from the entrance to an enormous throne. The knifelike edges of the chair drip impossibly upward to the ceiling. The overall effect is disorienting, as if gravity is constantly being broken and then re-formed to better suit the seated figure.

It is almost impossible to tell where the throne ends and the Imperator begins. Enitan's gaze rises from a pair of polished boots, up a black suit barely more ornate than hers, and finally to the Imperator's face. She *looks* serene, but the tightness around her eyes tells Enitan otherwise. She lifts a gloved hand to adjust the black band over her brow—the only sign of her rank.

The whole affair appears to be ending. The Imperator stands and looks out over the crowd, and the sentinels at the foot of the throne bang their shockstaffs against the floor. When her gaze meets Enitan's, her stern frown slips into a subtle smile. She steps from the dais and makes her way down the audience hall to the door at her left, the sentinels falling into line behind her. After the Imperator's departure, the petitioners begin to file out, a slow-moving river of people flowing through the exit. Enitan finds a cushioned bench by the wall and sits down, waiting for the room to clear instead of trying to wrestle her way out. But even when the chamber is empty, she remains seated.

There are colossal windows on the wall facing her, giving a spectacular view of the setting sun. The black floor glows under the golden-red light, its surface transmuted into a gilded mirror.

"Hey."

"Hey." Enitan doesn't turn around. She slides down the bench and leans back against the cold steel wall.

After a moment, the Imperator sits beside her. "What are you doing here?"

When Enitan glances over, the Imperator favors her with an amused arch of her brow.

"I'm watching the sunset," she says.

A sigh.

Enitan laces her hands together, watching the reflection of a vermillion cloud ripple over the floor. "I was trying to decide something."

"Regarding what?" Is that a hint of worry in the Imperator's voice? "I . . . wish you hadn't seen me like that," she says softly.

Enitan shrugs, the room cold around her. "I've seen people hurt far worse than a knife through the hand, and for far worse reasons." She lets out a bitter laugh. "And I've done my fair share of bloodletting."

"You're not comfortable with violence, though."

"Who is?"

"I'm desensitized to it," says the Imperator. "I'm sorry for exposing you to more."

"Everything I've done, I've done willingly. I chose to join the raid." Enitan turns halfway around, looking right at the Imperator. "I realize that violence is a necessary evil."

The Imperator crosses her arms. "I disagree."

Enitan raises a brow.

"You must think me a hypocrite. But violence isn't necessary." The Imperator lifts the onyx circlet from her head and drops it onto her lap. "It's just the easiest option, most times, but never the simplest. A life isn't the only thing lost when you kill someone."

"Hmm."

"You believe otherwise."

"No." Enitan closes her eyes for a few breaths. "I could've shown mercy to the shadow councilors I killed, but they would have destroyed everything I love."

The Imperator nods. "So. You've made a decision, then?"

Enitan turns back toward the window, away from the Imperator's gaze. The cloud is gone, having drifted beyond the edge of the farthest window. "I have."

TWENTY-EIGHT

Surrounded by blossoming trees and vibrantly pigmented bushes, burbling streams and rippling pools, chirping iyebirds and the twinkling song of wind chimes, Enitan can almost, almost, pretend that she's back in Ijebu. They're in the Imperator's secondary private garden, seated around a table in a shade-drenched gazebo.

When the Imperator invited her here for lunch, Enitan considered, for the briefest of seconds, pretending she hadn't seen the message. But now she's glad she didn't; this place is nothing like the hanging gardens a dozen levels below.

The gazebo sits on a small island at the center of a shimmering lake. The crystal-clear water is full of brightly colored fish, which pop up to the surface every time a particularly bright leaf or petal spins down and alights upon the water.

"Are you going to eat?" asks the Imperator.

Enitan surveys the midday meal between them: rings of fried nut butter, starchy root vegetable dumplings, spicy seared cubes of fake meat, and melon seed soup. At the center of the feast sits a crystal pitcher of mhimat, an ancient Vaalbaran delicacy. It's a sweet, chilled cordial made from fresh wild herbs, flowers, fruit, and seeds. It all looks and smells delicious, but the thought of eating tightens the knot in her gut. She forces herself to spoon a little of the soup anyway.

"Are you all right?"

"I'm fine," Enitan says, as pleasantly as she can. "I'm just tired." She watches the Imperator as she pours them both a cup of tea. The white uhie brew has a mellow, honeyed flavor, with just the faintest touch of tartness.

The Imperator helps herself to a heaping spoonful of sugar syrup. It smells faintly of inablossoms. "Even the sweetest fruit becomes bitter if its tree is planted in poisoned ground," she says.

Enitan fights a tiny smile. "Pardon?"

"You know, you've changed." The Imperator stirs in the syrup. "You're much more guarded than you were just a few months ago." Her voice is wistful.

"You'd rather I had remained naive?" Enitan asks, cocking her head.

"No. I know that if you hadn't adapted, you wouldn't have survived in the Splinter." The Imperator stares into her tea. "I experienced the same loss of innocence here. It's bittersweet."

"You're quite philosophical this afternoon," remarks Enitan. But so are most Vaalbarans on a given day.

"I finally have the time and space for it," says the Imperator. "No one's threatening my life or yours." She lifts her cup to her lips.

Enitan shoots a hand out. "Don't drink that."

"Why not?" The Imperator puts her cup down with a playful smile. "Did you poison it?"

Enitan laughs, though the question makes her heart feel like it's about to burst from her rib cage. "Don't drink that *yet*," she says, as calmly she can muster. "It's far too hot."

"Are you sure that's all?" The Imperator blows calmly on her tea. "I know you spied for the High Consul, and that they asked you to kill me."

Shock and shame rise into Enitan's throat. Every emotion she's tamped down since coming here falls from her mouth in two words: "I'm sorry."

"Don't be." The Imperator takes a sip of tea. Her expression is impenetrable. "If I were in your position, I would have done whatever it took to save my people."

Something in her carefully neutral expression makes Enitan worry that she's about to erupt, but then she notices that the Imperator's shoulders are shaking. She's holding back laughter.

Enitan's own shoulders do not relax. "How can you find humor in this?" she asks, bristling.

The Imperator chortles. "You didn't think I'd have a few synths hidden in the Ominirish capital? In the High Consul's own household, perhaps?" She smirks. "And you may have learned how to navigate the riptide that is this court, but you aren't as skilled as you think at masking your emotions."

Enitan says nothing. She grabs her cup and drains it.

"Another thing," says the Imperator. "I know you're aware by now that I killed Meayng and Banurra. Plus a few of my own faithless agents, sent by Sacha to kill me."

Enitan blinks. "I don't understand why you enlisted me in the first place."

"Meayng had . . . a stronger will than I anticipated," the Imperator says, adding another spoonful of syrup. "He died without revealing a thing, so I had to start over to find Banurra. And figuring out how best to kill the duke took ages. I needed someone who could gather information without triggering suspicion."

"May I ask you a question?"

"Of course. But know that you might not like the answer."

"Why the rings?" Enitan asks, recalling her discovery of Banurra's blood-flecked bands.

"Oh," the God of Vaalbara says, grimacing. "Well, I thought they might signal to you that you had an ally here. But I was also inordinately high when I sent those, along with the suits. I realized later that it might have seemed threatening. My apologies."

"One more question."

The Imperator nods.

"How did you really become Imperator?"

"I was wondering when you'd ask." She pauses. "It's a very long story, but the short of it is that I sided with some very influential people. You know of Obara Uloyiso?"

"All Korikese children born after the annexation do." She still can't reconcile the woman who once tried to eradicate her people with Jeong's mother.

"She was the Council's messenger and my handler. In some ways, their unofficial leader was far too high-profile to become a full member." The Imperator refills Enitan's cup. "But before that, she was my mentor. At least, she fancied herself as such. My plans for Vaalbara's future were formulated years ago, and I knew I needed the crown to see them through. Once I figured out that she and her invisible friends were really running things, I promised to support her goals, whatever they might be, though I obviously had no intention of following through. It was no secret she resented my predecessor for his surrender. I told her that she was right, that Ominira had to burn, that I'd carry the torch myself. She told me that if I meant what I said, she'd make me Imperator. And then she did." There is such deep regret in her voice; Enitan looks away. "By the time I discovered what her true goals were, it was too late. I was barely old enough to remember when she razed Koriko to the ground, but I should have known better. She'd begun kidnapping Korikese long before my coronation."

"Did you kill her?"

The Imperator runs a finger over the figure carved into her cup's handle. It looks like a saljutiger, bent over the rim to lap at the tea within. "Obara died in her sleep."

For a long time, the two women say nothing.

Enitan is the one to break the quiet. "The coming days won't be easy. Koriko means nothing to Vaalbara in any way that matters, but your people will see giving it up as a sign of weakness. Capitulation to the wishes of your barbarian mistress."

The Imperator winces but nods. "We need to convince the Empire that the moon's independence is both necessary and inevitable. With the Nlamiraan gone, I have the freedom to forge new policy, but I can't push things so far so soon. Kulta and his craft-siblings are still tracking down the councilors' underlings for arrest."

"You know this will hurt you politically. So why are you doing it?" Enitan asks.

The Imperator looks down as she considers her next words. "The biggest threat to Vaalbara is Vaalbara itself. A system built upon continued exploitation will not survive."

Enitan gives her a look. The system seemed to have been surviving just fine before she came along. But she has to admire the Imperator's integrity, optimistic as it may be. "That's it?"

Sadness bleeds into the Imperator's voice. "Is it not enough that this is the right thing to do? That I want to help end this suffering and find another way for my people?"

"I would like it to be enough. But it has *always* been the right thing, and that's made little difference."

"Well, I intend to make that difference." The Imperator looks over at Enitan, eyes glistening like two black stones underwater.

Enitan nods slowly. "Xiang and I owe you our lives." But they've also secured her position of ultimate power. "I do trust you, but we know each other primarily as allies rather than people. Perhaps we can change that."

"Yes, I'd like that." Menkhet's smile flashes like a faraway star. Then she looks down at her tea. "You've diluted this, haven't you?"

TWENTY-NINE

When the headwoman answers Enitan's call, her first words are: "We thought you were dead."

Despite it all, Enitan finds herself smiling. "Hello to you, too, *Mother*."

The headwoman wrinkles her nose. "Please don't call me that."

"I'm glad you're alive."

"Likewise." The headwoman crosses her arms. "The new governor told us they were going to kill you if anyone so much as breathed the wrong way. And when that farce of a rebellion spread from Lishtaqa to Tamoko, he stopped talking about you altogether. What happened?"

"You must have heard the rumors. I'm the Imperator's mistress."

The headwoman snorts. "No you aren't."

Enitan huffs a laugh. She should've known the headwoman would see right through her. "But we did become friends."

All mirth vanishes from the woman's features. "How could you become friends with that monster?"

"There's a lot I want to tell you that I can't say now," says Enitan. "But I promise you that she's not like her predecessors. Xiang wouldn't still be here without her." She looks away, heat inexplicably rising to her cheeks. "And we're going to work together to free Koriko of Vaalbaran rule."

For a moment, the headwoman says nothing. "Is this true?"

"It is." Enitan leans forward. "I'm having a hard time believing it myself."

"When will you be returning to Ijebu?"

"As soon as I can," says Enitan. "Once Koriko's independence is set in stone, I'm taking the first ship back. But right now, I'm afraid there's an ulterior motive to this call."

"Oh?"

"The Imperator has asked me to request, on her behalf, that you advise her on how best her people can make amends to the communities. We were hoping you could join our next meeting from afar."

She's well aware that this won't be a painless undertaking. But there's no better cause to devote her efforts to. She wasn't lying about going back home, though, and she intends to leave the politicking to the headpeople and the Imperator, helping only where she's asked. When she'd sworn to remain in Vaalbara for as long as it took to take down the Council, she'd genuinely feared she'd remain trapped here forever. The thought of finally returning to something resembling normalcy is a pleasant one.

The headwoman chuckles.

Enitan cocks her head. "What?"

The headwoman gives her the slightest of smiles. "How you've grown, Enitan Ijebu."

◆

"How do you feel?" asks Menkhet, donning a heavy gold bracelet.

Tonight is the last time she'll wear it. After tonight, every shiny treasure in the Imperial vault with even questionable history will be quietly returned to its land of origin. She'll still have more gems than she could wear in three lifetimes, but most of the crown jewels will be gone.

"Wonderful, for the first time in . . . I can't remember how long." Enitan, seated beside Menkhet on the settee in her second private drawing room, sighs happily. "I know it won't be overnight, but at least things are finally changing."

The Korikese people the Nlamiraan tore from their homes have been found and are finally headed back home. Saban and the others have already begun to organize the rehabilitation efforts, with Jeong acting as liaison between them and sympathetic nobles. Sentinels in recently annexed regions are slowly being summoned back to the Empire.

"You know, you don't have to attend the feast if you don't want to," Menkhet says, placing a soft hand on Enitan's knee. "I'd think you were rather sick of Vaalbaran parties by now."

"Oh, I am." Enitan presses her fingers over Menkhet's, tracing the pale scars etched over the other woman's knuckles. "But now I finally have a reason to celebrate."

Menkhet stands with a laugh, before pursing her lips. Her hand is still in Enitan's. "My attendants are waiting for me to get ready. You should go down first."

Enitan lets her go, a little reluctantly. "I'll see you later."

Menkhet nods. She brushes Enitan's arm with her fingers as she goes, a touch so light and fleeting Enitan wonders if she's imagined it. She walks out and steps into a tubelift, still smiling by the time she reaches the palace's great hall. Then the doors slide open, and Enitan barely manages to rein in her surprise. She knew to expect a great deal of pomp, especially after the last grand party she attended, but the decadence before her exceeds all expectations.

A thousand bright-blue flames burn within a thousand silver braziers, illuminating an ocean of artfully arranged divans and cushions. Lines of fire dance around fountains of alcohol, mimicking waving reeds beside a stream; rivers of rum flow around waterfalls of whiskey, all wreathed in more fluttering cobalt. The rich and powerful of Vaalbara meander around the colossal space, piling their jeweled plates high. And the food—Enitan has never seen so much of it all in one place. Towering pyramids of artificial iyebirds, glistening with fake fat and glittering with spun sugar. Gigantic, bloody hunks of lab-grown meat rotate on gilded spits, spilling roasted nuts and dried fruit with every turn. Mosaics of pan-fried dumplings, savory fillings tucked inside chewy, translucent skins. Shallow silver dishes of colorful curries, drizzled with fresh cream and sprinkled with seeds. An armada of crisp salads, rich soups, and crusty breads.

The guests have begun to notice her. There's nowhere to run, not that she needs to. Enitan moves away from the tubelift, squares her shoulders, and joins the festivities. Nobles descend on her like a pack of ravenous bloodhounds as she inspects an array of vegetables. They crowd around her, bodies pressed together as they lob question after question about how she convinced the Imperator to seek genuine peace with Ominira and Iëre. And what, exactly, is the God-Emperor going to do with Koriko? But this is far from the first time Enitan's run this particular gauntlet. Over these months, she's gathered an arsenal of weaponized manners, complete with proper facial expressions, tones, and body language.

When a particularly intrusive aristocrat asks her about the Imperator's "preferences" and Enitan tells him about the books Menkhet's recently recommended, the crowd finally disperses to rethink their questions. Before another flock of nobles appears, Enitan decides to sample the dishes. She selects some sort of neon-green tuber. She sinks her teeth in, doing her best to contain any embarrassing sounds. Spicy-sweet filling floods her mouth, sinfully buttery yet somehow refreshing. Enitan devours five before someone taps her on the shoulder.

"There are more of these three tables down," she snaps irritably, before the person laughs. It's Menkhet, whose entrance she somehow missed. Her simple silk suit is more dark green than pure black, and she's unadorned besides the single gold bracelet and the obsidian clips in her hair. "I'm surprised you managed to escape the horde."

"Only for a moment." Menkhet sets down one of the two goblets of mhimat she's holding and plucks one of the tubers off Enitan's plate. She pops it into her mouth and chews. "God, this is amazing!"

Enitan smacks Menkhet's hand away when she tries to purloin another. "Have you seen Xiang?"

"They said they were tired, and Katun agreed to escort them to their room." Menkhet gives her a mischievous grin. "They told me not to tell you."

Enitan heaves a sigh. "I wish you'd listened."

Menkhet hands Enitan a goblet and picks up the other. "To peace and justice." She holds her drink aloft before taking a deep sip.

Enitan does the same, watching the light dance in Menkhet's eyes. "Perhaps we should—"

Menkhet slumps forward, a hand shooting out to clutch the edge of the table.

Enitan grabs her by the shoulders and tries to haul her upright. "Menkhet? Are you all right?"

People have begun to notice the Imperator is in their midst. Out of the corner of her eye, Enitan sees a group of noblemen point at her and whisper something to each other. Enitan's grip tightens around Menkhet. Her skin, usually a warm golden brown, is beginning to look ashen.

Oh fuck.

Poison.

Enitan's heart seems to stop. Then all her calm, all her hope and excitement, shatters like a pane of glass struck by the blunt end of a shockstaff. She grabs her communicator, but before she can press the emergency button, Menkhet snatches it from her. She pulls out her own and rapidly types something out. Then she tosses both devices into the nearest brazier. The fire rears up like an attacking kinukmane, flames sparking violently as the electronics are consumed.

"What are you doing?" Enitan hisses, sickening terror shooting through her veins. "Menkhet—"

A choked gasp rips out of Menkhet's mouth. "Too late . . . I'm sorry . . . Enitan." Her eyes go unfocused and blank, their usual sharp gleam lost. "Please, promise me . . ."

She doesn't get to finish her sentence. Menkhet's knees give way, and she crumples to the floor before Enitan can catch her.

It isn't long before the sentinels arrive. A phalanx rushes in just after the Imperial physicians rip Menkhet from her arms. And at their head is Marchioness Zumas, who's bawling inconsolably. Panic thrashes in Enitan's chest as she watches the noblewoman.

"I saw her slip something into the Imperator's drink," she weeps, pointing at Enitan and scrubbing fat tears from her ruddy face. "Oh, God, is she alive?"

Enitan struggles not to collapse herself. "I didn't . . . I wouldn't—"

"Don't listen to her!" the marchioness shrieks. "I saw her do it! You filthy savage, you wanted revenge—"

One of the sentinels lifts a hand, cutting off her tirade. "All right, that's enough." He takes a single step toward Enitan. "You're under arrest, citizen."

No. *No.* She's not a citizen, not of Vaalbara. But before she can say or do anything, she feels handcuffs close around her wrists.

"Please," she whispers. "It wasn't me."

Another sentinel gestures at the marchioness. "She said she saw you poison the Imperator's wine. That's proof enough, *Korikese.*"

Though Enitan knows they're using her nationality as an insult, it's better than being called a citizen of this empire. Icy fingers close around her heart. "There won't be a trial, will there?"

"Due process only applies to full Vaalbaran citizens." She swears she hears the sneer in their modulated voice. "The Imperator will decide your fate once she recovers."

Once she recovers. Enitan allows herself a sliver of hope. She cannot bear the thought that she might be responsible for Menkhet's death atop Ajana's.

Her heart jumps into her mouth as the second sentinel grabs her shoulder and shoves her forward, past the row of soldiers standing at attention. She sees her own terror reflected back in excruciating detail by their visors. The sentinel drags her into a tubelift.

When they start moving upward instead of down to the palace dungeon, Enitan cranes her neck to look at the sentinel.

"I was framed," she says, her breaths growing rapid and shallow. "It's obvious. So you're planning to get rid of me before the Imperator can find the actual culprit, then."

The sentinel's grip on her shoulder tightens slightly. "Stop talking."

She only really begins to panic when the sentinel starts dragging her toward the abandoned floor.

"You don't have to do this." She stumbles over the uneven threshold. Sweat pools beneath her collar and inside her gloves. *Don't beg. Do not. Beg.* "My death won't benefit you. As soon as she's healed, the Imperator will hunt you down."

The sentinel steers her down a hallway. She recognizes the dark, dusty passageway—it's on the rough map she drew on her first trip down here. Soon, they'll be very far from anyone who might hear her scream. Not that anyone would come and rescue her anyway. Not that anyone would care.

"Save me and I'll save you," she chokes out, a last desperate plea.

The sentinel releases her. "Just like always."

Enitan twists around, eyes wide.

The sentinel reaches up and removes their helmet.

"*Xiang.*" Enitan flies toward her sibling—whether to hug or hit them, she doesn't know. Either way, her handcuffs restrain her. "What happened?"

Xiang pulls an electronic key from their belt. "Menkhet messaged me. I arrived just in time," they say, sliding the handcuffs from her wrists. "Everything's falling apart, Enitan. They're not gone. They lied."

"What?"

"The shadow councilors," says Xiang. "There's one more."

THIRTY

"I'll show you." Xiang pulls out their communicator.

Enitan's heart pounds furiously as she lurches forward, grabbing her sibling by the shoulders.

"Xiang!" she hisses. "You brought your communicator? They're probably tracking us right now—"

"Ancestors, I'm not a complete idiot." Xiang rolls their eyes. "It's an honor guard model; these can only be monitored by the Imperator." Before Enitan can whisper-yell at them some more, they hold up a hand. "But I made a few modifications anyway with Katun's help, so that we're completely invisible."

All of a sudden, their communicator pings. Their eyebrows draw together. "There's a new announcement." They tap twice on the screen. "From Menkhet."

Enitan settles down beside them, her heart rate skyrocketing. "Open it."

Xiang does, and a small holoscreen pops up. After a few seconds, Menkhet's tired face appears.

"Citizens and subjects," she croaks, "I have been betrayed. Enitan Ijebu, the Korikese I invited into my home, attempted to murder me at the ball I held to celebrate the restoration of Koriko's independence. She is an assassin, planted by Ijebu's headwoman with aid from the treacherous High Consul."

Enitan feels as though her throat is filled with ash. "She wouldn't—How could she—?"

"That footage is synthesized," Xiang interrupts in a voice so calm she knows there's a storm raging behind it. "The words—perhaps even down to the syllables—have been pieced together from multiple videos, and then carefully edited. It's masterful work, actually. Props to whoever designed the program."

"How do you know?" Enitan demands.

"Well, mostly because Menkhet would die before she turned on you like that," says Xiang. "And because the synthesis is excellent, but not *perfect*." They point at the top left corner. There's a tiny dark flicker there, a line between the edge of a tapestry and the wall. "For example, the AI didn't line up these two fragments properly."

Enitan squints; they're right—the back wall is from Menkhet's primary office, but that particular tapestry is from her fourth private drawing room.

"This cruel and cowardly attack has brought me to my senses. Koriko and the Ominirish Republic will pay dearly. I will finish what my predecessor started. Now is not the time for weakness. I will paint the Korikese swamps red with the savages' blood. Let what was once a lunar province of our Empire become ashes underfoot. And as for the Republic . . ." Here, Menkhet smiles. "They will suffer as they have never suffered before."

Enitan knows that it's not really her speaking, but hearing the hate in her voice, even stitched together and synthesized . . . "No, please, no," she whispers to the hologram.

Xiang takes her hand and grips it, staring just as intently at the false Menkhet.

"While I gather my strength and prepare to show the world the true power of Vaalbara's wrath, I have chosen a hand to guide the Empire."

The holoimager centers on Archduke Ta-Ji kneeling beside the Imperator in a robe so dark it's nearly black. Menkhet beckons to him, and he rises gracefully to his feet.

Menkhet declares, "I name as my regent and heir presumptive the archduke Yehana Ta-Ji."

He steps forward, hands open and welcoming at his sides. An offer, an entreaty. "I know I am not worthy of this honor among honors, my Imperator and my God, but I will spend every moment henceforth striving to deserve it."

His words fade into the background as Enitan looks on in abject horror. "It won't be long before he kills her," she whispers. "If he hasn't already."

Then a blurred image of Kulta appears, and Enitan strains to listen, fear seizing her lungs as Yehana continues speaking. "The High Consul dispatched a number of synthetic agents to support Enitan Ijebu's heinous mission, including these foul creatures."

Xiang freezes when the archduke gestures at another image, this one of Katun.

"Be not afraid," Yehana says, eyes glittering to match his politician's smile. All Enitan sees is malice. "We will hunt down these artificial abominations and tear them apart." Images of Enitan and Xiang appear beside the synths. "The failed assassin and her sibling have fled the palace and have hidden themselves in the bowels of the capital." He clasps his hands behind his back. "The Imperator is not without mercy. If these two Korikese individuals bring themselves before the Imperator, a few of their fellow savages may be spared." The holoimager centers on his face. "Anyone found withholding pertinent information will be punished as severely as Vaalbaran law allows. That will be all."

Xiang closes the holoscreen and opens their communicator's map. Unlike the version on Enitan's device, this one shows all the positions of sentinels and the honor guard throughout the palace. Little black dots, slowly moving, filling every hall and chamber.

Xiang shakes their head. "He's turned the whole Splinter into a police state. We can't escape."

"Of course we can," says a voice a few meters away.

Enitan leaps to her feet alongside Xiang, heart thundering. Her jaw drops when she sees who it is. "Deora?"

"Thought I might find you here," Deora says. "I remembered you telling me about it. Are you okay?" She blinks, her eyes growing teary. "I know you didn't do it, obviously. We'll sneak you out."

"*This* is your amateur cultural anthropologist?" Xiang whispers, cocking their dissection gun at her. "Can we trust her?"

"Yes, I think so. Ancestors, put that thing away," Enitan says, pushing Xiang's wrist down before rushing forward to pull Deora into a hug. The countess might be a pampered, woefully benighted aristocrat, but it's nice to see a familiar face—particularly one that doesn't want her and Xiang dead.

"I appreciate your concern, Deora," says Enitan. "I really do. But you have to leave."

Deora draws back, frowning. "Why?"

"Because I don't want you getting hurt. This isn't your problem."

"But I want to help make things right—"

"How could you possibly help?" snaps Xiang. "From what I've heard, you've done nothing but hoard and sell precious Korikese artifacts."

Deora glares at them. "I was trying to *preserve* your culture!"

Enitan tamps down a flare of irritation. "For whom?" she asks, her tone as even as she can manage.

Deora sighs, wilting like a dying blossom. "You're right. I'm sorry. It's . . . hard to unlearn."

"Oh, really," Xiang says flatly. "Can't imagine what that's like."

Enitan exchanges a look with her sibling. She's on the verge of turning the countess down when Deora steps forward and does the unthinkable. She kneels at their feet.

"I've only ever wanted to help," she whispers, ducking her head. "Even though I've failed you miserably. You know that, don't you?"

Despite everything, Enitan does. "I know."

Deora looks up at her. "Then please, let me do something good for once. Let me make it up to you in some small way."

"How?" snaps Xiang. "And get up, will you?"

Deora rises gracefully and gestures at their sentinel armor, all still donned save for the helmet. "I had a plan, but since you already have a disguise, I have an even better idea."

Enitan crosses her arms. "What do you have in mind?"

"I'll say I'm taking you to Yehana," says Deora. "My private shuttle is only two floors down from here. If we can get to it, I can activate it and take you two wherever you want to go, as long as it's on Gondwana. All my space-worthy ships are under repair, I'm afraid."

"That's barely a plan," says Xiang, frowning. "We have no idea where we'd be safe on-world. And how do we know this isn't a trap?"

"If I wanted you dead, I'd have brought sentinels with me and had you killed here and now," Deora says, a hint of indignation in her voice.

Xiang's frown deepens. "If you betray us, I'll kill you."

Deora sniffs, tilting her dainty nose upward. "Well, I won't, so that shouldn't be a problem."

"Can your shuttle be accessed at any time?" Enitan asks.

Deora nods firmly.

"Then let's go."

Xiang carefully handcuffs Enitan again and shoves on their helmet. Deora pulls herself together, her face taking on a determined expression. "All right, follow me."

Xiang pulls Enitan back a little as they find their way to the main entrance. "What do we do if this *is* a trap?" they whisper.

"I don't know," says Enitan. "We'll have to figure it out then. Come on."

Deora leads them toward a tubelift, looking back every few seconds—to check either that they're still following her or if anyone's following all of them.

She takes Enitan's arm and pulls her into the lift, stepping in just after Xiang, then straightens her posture, brushing off her pearl-encrusted shirt. "The shuttle's just two hallways down from the tubelifts."

But then the transport lurches violently to the right, throwing the trio into its opposite side as it shifts without warning into another track.

Enitan shoves herself upright, her mind spiraling. She's played right into their hands.

"What's happening?" demands Xiang. They stare at Deora. "I knew it. You traitor—"

The tubelift slides open with a cheery chime. Five sentinels stand right outside, dissection guns all cocked and aimed at the trio's faces.

"You fools," sneers the nearest. "The Lord Regent had holoimagers installed in all of the passageways this morning. Step away from the countess."

Xiang grabs Deora's shoulder with one hand and presses the muzzle of their gun to her temple with the other.

A burst of adrenaline stabs into Enitan's chest. "She's our hostage," she declares, keeping her tone coolly bland. "Step away and let us through. We'll release her as soon as we're out of range of the Splinter."

"Do you not care about your swamp and the other Korikese?" demands another sentinel, stepping before the first. "The Lord Regent is open to negotiating if you and your sibling turn yourselves in."

Enitan presses her lips together. "That's clearly a lie. Now *move*, or you'll be responsible for the Lord Regent's closest friend being sliced into mincemeat."

For a moment, the sentinels do nothing. Their guns remain trained on Enitan and Xiang, hands held firm around the polished grips. Then Deora bursts into tears.

"I don't want to die," she sobs, wringing her gloved hands. "Oh my God, please, don't let them kill me."

The second sentinel slowly lowers his gun.

The first turns to look at him, shoulders lifting. "What are you doing?" she hisses.

"It's true. She's close to the Lord Regent. And her uncle is the Supreme Abbot's second cousin. We can't risk getting her killed."

"Sir, you don't have the authority to make this decision," the first sentinel retorts, but she lowers her gun too. "The Lord Regent's orders were clear—"

"I'm aware." The second pulls out his communicator. "I'm calling him now."

Enitan uses the distraction as an opportunity to move toward the exit, but the first raises her gun again. "Try it, then. Run and see what happens, *citizen*."

"He's not answering," says the second.

"Try again." She doesn't even bother with her superior's honorific.

"I *did*. Stand. Down."

"But—"

"I'm giving you to the count of five to decide," yells Xiang. "Drop your weapons or the countess dies."

"You wouldn't dare."

"Five." Xiang cocks their gun.

"No!" The second drops his gun and lifts his hands. "Don't. *Don't.*" He turns to the other sentinels. "Move!" he barks. "Disengage, let them leave. That's an order."

The first spits out a curse, but she does as commanded. The sentinels step away, giving Enitan, Xiang, and Deora just enough room to run past them.

"Would you really have shot me?" Deora pants, racing down a hallway and swinging herself around a corner.

"Yes," Xiang replies simply, easily outpacing her.

Deora mutters something, coming to a sudden stop before a large triangular door, and slaps her hand onto the screen-surface. It slides open, revealing a small hangar. There are only five shuttles resting on the stone floor, their featureless surfaces dark and glassy. The countess dashes over to the one in the center and commands open the ramp. Enitan and Xiang throw themselves in after her. Deora's fingers fly over the holographic console, and the engines come to life with a low purr.

Enitan scrambles into a seat beside Xiang as the shuttle lifts off from the ground. After punching in a few commands and flying them out of the hangar, Deora joins them.

They've made it.

Deora brushes a lock of hair from her face. "So, where to next?"

Enitan looks at Xiang. "I don't know."

They pull off their helmet. "Even if we had access to a space-worthy ship right now, they'd hunt us down on Koriko."

Enitan grimaces. "And if we tried Ominira, the High Consul would turn us over to Yehana if they thought it'd delay the war by even a day."

"So, what?" Deora spreads her hands. "We just fly around until the solar cells stop working?"

"The archipelago." Enitan rubs at her eyes for a moment. "How about there? We can at least hide out until we figure out a working plan."

Xiang purses their lips. "There are nearly a thousand islands just off the southern coast."

"And over a hundred populated ones." Deora nods. "I'll drop you two off, then land the shuttle somewhere in Vaalbara. I'll say you incapacitated me and ran off into the wilds or something."

"Thank you." Enitan holds out a hand to her sibling. "Let me see your communicator."

They hand it over, and she opens up the holomap. "So which one?"

Xiang lifts a hand to zoom in on an island. "Mmrioa looks nice."

Enitan summons up a smile. "So that's settled. Mmrioa it is—"

She's cut off by the blaring of a thousand alarms going off, the side panels of the shuttle flashing with a hail of sparks. Enitan is thrown back into her seat as the shuttle twists sideways. Xiang unbuckles themself and runs over to the console to gain control of the aircraft.

"Merciful God." Deora wrestles with her safety restraints and throws herself out of her seat. She pushes Xiang aside and shoves her hands into the midst of the flickering console. "How the hells—"

The shuttle shudders violently and roars in protest as it tilts slightly upward. But it's not enough. The aircraft screams and plummets down, like the strings suspending it have all snapped. Enitan stares at the window facing her, terror roiling in her gut as a sea of turquoise trees races up to meet them.

"It won't work," she whispers.

"What?" Deora cries out, throwing a wild-eyed glance back at Enitan.

"Yehana." Enitan closes her eyes, trying to force words through the waves of adrenaline threatening to drown her. "He's doing this remotely somehow. It's possible he disabled all the shuttles using the Imperator's access codes."

Deora pulls her trembling hands from the console, her face ashen. "We're going down. Brace yourselves!"

She and Xiang fall into their seats and strap themselves back in. The shuttle lets out a final piercing cry, announcing its death. And then fire swallows them whole.

THIRTY-ONE

Enitan wakes up covered in dirt and blood, a dozen meters away from the still-smoking shuttle. Her ears are ringing. Light stabs at her eyes. Her mouth is full of ash.

She drags in a breath. It's agonizing. Her lungs feel both shrunken and swollen as she forces another inhale. The smell of crushed grass and burning rubber floods her nose.

She has no recollection of the crash. All she knows is that she was conscious one second and gone the next. Everything on one side feels wet and cold. It's probably blood. She fidgets.

A hand curves around her shoulder. "Oh, thank the Ancestors." Xiang's soot-smeared face appears at the edge of her vision.

"Where . . . ?" Enitan coughs, moistens her cracked lips. "Where are we?"

"I don't know. But you've been out for the better part of a day," they tell her. They lean in. "Enitan, I'm so sorry."

This isn't Xiang's fault. Once again, Enitan has failed them. Only a miracle can keep them from a Vaalbaran prison cell, or worse.

"None of this is your fault," she chokes out. "It's mine. Ancestors, I'm so stupid."

She lifts her left hand to rub at her eyes, which are stinging with tears. Or at least, she tries to. She feels nothing there. Xiang makes a pained face.

"What happened?" she asks.

"Part of the shuttle ceiling fell on your arm," Xiang whispers, tightening their grip on her shoulder. "Deora and I couldn't move it."

Enitan stares up at them. She can't bear to look down. "So it's gone, then?"

Xiang draws in a slow, deep breath.

Enitan closes her eyes. "I don't feel any pain."

"That's the drugs from the medkit," she hears Xiang say. "You'll be okay, I promise. We'll have your arm regrown when we get home."

Home. She almost laughs. Koriko wasn't an option even when they had a fully operating shuttle. Their community is hundreds of millions of kilometers away, and the moon will probably be crawling with sentinels in a handful of hours. They'll be sent from every asteroid station to crush dissent before it boils over into a real rebellion. She can only hope they won't just set everything and everyone ablaze and be done with it.

In this moment, Enitan wants nothing more than to lie here. To sink into the soil and let herself rot. Silent sobs coagulate in her throat. She is everything Vaalbarans tell her she is: worthless and witless. She's failed. She's killed them all.

But to her surprise, a shard of resolve returns with her next breath, cutting through her drug-addled haze.

No, she tells herself. *You are not worthless. You are Enitan Ijebu of Ijebu Community, and you will not let yourself or your sibling or your friend die.*

Some of this must show on her face, because Xiang's hold on her loosens. "Please, don't push yourself."

Enitan shoves herself upward with her right arm until she's sitting upright. "I'm fine. I don't even feel anything. Where's Deora?"

"The drugs will wear off soon," warns Xiang. "She's out foraging for herbs that might help. We'll need to—" They stop abruptly, their mouth thinning into a sharp line as their eyes go wide.

Enitan has never seen her sibling look so frightened. She twists sideways. She's peering into the shadowy turquoise distance when sees it: a shevvaskull. An apex predator and, historically, a popular pet of the Vaalbaran elite. They became illegal to keep once one ripped out the intestines of a former Imperator's beloved husband. Every hair on the back of her neck prickles.

The beast resembles the Homeworld wolves of Enitan's old textbooks, only five times as tall and covered in dark-cyan fur. Hair coats all of the beast's bulk except for its head, which is plated in bare, yellow-gray bone. Six bright-orange eyes glow beneath the plating's ridges. The shevvaskull is staring right at them.

"Where's your gun?" Enitan hisses.

"Somewhere under the shuttle," Xiang whispers. They rise slowly to their feet, pulling Enitan up with them. "Maybe we should make a run for it."

The animal begins to circle them, a bloodcurdling keening noise slipping between its razor-edged teeth. It sounds like a weeping child. If Enitan was not shaken before, she certainly is now. And then it charges, its massive paws tearing chunks of grass and dirt from the ground beneath it.

Xiang grabs Enitan's arm and drags her back. They run. Xiang curves toward the trees, and Enitan races just after them, her sibling's grip a vise around her limp wrist. The beast is gaining, and she's falling behind. She can hear the shevvaskull close the paltry distance between them, its eerie sobbing growing louder and sharper. And she can feel her body falter. The drugs are too powerful. The desire to stop and lie down is overwhelming.

"Xiang," she gasps. "Xiang. Let go."

They don't even turn around to look at her. "No, Enitan." They yank her forward, and she stumbles to catch up to them. "Never. If you die, I die with you."

A shot goes off just behind Enitan, nearly bursting her eardrums. That was far louder than a gun. Xiang pulls her around, her bones still rattling in their sockets.

Between her and the dead shevvaskull is a tall man with gray hair. There's a dissection blaster in his hands, an unwieldy hunk of battered metal still smoking at its muzzle. He shoves the blaster into the frayed holster at his hip and turns to Enitan and Xiang. His lined brown face is square and weathered. Enitan squints at him. He looks oddly familiar. Perhaps an escaped sentinel who once served in the communities? It's the only possible explanation, but it still doesn't feel quite right.

He sighs and gestures at the faraway shape of the shuttle behind them.

"You kids crashed right into Old Blue's territory," he says. "Who was flying that? Are you drunk or something?"

Xiang crosses their arms. "Who are you?"

"I'm Hkon," he says, a hand pressed to his chest. "A sworn scavenger, on a sacred path to aid anyone I find in need. When I was a young boy—"

"Thank you for saving us," Enitan cuts him off, knowing she won't be able to remain standing for the full story. Even his name sounds familiar. "How did you—?" The drugs have begun to wear off. Her head feels like it's being slowly lowered into a flame. She presses her only hand to her temple. "How did you find us?"

"I saw the shuttle go down," says Hkon. "Thought I'd go and check out the wreck. If you were alive, I'd help. If you were dead, I'd scavenge the vessel. A win-win scenario."

Xiang snorts. "I don't know about that."

"Oh, I . . ." His words fade away as the pain radiates down from Enitan's head to the stub of her arm.

Deora's startled voice cuts through the woods: "I'm back— Oh my God, what happened?"

Enitan tries to suppress a moan and fails, a pained hiss escaping from her clenched teeth. She shuts her eyes and tries to breathe. She feels Xiang hold her tighter. They're saying something, but she can't understand them. The white-hot agony stabbing through every cell in her body drowns out the world.

A hand grips her arm. And then Enitan finds herself being pulled over someone's back like a sack of root vegetables.

"My homestead isn't far," she hears Hkon say, as if through churning water. "Follow me."

Enitan's vision splinters when he begins to move. Every muscle fiber screeches in protest at even the slightest shift, and Hkon isn't exactly light-footed. She spends the entire trek writhing over his shoulder and gasping in pain. She knows Hkon said his home wasn't far, but the journey feels like it takes hours. Few things cut through the suffering: an orchestra of birds and insects, the crunch of feet over crisp vegetation, the smell of sweat and dirt and inablossoms. The thundering roar of some great river. When Hkon slides down a mossy slope, she glimpses a dark blocky shape crowning a looming hill—the palace ruins she spotted all those weeks ago, not long after she poisoned the magistrate.

There's a break in Enitan's memory after that. The next thing she knows, she's sprawled on a lumpy mattress with a mouth full of horrendously bitter herbs. When the pain subsides enough for her to feel human again, she sits up.

She's in what must be Hkon's bedroom. The chamber is stuffed with paraphernalia: at least four different shovels, messy bundles of holosheets, an array of battered walking sticks. There's a heap of tattered blankets at the foot of the mattress.

From their cushion on the floor, Xiang reaches over to gently pat her shoulder. "Feeling better?"

"Much." Enitan manages not to whimper in agony as she leans closer. "But look at this place," she mumbles.

Xiang peers upward. "You mean this second-century Nri castle-fortress? You can tell by its coved ceiling and the triumphal arch outside."

"You still care about architecture?" she blurts out.

"I'm not just a victim, Enitan," Xiang says with a low laugh. "I'm still me, just with a few more scars."

"Of course. I'm sorry, I didn't mean—"

Someone coughs awkwardly and Enitan looks up to see Deora and Hkon lounging in the corner. He meets her gaze and walks over, a chipped cup of tea in hand.

"Good thing your friend found that xaalufern," he says.

Enitan sets down the vessel with a clink, as if parrying his apparent kindness. "I know who you are."

Hkon's easy grin vanishes. His dark eyes harden into a glare. "And who is that?"

He might be old and gray now, but Enitan can still see the remnants of the man he once was.

"You're the one who ravaged my homeland. The one who sought to beat my people so that we'd never stand again." Unsteadily, she rises to her feet and leans against the cracked wall. "You're the last Imperator. Adehkonra."

Adehkonra the Once-Great, now neither a god nor much of a human.

Deora gasps. Xiang throws down their tea and surges to their feet. They drive their boot into Adehkonra's chest, pinning him to the dusty floor.

The former Imperator claws at Xiang's calf, to no avail. "How did you know?" he wheezes.

"The statue in Sun's sepulcher. She takes after you." Enitan crosses her arms. "You should've changed the color of your eyes at least. And your name—Hkon? Really?"

Adehkonra sputters, "You were in her tomb? In the palace? Who . . . ?" He goes still under Xiang's boot. "You're the Korikese hostage."

Enitan smiles, though humored is the last thing she's feeling right now.

"Oh, God." Adehkonra's arms fall flat at his sides. He closes his eyes. "Kill me, then. Take your revenge."

Xiang makes a disgusted noise, stepping off the man as if his chest has sullied their boot. "We're not monsters," they snap. "Unlike you."

Enitan slumps back onto the mattress. "What are you really doing out in the wilds? I don't buy that wandering hermit nonsense for a second."

"I was banished here by powers invisible to all." Adehkonra gets up and takes a shallow sip of tea.

"We know about the Nlamiraan," Enitan says. "We were working with Menkhet to try to take them down."

His eyes widen in shock at the mention of her name. "Menkhet. You know her well, then." He looks down. "I wanted to protect her, but . . ."

"Ancestors." Xiang's lip curls. "I thought your only redeeming quality was that you *weren't* a coward."

Adehkonra weathers the insult like a blow. "The suffering I carried out at their command . . . I wish I could blame the Nlamiraan for all of it, but I did nothing to stop them." He pauses. "I'm sorry, Enitan."

Her name in his mouth feels like a slap.

"*Don't*," she says softly, "say my name."

Adehkonra ducks his head. "I know no apology will suffice. But I will do my best to make amends. For now, you all need rest. We'll talk in the morning."

Xiang opens their mouth, probably to protest, but Enitan cuts them off with a raised hand as she looks around the room.

She whispers two words: "Where's Deora?"

THIRTY-TWO

Adehkonra checks the power level on his blaster before returning it to its holster. He snatches up the nearest walking stick and grabs his cloak from where he dropped it on the floor. "I'm going to go find her," he says, flicking the neatly patched hood over his head. "Stay here."

Xiang shrugs. The moment he steps out the door, they turn to Enitan. "He's just going to run away, isn't he? He'd probably even turn us in if he could."

Enitan lets herself fall back onto the mattress. "Probably." She isn't in brain-wringing agony anymore, but fatigue has subsumed her. It feels like there isn't a single bone left in her body.

Xiang purses their lips. "Do you trust Deora?"

"I think so." Enitan groans, rubbing at her eyes. "I don't know. I barely even trust myself nowadays."

Xiang squeezes her hand. "I might know what that feels like." Then they stiffen. "Do you hear that?"

"Hear what?"

Enitan sits up, straining to catch whatever noise Xiang's noticed. And then she realizes that it's not that her sibling is hearing something, but rather that they *aren't*. A chill runs through her. The evening song of nocturnal birds and insects has vanished. There is only all-consuming silence. It's as if the planet has rolled to a perfect, noiseless stop.

And then a sound: the echoing, regular patter of heavy footsteps on stone. Enitan recognizes them; she's heard them every morning and every evening since Vaalbara took her homeland.

She forces herself to her feet, groping for the wall to brace herself as unease pierces her heart. "Deora."

The countess glides through the door, a rapidly blinking communicator in one hand and a dissection gun in the other. "Enitan, Xiang. I wish I could say I'm sorry."

Xiang flies to their feet. A squad of sentinels in shimmering armor marches in after Deora, a scene pulled straight from the blood-soaked records of Enitan's memory into the nightmare of her present.

"You traitor," Xiang hisses. "You—"

"Oh, save it," Deora snaps.

Enitan pushes herself off the wall, stumbling as she wills her body to find balance with one less arm. She stares at the flashing communicator in Deora's hand. *"Why?"*

But even as she says it, she knows. It was all a lie. Deora's friendship. Her shallow understanding of Vaalbara's wrongs. Her epiphanies of kindness and compassion. Enitan feels her eyes burn with unshed tears and loathes herself for it.

Cold clarity cuts through dull, aching numbness as the truth stitches itself together in her head, piece by bloody piece. Banurra's anthropological "work." Erseydis's stolen treasure, on loan. Vidra's patronage. Sacha's appearance at every fundraising gala. All of the Nlamiraan were connected to the Imperial Museum. And at the center of it all was Deora.

Of course. From the start, one thing has been clear about the countess: that she believes in the Empire's right to every world. To other lands, other cultures, other *people.*

"It's you," Enitan whispers hoarsely. She tastes stomach acid at the back of her throat. "You're the last shadow councilor."

Deora claps her hands together with a radiant smile, the action only slightly hampered by the gun in her hand. "Ah, you've finally figured it out! Just as Sunnetah did, right before her little . . . accident." She brushes aside a lock of hair.

"You murdered her," says Enitan. "Like you tried to murder Menkhet."

"As if you haven't been going around killing the rest of my council. Why do you think I *let* you do that? Hmm?"

When Enitan says nothing, Deora laughs aloud. "That's all right, I'll tell you: because they were a nuisance. It took so long for us to agree on anything, we could barely function. Two of them thought Obara's plan was too much of a headache to even attempt, and I suspect others might've even felt guilty. But you've taken care of them for me, haven't you? Them, and their *children*, of course."

Enitan closes her eyes, shaking. "Why, Deora? All we want is to be free." She's just trying to buy them time, and the countess knows it. But no one is coming for them. Deora has all the time in the world.

"You may not believe me, but my intention has always been to help Koriko. Your speck of a moon colony shows *so* much promise. But the only way it can ever equal Vaalbara is by becoming *part* of Vaalbara." Deora clasps her hands behind her back, serene and still, a field general surveying the terrain of a coming battle and finding it to be in her favor. Her eyes gleam with purpose. In this moment, there is not a single thread of cruelty or contempt in the tapestry that is the countess Deora Edwan. In the woman Enitan thought was her friend, she now sees the entirety of the Empire. Vaalbara, at its heart, is not merciless. It simply does not know mercy, cannot hear the screams of those it tramples in its quest for glory.

"Anything worth anything requires sacrifice." Deora's voice is drowned in conviction; it drips with the certainty that Korikese are less than people and Vaalbara is right to treat the communities accordingly.

"Oh, and don't worry about Yehana. His time will come. But not before yours, alas." The gentle curve of her mouth vanishes. "I really liked you, Enitan. My one comfort is that, in the grand scheme of things, you're just one small casualty of progress." Her gaze locks onto Xiang. "*Gray sky, black soil. Homeworld, new world—*"

"I broke conditioning, asshole," Xiang snaps, cutting her off. "Your code words won't work on me."

Deora shrugs. "No harm in trying." Then she lifts a gloved hand. "Shoot them."

The sentinels do nothing.

She whirls around, eyes flashing. "Fire."

They don't. As Enitan watches them with bated breath, the pieces of another puzzle fall together.

"I said, *fire*."

Enitan moves in front of Xiang. Her heartbeat thuds in her ears, so fast she can hardly breathe, let alone speak. And yet, she does.

"They won't, not yet." She keeps her voice firm, holding it so tightly the waver in it is almost entirely squeezed out. "You don't have as much power as you think you do, Deora. Half of them serve Yehana. They might even be here to eliminate you."

As if on cue, several of the sentinels angle their guns at Deora. She in turn aims her own at Enitan. "You—"

One of the sentinels fires, barely missing the countess. The shovel just beside her bursts into splinters with a bang. Deora pivots with a snarl, lifting her gun and slicing apart his head with a shot. She bursts into a run, dodging return fire.

Enitan doesn't waste another second. It's impossible to tell who serves Deora and who serves Yehana, but all of them are here to capture her and Xiang. She throws herself forward, grabbing Xiang's arm as she rushes to the door. They're less than three meters away when the tiles at their feet shatter into a thousand fragments. Debris flies everywhere, several shards slicing deep into Enitan's outstretched arm. It's as if she never had the xaalufern at all. Her vision flashes white, a blaze of pain consuming her entire body.

Xiang is atop one of the sentinels as his gunshot goes wide. They strike him in the gut, driving a fist into the weak spot between two armor plates. Their other hand wrenches the gun from his momentarily weakened grip. They shoot, slicing his body in half.

They reach back, take hold of Enitan, and pull her toward the door. Even though they're being as gentle as possible, her body is screaming in pain. Enitan scrapes together the very last of her strength and runs as fast as she can.

The fight spills into the adjoining chambers. Enitan and Xiang dodge sentinels and stray blasts, shoving aside ragged curtains and leaping over cobbled-together furniture. They barrel outside. Panting, they sprint through a field of violet grass.

Xiang yanks out their communicator as they run. Their fingers fly over the holographic display. "I found their shuttle's signal! It's just on that boulder."

Enitan's eyes follow the line of their raised arm. There it is, a gleaming black shape less than twenty meters away now—

"Stop!" Deora shrieks.

The countess dashes into the spot right before them, a blur of torn silk and red-smeared skin. She lifts her gun, shivering violently despite the heat. Shoulder-high blades of grass stick to the blood on her arms and legs, only to fall away as she trembles.

Xiang aims their own weapon. "Step away, Deora."

She ignores them. "Don't you want to know what happened to Ajana?" she coos to Enitan.

Enitan watches Xiang's fingers flex around the grip of their gun. "Deora, move. You know I'm a better shot. I have you to thank for that, I suppose," they say bitterly.

The countess spits blood, eyes wild. Xiang begins to circle her, stepping closer to the shuttle. Enitan moves with them.

"Ajana simply wasn't a leader, no matter how much effort was expended molding her into one," says Deora with a smirk. "You know, if you were anyone else, I'd advise you to stop falling for enemy figureheads. But you seem to doom everyone you love, and that's worked out perfectly fine for me."

Enitan can't feel her fingers, but she watches them tighten into a fist anyway.

Deora lets out a cutting laugh. "Did you know she called out for you, when the end came?"

The fate of the Empire—the fate of the whole system—might hang in the balance, but fuck it. Enitan's blood burns as hot as boiling oil. She stops in her tracks.

"Don't fall for this!" Xiang shouts. "If we stay here any longer, she wins."

The words slip right off Enitan. She shoves past her sibling.

"We only needed her pretty face to rule Ijebu," Deora says with a sneer. "It was *you* who made us take her life by asking questions, challenging the order of things. *You. Made. Us. Kill. Her.*" She shrugs, gun still in her hand. "But may her soul find peace."

Out of the corner of her eye, Enitan sees Xiang move. Deora's gaze flicks from Enitan to her sibling. But before Enitan can shout a warning, Deora fires.

THIRTY-THREE

Enitan hits the ground. Hard. Adehkonra falls atop her with a blood-curdling shriek before going silent. It takes a moment for her to realize he's shoved her out of harm's way. Xiang roars a battle cry, and Deora snarls out a curse. Enitan's vision swims.

How ironic, she thinks, her lungs burning as she struggles under Adehkonra's crushing weight, *that the Imperator who ravaged my home and then saved my life might yet be the one to end it.*

Deora grunts. Another shot goes off. And then another. Xiang hisses out a string of profanities. Enitan worms her remaining arm beneath Adehkonra's body and pushes with everything she has left. She feels a dozen tile shards tear through her flesh like teeth. A scream erupts from her throat.

"Enitan!" Xiang yells. A response to her howling or a cry for help?

Enitan gives one final shove. Through sheer desperation alone, she manages to push the former Imperator off. She staggers to her feet, ready to fight or flee, just in time to see Xiang dodge a blast from the gun and disarm Deora. They punch her square in the face, sending her stumbling. The countess has almost regained her balance when they deliver a roundhouse kick to her side. She crumples halfway to her knees before she manages to push herself upright. She lurches back, hands up. Xiang raises the gun.

"I was trying to save you," Deora snarls. "Remember that."

"Save us?" Enitan chokes out. "Before or after you used us as cannon fodder?"

"Until you are elevated," Deora says, "until you are cultivated by the Empire, you're not good for much else. But after—"

"Give me the gun, Xiang," says Enitan, cutting her off. She will spare them from this, at least. She holds a hand out to her sibling. Without hesitation, they drop the weapon into her grasp. "That's the problem, Deora. We don't *need* to be saved. And certainly not by you."

Deora clasps her hands together. "No, Enitan, wait—"

The crack of the gun cuts through the air. Deora flies backward and falls to the ground, lifeless.

A broken laugh rises up out of the grasses. "Is . . . is she dead?"

Enitan spins around—it's Adehkonra, who is somehow still alive. He must have partly dodged the blast himself. He's still breathing, but by the look of it, not for long. His cloak conceals the worst of his wounds, but blood bubbles up over his lips, thick and crimson.

"Yes," Enitan says. "She is."

"Finally," he croaks. "Xiang, you were right. I am a coward. And before that, a fool who thought beating others down would make me taller. I am sorry." His breaths are growing shallower. "I'm . . . sorry." His whole body stills, as if he were being slowly encased in amber.

After a moment's hesitation, Enitan passes Xiang the weapon and bends down. She closes his eyes with a brush of her fingers. Xiang throws an arm around her middle, supporting her, and together they clamber up the giant rock to the sentinels' shuttle.

"So . . . how do we get in?" Enitan asks.

Xiang hands back the dissection gun. "Shoot anyone who comes out of the grass. I think I can reconfigure the controls and commandeer the ship via my communicator."

"Who taught you how to do that?"

"The same people who taught me how to pick old locks," Xiang says with a devious smirk. "The same people with pockets full of skey-root."

"Fine, I was wrong about them. Happy?" Enitan huffs and lets her sibling go, leaning back against the cool hull of the shuttle. The gun feels so, so heavy.

The first sentinel crawls out of the grass, little more than a moaning, smoking heap of charred muscle and armor. Enitan fires—a mercy kill. The second bursts out at full speed. By the time Enitan has the gun switched to stun, he's already thrown himself at the rock and is scrabbling up with terrifying swiftness. She aims, shoots, misses. She fires again. He dodges. His outstretched hand is mere inches away from her ankle, ready to drag her down, when she finally gets in a shot. He slides off the rock and flops onto his back with a grunt.

Two more sentinels spring from the grass.

"How long?" Enitan yells, her eyes trained on the approaching soldiers.

The shuttle gives a series of high-pitched beeps.

"Just give me . . . a few . . . more . . . seconds . . ."

Enitan fires twice, catching one sentinel in the leg. The woman stumbles but doesn't stop. Ancestors, this would be so much easier if she weren't shooting on stun. Her third blast hits the other sentinel in the head by luck alone. The first sentinel is still advancing toward them. She's clutching one of Adehkonra's shovels, the handle end broken off into a jagged point. There's gore still dripping from it.

Enitan pulls the trigger, her bloody hand raw around the grip. The gun makes a pathetic whine.

"Xiang," Enitan grinds out, "we're out of juice. You better be—"

The shuttle's ramp flies open. Xiang grabs Enitan and swings them both up into the shuttle. Xiang taps something on their communicator, and the ramp closes with a loud *thunk*, far faster and harder than the standard sequence would have dropped it.

Enitan throws herself into a seat. "We can't go to the islands," she says, buckling herself in as Xiang slides into the pilot's seat. "Deora must have told the sentinels about that plan, which means Yehana knows." Her head falls into her hand. "I'm sure by now he knows we have this shuttle, too."

Xiang coaxes the shuttle off the ground. "Actually, the first thing I did was jam all their signals from the shuttle. I even looked for recent communications, and nothing got out. They're too busy killing each other to request backup."

"Xiang," says Enitan, beaming. "Have I ever told you how proud I am of you?"

They chuckle as the shuttle glides up into the sky. "Not frequently enough."

Enitan leans forward. "I have an idea. Let's go back to the Splinter."

Xiang stares at her, their mouth agape. *"What?"*

"We need to end this, today. There'll be a target on our backs for the rest of our lives if we don't. And Yehana will obliterate Koriko in the meantime. Right now, the last place they expect us is the same place we need to go."

Xiang tilts their head. "So what's the plan?"

"Can you find out which landing pad this shuttle came from?"

Xiang nods.

"Contact the archduke. Tell him the mission was a success. That Deora is dead, and the savages are our captives," says Enitan. "I'm betting he'll make an appearance to gloat the second we land. And when he does . . ." She gestures expansively at the array of dissection blasters on the polished walls.

"Enitan, there are about a billion ways this could go wrong."

"Well," she replies, "do you have a better plan?"

Xiang huffs. "No."

"Come on." Enitan grabs their hand with her remaining one. "We've got this. Are you with me?"

They squeeze her hand back. "Always."

Xiang activates the autopilot. The shuttle turns and glides back toward the Imperial capital. They push out of their seat and pull the two largest blasters off the wall. They hand one to Enitan. She drops her gun and slides her hand around the blaster's grip. When she tries to lift the weapon, it clatters to the floor.

Xiang's eyes widen in concern. "Oh, Enitan, you're bleeding everywhere."

"I'll be fine," she says, gritting her teeth as she hefts the blaster. "I promise."

She leans back into her seat and lets her eyes drift closed. She doesn't remember the trip from the Splinter to the wilds taking nearly as long. But then again, she and Xiang were flying from certain death to freedom before, and now they're doing the exact opposite.

It's not long before they see the Splinter floating above them, no less impressive than when Enitan first laid eyes on it. The shuttle rises smoothly upward just as a discreet private landing pad materializes from one of the monolith's facets. Five figures emerge from a shadowed passage and stride over to the edge of the pad.

The archduke and four sentinels, if they're lucky. If they're not, all that awaits them is imprisonment, torture, and whatever horrors the archduke decides to visit upon them.

"No one else dies," Enitan says, as Xiang reaches over to command open the shuttle. "Put your blaster on stun."

They raise an eyebrow at her. "You can't be serious. We *can't* let him get away with this."

"I am." Enitan unbuckles herself and flicks off the lethal setting on her own weapon. "And he won't, I promise. Please."

There are so many words Enitan should have said to Ajana, the night before she died. She remembers five of them now: *There is always a choice.*

"Why?" Xiang grits out.

"A wise woman once told me that bloodshed is never necessary," says Enitan. "It's just the easiest option. Deora had to die. These people don't. I'm tired, Xiang. Aren't you?"

They curse but do as she asks. The ramp lowers.

The archduke's face comes into view, a smirk plastered over his features. "Excellent work—"

Enitan launches herself upward, letting momentum guide her. She pulls the trigger. The archduke is thrown down with the force of the blast, knocking a sentinel flat on their back. The archduke groans, still conscious; she caught him in the gut, not the head. Xiang rushes out of the shuttle, firing blast after blast at the sentinels, taking down two more.

Enitan drags herself after them, shooting wildly. The sentinel who went down with Yehana rolls the archduke off themself, giving Xiang just enough time to blast them in the head.

The edge of the shuttle's ramp bursts into a shower of metal and sparks. The last sentinel. Enitan whirls around. If she still had her left arm, that shot would've taken it right off. Xiang fires, and the sentinel flies back with a wail.

The archduke groans as Enitan steps over to him. She looks down. "For your sake," she says, "I hope Menkhet's still alive."

She shoots him between the eyes.

THIRTY-FOUR

Zuhura fills Enitan's cup to the brim. They're having an emerald-green uhie blend, the unoxidized leaves stone-ground into an ultrafine, antioxidant-packed powder. The final product is smooth and lightly frothed, with a slightly bitter but rich, almost buttery flavor.

With her newly regrown arm, Enitan gingerly raises the enameled porcelain to her lips. The cup trembles, but she doesn't spill a single drop. *Progress.* The Imperial physicians took the brace off only two days ago, and the entire limb still cries out in protest whenever she moves too quickly. The doctors have promised her that in a few weeks, she'll forget her arm was regenerated from scratch. Somehow, she doubts that.

Zuhura raises a brow, impressed. "How are you feeling?"

Enitan takes another sip. "I'm good."

The arched brow lifts higher, in incredulity now.

"No, really. I'm good." Enitan starts ticking things off on her fingers. "Xiang and Menkhet are safe, my people are about to be free, we've taken down the Nlamiraan. And I got my arm back." She folds her hands over her new tunic. Though the thick cloth is Vaalbaran made, the cut and colors are Korikese. "What else could I ask for?"

Zuhura inclines her head, a knowing look to her crinkled eyes. "Well, I'm sure you'll miss Menkhet."

Enitan looks down at her tea. "So you knew. Does it . . . bother you?"

Zuhura shakes her head. "I know Ajana would've wanted you to be happy." Here she offers a small, sad smile. "Love doesn't die; it can't. It changes shape, that's all."

Enitan shuts her eyes, and suddenly she's back in Ijebu, pulled home as if by a gust of warm wind. She's there on the humid, otherwise inconsequential afternoon she first met Ajana.

"Enitan?" Zuhura asks softly.

She blinks furiously for a moment, willing her tears back in. She mostly succeeds. She clears her throat. "I hear Ominira has a new High Consul—one who's truly committed to peace."

"What convenient timing." Zuhura snorts, picking at the silver embroidery of her black robes. "Still, you're right—a significant improvement. Kulta's report suggests that the Supreme Senate is leaning toward exile for his predecessor, active as soon as the second impeachment trial goes through."

Enitan folds her hands together. "Good. Maybe they'll repent and become a sworn scavenger too."

Zuhura laughs. "Somehow, I doubt that. But the new Consul is flying here next month to sign the revised treaty, though he's requested to bring what looks like a battalion of guards." She shakes her head. "I forgot what politicians were like. I want to resign."

Enitan carefully refills her cup. "You've only been Imperator for a week."

"*Vice*-Imperator," the former duchess corrects. "And not for long, I hope."

"Pardon me, but you're not allowed to quit," says a familiar voice. "Especially after I went through all the trouble of creating your position."

Enitan turns in her chair, a smile tugging at her lips.

"I need someone to handle Ominira and Parliament and the rest of our incompetent bureaucracy," Menkhet continues, crossing her arms, "while I drag sentinels and monks off of Koriko and make sure those reparations actually get paid from the Imperial coffers. Oh, and there's the new hospital in the lower city."

"We still need a plan for that, by the way," Enitan says. She doesn't bring up the other, harder problems, the ones they've already debated ad nauseam. For now, at least, she lets them all pretend that protests haven't broken out across half the Empire, many incited by disgruntled nobles. The Nlamiraan may be gone, but their attitudes and influence run deep within the Empire. The truly hard work is up ahead, and they haven't even formally announced Koriko's independence yet.

Menkhet sits down beside her and plucks her cup from the table. Enitan catches a split-second of hesitation before the other woman drains the last of her tea. Menkhet very nearly died that night. She was laid in her healing pod moments before her life was snuffed out for good. She's still very much in recovery, despite her disconcertingly good show of being back to health.

"Right, I'm thinking we could have a stretch of green space around the whole hospital," Menkhet says. "Plus, we'll need some sort of structure to replace those awful hanging skulls in the palace. Do you think Xiang would be willing to design for us?"

Zuhura sighs. "You know exactly what she means. We have the support of half of the Imperial parliament, and even that hardly amounts to much. We need to persuade the rest of the Empire that Koriko's independence is imperative to everyone, and soon, before we have a full-blown insurrection on our hands."

From the look on Menkhet's face, it's clear that the Imperator would love nothing more than to squash such a revolt. But she sighs. "Let's get to work, then."

◆

"I forgot what it felt like to *really* be safe," says Xiang, throwing their arm around Enitan's shoulders.

"As did I," says Enitan, tucking her arm around their waist as they turn a corner. "But we made it through."

She's giving them a tour of the palace. Xiang has seen bits and pieces of it, but this is the first time they've been able to look around freely.

"Excuse me," someone calls out.

Enitan freezes. She recognizes that voice. She spins around to face Ajana's former sentinel, the woman who gave her the funerary box and helped her get here in the first place.

"What do you want?" Xiang demands. Enitan has told them the story, but they don't know the woman's face.

The sentinel holds up her hands in a placating gesture. "My name is Wulen. I need to speak to you, Enitan Ijebu."

A familiar cord of anxiety tightens around Enitan's chest. "About what?"

"About what you've done here."

"And if I refuse?"

"Then everyone will find out you're not the headwoman's daughter."

Xiang surges forward. "Are you *threatening* her—?"

Enitan grabs their elbow and pulls them back. "No one will care," she says. "But fine. Consider this a favor. After this, we're even."

Wulen nods stiffly. "I would like to speak to you privately. Please come with me."

"We're not following you anywhere," says Xiang.

Enitan sighs. "There's a public drawing room this way."

Xiang and Wulen follow her to the chamber, glaring at each other the entire way. She presses her hand to the screen-surface of the door, and it slides open. When Xiang moves to step in after the sentinel, Enitan holds up a hand.

"Absolutely not," says Xiang. "I'm coming in."

"Let me just see what she's here for."

"No. What if she—?"

Enitan places a calming hand on their shoulder. "I'll yell if she tries anything. I promise."

"But it might be too late—"

Enitan steps back and lets the door slide shut in their face. She turns toward Wulen and sits down on the cushion before her.

"So, what do you want?"

The sentinel pulls off her helmet. Her angular, freckled brown features are pinched. "I expected you to save your sibling here. I did not anticipate that you would seduce our God."

Despite her best efforts, Enitan laughs in her face. "Oh, Ancestors, I'm sorry," she wheezes. "Please, go on."

Wulen fidgets, her frown deepening. "Her Imperial Majesty is hardly the first to seek . . . relations with one of your kind. Neither was the Lady Ajana. I have to assume it's the exoticism of it all. But it's . . . it's not proper."

To Enitan's surprise, the words sting. She swallows a burst of unexpected hurt, trying not to let it show on her face. "I don't know what rumors you've heard, but my relationship with the Imperator is completely and utterly—" *Professional* isn't the right word, at least on her end. Her feelings about Menkhet are . . . complicated, to say the least.

"Nothing like that has happened between us," she says finally.

"Then you should leave the Splinter."

Enitan sucks in a deep breath. The sentinel can believe whatever she wants. "Listen. She and I are not romantically involved, but if your God-Emperor is so unquestionably perfect, then any partner she chose would be the right one. That's all I have to say on the matter."

She steps out, leaving the sputtering sentinel behind her. They both know she just made that up, but it's not as if the woman can refute her without committing a little heresy.

Xiang turns toward her, arms crossed petulantly. "So, what did she want?"

"She got caught up in the hearsay. Thinks Menkhet and I are lovers."

"Aren't you?"

"Very funny. I'm pretty sure she wants me put into a convent."

"Hmm." Xiang narrows their eyes at her. "Then why are you in such a good mood?"

"Well." Enitan grabs their arm and steers them toward the nearest tubelift. "I've figured out how to save Koriko."

THIRTY-FIVE

Enitan bursts into the Imperator's office.

Menkhet looks up from the datapad in her hands. "Hello."

"Hi. I noticed that your bimonthly pilgrimage is coming up. Can I come with you?"

"You don't have to do that," Menkhet says, though her eyes brighten. "I was actually planning to cancel it. We still have so much to do."

"It's not just to keep you company. I have an idea."

"Ah. Right." Menkhet turns off the datapad and sets it aside. "So, what's your plan?"

"Well, first, I have to admit that it's pretty impious. How religious are you?"

"Do you really think I'm such a raging narcissist that I genuinely believe I'm a god?" Menkhet snorts. "In short: not very religious. I was the perfect devotee as a child, but faith gets harder once you see the atrocities connected to it—and become the face of them."

Enitan pulls herself up to her full height and begins speaking rapid-fire. "But you can also change things that way, right? As the Vaalbaran God, you lead the way for the Church; you set the canon."

Menkhet pauses. "In a sense. The rank-and-file monks and senti-nels will follow any edicts I put into place, but few of the leaders are so religious. They feign loyalty for the power their positions grant them."

"But your authority trickles down to them. They follow your lead or risk undermining their own influence. So you already hold sway over much of your country."

"But not the majority," says Menkhet. "I doubt that the average citizen truly believes in my infallibility. And you've heard how much of the aristocracy speaks of me. They value religion only when it suits them."

Now Enitan smiles. "But how they speak of you is different from how they speak of the First God-Emperor. Your people worship her as fervently as the people of Homeworld worshipped their gods."

"I hate to break it to you, but she's long dead, and I wield none of her influence."

"That last part isn't quite true." Enitan places her communicator on the desk and opens up a hologram. It's a collection of black statues, all of past Imperators reaching out to touch a floating woman with an axe. "You must be familiar with these?"

"I have no idea what those are."

"They're the Statues of Ruya-Tesh," says Enitan. "Deora taught me about them a while back. They depict past Imperators receiving visions from the First God-Emperor."

Menkhet's eyes widen in recognition. "Yes, I remember now. We learned about these in crèche. But those visions—they've only ever been used to justify war. I can't use the same tactic to pursue peace."

"Actually, Deora once told me that some Imperators claimed holy visions to grant Imperial pardons."

"To friends and family members, no doubt." Menkhet sighs. "So you want me to go to a church, claim to have a vision of the First God-Emperor commanding me to relinquish Koriko, and then use that to formally support the moon's independence?"

"Yes, exactly. We haven't made all of our intentions public yet. Your greatest power as Imperator isn't that you're the commander of the largest army in human history. It's that you're the voice of the First God-Emperor."

"No one's going to buy that. They're going to say I've deceived them just to please my lover." She makes a face, turning away. "Besides, we're just skirting around the central issue: at least half of all Vaalbarans, along with nearly the entire aristocracy, genuinely believe in the Empire's superiority over all other nations."

"That doesn't matter," Enitan promises, dropping into the chair on the other side of the desk. "You'd be surprised at the number of families, both noble and commoner, who've benefited richly from these visions."

"I'm not."

Enitan snorts. "Well, hundreds of today's aristocratic lineages were founded when officers were promoted during holy wars. Entire palatine families survived only because the Imperator at the time said the revered First God-Emperor called off the executions. Were you to nullify these, your average citizen would be affected, too—everything from tax breaks to the removal of corrupt officials is said to be the first Imperator acting through your predecessors. The only reason the average Vaalbaran cares about a tiny moon habitat in the first place is because they've been told to."

Menkhet makes an impressed sound. "That's a little optimistic, but you've done your research, haven't you?"

"We're talking about my home, Menkhet," Enitan says. "Do you think this could work?"

"With the clergy, armed forces, and aristocracy on our side . . . perhaps." Menkhet rises to her feet. "Very well. We can leave tonight. Is Xiang coming?"

"No. I think they'd like a night to themself."

"And Katun, no doubt."

Enitan huffs. "If they get married someday, I'll blame you."

Menkhet laughs. "What can I say? Their love has bloomed as brightly as—"

"That's my cue to go," says Enitan. "I have to pack." She pauses right before the door. "I'm grateful, Menkhet Ta-Miu."

"I made you a promise, Enitan Ijebu."

Enitan holds back a smile as she walks out.

◆

Enitan steps out onto her balcony for what she knows will be one of the last times. It's freezing at first, as always. It is now officially midsummer in Vaalbara, though the weather seems unaware of that. The chill on the eastern part of the supercontinent has risen by only a few degrees.

Enitan tilts her head up toward the sky. The stars shine like a million tiny pinpricks poked into the dark canvas above, each letting one of the Ancestors' souls peek through. That's what Xiang used to tell her, when she was smaller and innocent and all too eager to believe her new elder sibling.

She leans back, and there's a wonderful, vertiginous second where she feels like she's about to tumble into the stars. But then her feet find balance and she's back on the balcony, swaddled in a blanket of warm air from the heaters. She hears footsteps behind her. She doesn't bother turning around; she keeps her eyes on the tapestry of constellations above. She knows who it is by the sound of their steps alone.

At the periphery of her vision, she sees Menkhet looking at her. She's wearing another set of comfortable travel clothes: a knee-length black tunic over loose trousers. A thin robe sweeps the stone behind her like a cape.

Enitan turns, meeting Menkhet's eyes. "The shuttle is ready?"

"It is. Are you?"

Enitan surprises herself by breaking out into a smile. "More than."

The women walk back into the bedroom, where Menkhet snatches Enitan's bag up from the floor before she can stop her. They take a tubelift to the Imperator's private landing pad, where a phalanx of sentinels in black armor awaits them—the Imperator's new and improved honor guard. With the Nlamiraan gone, Menkhet replaced all of her personal protectors with trusted synths.

Three identical shuttles sit side by side, humming in the cool midnight air. Ordinarily, the Imperator takes hundreds of people with her on her pilgrimages, but this journey has been announced as one of quiet reflection. Enitan follows Menkhet into the central shuttle, sliding into the seat across from her. This model is made for comfort, not for speed or for war, unlike the other craft she's traveled in. The aircraft's interior is as black as the outside, stuffed with velvet cushions and damask upholstery.

They don't speak much on the two-hour journey to the Church of Sitaare, and that's fine. The silence that falls between them is a comfortable one. Enitan occupies herself by trying to pick out the scattered ruins below before her communicator notes them. There are churches and castles and cities, all broken down and reshaped by overgrown vegetation.

In the morning, they reach their destination. Unlike most places of worship in the Empire, Sitaare is housed within its own monolith monastery, rather than a full settlement. The only people here are ascetic monks and their scribes. Enitan and Menkhet don't have to worry about the prying eyes of gossiping nobles or power-hungry officials. Together, they watch the monolith as it swells in their line of sight. It is vast and blade-sharp, its myriad facets glinting in the sunrise.

Menkhet leans over as the shuttle touches down on a landing pad. "I had my first ritual cleansing as Imperator here. I hope the food is still as good."

"How did you feel afterward?"

Menkhet sighs. "The ritual was supposed to wash away my humanity, leaving only my nascent divinity." She steps out of the shuttle when the ramp slides open. "But when it was over, I felt much the same, only cleaner."

A single monk greets them wordlessly, plastering himself to the floor at Menkhet's feet. According to the God-Emperor, all the monks here have taken a rigid, lifelong vow of silence; the only people the two of them will be speaking to are each other.

The monk shows them to their rooms, identical chambers connected by a door. Low beds sit at the center of smooth stone floors, little more than lacquered wooden frames layered with thin homespun sheets. Plain black hangings line the gray walls, and each chamber contains a humble carved desk.

They have breakfast in Menkhet's room. She calls for food, and another silent monk brings a little metal grill, along with a dish of raw vegetables and small bowls of scarlet grain. Enitan has grilled two pieces of some yellow-striped root when she notices that the monk hasn't left. He's staring wide-eyed at her, and it takes a second for her to recognize him.

"Stijena?" She puts down her fork. "I see they promoted you."

Stijena opens his mouth before snapping it shut. Color rises to his pale cheeks. He bows at Menkhet and scurries out.

"An old friend?"

"More like an old menace," Enitan huffs under her breath. When Menkhet's lips tighten into a thin, threatening line, she quickly adds, "But completely harmless. He served at the mission in my community. He always bragged about how he'd go back to the Imperial interior and become an abbot. Seems like he's on his way there."

Menkhet shoots a glare at the door. "Not if I have anything to say about it."

"Don't. Please, it's all right."

"Fine," Menkhet grumbles, plucking a purple-swirled cube of koradish from the grill. "Could you pass the pepper sauce?"

Enitan reaches for the bowl, then freezes. It's not that she's opposed to the request. It's that Menkhet just spoke in nearly flawless Korikesian.

"When did you start learning?" asks Enitan, in her own tongue.

"When I first became Imperator," Menkhet replies, still in Korikesian. "But I began studying in earnest after we first met. Respectfully, the twenty tones you use are a pain in the ass."

Genuine laughter, a rare phenomenon in Enitan's life these days, bubbles out of her. "I could drop you in Ijebu right now, and no one would suspect you're Vaalbaran."

"Flattery will get you nowhere," says Menkhet, but she's beaming over the rim of her cup.

"It's not flattery. I'm impressed." Enitan picks up the pepper sauce. "Now, did you actually want this, or was it just an excuse to show off?"

◆

They've planned to stay at the Church of Sitaare for three days. Any less would be too convenient, making the true purpose of the excursion even more obvious than it already is. And any more would be another day the people of Koriko suffer under Imperial rule—tensions have likely risen upon the return of the kidnapped soldiers.

The first day passes by uneventfully, as does much of the second. Enitan and Menkhet remain mostly in their rooms, discussing how best to heal the deep wounds Vaalbara left to fester nearly two decades ago.

In the evening, they travel to the inner sanctum of the church, where Menkhet is to receive her vision. The sacred chamber is empty, save for a silver icon that takes up a whole wall. According to Menkhet, it's a perfect replica of the Imperial city at the height of the First God-Emperor's reign. Even the roofs are rendered in exquisite detail;

the tiles are carved from minuscule onyx shavings rather than etched into a single piece of stone.

The women sit on the cold stone floor, leaning their backs against the wall at the other end of the room.

"I feel like I'm not a good person." Enitan stiffens as soon as the words leave her mouth. She has no idea why she's just said that, nor why she thought it in the first place. Every terrible thing that she's done, she's done for Xiang and Koriko.

If Menkhet finds the statement odd, she doesn't show it. She stretches out her legs and says, "Someone used to tell me that you shouldn't strive to be a good person, but rather to do good things."

"Who told you that?"

Menkhet favors Enitan with a wry, lopsided grin. "Adehkonra, of all people." Her smile falters. "He raised me, actually. Sun and I really were like sisters, contrary to popular belief."

For some reason, the news does not come as a surprise to Enitan. "All the stories about your family say your parents are too humble to move from the middle territories to the palace, and that they'd prefer to remain anonymous," she remarks. "I always thought they sounded too . . . perfect, I suppose."

"Well, you're right. They're dead." Menkhet crosses her legs at the ankle. "The Imperator saved me from a raid on Iëre when I was four. Pulled me from the rubble himself and raised me as his secret ward."

That is a shock. Enitan remembers the bloodless invasion Menkhet led on the islands like it was yesterday. A thousand thoughts burst into her head, the first and foremost of which is that in the eyes of her own subjects, the God-Emperor of Vaalbara is even less Vaalbaran than Enitan. Koriko has been part of the Empire for most of her life. The islands were only just annexed. If this were to get out, there would be chaos. But she says nothing, giving Menkhet the space she needs.

"I don't remember any of it." Menkhet smiles, though her words sound forced. "My therapists say the whole ordeal was so painful I simply made myself forget." She says nothing for a very long time. "I didn't find out until I was an officer in the fleet, leading my own attack against Iëre. I was throwing a man in chains when his wife ran out of their hut. She couldn't have been a year older than me." She presses her hands to her mouth and pulls in her legs, folding herself into a ball and squeezing her eyes shut. "Enitan, she looked exactly like me. But before I could say anything, do anything, my second-in-command shot her. And my third set the hut on fire." She drags in a deep, shuddering breath. "The day I got back, I confronted the man I called was my father. You know that no one in the Empire uses their own body to have children. He'd always told me that I was the secret biological daughter of his late best friend. Fed me some paper-thin story about the couple deciding not to use a birthing vat in order to protect their family from the scandal of their elopement. But when I demanded answers that day, he didn't even attempt to lie."

At some point in the conversation, they shifted closer to each other; Enitan's knee almost brushes Menkhet's.

She reaches over to hold the other woman's hand. She squeezes. "It wasn't your fault."

Menkhet goes stiff and stares at her, surprise etched across her features. A tear rolls down her cheek.

"I try to tell myself that." Her voice is thin and soft and almost intangible, smoke in the shadows. "But I killed my sister, even if I didn't pull the trigger myself."

Enitan brings her other hand to their intertwined fingers, cradling Menkhet's hand between hers.

Menkhet drags in a deep breath. "When Sun and I were little, Adehkonra would pop in on our lessons whenever he had a spare moment. He never said a word while he was there, but sometimes, if the instructor had been particularly jingoistic, he'd take us aside later. He'd offer us a few inane, hollow words about how all humans are people, or that bigotry wasn't very good, or that we should try to respect all our subjects, even the ones that hadn't been beaten into submission yet." She frowns. "It was the great mystery of my childhood: that my God-Emperor found fault with his own Empire, yet never lifted so much as a finger to stop it. But the moment I learned of my true heritage was when I finally, finally understood: he was simply too afraid to do anything. He admitted as much to you when you met him. It was the moment I decided to be better than him.

"Anyway, what I was trying to say, earlier, is that we all wish we were better people, but the sad truth of it is that wishing does precious little. You can't just *be* good, you have to *do* good. And in the meantime, we must try to love ourselves and each other. That's all." Menkhet squeezes back. "You've mastered the first part, Enitan. You've done more for both our worlds than could ever be repaid. It's the rest you could use some work on. Be kinder to yourself."

Menkhet sticks a hand into one of her pockets and pulls out a compact holoprojector. It's dented and there are burn marks around the edges, as if someone pulled it from a fire right before the metal began to melt.

When she activates it, the projected beam resolves into two tall men standing beside two young daughters. The hologram flickers before color floods the image, revealing bronze-brown skin and black hair. Menkhet stands and sets the holoprojector within a recess at the icon's center.

Her posture straightens and she kneels, folding her hands together and bowing her head. Enitan sits patiently as Menkhet pays respect to her family. Enitan hasn't prayed or meditated in years, and she feels no need to begin again now. But she closes her eyes anyway.

She opens them again when Menkhet stands with a soft rustle of fabric.

The God-Emperor dusts herself off, though there isn't so much as a mote there. "Time for the performance of a lifetime. Be sure to look shocked."

"Of course." Enitan rises to her feet, opening her eyes as wide as they'll go.

Menkhet sweeps back her braids. Then she throws open the doors of the inner sanctum and cries out, *"Praise be!* I've seen the First God-Emperor!"

THIRTY-SIX

Menkhet spends the third day at Sitaare "consulting" with the monks after her divine visitation. In reality, she and Enitan spend their final hours planning for the storm they know is on the horizon. They hope that the nobles, sentinels, and votaries of Vaalbara will go along with the Church, keep their mouths shut, and stay out of the way, but that's all they have—hope. The other factions of the Empire might indeed have a great deal to lose by arguing against Menkhet's supposed vision, but that doesn't mean they won't. Koriko was mostly profitable for the Nlamiraan alone, but for everyone else, its freedom is a matter of wounded Imperial pride.

It's almost midnight by the time Enitan remembers that their return shuttle is coming for them at dawn. Tomorrow, she'll be in charge of announcing the communities' victory to them with the help of Ijebu's headwoman, and Menkhet will have to wrestle with a legion of angry reporters and angrier aristocrats. Enitan's already argued that she should be there to help with damage control.

"We should probably go to bed." A good night's rest may be out of reach for her, but she knows she ought to try anyway. She pushes aside the wooden trays between them, which were previously laden with strong black tea and whimsically plated pastries. Ancestors, all that caffeine and sugar after sunset was a terrible idea.

"Right." Menkhet stands, tucking a few datapads under her arm and turning toward the door. "I'll see you in a few hours."

"Wait." Enitan rises to her feet. "You . . . can stay." She pauses. "If you want."

The air between them feels like it would break into a thousand glittering shards if she tapped at it. Menkhet's black eyes are fixed on her.

"Are you sure?"

Enitan sits on the bed and lies back, patting the spot next to her. Menkhet joins her after a moment, rolling onto her side and propping herself up with one elbow. With painstaking slowness, she reaches over and brings her fingers softly to Enitan's jaw. The lightness of Menkhet's touch reminds Enitan of the way she held her after Erseydis. She covers Menkhet's hand with her own and presses it into her cheek. "It's okay. I'm not made of glass."

"I know." Menkhet scoots just a little closer, tucking Enitan's head under hers and wrapping her arm around the other woman's shoulders. "This is fine?"

Enitan, already on the verge of sleep, makes a contented sound. "Very."

"In Iëran," whispers Menkhet, "the word *I* simply doesn't exist. The closest thing is an entire phrase: *this one part of the whole.* I always thought . . . Well, I never truly understood, until now."

"I'm glad," Enitan mumbles gently, yawning as the tides of slumber pull her down deeper into the realm of unconsciousness.

"I care for you, Enitan. Quite a bit."

This yanks Enitan back from the brink of sleep.

But before she can say anything, Menkhet continues. "It's okay, you don't need to respond. I don't expect you to feel the same." Her hold on Enitan loosens, though she doesn't let her go. "Considering what I've been responsible for, knowingly or not, I couldn't fault you for considering me the enemy."

◆

When Enitan wakes up after the best sleep she's had in months, Menkhet is crying. Enitan hears the sound of sniffling and extricates herself from their tangle of limbs to get a good look at the other woman.

She's still asleep. Menkhet's tear-streaked face is furrowed in agony, and every few moments, her entire body spasms, her fists clenching as the rest of her convulses. She's having a nightmare.

Enitan isn't quite certain what to do. Watching Menkhet in such pain makes her feel physically ill, but she knows it's best to let the night terror run its course. When Xiang started crying out in their sleep years ago, the headwoman advised Enitan to simply leave them be. According to her, their sleeping mind was dealing with the trauma their waking one could not. She suggested meditating with them before bed, and after Enitan started brewing calming teas, her sibling's rest eventually grew peaceful. She decides she'll start doing the same for Menkhet. For now, though, all Enitan can do is watch over her.

Menkhet eventually comes to with a slight jolt. Her eyes fly open, every inch of her tensing as if she's about to flee or fight. Enitan hugs her closer, lifting an arm to tangle her fingers into Menkhet's dark braids, each like a strand of woven satin.

"It's me. I'm here," she whispers, cradling her head. "I'm here. You're all right. I've got you."

Menkhet relaxes slowly, letting out a warm puff of air that tickles Enitan's nose.

"Menkhet," Enitan whispers. "I care for you too."

Menkhet's eyelids flutter in surprise but she says nothing, just pulls Enitan in tighter. Then her communicator chimes, ruining everything, and they both roll off the bed with a groan.

"The shuttle," Menkhet says, stretching. "We should go."

Enitan rolls her neck and yawns. She picks up her bag and then Menkhet's. They clamber out into the plush aircraft, and this time Enitan sits on the same side as Menkhet.

"You look tired," says Menkhet. "I'm sorry I woke you—"

"I slept quite well, actually," Enitan replies, though she yawns again. "I guess my body's just catching up on what I missed."

"Why don't you take a nap?" Menkhet taps her arm. "You can sleep on my shoulder."

Enitan melts like a glacier under the spring sun. She slides over and curls up against her.

◆

Enitan wakes up to Menkhet patting her knee with the softest of touches. She begrudgingly lifts her head from the other woman's shoulder, which served as an excellent pillow. The honor guard sees them safely to Menkhet's quarters, where Xiang, Katun, and Kulta are already waiting.

"How was the trip?" asks Xiang, wiggling their eyebrows at her.

Sprawled halfway over her sibling, Katun grins.

"It was very good," says Menkhet, and Enitan looks away, feeling her cheeks grow warm.

"Glad to hear it," Kulta says flatly, pulling a sheaf of holosheets from his bag. "Menkhet, you have back-to-back meetings with the various factions of Parliament until the evening, when you'll give a speech that will be broadcasted across the Empire. And then we'll get all the assholes of import too drunk to complain at the ceremony immediately after." He hands the Imperator a holosheet. "Read that and let me know if I should make any changes."

Menkhet looks it over before passing it to Enitan. "What do you think?"

Enitan skims the floating words. "I think it's perfect."

"Great." Menkhet folds up the holosheet and stuffs it into her pocket. "When's my first meeting?"

Kulta hands her a crisp black suit. "In two minutes. You should get changed."

With a long-suffering moan, Menkhet grabs the suit and drags herself toward the finely carved door. "I'll see you all this evening." She looks back at Enitan.

Xiang and Katun snicker as Enitan grabs Kulta by the arm and pulls him outside.

"I'm glad you two have grown close," says Kulta.

Enitan grimaces. "Not you too."

"My craft-siblings and I are Menkhet's friends, but we can't give her everything she needs."

Enitan's mouth twists into a thin, wry smile. "And what might that be, exactly?"

"Human companionship." Kulta leans against the wall. "None of us would change our nature even if we could, but . . . while we may be close with her, our primary duty is to protect her and help her fulfill her duties as Imperator." He smiles at Enitan. "I wish it were under different circumstances, but I'm glad I met you."

"As am I." Enitan leans against the cool stone beside him. "The world hasn't been kind to either of us, has it?"

"No," says Kulta. "No, it hasn't. But I'm hopeful."

Enitan turns to meet the synth's eyes.

"The Republic has a long way to go, just as Vaalbara does," says Kulta. "It won't get there today, or tomorrow, or even in a century, but the world is changing. Already, synths in Ominira are being treated with far greater dignity each year. My kind is patient. We'll outlive our creators and push the necessary changes forward, to the extent we can, as we have always done."

Enitan almost envies Kulta. Her people, mortal as they are, need change sooner than that.

"Do you miss Ominira?" she asks.

Kulta's answer is a certain one. "No. My siblings and I transferred ninety-seven percent of our memories of the Republic to a hidden pocket of the net and deleted the rest." He shrugs. "Home is where you can live freely as yourself, and Menkhet has provided that for my family."

"I can sympathize with that, even if I can't truly understand everything you've been through," says Enitan. "I imagine the same goes for you. But if I ever say or do something that crosses a line, I hope you'll tell me?"

"Of course. And please do return the favor."

Enitan smiles. "Can I give you a hug?"

Kulta laughs and opens his arms.

◆

For the past century, the God-Emperor has delivered all official speeches from the safety of their residence. In the past, Vaalbara's rulers spoke from a balcony overlooking a vast plaza, up until an armed force of disgruntled leaders from recently conquered tribes blew up half the square and stabbed the then-Imperator.

"You should be here with me," says Menkhet, adjusting the layered sleeves of her tunic and tugging on the wide belt securing her formal tabard. "God, this thing is tight."

She's standing in front of a massive mosaic map of Vaalbara, identical to the one lower in the Splinter save for its base metals: silver and steel instead of copper and iron.

Enitan shakes her head, wiping her sweaty palms over her own, far more comfortable garb: the robe Xiang gifted her all those years ago, accompanied by Ajana's headscarf and ring. "And make everyone think I hold even more influence over you?"

Menkhet sighs. "You probably do."

"Menkhet—"

"It's true, though, in the best way. You've made me better, Enitan." She stops pulling at her raiment. "I may never be able to undo the pain Vaalbara has caused you and Koriko and the rest of the system, but I'll spend the rest of my life trying."

The words are startlingly similar to Adehkonra's, but this time they ring true to Enitan. Menkhet has the conviction that her adoptive father lacked.

"Please don't make me cry," Enitan says, willing away the heat behind her eyes.

Kazu, the remarkably tall synth, gets up from a nearby couch. They hold out a palm and spread their fingers, and the skin of their hand slides away to reveal a compact holoimager.

"Are you ready?" Enitan asks.

Menkhet takes a deep breath. "I am."

"Recording in three, two, one . . ."

"Citizens and friends," begins Menkhet, "it is an honor to be your God and Imperator. But it is also a challenge. We call ourselves the greatest empire in history, but that title was not easily won. Just as our ancestors fought for this distinction, I have fought and spilt blood for the glory of the Empire. And I tell you today that I regret almost every drop of it. When the greatest of all our forebears, the First God-Emperor, appeared to me in a vision at Sitaare during a moment of prayer, I was bewildered. Over the course of our nation's history, only a handful of our mightiest rulers have received such a visitation. What had I done to deserve such favor? I, who had served only three years in the fleet. I, who had ruled for scarcely a few months. I, who even then harbored great doubts about my own throne. I expected to be chastised, if not struck down. But the God-Emperor did not descend from the highest heaven to condemn my reign, nor did she call upon me to wage yet another holy war. Quite the opposite, in fact."

Menkhet pulls herself up to her full height. When she speaks, her voice is loud and clear and unflinching. "She demanded peace. The God-Emperor who built Vaalbara transformed the iron of our people into steel. Steel to build and to defend, but not to kill without reason. We were never meant for that. And yet, what have we done?" She shakes her head. "We have conquered our peaceful neighbors for no other reason than that there were no more battles to fight. We plundered and pillaged their homes and forced them to their knees. But this era of senseless bloodshed is over. Now is the time for reflection, redemption, and reconciliation. We are so much more than soldiers. We are inventors and innovators, artisans and architects of our own future. Koriko is so much more than a province. It is a people and a culture, no less great than ours. One we would do well to befriend in truth. And so, guided by the perfect and omnipotent hand of the First God-Emperor, I—Menkhet Ta-Miu, First of Her Name, the two hundred and twenty-eighth Imperator of the Holy Vaalbaran Empire, Lord of the Church Undying, Queen of the Splinter and All the Lesser Monoliths, True Heir of Homeworld, and Vowed Mother of All Humanity—affirm the independence of Koriko, a sovereign state wrongfully and violently annexed under our power. I have been shown true strength." She turns to Enitan, who can barely contain a gasp. "And it is not in the tears of the conquered or the blood of the slain. It is in heroes who rise up against the cruel and powerful, even when it seems as if the whole world is against them." She draws in a deep breath. "My people, you have my gratitude, my loyalty, and my love. Let us begin this bright future together."

Kazu retracts the holoimager and closes their hand. "You didn't follow the script."

"I know." Menkhet returns to fidgeting with her belt. "But I don't want to pretend that what we did was right. The Empire needs to confront its past." She turns to Enitan. "What did you think?"

Enitan's heart beats just a little faster. Warmth flows over her, gratitude and relief and something else, something soft and fleeting like a warm summer rain. But she hasn't the slightest idea how to convey those muddled feelings, so all she says is, "I'm impressed, Menkhet."

Menkhet beams back at her.

Stone-faced, Kazu says, "All right, I'm leaving. Kulta says you both better be in the great hall in one-point-five minutes or he'll come up here and drag you down himself."

They step out the door.

THIRTY-SEVEN

"Enitan. Enitan. Wake up."

Enitan yawns and opens her eyes. She blinks blearily up at Menkhet, tucked beside her on the chaise longue in the sixth private drawing room of the Imperial suite. "Sorry for falling asleep on you," she murmurs. "Though it's your fault for being so comfortable."

"Is that so?"

"Quite."

Menkhet flashes a smile at her, as fleeting as the sun glinting off steel. If Enitan didn't know her better, she'd think it was genuine. But she *does* know her better; she catches the sadness in Menkhet's eyes.

"What's wrong?" Enitan whispers, cupping the side of Menkhet's jaw.

"Your shuttle's here," Menkhet replies, her tone painstakingly smooth. "Even though I threatened to shoot it down if it landed."

Enitan reaches for her communicator with her other hand. "I'll tell Xiang."

"Xiang's already inside."

Enitan snickers. "How long did you make them wait?"

"As long as I could." Menkhet disentangles herself from Enitan and rises from the cushions. "I have something for you. I'll be back in a moment." She returns a few minutes later, a silk-wrapped parcel in hand. Enitan pulls loose the badly tied ribbon, revealing a journal bound with Korikese cloth and filled with real paper.

Menkhet kneels at Enitan's side. "Do you like it?"

"I love it. It's beautiful," Enitan says, her voice nearly breaking on the last word. "Why?"

Menkhet huffs out a laugh. "Normally, the proper response to someone giving you a gift is to thank them."

Enitan sighs.

"I thought you might benefit from writing down your thoughts, at least until you find a good therapist in Ijebu." Menkhet glances away for a heartbeat. "Maybe even after that. It's just a small present, a symbol of our . . . friendship."

In Vaalbara, a friendship is one step down from a romantic bond, and two from a familial one. On Koriko, the three are equal in importance. Friends are the family you choose, no less. The tender look in Menkhet's eyes makes it clear what she means. This is the real gift.

It's too much. Enitan feels overwhelmed, undeserving.

"Thank you." She averts her eyes, tucking the journal into her satchel. "I'm sorry I didn't get you anything."

"All the better. You've already given me far more than I could ever hope to repay."

Enitan is caught between lifting her eyes to the ceiling or breaking into tears. Either way, she'll be sure to send Menkhet a potted alabaleaf for her rooms as soon as she's back home, along with some tea to help her sleep. They meet Zuhura on their way to the landing pad. The Vice-Imperator pulls Enitan into a tight hug the second she lays eyes on her. "Safe travels, my dear."

"Thank you, Zuhura. I hope to see you again soon; you're always welcome in Ijebu." Enitan cants her head at Menkhet. "Good luck with her."

"She'll need it," says Menkhet with a grin. "And before you leave, I'd like to discuss something with both of you." Her voice drops to a near whisper. "I meant what I said in the gardens, Enitan. The institution that allowed such atrocities cannot carry on. The Nlamiraan was chock-full of monsters, certainly, but they only got away with it because of the system at large. Every territory that desires independence will have my support. I'm going to dismantle the Empire, piece by piece."

Enitan is speechless. From the look of it, so is Zuhura, at least for a moment.

Then the Vice-Imperator nods, taking the revelation in stride. "I don't disagree. To build a new world, the old one must die."

"And what will be put in its place?" Enitan asks, the words hushed. She hadn't dared to think of what they've done as not only an ending, but the start of something entirely new.

"That's hardly a question any one of us can answer," Menkhet says. "But we know where to start."

"Well, in the meantime, we have our work cut out for us," says Zuhura, already looking exhausted. "At least my abilities are being put to good use."

She says her goodbyes and leaves. As soon as she does, Menkhet takes Enitan's hands in hers and kisses her knuckles. "What about us?" she asks, very quietly. "I know right now isn't the best time, but . . . perhaps I could visit Koriko too."

Enitan's cheeks grow hot, though she almost laughs—she's never seen the Imperator so bashful. They make their way toward the shuttle, and as they round a corner, Enitan feels Menkhet slip a hand to her lower back to steer her. The hand stays there.

Menkhet's presence is a warm fire on a cold night. But . . . "Menkhet, I don't see how it could work."

"If I can't come to your moon, perhaps we could meet in the middle. Somewhere in the asteroid belt."

"What reason have I to leave Koriko?" Enitan says, lifting a brow. She's grinning, though. "My job here has finished."

Menkhet's eyes are diamond-bright. "The Republic may no longer require a spy or an assassin, but the Empire would be honored to have you as Koriko's ambassador."

Enitan chuckles, more than a little amused. "I'm even less qualified to do that than I was to be your advisor."

They reach the landing pad.

"And yet you performed admirably as such."

Enitan sighs, resting her back against the shuttle's hull. "If you insist."

"I do." Menkhet reaches for her, just a brush of the back of her knuckles down the side of Enitan's face. "I may not know what the system's future will look like, but I want you in mine. Will you at least consider it?" The touch is affectionate. And then she does it again, drawing a finger along the curve of Enitan's jaw.

Enitan blushes furiously, registering the woman's familiar half smile. "All right. I will."

"I can't tell you how much you mean to me," Menkhet whispers. "Take care of yourself."

"You too." Enitan can practically taste her own heartbeat. For a moment, they simply gaze at each other. Then Enitan reaches up and tucks a stray braid behind Menkhet's ear. Menkhet leans over Enitan and . . .

She presses her hand against the screen-surface of the shuttle. The ramp slides open with a hiss of air.

Xiang makes a retching noise when they see the pair. "Ancestors, get a room already."

"Oh, as if you two are any better." Enitan's gaze latches on to Katun, who is sprawled comfortably on the padded bench beside her sibling. "I believe that's my seat. You can go now."

"Actually, I'm coming too," says Katun.

"Pardon?" Enitan asks, as calmly as she can.

"I invited him to stay with us," says Xiang, only a tad sheepishly.

"Absolutely not! Where will he stay?"

"Don't worry," says Katun, "Xiang said I could share their mat while they renovate our housepod."

"*Our* housepod?" Enitan drags in a long, deep breath and decides that she can live with this. She looks over at Menkhet.

Menkhet smiles at her.

Enitan takes her hand and squeezes it before letting go. "I'll see you in the belt, then."

She sits beside Xiang. They lean against each other as the shuttle lifts into the air and the viewport fills with sky.

This is how it begins, she thinks. There is so much to be done. There are worlds to mend, and no shortage of dangers to face. But for now, Koriko calls her name like a song, and she will answer.

She is bringing home back with her.

ACKNOWLEDGMENTS

I'd like to express my deep appreciation for my agent, Tricia Skinner, and for her expertise, encouragement, endless patience, and everything else. She's the best literary agent in this world and every other. Team Vader really lucked out. I'm also grateful to Ernie Chiara, who picked my manuscript out of the slush pile and gave me a metric ton of excellent feedback. And many, many thanks to my editor, Amara Hoshijo, whose eye for detail and excellent suggestions brought this story to a new level.

Thank you to the whole team at Saga Press/Gallery Books—especially Jéla Lewter, Kayley Hoffman, Nicole B., Yvonne Taylor, Caroline Pallotta, Emily Arzeno, Sydney Morris, and Tyrinne Lashay Lewis. Thank you to Andis Reinbergs for the stellar (haha) cover.

Additional thanks are due to my critique partners and earliest readers, including (in alphabetical order): Bill A., Alan A., Kelly A., Michaela B., Zach H., M.W. Patterson, B.S. Roberts, John S., Ari S., Nihar S., L. K. Tyson, Max V., Nicole W., and Jay Y.

This book would never have been written without the teachers who inspired and encouraged my love of storytelling: Ms. Johnson, Mrs. Nepf, Ms. DeVine, and Ms. Gomez (my first and only creative writing teacher). I owe them all quite a lot.

Because I try to base my science fiction on, well, science, I'd be remiss if I did not also thank the teachers and researchers who most influenced me as a scientist-in-training. In semi-chronological order, they include: Mr. Dev, Ms. Peters, Dr. Pal, Dr. Kovalenko, Dr. Berry, Dr. Wooldridge, Professor Hoekstra, Professor Fischer, Professor Sasselov, Katherine K., and Professor Pearson. Thank you especially to Ms. Tighe, Professor Kittles, and Professor Knoll. For the sake of storytelling, I was forced to occasionally fudge some of the background science. Anything true and interesting in here is due to the aforementioned mentors, and anything false or even outright ridiculous is my fault alone.

Special thanks also to Shane, Ashley, and Mariah at the Ku Cha House of Tea in Denver for their extensive knowledge and willingness to let me sample half the store.

Last, but certainly not least, I'm grateful for the love and support of my family and friends. I love you to the moon and back.